Point Romance

THE LOVE COLLECTION

THREE HOT ROMANCES

D1160517

Have you read these *sizzling* romances:

First Comes Love
To Have and to Hold
For Better, For Worse
In Sickness and in Health
Till Death Do Us Part

Last Summer, First Love
A Time to Love
Goodbye to Love
Jennifer Baker

A Winter Love Story
Malibu Summer
Winter Love, Winter Wishes
Jane Claypool Miner

Two Weeks in Paradise
Spotlight on Love
Denise Colby

Saturday Night
Last Dance
New Year's Eve
Summer Nights
Caroline B. Cooney

Cradle Snatcher
Kiss Me, Stupid
Alison Creaghan

Two-Timer
Love Triangle
Lorna Read

Summer Dreams, Winter Love
Mary Francis Shura

The Last Great Summer
Carol Stanley

Lifeguards
Summer's Promise
Summer's End
Todd Strasser

Crazy About You
French Kiss
Ice Hot!
Russian Nights
Robyn Turner

Hopelessly Devoted

Dream Ticket
1: Blazing Kisses
2: Freezing Heart
3: Follow the Sun
Amber Vane

Summer Sizzlers
Summer Scorchers
Winter Weepies
Winter Warmers
(short stories)
Various

Secret Love
Sue Welford

Point Romance

THE LOVE COLLECTION

THREE HOT ROMANCES

Crazy About You
French Kiss
Ice Hot!

ROBYN TURNER
Cover illustration by
Dennis Ryan

SCHOLASTIC

Scholastic Children's Books
Commonwealth House, 1–19 New Oxford Street,
London WC1A 1NU, UK
a division of Scholastic Ltd
London ~ New York ~ Toronto ~ Sydney ~ Auckland
Mexico City ~ New Delhi ~ Hong Kong

Crazy About You
First published in the UK by Scholastic Ltd, 1995
Copyright © Robyn Turner 1995

French Kiss
First published in the UK by Scholastic Ltd, 1994
Copyright © Robyn Turner, 1994

Ice Hot!
First published in the UK by Scholastic Ltd, 1996
Copyright © Robyn Turner, 1996

This edition published by Scholastic Ltd, 1997

ISBN 0 590 19416 X

All rights reserved

Typeset by TW Typesetting, Midsomer Norton, Avon
Printed by Cox and Wyman Ltd, Reading, Berks.

2 4 6 8 10 9 7 5 3

The right of Robyn Turner to be identified as the author
of this work has been asserted by her in accordance with the
Copyright, Designs and Patents Act, 1988.

This book is sold subject to the condition that it shall not,
by way of trade or otherwise be lent, resold, hired out, or
otherwise circulated without the publisher's prior consent
in any form of binding or cover other than that in which it
is published and without a similar condition, including this
condition, being imposed upon the subsequent purchaser.

Contents

Crazy
About You

1

French
Kiss

177

IceHot!

357

Crazy About You

1

December

The snow fell softly around Astor College, covering the sports fields in a crisp blanket of white, and transforming the school's rolling grounds and old stone buildings into a scene from a Victorian Christmas card.

It was late afternoon, and already dark; inside the brightly-lit centrally-heated classrooms there was a feeling of well-earned indolence. After all, it was nearly Christmas and there were only two days to go before the end of term. If you couldn't start to slow down a bit before Christmas, then when could you?

The large school and sixth-form college in the Midlands, built on the site of a former country mansion for the landed gentry, had a reputation for turning out some of the best and brightest students in the entire country.

You certainly didn't need money to go to Astor College, even though the parents of many of the college's students were very well-off indeed, but you did need brains, and something which the teaching staff and the Board of Governors – self-made men and women every one of them – valued even more.

Individualism, thinking for yourself, standing on your own two feet – or stubbornness and sheer bloody-mindedness as some were inclined to call it – was something which was positively encouraged at Astor College. School work was important, certainly, and nothing but the best possible grades were expected from each and every student; but preparation for adult life and work was deemed just as important and therefore there was a whole host of extra-curricular activities from which Astor students could choose.

At the end of the school day when the corridors were packed with students, only half of those students were in a rush to go home; the other half were off to work on the school paper, go to a rehearsal of the school's drama society, or help out in Astor's community care scheme at the nearby Cuttleigh Hall.

So immersed in her own thoughts was one tall dark-haired girl at the end of this particular day that she wasn't looking where she was going, and she collided into a fellow student, a pretty and petite blonde-haired girl. As they ran into each other, the pile of files and folders the dark-haired girl was carrying fell tumbling to the floor.

"Damn!" cried the taller girl, and bent down to pick up the files and papers.

"Sorry, Angie," the blonde girl said, as she knelt down to help her friend gather up her papers.

Angie ran a hand through her short black hair, which she'd recently had cut into a stylish bob by one of the top hair stylists in town.

"It's not your fault, Bec," she said, and smiled ruefully. "If I stopped charging around Astor like a bat out of hell it wouldn't have happened."

"It is Christmas, you know," Rebecca said, handing the files over to her best friend. "You are allowed to take a little time off, wind down. That's what holidays are for."

Angie stood up, and smoothed the creases in her sharp deep-blue Katharine Hamnett suit. "You know that Christmas is the busiest time of the year for me," she reminded Bec. "For starters, there's revision for next term's exams—"

"Don't remind me," Rebecca said glumly. Christmas was supposed to be a time of goodwill to all men, but obviously no one had informed Old Mother Greystone, their maths teacher, when she had set them their holiday homework.

"And there's Cuttleigh Hall's New Year's Eve party," Angie continued. "You promised to help me out this year."

"I know," Rebecca said. In fact, she had secretly been wishing that Angie had forgotten about the promise she had made her in the summer, when the thought of helping to organize a party for the disabled kids at Cuttleigh Hall hadn't seemed so bad. Christmas and New Year were supposed to be times for enjoying yourselves, not for spending most of your time elbow-deep in someone else's jelly and custard!

"Plus there's stories to prepare for the *Recorder*," Angie finished. "The New Year issue's due out in the first week of next term." She sighed theatrically and chuckled. "Holiday? What holiday?"

"Don't you ever rest, Angela Markowski?" Rebecca asked in a mock-stern voice. "Straight-A student, part-time charity and care worker, and assistant editor of the student newspaper. I mean, do you ever get time to do the things we normal people do – like eat?"

For a moment Angie looked serious. "Bec, if my grandad hadn't worked hard, and raised enough money to move his entire family out of Poland just after the end of the Second World War, I might not be here now. My dad's family were poor: it's only through sheer hard work that we've got to where we are today – I don't want to waste the opportunity I've been given."

Rebecca nodded, taking Angie's point, but still giggled. "Where you are today?" she repeated. "Living in the posh house on the hill, and having so little free time that you don't even get the chance to use your father's credit cards? Now that's what I call a waste!"

Angie gave Rebecca a friendly cuff on the shoulder: it was a long-running argument between the two of them.

"Bec, next year when you're at university reading soppy Victorian love poetry—"

"Alongside some soppy Victorian love-god, I hope," Rebecca said dreamily, and even Angie smiled.

"When you're at university, I want to be working as a journalist," Angie continued, sounding a little too earnest for her own good. "And every hour I put in on the student newspaper, every minute I spend experiencing some of the social problems of this town, every moment I'm helping someone less fortunate than myself, is going to stand me in good stead. Think of it as a sort of work-experience."

"But you could walk into a reporter's job as easily as that," Rebecca said, clicking her fingers.

"And what gives you that idea?"

"Well, your dad," Rebecca replied. "He works for the BBC in Birmingham, doesn't he? He could pull a few strings for you, and the next thing you know you'd be reading the Nine O'Clock News on the telly!"

Angie shook her head. "No way. He says that if I want a job in journalism then I've got to get it myself, the hard way. The way he got his own job."

Rebecca pulled a face, as if to show that she didn't think much of Peter Markowski's refusal to help his only daughter, but Angie smiled.

"And of course, he's right," she said. "If I can't get a job on the strength of my own talents, and can only get one because of who my dad is, then I'm simply not good enough!"

"You're determined, Angie, I'll give you that," Rebecca said, and started walking with her down the corridor towards the Senior Common Room.

A couple of boys from the lower sixth wolf-whistled as they passed by. Angie ignored them snootily; Rebecca, on the other hand, winked flirtatiously back at them.

"You've got to be determined in this world," Angie opined. "You've got to recognize exactly what it is you want, and then go out there and get it."

"You sound exactly like some of our teachers!" Rebecca said, and mimicked the accent of one of the more earnest careers advisers at Astor. " 'Gang your ain gait, mae wee children, gang your ain gait!' "

"Shut it!" Angie said, and punched her playfully in the ribs, as they reached the Common Room.

"But you're right," Rebecca agreed enthusiastically. "I've decided what I want and I'm going to go right out there to get it!"

Angie sniggered: she knew exactly what was coming next. "So who is he this time, Bec?"

"He's six-feet-two, has just turned nineteen, has the bluest, biggest eyes in the whole universe, and the cutest curly hair you've ever seen," she said animatedly, without pausing for anything so boring as a breath. "He's studying Physics, Chemistry and Engineering at the technical college down the road, he drives a second-hand Metro, his dad's something in computers, and, Angie, he is simply the hunkiest and most gorgeous creature on the surface of this entire planet!"

"I don't suppose you've found out his name yet?" Angie asked sarcastically.

"Adrian Fowler," Rebecca said smugly. "I tell you, Angie, this is it, this guy is going to be the biggest love of my life!"

"And have you actually met this sex-god yet?" Angie asked practically.

Rebecca's face fell. "Well, no, not exactly..."

"I thought not," Angie said wisely, and grinned. Rebecca was always falling in love at the drop of a hat. *Come to think of it*, Angie realized, *Rebecca Penswick doesn't even need the hat!*

"And that's where you come in, my bestest, bestest friend!" Rebecca said, and took Angie's arm.

"I do?" Angie suddenly had a sinking feeling in her stomach. She'd done favours for Rebecca before, favours which had usually landed her in a whole lot of trouble.

"I'm helping you out with your charities over Christmas," Rebecca reminded her, "so you owe me. Adrian's going to be at the Christmas dance tonight. Come with me, will you?"

"Bec, I haven't got the time..." Angie began, and then smiled. Rebecca was looking at her pleadingly, like a cute little kid deprived of her favourite teddy bear. Maybe Bec was right, maybe she did need to unwind just a little.

"Well, OK," Angie finally gave in, and Rebecca clapped her hands triumphantly. "But what about tickets?" she asked, sensibly. "I thought the dance had sold out weeks ago."

Like a conjurer pulling a rabbit out of a hat, Rebecca whipped a pair of tickets out of the back pocket of her Levis. In response to Angie's puzzled look she explained that she had bought them several weeks ago when they had first been put on sale. Then she had been planning to go to the dance with Rod, a good-looking fellow student on Rebecca's English Literature course.

"I seem to remember you calling Rod the greatest love of your life only a couple of weeks ago," Angie mischievously reminded her friend.

"Puuh-*lease*!" Rebecca said and shuddered. "He had spots like you wouldn't believe..."

"You didn't seem to mind that when you were kissing each other by the lockers," Angie recalled. "You didn't come up for air for hours!"

Rebecca glowered at her best friend: Angie had an infuriating habit of always reminding her of her past mistakes. "Anyway, he was *sooooo* immature," she said loftily.

"He was two months younger than you!" Angie giggled.

"That's what I mean," Rebecca laughed, and then was suddenly serious again. "But believe me, Angie, Adrian is it!"

"Sure, Bec." Angie nodded her head, clearly not believing at all. She'd give Bec's infatuation with Adrian about two weeks, before her dizzy friend fell for some other hunk. Bec was always flighty and changeable, unlike the ever-dependent and determined Angie, and that was probably why they got on so well.

Angie had only ever had one serious relationship with a boy before and that had been with Guy, the son of one of her stepmother's friends. He'd been solid and reliable ("boring" and "stick-in-the-mud", Rebecca had called him), and they'd gone out together for almost two years before he moved down to London to study for his accountancy exams. The split had been amicable, and although Angie had been out with a couple of boys since Guy, there had been no one she had really cared for enough to give up her work on the *Recorder*.

What was more, Angie had seen what happened when people embarked on heavy relationships in their final year of college: their grades inevitably went down, because they were spending more time with their beloved than studying for the all-important A-levels. Journalism was a tough enough profession to enter at the best of times: she didn't want to mess it all up by falling in love with some hunk and getting anything less than the straight As she always got.

"So I'll meet up with you tonight?" Rebecca asked, as she said goodbye to Angie, who had to go off to another class. "And Angie...?"

"Yes?"

"Adrian's mine, OK?"

Angie frowned, but nodded anyway, and walked away, promising to pick Rebecca up at half-past seven that night. As Rebecca watched her friend disappear, she smiled stoically to herself.

Life wasn't fair, she thought. Here she was, Rebecca, chasing after all the boys at Astor (admittedly catching quite a few of them), when Angie, who wasn't interested in a relationship at all, could have had any one of them she wanted.

One day, Rebecca knew, Angie was going to wake up and discover just how beautiful she really was, if she'd only loosen up on her ambition and planning for her future career.

Rebecca turned and entered the Senior Common Room. She had more important things to occupy her mind now, like what to wear for the dance tonight, and the best chat-up line to try out on Adrian. Who knows? She might even manage to fix Angie up with a date as well!

*   *   *

The throbbing beat from the latest chart-topping sounds reverberated through the assembly hall as Astor College's Christmas dance got into full swing. The hall had been decked out with bright silver bunting and balloons, which sparkled and twinkled in the strobe lights reflected off the giant mirror ball in the ceiling.

At the side of the main dance area tables had been set out, and people were sitting round them and gazing out on to the dance floor, to see who was dancing with who, and who had sneaked off together to some dark corner, to kiss under a strategically-placed sprig of mistletoe.

At the far end of the hall, a bunch of teachers sat, looking distinctly uncomfortable and out-of-place. They were there to make sure that things didn't get too out of hand, although none of them had been vigilant enough to spot the carrier bags full of wine that several students had successfully smuggled into the hall, to supplement the Cokes and soft drinks available at the bar.

It was almost nine o'clock now and the dance floor was packed with couples bopping and gyrating to the latest in disco, house and techno. Angie, dressed in a white Nicole Farhi top and trendy Calvins, was sitting at a table by herself, after having turned down the third invitation to dance in as many minutes.

She was scribbling in shorthand in a reporter's notebook, occasionally looking up to see Rebecca and Adrian dancing on the dance floor. Angie smiled to herself: her best friend hadn't wasted any time, and had been monopolizing the handsome college student for the best part of an hour.

The dance track faded, to be replaced by a sugary-sweet piece of nonsense from one of the latest Aussie soap stars, and Rebecca and Adrian left the dance floor in disgust, to rejoin Angie at her table. Rebecca glanced down at the notebook, unsuccessfully trying to decipher Angie's shorthand notes.

"Don't you ever stop!" she said and raised her eyes

heavenwards in despair. She closed Angie's notebook for her, before reaching out for her plastic cup of red wine.

"Sorry!" Angie laughed guiltily. "I was working on some ideas for an article for the *Recorder!*"

"You should be out there on the dance floor, enjoying yourself," said Adrian, who, if not quite the love-god that Rebecca had described, was still extremely good-looking and very pleasant. He was showing more than a friendly interest in Angie too, Rebecca noticed; but then, so were most of the boys at the dance. Some girls had all the luck!

"Angie wants to become the next Lois Lane," Rebecca announced, and added pointedly: "And until she does she's not going to allow even Superman to get a look-in!"

"That's a shame," oozed Adrian. "And such a waste too..."

Rebecca listened in, horrified. *Was Adrian actually coming on to her best friend?*

"Look, why don't you two go back and dance?" Angie suggested tactfully as the DJ started to play a smoochy tune. "I'll be fine here."

"You're sure?" asked Adrian.

"Of course she's sure!" said Rebecca and grabbed Adrian's hand, dragging him back on to the dance floor.

Angie smiled as she watched them join the other couples who were swaying gently to and fro. The song was unfamiliar to her, sung by a deep male voice against some average male harmonies, telling of how the singer had known lots of girls but thought he'd never meet the right one.

It was pleasant enough, Angie thought, but a little too sentimental and slushy for her taste; it was probably just an attempt by another band of pretty boys to cash in on their good looks, and write a song which would appeal to all the pre-pubescent teenagers out there. She was far too grown-up to be taken in by all that pop-music hype!

"Would you like to dance to Zone with me, Angela?" asked a dark-brown voice above her.

Angie looked up to see the smiling face of Dominic

Cairns, the captain of the college football team. They'd known each other by sight for a couple of years now, but had never really spoken to each other before.

"Excuse me?" said Angie. "Zone?"

"That's who's playing now," Dominic said. "They're a new band, and it's their first single."

Angie looked back at the dance floor: Rebecca and Adrian were getting involved in what looked like a pretty serious clinch. She felt a pang of envy.

"Well, I don't know…" she said unsurely.

"I'd be honoured if you did," Dominic smoothed. He smiled at her, displaying a set of dazzling white teeth. "It's so rare that I get a chance to dance with such an attractive girl…"

"Then how can I say no?" Angie said and allowed Dominic to take her hand and lead her out on to the dance floor.

As they passed through the throng of couples, Rebecca released herself from Adrian's passionate embrace, and her eyes glanced over at them.

So, for that matter, did the eyes of every other girl on the dance floor.

"Will you just look at that!" Rebecca said to her companion, as Angie and Dominic began to slow-dance in time to the sensual beat of Zone's first single. "Angie and Dominic Cairns!"

Adrian nuzzled Rebecca's neck. "So?" he asked, his mind obviously on much more interesting things. "What's the big deal?"

"The big deal is that Dominic is the most gorgeous, scrumptious boy in our entire school," she said. "He's the guy everyone says could make the big time as a male model if he wasn't captain of the football team."

Adrian grunted noncommittally, and returned to stroking the small of Rebecca's back, sending frissons of pleasure coursing down her spine. That was the trouble with boys, Rebecca thought ironically; they were only ever interested in one thing. They just didn't appreciate the delights of a good gossip.

"Every girl's been running after him for ... well, for ever. And who gets to dance with him without even trying?" Rebecca asked rhetorically. "What a lucky so-and-so Angie is! But I never even thought Dominic was interested in girls; the only thing he seems to have time for is kicking that football of his around. Adrian, this is the start of something big!"

Unaware of all the attention being focused on her, or the fact that she had suddenly become an item of envy for practically every girl in the room, Angie was enjoying herself immensely.

Despite his heavy football-player's build, Dominic was a surprisingly good dancer, leading her smoothly across the floor as if he had been doing it for years, and it felt good to have his body alongside hers. Beneath his open-necked cotton shirt she could feel his firm and strong pectoral muscles, and the biceps in his upper arms were hard and pumped. There was a hint of cologne about him: not one of those fancy and expensive foreign scents, but down-to-earth and masculine, making her think of rugged countryside and clear mountain streams.

Dominic looked down at her, fixing her with those brilliantly blue eyes which he knew could make almost all the girls at Astor weak at the knees.

"You're a very good dancer, Angela," he said approvingly.

"My mother taught me when I was a child," Angie replied, and held Dominic even more tightly. They weaved in and out of the other couples, and she ran her hand down the small of his back to the base of Dominic's spine, to the top of his smart Armani trousers. "She used to be a professional dancer – before she died."

"I'm sorry," said Dominic, and even sounded as though he meant it, Angie thought. Angie had always steered clear of Dominic before, distrusting his undeniably devastating good looks – *let the other girls giggle and make fools of themselves over him*, she had always told herself. But here on the dance floor, he seemed a very nice guy indeed, charming and modest, and blissfully unaware that he was probably the most handsome guy in the entire hall.

"You needn't be sorry, Dominic," she said. "Mum died a long time ago. And Stephanie – my dad's new wife – has been as good as a real mother to me…"

They danced in silence for a few moments, and Dominic pulled her closer to him. Angie looked up into his eyes: he really was most extraordinarily sexy, she decided, with thick dark hair, just curling over his collar, a firm jaw, and a swarthy Mediterranean complexion. Just her type, in fact; she hated pasty-faced blonds. She giggled.

"What's so funny?" Dominic asked, wanting to share in the joke.

"Bec was trying to fix me up with a date before," she said, wondering if the wine she had been drinking was starting to go to her head. "With some spotty fifth-former. She's convinced that I need a boyfriend for Christmas…"

"Well, I'm glad that she was unsuccessful," Dominic said, and then looked at her seriously. "And *do* you?" he asked.

"Do I what?" Angie said coyly, although she knew perfectly well what Dominic was asking her.

Near them, Rebecca and Adrian had manoeuvred themselves within listening distance: Rebecca had decided that this was going to be too good to miss out on!

"Need a boyfriend for Christmas?" Dominic breathed huskily.

A look passed between them, a look which said everything they needed to know. Thirty pairs of envious female eyes glared green with jealousy as the handsomest, sexiest and hunkiest guy at Astor Sixth-Form College bent his head down to kiss Angie.

Angie felt her heart pound in her breast, inhaled Dominic's warm and sexy smell, felt the taut muscles flex in his broad, strong back. Suddenly her entire world had become centred on this one spot on the dance floor. There was no one else here but her and Dominic, no other sound than the seductive and romantic tones of this new band, singing about the search for their one true love. It had been such a long and lonely time since Angie had allowed herself to be affected this way by any boy, and she realized now just how much she had missed it.

She closed her eyes, raising her head to meet Dominic's lips.

And then suddenly she broke away.

"Omigod!" she cried. "I'd forgotten all about it!"

"Angela, what is it?" asked Dominic, his voice full of concern. "Are you all right?"

Angie looked down at her Swatch. It was a quarter to ten. If she rushed she might just make it!

"Look, Dominic, I'm really, really sorry," she started to babble. "But the new Christmas hospice..."

"Christmas hospice?" Dominic was confused.

"Yeah, it's being opened tonight," she said. "By the Social Security Minister who's come up especially from London..."

"So?"

"Well, if I can get an interview with him for the *Recorder*, that would be a real scoop!" she said, and pushed her way through the smooching couples to the edge of the dance floor. She rushed over to her table, and grabbed her reporter's notebook, then turned to Dominic who had followed her.

"Look, I'm really sorry, Dominic," she said, and kissed him – a friendly peck on the cheek and not the long, deep and passionate kiss he had been expecting on the dance floor. "But you do understand, don't you?"

The look on Dominic's face made it plain that he didn't understand in the slightest. He was speechless: nothing like this had ever happened to him before. Usually he couldn't get rid of the girls: no one had ever walked out on him before!

"I'll make it up to you," Angie promised as she picked up her coat from the back of her chair, and the hapless Dominic helped her to put it on. She kissed him on the cheek again. "Have to dash now. See you!"

And with that Angie Markowski left the most gorgeous boy in the whole of Astor College standing alone, and rejected, and feeling more than a little puzzled and foolish, and raced out into the cold and biting winds of an English winter. Thirty girls who had been watching the whole scene decided that she was the biggest fool it had ever been their misfortune to know.

From the dance floor Rebecca and Adrian watched her go. Rebecca shook her head in amazement and, it has to be said, a little bit of perverse admiration. She turned to Adrian, who, in common with most of the boys present, wasn't quite sure what all the fuss was about.

"My best friend is the craziest, dumbest, most brain-dead person in the history of the world. Dumping Dominic Cairns for a fusty old Government Minister!"

"It's her job, so you were telling me," Adrian said.

"This is Christmas, Adrian," Rebecca replied. "We're allowed to switch off for the holiday season!"

"Angie doesn't seem to me to be the sort of girl who can switch off, or who does things by halves," decided Adrian. "Either she's going to go right to the very top in her career, or she's going to fall so head-over-heels in love that journalism is going to be the last thing on her mind!"

"You really think so?" asked Rebecca, and regarded her new boyfriend in a different light.

Not only was he a major hunk, the second cutest guy here tonight, but it sounded like he was also something of a secret romantic.

"Sure," he said, and then added: "And on that day you're going to see pigs flying in close formation over Astor College. Now come on, Bec, and let's dance!"

2

"**Y**ou do know I'm mortally ashamed to be your friend, Angie Markowski?" Rebecca announced loudly the following morning. She had met up with Angie in the offices of the school newspaper, where Angie had spent most of the morning typing up a story on one of the paper's two Apple Macs.

"Yeah, that's the third time you've told me –" Angie looked up at the digital clock on the wall – "in twenty minutes."

She glanced down at her spiral-bound notepad to check up on a fact and then, satisfied that her article was as perfect as she could make it, pressed the "Command-S" keys to save it on the hard disk, and started to print it out on the laser printer.

She swivelled around in her chair to look at her friend. "Look, Bec, what's the big problem?"

"What's the big problem?" Rebecca couldn't believe what she was hearing. "The big problem is that you dumped Dominic Cairns at the Christmas party!"

"So?" asked Angie, and smiled fondly as she recalled the special way she had felt in Dominic's arms. "What's so brilliant about Dominic Cairns? He's only the captain of the football team, after all."

Rebecca sighed: her best friend could be so dim at times.

"Angie, it may have escaped your notice but Dominic Cairns is not just the captain of the school football team. He's also SuperHunk, Sex On Legs, the guy most girls at Astor would kill their grandparents for! They say that some national magazine is even interested in him doing some modelling for them, so gorgeous is he. And you went and left him standing there! The official verdict is that you are seriously off your head!"

Angie shrugged, but couldn't help but be amused – and more than a little flattered – by all the commotion she seemed to have caused by ditching Dominic last night.

"I'm a journalist, Bec, or at least I hope to be one some day," she reminded her loftily. "I had a story to get!"

"And did you?" Rebecca asked pointedly.

Angie laughed ironically. "The Social Security Minister didn't make it in the end," she admitted. "Got caught up in the snow. Some boring old councillor opened up the Hospice instead!"

"See!" Rebecca crowed. "So it was all a waste of time after all! If you'd've listened to me you could have stayed with Dominic last night, and this morning you'd be the envy of every single female in the world!"

"You know something, Bec?" Angie laughed. "You're obsessed with men!"

Rebecca nodded happily. "Adrian – you know the guy I met last night?"

"How could I forget?" Angie asked sarcastically. "You haven't stopped talking about him!"

"Adrian is just one of the most wonderful guys in the world," Rebecca oozed. "Kind, gentle, intelligent, and so good-looking it just isn't true!"

"That's what you said about Rod," Angie reminded her, laughing. "And the one before him. And the one before him…"

Rebecca stuck her tongue out at her: Angie was always reminding Rebecca about her past boyfriends. It wasn't her fault that they didn't last so long; there was always someone just a little bit cuter, just a little sexier for

Rebecca to fall head-over-heels in love with. Adrian, she was sure however, was going to be different.

"At least I go out with boys," she said sulkily. "Unlike you – always chasing after the next big story."

"I have been known to go out with boys too, you know," Angie reminded her best friend.

"Guy? That was over almost twelve months ago," Rebecca said. She looked seriously at Angie. "Listen, Angie, we're seventeen. In another couple of years we're both going to be over the hill. We've got to have fun now while we can and before it's too late!"

She sauntered over to the editor's desk, which was littered with computer disks, bulging ring-binder files, and press releases. One press release in particular, paper-clipped to a glossy black-and-white photo, caught her eye, and she snatched it up. She rapidly scanned the press release, which had been sent to the paper's offices by a small record company based about a hundred miles away in Manchester.

"Zone are coming to town?" she asked. "I don't believe it!"

Angie, who was tidying up some files at her own desk, shrugged. "Zone? Who are Zone?" she asked.

"You danced to them last night!" Rebecca reminded her and gazed down at the seven-by-eight glossy. "When Dominic Dreamboat dragged you out on the dance floor!"

"Oh, yeah, I remember," Angie said and smiled. Dominic's body had been so warm and comfortable pressed up against hers. "So who are they?"

Rebecca passed over the photo for Angie to take a look. Angie nodded wisely to herself: she had been right last night when she guessed that the four guys in the band were a bunch of opportunists who were banking that their pretty-boy looks would take the place of talent and make them into stars.

Rebecca sighed, and pretended to swoon. "Zone are just the best band ever to have appeared on the scene in the past twenty years," she enthused.

"So why haven't I heard of them?" Angie asked. "Before last night, that is."

"They only formed a few months ago," Rebecca explained knowledgeably. "That was their first single – "Lost Without You" – that you heard last night."

Angie smiled and handed the photo back to Rebecca, who gazed dreamily at it. "So if they've only released one track, how come you think they're the greatest band in the world?" she asked, although she had a pretty good idea of what Rebecca's answer would be.

Rebecca shook her head sadly: if Angie was going to ask such stupid questions she was going to be middle-aged before she even reached twenty! "Angie, with looks like these boys have got, they're bound to be big!"

"Far too pretty for me," Angie said dismissively. She remembered Dominic's rugged handsomeness. She could certainly imagine him as a model advertising a new brand of jeans, all tough and masculine. Maybe she'd been wrong last night to ditch him for that non-existent scoop.

"Pretty? *Pretty?*" Rebecca scoffed. "Calling these guys pretty is like saying the Sistine Chapel is kind of nice. These guys are to die for!" She pointed out the individual members of the band one by one.

"That's Danny," she said, pointing to a cute Italian-looking guy, dressed in a trendy T-shirt, designer-ripped 501s and a back-to-front baseball cap. "He plays drums and does backing vocals."

Angie nodded: in the photo Danny was trying to look tough, but with his baby-face it wasn't quite working. He looked about seventeen which made him, Angie guessed, at least two or three years younger than the other members of the band.

Rebecca indicated a black boy, whose baggy linen shirt had been undone to his waist, displaying his muscular torso to his adoring female fans.

"That's Marco – he plays bass guitar – and this mean and moody hunk with the designer stubble is Luke on keyboards…"

Angie then pointed to the fourth member of the group, who was standing in the foreground, removed from the other band members. He was tall, dressed in black leathers, and a white muscle shirt. He had dishevelled blond hair, which Angie immediately (and correctly) suspected hadn't been washed for a few days, and which curled over the collar of his leather biker's jacket; there was a tiny crucifix-shaped earring hanging in his right ear.

Angie found herself instantly disliking him: this guy oozed attitude, with a capital "A", and looked as though he had an over-inflated opinion of himself too. Even so, he dominated the photograph and it was hard to take her eyes off him.

"And who's this?" she asked casually, trying not to give away just how interested she was.

"I've left the best to last!" said Rebecca, sounding just like a star-crazy, love-struck schoolkid. "That's JJ, Zone's lead singer. He writes all their songs too. Isn't he the hunkiest thing you've ever seen in your life?"

"I wouldn't let Adrian hear you say that!" Angie advised her. "And what sort of name is JJ anyway?"

Rebecca shrugged, and picked up the press release again. "No one knows," she said, and then suddenly had a great idea. "Hey, Angie, you think you're such a good reporter! Why don't you try and find out?"

"Somehow I don't think discovering the real identity of a second-rate pop singer is going to get me a job on the local paper when I leave school," Angie replied.

God, did that really sound as pompous as I think it did? she immediately asked herself.

Rebecca finished scanning the press release. "You'd have no chance anyway," she told her flatly.

"And why's that?" Angie asked.

"The boys are coming to play at the local town hall – I must get some tickets," Rebecca said, reading from the press release. "But there's a strict ban on interviews. No one is allowed to get near them, not even the national papers. As far as the Press is concerned Zone are strictly off-limits."

Angie grabbed the sheet of paper from Rebecca, and read it more closely. There was an eager and challenged look in her blue eyes.

"Off-limits, are they?" she said scornfully. "We'll see about that!"

Rebecca looked at her best friend warily. She might have known: if something was forbidden to Angie Markowski then she went right out there and got it.

Rebecca recognized the gleam in Angie's eyes. She had seen it once before, a couple of years ago when Angie had been going out with Guy. Her grades had fallen off and Mrs Greystone had given her a severe telling-off in front of the rest of the maths class. The teacher had told Angie that her recent string of Cs wasn't acceptable, and that she had better start improving her work.

Determined to prove the teacher wrong, Angie had set about her work with a determination that was almost frightening: the next term she got nothing less than perfect As for every single one of her papers.

If Angie Markowski wanted something then she usually got it. Zone had better watch out!

What was the point of having a father when he didn't help you out when you needed him the most? Angie asked herself later that evening. She had returned home, through the snow, to ask her dad one tiny favour, and he'd turned away and told her in no uncertain terms that he had no intention of doing any favours for her at all, no matter how small.

Angie turned away angrily from her father and stamped her feet in frustration. Peter Markowski was still a good-looking man of fifty-one, and the greatest dad in the world, Angie knew; he was also one of the most stubborn adults she had ever known!

"Come on, Dad," she pleaded. "I've tried every other way I can think of. I've rung their record company, their management company, I've even bought a ticket for their concert! But there's no way that I can get an interview with Zone!"

Her dad smiled, and shook his head sympathetically. "Then you'll just have to be philosophical about the whole thing and accept that you can't interview Zone," he said.

Angie, however, wasn't prepared to be "philosophical" about anything. "If I got an exclusive interview with them, I could sell it to the papers!" she said. "It would look so good on my CV – the only reporter in the country to get an interview with the most up-and-coming boy-band around. And not just any reporter but a school reporter at that!"

"I know it would," her father agreed. "I'm sure the local paper would be interested in it – after all, even though they're based in Manchester now, Zone do come from this area. I imagine they'd love an exclusive story about the local boys made good..."

Angie looked curiously at her fifty-one-year-old dad: she hadn't thought that he would know something like that: she'd only found out that all four members of the band were local guys when Rebecca had told her.

"Oh, I keep an open mind," he said, in response to her unspoken question.

"You could help me, Dad," Angie continued.

Her father gave her a look as if to say *Oh, can I now?* and Angie continued.

"You work in TV, Dad, everyone says that you're one of the best TV arts producers around!"

Peter smiled but didn't say anything: after all, having worked for almost thirty years on late-night arty TV programmes, he'd been flattered by experts!

"You know everyone who is anyone," Angie reminded him. "You could use your connections, pull a few strings. If anyone could get me an interview with Zone you could!"

Peter glanced down at the press release Angie had brought home with her. "I probably could," he agreed, and read the name of Zone's management company, which was printed at the foot of the sheet of paper. "Krupp Promotionals." The name rang a bell, and he cast his mind back a few years.

"I met Joe Krupp once, just before your mother died. He was interested in signing her up for a dance special on TV. I've probably still got his phone number somewhere in my Filofax."

"Then you'll help me?" Angie asked. "You'll phone up Joe Krupp?" She leaned over and kissed her father gratefully on the cheek. "Oh, Dad, you're the best dad in the world and I know you're going to be so proud of me when you see my interview printed in the papers!"

Peter shook his head. "No, darling, I'm not going to help you," he stated firmly.

"*What?*" Angie couldn't believe what her dad was saying.

"If you want your interview with Zone, then that's fine by me," he said, and stood up from his chair. "But get it yourself. If you're really cut out to be a reporter then you'll be able to interview Zone without my help."

"But—"

"Sorry, darling," her dad said, "you're on your own on this one."

He walked out of the room.

"Of all the pig-headed, arrogant, selfish, old-fashioned—" Angie spluttered.

She turned to Stephanie, her dad's second wife, who had been silently following the conversation from her armchair. Stephanie was a research physicist at the local University. She was several years younger than Angie's dad and Angie often regarded her as an older sister rather than a stepmother. The fact that she wore her ash-blonde hair in a short and trendy bob made her look even younger.

"Can you believe that, Steph?" she said. "How can he be so cruel?"

Stephanie put down the research papers she had been working on, and patted the chair next to her, indicating that Angie should sit down and talk to her.

"He's only got your best interests at heart, Angie," she said. "And deep down you know he's right."

Angie sighed. "I suppose so," she admitted reluctantly. "But an interview with Zone would be so good for me."

"Then go for it," Stephanie said. "Prove to your dad that you can do it. Prove it to yourself."

"Security around Zone is so tight I'd have a better chance of breaking into the Bank of England," Angie said glumly. "If only that so-and-so had agreed to help me!"

Stephanie chuckled. "That so-and-so is your dad – my husband – who's only interested in your welfare. If it's any consolation I'd happily give you Joe Krupp's telephone number," she said.

"You have his number too?" Angie asked, immediately hoping that Stephanie would prove an ally in her attempt to secure an interview.

"Well, yes – on my computer," Stephanie said. "You know how absent-minded your dad is. I'm sure that one day he's going to lose that Filofax of his, so I had him copy all his important phone numbers on to my hard disk for safe-keeping." She paused, considered, then added hastily: "On second thoughts, don't ask me for the number – not even I'm prepared to face your father's wrath!"

Angie laughed. "Thanks anyway," she said. "At least you're different from the Dad from Hell..."

"Different?" Stephanie smiled.

"Yeah," Angie said. "You don't always push me to the limits like Dad does. You're much more easy-going." She indicated the sheaf of papers Stephanie was working on. They were filled with numbers and symbols which Angie knew she'd never have a hope of understanding. "You even have a totally different gobbledygook!"

Stephanie laughed. "That 'gobbledygook' is my work!" she said. "As far as I'm concerned, all the arty novels and intellectual films your dad reviews are gobbledygook to me!"

"But you're both so different," Angie said. "I mean, for most of the time Dad goes around with his head in the clouds, talking about literature, and black-and-white foreign films, and classical music and dance. And you go on about quarks and anti-quarks, and protons and neutrons and tau-mesons and a thousand other things I don't understand."

Stephanie chuckled. "The only difference is that your father deals with the abstract, and I look after the concrete," she said. "What more perfect match could there be?" She smiled again. "But what you really mean, Angie, is that I'm different from your real mother..."

Angie turned away shyly, uncomfortable at the direction the conversation was taking. "It's just that my dad and my mum were always interested in the same things," she said. "When they met she was training to be a classical dancer and he was a trainee arts producer for the BBC. They moved in the same circles, went to the same concerts and ballets and films, and they just seemed so right together, so perfect for each other..."

"Meaning I'm not?" asked Stephanie mischievously.

"Oh, I don't mean that!" Angie said and turned back to her stepmother. "You know I love you, Steph, and I'm really glad that you and Dad got together after my mum died." She lowered her eyes, so as not to look Stephanie in the face. "But you'll never take the place of my real mum..."

"I don't intend to," Stephanie said gently. "Your mother was a very special person for you, and your father, and no one can ever replace her."

"You make Dad happy, and that makes me happy too," Angie said. "But if someone had told me that you and he were going to get together, I'd never have believed it! I mean, how many times have you been to see *The Nibelungenlied*, or watched a scratchy copy of an arty-farty French movie on late-night telly?"

"Never," Stephanie admitted cheerfully. "But then how many times has your father discussed the logistical and ethical problems of nuclear fission or questioned the validity of Einstein's theory of relativity?"

"Point taken."

"Opposites do attract sometimes, Angie," Stephanie said. "And three years ago, if someone had told me that I would end up marrying your father I would have thought that they were crazy too. The first time I met him I thought he was pompous, arrogant, conceited, and much too full of himself."

"You're not far wrong there," Angie said cheekily.

Stephanie chose to ignore her stepdaughter's remark and continued: "But as I got to know him better I found that that was only the impression he gave to the world because he was shy about meeting other people."

"Dad? Shy?"

Stephanie nodded. "His stand-offish manner was just a front, a form of self-defence, if you like, for those times he was confronted with people like me who he didn't know what to make of," she explained. "But as I got to know him better I discovered that he was the sweetest, gentlest, most lovable man I had ever known in my life. And, in spite of all our differences, soon I found myself falling helplessly in love with him.

"Love's like that, Angie: it's got no prejudices, it never plays by the rules. You might have known someone for years, and have never felt anything for them; you might not even be able to stand that person, or at the very least think that they're not your type; and then suddenly little old Cupid goes and fires his arrow, and – well, you know the rest..."

Angie thought about this for a second and then laughed. "Little old Cupid and his arrow?'" she said flippantly, and pulled a face of mock-disgust. "That's the sort of slushy nonsense my dad might come out with! You're learning from him, Steph!"

"Not as much as he's learning from me," Steph said, joining in the joke. "Why, only the other day I caught him trying to mend the washing machine! This from the man who had to be told only a couple of months ago how to wire a plug!"

"Now that really is something!" Angie remarked.

"When two opposites meet they learn from each other," Stephanie said. "And the most important thing you learn is that, no matter what your superficial differences are, you can never stay apart for long. It's no use fighting the attraction: you're drawn to each other like a magnet is to a piece of iron.

"All you can do is give in. If you don't, if you struggle against it, then you're going to be miserable for the rest of your life. And I, for one, am glad that I didn't fight against that attraction..."

"And I'm glad too," said Angie, and gave Stephanie a daughterly peck on the cheek. She looked towards the door through which her father had left. "He's still the Dad from Hell though!"

Stephanie burst out laughing as her stepdaughter lightened the tone of the conversation. "He's your father, and he wants to look after you!" she repeated.

"If he's interested in my welfare he could have got me my interview!" she said lightly.

"Like he said, this is your chance to prove what a crack reporter you are," Stephanie said. "And besides, maybe there's another reason for him not wanting you to get the interview..."

"And what's that?" asked Angie, suddenly serious.

"Well, you're his only daughter and he loves you more than anything else in this world," the older woman said, with a wicked twinkle in her eye. "And you know what they all say about rock stars, don't you...?"

"No," Angie said, all coyly, and grinned as she put her stepmother on the spot. "What do they all say about rock stars, Steph?"

Stephanie was about to answer when the telephone rang. She answered it, and passed the cordless receiver over to Angie.

"Hello?" Angie frowned, wondering who could be asking for her at half-past eleven at night.

"Angie, is that you?"

Rebecca's voice crackled down the receiver. In the background Angie could hear the buzz of people talking and the throbbing rhythms of some heavy house and techno music: she remembered Rebecca telling her that Adrian had promised to take her to the town's trendiest and most happening club tonight, and guessed that that was where Rebecca was phoning her from.

"Listen, I told you that Adrian was a catch and a half, didn't I?" Rebecca said excitedly, shouting to make herself heard above the sound of the techno beat.

"He's a nice guy, Bec," Angie agreed, smiling to herself. Rebecca was always like this in the first few days of a new relationship, ringing everyone up to tell them just how wonderful her current boyfriend was: she'd calm down in a few days' time, after the first flush of "love" had faded away.

"We have just had the most fantastic conversation ever," Rebecca continued.

"I'm surprised you can hear him above all that noise," Angie joked.

"We've learned so much about each other," Rebecca said. "He's kind, he's charming, he's intelligent and witty—"

On the other end of the line, Angie nodded impatiently. "All your boyfriends are, Bec. What's so special about him?"

"Listen, Angie, we got talking about our families, right?" Rebecca said, determined to make Angie wait as long as possible for her devastating piece of gossip. "I told him all about how my brother's two-timing his girlfriend..."

For Heaven's sake, Bec, get to the point! Angie thought irritably.

"And Angie, you are never in a million years going to guess who Adrian's cousin is!"

From her armchair Stephanie watched Angie's expression turn into one of delighted incredulity as Rebecca announced her news.

"Adrian is related to *who*?" Angie asked down the phone. She could scarcely believe her good luck. She glanced over to Stephanie and, with her free hand, gave her a thumbs-up gesture of victory.

Her exclusive interview with the four guys from Zone was as good as guaranteed!

3

The thuggish-looking bouncer, who was wearing a black T-shirt and black leather trousers, looked down at the backstage pass Angie had presented him with. He studied it carefully – *probably because he's only just learned how to read joined-up writing*, Angie thought rather uncharitably – and then he glanced back up at Angie's anxious face. Angie gulped, wondering whether he would see past her deception.

She was dressed in a leather jacket to protect her against the cold, a loose-fitting Katharine Hamnett blouse, and well-cut blue jeans, which she imagined made her look sophisticated and self-assured, and not at all like the giggling schoolkids who were gathered around the stage door of Astor Town Hall, in the hope of catching a glimpse of their pop-star heroes. Even though it was bitterly cold and snowing they had been huddled outside for hours now. In Angie's shoulder bag was a small tape recorder and a list of questions that she and Rebecca had thought of that morning to ask the boys from Zone.

The bouncer regarded her through narrow, suspicious eyes. "A. Fowler," he read from the pass. His breath hung in clouds in front of his mouth. "And that's supposed to be you?"

"That's right," she said nervously and shivered in the cold. "Angela Fowler."

It had been Rebecca's idea to use Adrian's backstage pass; after all, Adrian, who had unexpectedly had to visit some old maiden aunt with his Christmas presents, wouldn't be able to use it.

Angie gulped: this sort of thing always looked so easy on TV, but it was a lot more hair-raising in real life. Was the bouncer going to believe her? Or was he going to turn her away like she had already seen him turn away scores of fans desperate to get backstage for a chance to speak to their idols?

The bouncer obviously wasn't convinced. "You got any other ID?" he asked gruffly.

Aha! Angie thought triumphantly. *You thought you'd catch me out on that, didn't you?*

She beamed and rooted in her bag for her school press pass. She passed it to the bouncer who read it and checked Angie's photo in the top right-hand corner. He shrugged.

"Angela Fowler," he read again. "Seems like you're on the level after all."

Angela gave herself a congratulatory pat on the back. She'd guessed that the bouncer would have needed some additional ID to identify her as "A. Fowler", so she had spent the afternoon producing a fake press card in that name on one of the *Recorder*'s Apple Macs.

Lois Lane, eat your heart out! she crowed to herself. *They don't call me an ace reporter for nothing!*

The bouncer handed the backstage pass and the fake ID back to Angie. "So you're Luke's cousin, are you?" he grinned, his manner now much more friendly as he realized that Angie wasn't a pushy fan or a tiresome groupie.

"That's right," she breezed. "Luke and me, we're like that." She crossed her fingers together to illustrate her point – and for luck.

The bouncer stroked his chin which was covered with a few days' beard growth. "Funny he never mentioned you before, though," he said. "He's always been one for the girls, has our Luke. I'm sure he would have mentioned someone as pretty as you..."

Good grief, he isn't coming on to me, is he? Angie asked herself in disbelief. *This bouncer's almost old enough to be my dad!* She laughed nervously. "I ... er, I like keeping a low profile."

"Sure," said the bouncer who still hadn't let her inside. "I suppose you've met the other boys as well?"

Angie nodded. "Naturally," she said. "We're all great pals. We see each other all the time. Marco. Danny. And, of course, EJ."

"JJ," the bouncer corrected her.

"Yeah, that's right, JJ..." Angie said, and kicked herself.

The bouncer looked at her for a few more seconds, eyeing her up, Angie thought ... and then stood aside.

"OK," he said, "go in!"

Done it! Angie whooped to herself. *Pulled the wool over your eyes well and good! Scoop of the year, here I come!*

She skipped lightly past the bouncer and started to head off down the corridor to where he had told her the boys' dressing room was. Suddenly a short, fat man emerged from an open doorway, as silently as a cat, and Angie ran straight into him.

"I'm sorry," she said, and looked up at the man's podgy face. He had piggy eyes, and a narrow, unpleasant mouth; he reminded Angie of the baddies she had seen on some of the late-night trashy movies she and Stephanie loved to watch.

"And who have we here?" the man asked, looking not at Angie but at the bouncer standing by the open door.

"Angela Fowler, boss," the bouncer said. "She says she's Luke's cousin."

"Indeed?" The fat man stared down at Angie, a look of disbelief on his ugly face. Angie dived into her bag again and pulled out her backstage pass.

"See?" she said, pushing the card under the fat man's pug nose. "A. Fowler – Access All Areas."

The fat man took Angie's arm – a little too roughly –

and marched her towards the door. Angie shook him off.

"I've got to see my cousin," she protested. "He's expecting me..."

"Luke is not expecting you, nor is any other one of my boys," the fat man said roughly.

He grabbed Angie's backstage pass and tore it in half and threw it on to the floor. "You are also not Luke's cousin – unless you have recently had a sex change which I have not been informed about! Luke's cousin is called Adrian, not Angela—"

Angie's face fell, but she was still determined to stick to her story. "How come you know so much about Luke's family?" she asked the fat man defiantly, as the bouncer marched up to escort her out.

"My name is Joe Krupp and I am the manager of Zone," the fat man announced. "And I make it my business to know everything about my boys. Now, goodbye, Ms Fowler – or whatever your real name is!"

The bouncer escorted Angie unceremoniously out of the theatre and back into the cold. The fans who had been waiting outside gave her sympathetic looks: it had been a nice try, but didn't she know that Joe Krupp was famous for making sure that no one ever intruded on his clients without his written permission? That was why he was one of the most successful managers in the business: he kept tight control over every single detail of his clients' lives. They said you couldn't even sneeze without Joe Krupp knowing about it.

Angie glared at the stage door, which was now firmly closed. Krupp didn't know it, but he had just made her even more determined to get an interview with the boys from Zone.

JJ strutted along the edge of the stage, in tight, tight leather pants, his shirt unbuttoned to the waist, revealing a muscular, hairless chest, and a lean and gym-trained torso.

A hundred teenage girls in the first few rows squealed

their approval. Few of them were over fourteen, even fewer of them had ever had a boyfriend, but every single one of them knew that JJ was without any doubt the sexiest thing that had ever taken to the stage.

JJ bent down, reaching out to touch their outstretched arms, and then pulled away suddenly, teasing them, exciting them, making them beg for more. He swayed his hips suggestively, and then spun around on his heels, turning to the other boys in the band. With the hand that wasn't holding his mike, he directed them, like the master-conductor of a world-famous orchestra.

Danny on drums, his face already drenched with sweat, grinned and pounded out the beat, while Marco cut a mean riff on his electric guitar, and Luke went wild on the synthesizer.

But great-looking as the others were, all eyes were on JJ, as he turned back to his audience, and sang out the words to Zone's opening number, a raunchy rocker called "Are You Ready For It?" It seemed that he was born to sing the song, as he wrenched every ounce of emotion out of its lyrics and the audience screamed out their approval.

At the side of the stage, hidden from the audience, Krupp watched, with a satisfied smile on his face. This song was designed to whip the audience into a frenzy from the very start, and it was succeeding.

Zone were assured of a warm welcome in their home town, he knew, but if JJ and the others could work this sort of magic on the nationwide tour he was already planning for them, then they could be the biggest thing in pop music within the next two years. And Joe Krupp would be richer by several million pounds.

JJ was undoubtedly the star of the show, and was revelling in all the adulation coming his way. It seemed that the more the audience screamed his name, the sexier he became.

He had them eating out of the palm of his hand, and, as he launched into the second number, a sharp-sounding tune called "Will You Be The One?", practically every member of the audience wished that she could indeed be the "One".

Towards the back of the hall, Rebecca, who was already clapping her hands and dancing in the aisle, turned to Angie. "Aren't they just great?" she asked, above the music and the screams of Zone's younger fans.

"They're OK," Angie said dismissively, even though her feet were betraying her feigned indifference by tapping along to the rhythm of the beat. "But take away their good looks, and JJ's dance routine, and what have you got?"

"Loosen up, Angie!" Rebecca chided her. "You're just being grumpy because you couldn't get backstage to interview them!"

Angie wagged an admonishing finger at her friend. "I'm not defeated yet, Bec Penswick," she said. "I promised to get an interview with them, and I'm not going to give up until I do!"

Angie sneaked around the back of the town hall, past the gaggle of adoring girls hanging around the stage door, to a tiny yard which backed on to the building. This was where the brewery van parked when it was delivering barrels of beer to the Town Hall bar.

Making sure that no one could see her, she bent down and tugged at the iron grating which she guessed led down to the cellars. Her plan was to get into the town hall via the cellar and, once inside, and out of the public area, she could try and track down Zone's dressing room, and get her prized interview with the boys.

Damn it! she cursed. The grating was too heavy and was barred from the inside. As she stood up she noticed a tiny window, set about thirteen feet up in the wall. She put her hands on her waist, grateful that she had the sort of slim physique which was the envy of most of the other girls at Astor College.

An empty beer barrel had been left in the yard, and she rolled that underneath the window. Standing on tiptoe, she reached up for the sill of the window and, with muscles aching painfully, hauled herself up to the open window.

It was a tight squeeze but she managed to get through, although not without ripping the legs of her jeans in the process. *This interview had better be worth it!* she thought, as she clambered through and dropped carefully to the ground on the other side.

She was in some sort of store room. She crossed over to the door, thankful that it wasn't locked, and peered out into the corridor.

At the far end she could hear Krupp arguing with one of Zone's fans. No, he didn't care who she was, Angie heard him say, she couldn't have a quiet chat with his "boys". They would be signing autographs later and that would have to do.

This was Angie's chance, while Krupp and the bouncer were occupied. She ran down the corridor, in the direction of the stage, guessing that that was where the boys' dressing room would be.

She heard Krupp bid the fan goodbye, and march off down the corridor. Panicking, she opened the first door she came to: as luck would have it, it was the very room she had been searching for. Krupp's footsteps came echoing down the corridor. It was obvious that he was headed for the dressing room as well.

There was a large wardrobe in the corner of the room. Angie raced over and hid herself in it, huddling against the stage costumes belonging to the boys from Zone. Her heart pounding, she heard the door to the dressing room swing open. Krupp's footsteps marched across the stone floor. Coming right for her. The door to the wardrobe creaked open.

"Well, well, well, and what do we have here then?"

Angie breathed a sigh of relief. It wasn't Krupp! The manager had not been making for the dressing room after all. Instead, grinning at her, and obviously incredibly amused, was that handsome lead singer. He offered her his hand and she stepped out of the wardrobe.

"Thanks, EJ," she said.

"It's JJ, babe," he corrected her, and then turned to the other members of the band who were just filing into the dressing room. "Hey, gang, look what's just come out of the closet!"

The three others grinned; Luke even wolf-whistled. They then carried on as though nothing unusual had happened. Marco started stripping off, to get ready for his after-gig shower.

"And what are you doing here, babe?" JJ asked.

If he calls me babe again, I'll kill him! Angie thought.

"My name's Angie," she said. "Angie Markowski."

"That's an interesting name," JJ said.

"My dad was born in Warsaw," she explained. "I'm half Polish."

"The pretty half, of course."

JJ looked Angie appreciatively up and down, smiling that wicked little half-smile which he knew made him look really sexy. That smile was guaranteed to make his fans swoon in a second, and he frowned when Angie showed not the slightest sign of being impressed by it.

"So what do you want?" he asked again.

"I'm a journalist," she said, suddenly aware that her hair was a mess and her face was black and dirty from having climbed through the window, "for the local student newspaper."

"Aha!" said JJ smugly. "So you want to interview me, is that it?"

"Not just you, JJ," she said. "The others as well."

"What d'you say boys?" JJ asked. "Should we let this pretty young thing talk to us?"

Of all the patronizing, big-headed...!

The others shrugged. "It's up to you, JJ," said Danny, the cute young one. "As long as Joe doesn't find out."

"How did you get in here in the first place?" JJ asked Angie.

"Through a back window..."

JJ laughed. "That's crafty," he said. "I admire that."

"So you're quite willing to do an interview, JJ?" Angie asked, all business-like as she tried not to notice Marco's athletic body: he was crossing the dressing room on his way to the showers, dressed only in his white Calvin Kleins.

"Sure, why not?" said JJ. He sat down, and offered Angie a seat. He leaned back in his chair, and placed his leather-clad legs on the coffee table which was between him and Angie. She took the tiny tape-recorder out of her bag, and set it up on the table. "There's nothing I like better than pleasing the Press..." He chuckled, and winked over at Luke and Danny before turning back to Angie. "You did say you were a journalist, didn't you? You're a lot prettier than most of the *real* reporters I've seen..."

Angie glared angrily at him. She'd caught JJ's suggestion that she wasn't quite the professional lady of the press that she liked to think she was.

Resisting her natural urge to tell JJ just what she thought of him, Angie simply smiled sweetly and said: "I might not be working for Fleet Street or the BBC, JJ, even though I hope to one day, but let me remind you that I succeeded in getting past your manager's security, and the other members of the Press didn't."

Danny, the drummer, who had been listening in on the conversation, took a sip from his can of diet Coke, and laughed. "She's got you on that one, JJ," he said. "Not even the SAS can get past Joe when he's in a bad mood!"

"And what's more, JJ," Angie continued, still smiling, "it's perfectly true that I'm only working on a newspaper for unimportant schoolkids and college students. But just remember that it's those unimportant schoolkids and college students who are going to buy your records, and, if you're really lucky, make you rich and famous one day..."

She suddenly dropped her smile and fixed the handsome young singer with stern and reproving eyes. "Now, shall we get on with the interview?" she asked brusquely.

JJ looked strangely at Angie. No one had ever stood up to him like that before, especially not a girl as attractive as Angie. After all, he was the star of Zone, their lead singer and their songwriter. He was the one, Joe Krupp had promised, whose face was going to be in all the teen magazines within twelve months.

Hey, he needed a little respect! And then JJ realized that respect was exactly what Angie was demanding too.

She had spirit, this girl, JJ thought, and he found he liked that. He liked it very much indeed.

"OK, sure, let's get it over with," he said grumpily. Angie might have won the first round, but there were several more to go!

"Great!" Angie grinned, and switched on the tape recorder. "Now first question—"

JJ interrupted her and turned around to shoo Danny away. The young drummer had settled himself down in a nearby chair to listen to the interview.

"This is private, Dan!" JJ said jokingly. "I'm gonna tell –" he looked at Angie – "what did you say your name was again, babe?"

"Angie." *And don't call me babe!*

"Yeah, that's right, Angie," he said and turned back to Danny. "I'm gonna tell Angie all my deep and darkest secrets, and I don't want you or any of the boys to get to hear them, do I?"

Danny shrugged and stood up. "Sure," he chuckled, and walked away out of earshot. As he did so, and from behind JJ's back, he gave Angie an encouraging thumbs-up sign. Angie grinned: it seemed as though she had an ally in Danny already.

JJ turned back to Angie, and smiled sexily at her once more. Once again, it didn't make the slightest impression on her. What *did* make an impression on her, however, had been JJ's brief words to Danny. It had been interesting to see the lead singer drop his brash and self-assured mask for just a moment, and reveal the real JJ – who was genuinely embarrassed at having one of his mates listen in on his interview.

But when he looked at Angie again, he was the cool rock star he played on stage once more.

"OK, let's roll, babe—"

"The name is Angie," she said sternly.

"Whoops, sorry, ba— Angie!" JJ teased. Angie found it impossible not to smile. She glanced down at her notes.

"What does JJ stand for?" she asked.

JJ held his hands up, palms facing Angie, in a mock gesture of defence. "Top secret," he replied. "Next question please!"

Angie glowered at JJ through narrowed eyes. If this second-rate pop star was going to answer all her questions in a similar manner she might as well go home now!

"OK, let's try something which you might be able to remember," she said patronizingly.

JJ grinned. Angie was treating him like a particularly irritating baby brother! She sure was a refreshing change from all those people who kept on telling him exactly how wonderful he was!

Angie asked him about how he and the others had got together in the first place and formed Zone. Marco had been studying classical music at a private school in the area, he told her, and Luke and Danny were fellow students in a stage school in Birmingham, although not in the same year. They'd formed a rock group and started playing the odd local gig.

"Then Joe Krupp came along," JJ said. "And he saw the guys' potential, and signed them up. But they lacked something, you know..."

"And what was that?" Angie asked and found her eyes wandering from JJ's face to his open shirt. A tiny crucifix hung from his neck, and nestled in the groove between his pectorals. The muscles were firm and well-defined, obvious evidence that JJ spent a lot of his free time in the gym.

"What were they lacking?" JJ asked, in a blasé fashion,

and leaned even further back in his chair. "Good songs – anyone can play that top twenty trash: the public wants something different and original, you know. Plus they needed a dancer. And, of course, an impossibly handsome and sexy lead singer!"

"So I take it they're still searching for one, are they?" Angie asked sarcastically.

For a second JJ looked as though he was about to explode with indignation; and then he relaxed and grinned, realizing that not only had Angie won round one, but round two was hers as well!

"So Krupp found me," he continued. "I'd been a friend of Danny's from way back – I knew his sister, Eva..."

"Eva?" The Germanic name was an odd one for the sister of someone like Danny, whose family was obviously of Mediterranean origin.

"Yeah," JJ said. "Danny's mother was half-German – he speaks the language like a native. They named his sister after her maternal grandmother." JJ suddenly coloured, as though he was embarrassed about something. "Look, I thought we were supposed to be talking about me?" he said quickly.

"Sure. Go ahead, JJ," Angie said, interested, detecting a possible romantic angle for her story. She made a mental note to ask JJ about Danny's sister later.

"I got on well with the other guys," he continued, "I started writing their songs, organizing their dance routines, and that's how the best-looking pop band in the history of music came about!"

"And what about the mysterious JJ? Why do I get the feeling you're keeping something from me? Exactly where did Krupp find you?"

JJ leaned forward and reached out to switch off Angie's tape recorder. "I've got a better idea," he said huskily, and gazed into her blue eyes. "Why don't you tell me where *you're* coming from – like maybe over dinner tonight?"

Angie switched the tape recorder back on. "Sorry, I conduct interviews – I don't give them," she said smartly.

"You'll be sorry," he told her, trying to sound as if Angie's refusal hadn't disappointed him at all. "All my other girl-friends have had no complaints."

"They like hamburger and chips in a greasy spoon then, do they?" Angie asked patronizingly, and followed up JJ's remark with: "So, JJ, do you have a girlfriend at the moment?"

JJ smirked, and silently congratulated himself for managing to change the subject so successfully. *Round three to me, babe!* he thought. *You're not quite so on the ball as you like to think!*

JJ ran a nonchalant hand through his thick, uncombed dark-blond hair, which, Angie noted, curled so cutely over the top of his shirt collar.

"Too much of a hassle, you know," he said, sounding like an experienced man of the world, although a quick glance at Zone's official biography would have revealed that he wasn't yet twenty-one. "You see a girl a couple of times and then the next thing you know she wants to go steady with you. Or she's only interested in you because she thinks you'll be famous one day." He shrugged philo-sophically. "Love 'em and leave 'em, that's my motto…"

You arrogant, self-opinionated chauvinist pig, Angie wanted to say. With his perfectly proportioned body, mischievous eyes, and that divine little dimple in the middle of his chin which she couldn't take her eyes off, Angie knew that JJ could have his pick of girls.

Yet she controlled her anger, because there was some-thing about JJ's manner which jarred. Maybe it was the fact that he didn't look her in the eyes when he spoke about his "girlfriends"; maybe it was his body language as he crossed and then uncrossed his legs; but something told Angie that JJ wasn't telling her the entire truth.

"'Love 'em and leave 'em'," Angie repeated JJ's words, and watched as he shifted uncomfortably in his chair at the sound of his own words. "Can I quote you on that?"

"You will be quoting JJ on nothing," said a stern and familiar voice behind her.

Angie saw JJ's face fall, and she turned to see Krupp standing behind her. Once again he had crept up silently on her, like a hungry puma stalking its prey.

"Er, hi, Mister Krupp," she said weakly, and stood up.

Krupp didn't return her welcome, but reached down and switched off Angie's tape recorder. He took the cassette out and put it into the pocket of his jacket.

"I believe I banned you from my boys' dressing room," Krupp said, grimly.

"Joe, she wasn't doing any harm," JJ pleaded on Angie's behalf. Angie thought she could detect a note of fear in his voice. "She was just interviewing me for her school paper, that's all."

Krupp shook his head sadly. "How many times must I tell you, JJ? There are to be no interviews until I decide the time is right," he said. He patted the pocket into which he had dropped Angie's cassette, as if to reassure himself that it was still there. "Trust me – I have only your best interests at heart. Have you ever known me let you down before?"

JJ hung his head. "No, Joe, of course not..."

Krupp smiled at JJ, and then turned his attention to Angie. He stopped smiling. "And as for you, young lady, you are guilty of breaking and entering. Perhaps I should inform the police..."

"No, Joe, you can't do that!" JJ cried, taking even Angie aback by the urgency in his voice.

Like he's frightened of something, she realized.

For a second JJ and Krupp stared at each other, as though engaged in a battle of wills. Finally Krupp conceded defeat by averting his eyes, and took Angie's arm.

"You have a convincing defender in JJ," he said, and led her to the door. "But pull a stunt like this again and I shall have no hesitation in reporting the entire matter to the police!"

Angie just had the chance to nod her thanks to JJ before Krupp escorted her out of the dressing room, and slammed the door shut behind her.

Left alone in the room, JJ breathed out a sigh of relief. The door to the adjoining dressing room opened, and Luke, Danny and Marco came out.

"You sure lucked out on that one, didn't you?" Danny chuckled, and went over to give JJ a consoling pat on the back.

"Were you miserable scumballs eavesdropping at the door?" JJ asked, pretending to be shocked. Danny nodded happily.

"What's wrong, my man?" Marco, who was drying his hair after his shower, asked evilly. "The old JJ magic not workin' any more? I thought you could get any babe you wanted."

"She's not a babe," JJ corrected him, "her name's Angie..."

"So she's got a name," Luke said dismissively. "You still didn't get a date with her, SuperStud!"

Before JJ had joined the band, Luke had always been the one the fans swooned over, and now there was an element of not entirely friendly rivalry between the two of them.

"Leave it out, Luke," JJ said. "Angie's different. She's got brains, for one thing; and she's her own person. She stood up to me – no one else has done recently. She's not like all the others."

"I'll say that," agreed Marco. "She said no to you for one thing!" By Marco's side, Danny didn't say a word.

"It looks like you've lost your touch, JJ," Marco continued to tease. "Maybe we should think about getting us a new lead singer..."

"Let me tell you, Marco, my man, that JJ never loses his touch," JJ bragged, now that his chatting-up skills had been called into question. "If I'd really wanted her, I could have got her to agree to go on a date with me."

Luke looked his friend in the eye. "So prove it," he challenged.

"Prove it?" asked JJ, puzzled. "What d'you mean?"

"If you think you're such a gift to womankind, get this babe—"

"Angie," JJ corrected him.

"—get this Angie to agree to go out with you."

JJ shook his head. "Hey, I don't know that that's such a good idea," he said.

"What's wrong, JJ?" asked Marco, and mischievously added his own voice to Luke's challenge. "Think you're not up to it any more?"

"Yeah, JJ," Luke taunted, "what's the trouble? *Scared?*"

That did it. JJ took a step towards Luke.

"No one says that I'm scared," he snarled menacingly. "Not even you, Luke."

"Oh, yeah?" spat back Luke. "Well, I'm saying it."

"Cool down, guys," Danny said, coming between them. "Let's just forget about it, shall we?"

JJ shook his head. "No way am I going to forget it, Dan," he said. "I'll get a date with that girl."

Danny shook his head sadly. JJ's ego had been injured, and he wouldn't rest now until he had seen Angie again. Danny might have been three years younger than JJ, but he knew him much better than the other two guys in the band; and he knew that JJ felt a need always to prove himself. He also knew that if JJ went after Angie someone was bound to get hurt.

But who that "someone" was, Danny wasn't quite sure.

4

"**Y**ou're crazy, Angie!" Rebecca announced the following day, as she and Angie walked down the corridors leading to the office of the *Recorder*. There were only two days to go until Christmas, but the newspaper's office was still open.

Angie stopped, and made an exaggerated point of looking at her Swatch. "Congratulations, Bec," she said in a voice dripping with sarcasm.

Rebecca was puzzled. "Congratulations?" she said. "What for?"

"It's half-past eleven in the morning, and I picked you up from your Aunt Lizzy's house one and a half hours ago," Angie sniggered. "And it's taken you that long to tell me that I'm crazy!"

"I was practising phenomenal self-control," Rebecca explained without even a hint of sarcasm. "Adrian rang me up from his aunt's last night…"

"And how is he?" Angie asked.

Rebecca shuddered with pleasure. "Still as mind-numbingly gorgeous as ever," she said. "He said he was sorry about the mix-up with the backstage pass…"

"That's sweet of him," Angie said. "He's a really considerate guy, Bec. Good-looking too."

"Yeah, I suppose he is," Rebecca said off-handedly, causing Angie to wonder if, despite all her words, her best friend might already be losing interest in her new boyfriend: after all they hadn't seen each other for almost forty-eight hours now, and for the love-struck Rebecca that was something of a record!

"He got a phone call last night," Rebecca went on. "From his cousin."

"From Luke?" Angie had only seen Zone's bass player briefly, and hadn't had the chance to tell him that she knew Adrian.

"That's right," Rebecca said. "He told Adrian everything about your interview with JJ last night after the concert."

"Yes, I was a bit of an idiot, wasn't I?" Angie admitted. "Letting their manager snatch that tape off me like that..."

"*Idiot?*" Rebecca couldn't believe what she was hearing. "Compared to you an amoeba has brains! Angie, you turned down a date with JJ himself!"

"Oh, yeah, I suppose I did..." Angie said calmly, secretly enjoying Rebecca's dismay.

"Is that all you can say, Angela Markowski?" Rebecca cried out. "There are thousands of girls out there who would die to have been in your position last night, and all you can say is 'Oh yeah'?"

"He's a good-looking guy, I'll give you that," Angie admitted, and remembered JJ's hazel-brown eyes, his shock of dark-blond hair, his teeth whiter than any she ever seen before... *And that divine little dimple right there in the middle of his chin.* "But he's an egomaniac. Thinks he's God's gift to women."

"And isn't he?" Rebecca definitely had her own views on that particular subject.

Angie ignored her, and started walking again. "He's found a little bit of fame, has a few lovestruck girls sending him adoring fan letters and hanging around the backstage door—" she continued.

"Like us, you mean," piped up Rebecca, until Angie silenced her with a threatening glare.

"—and he thinks he can call all the shots, and go out

with whichever girl takes his fancy." They reached the *Recorder*'s office, and Angie started to open the door, still talking.

"Zone are still only a local band, Bec, remember that. They're nothing but a bunch of pretty boys who can vaguely sing in tune. They're a flash in the pan, and tomorrow no one will remember who they are. So if that arrogant, self-centred streak of ditchwater thinks he can turn my head by pretending to be some sort of great and famous rock star, then he's got another – Omigod, who died?"

She had opened the door, only to be confronted by a newspaper office, the greyness of which usually bored Angie to tears, but which was now a vibrant shade of red, and whose normally stuffy atmosphere of printing ink and paper had been replaced by the sweet and heady fragrance of flowers.

Bouquets of red roses covered every available surface. There were scarlet blooms on Angie's own desk, even on the fax machine which had recently been given to the paper by a generous parent. The photocopier in the corner was piled high with bouquets too, as well as the bank of two Apple Macs which lined one wall.

In the middle of all the redness stood the tall, lanky figure of Steve, the eighteen-year-old editor of the school newspaper. He was holding in his hand a sealed envelope, and as soon as Angie entered the room, he handed it over to her.

"Yours, I believe? They arrived about an hour ago, by special delivery," he said in a sardonic voice, which suggested that he was not in the slightest bit amused by the fact that his office seemed to have been turned into a branch of the local florist's.

"All these roses are for me?" Angie asked incredulously as she tore open the envelope.

"Your name's on the envelope, isn't it?" Steve said. "At least I presume they're for you – you're the only Angie I know."

Rebecca peered over Angie's shoulder as she started to take the card out of its envelope.

"They're from Dominic Cairns, I know it!" she said definitely. Angie stopped in her tracks.

"Dominic Cairns? What do you mean?" she asked.

"Ever since you ran off from him at the Christmas dance he's become obsessed with you!" Rebecca said. "He never talks about anything else!"

"Really?" Angie was suddenly very interested, so much so that she forgot about the envelope in her hands. "Dominic Cairns is obsessed with *me*?"

She remembered once again how much she had enjoyed dancing with Dominic a few nights ago: it had felt so good, and Dominic had been so kind and considerate even when she had suddenly run off and left him. He was so handsome too, with his curly, freshly-washed hair, and his dark Southern complexion. Any girl would be so lucky to go out with him.

Rebecca nodded furiously. "Well, come on!" she said impatiently. "Read his card!"

Angie smiled and took the card out of the envelope. "A hundred red roses from Dominic Cairns! It's quite a Christmas present, isn't it?" she said, as she turned the card over to read the message.

"Fifteen bouquets to be precise," came Steve's sarcastic comment as he tried to clear a space at his desk.

"Wait a minute," said Rebecca. "It's December the twenty-third!"

"So what?" asked Steve.

"It's the middle of winter! Roses are out of season!"

Angie shook her head, as she read the message on the card. "Not in Australia," she sighed, and raised her eyes heavenwards. "These were flown in especially from Sydney last night."

"*What!*"

"Take a look at the card, Bec," Angie said and handed it to Rebecca. There was a delighted grin on Angie's face which she tried unsuccessfully to hide.

Rebecca's normally large eyes grew even bigger as she read the message on the card. She looked up at her best friend in amazement. "These are from JJ?" she gasped.

"That's what it says," Angie said, and took the card from Rebecca and read the message aloud: " 'To the best lady reporter there is. Sorry about the interview. Maybe we can hold it again over dinner. Thinking of you, JJ'."

"Angie, you have got it made!" Rebecca enthused. "JJ still wants to take you out to dinner!"

Angie picked up one of the bouquets and brought the flowers to her face. They smelt fresh and sweet. It had been a long time since anyone had bought her flowers, and roses had always been her favourites. It was a lovely idea of JJ's to apologize for last night: maybe he wasn't such a bad guy after all...

Angie Markowski, what are you thinking? she instantly scolded herself.

Angie replaced the card inside its envelope and casually tossed it on to her desk. "If I know him, dinner will probably be egg and chips at the local caff, and then a quick grope in the back of his car," she said dismissively. "The guy's got no style."

"Ten million red roses isn't style then?" Rebecca asked, and smelled their fragrance.

"It's showing off," Angie replied, "and don't exaggerate. He's just proving that he's flash and has got a bit of money to throw around. A single red rose would have been much more effective. But not even that would have worked 'cause I'm not going out with him."

"You're not?" Rebecca asked in amazement. "The hunkiest guy in the world wants to take you out to dinner and you're turning him down?"

"That's right," Angie said. "Let him go out with one of his fans who can spend the whole evening telling him just how wonderful he is and gazing into those big hazel eyes of his..."

"Hazel eyes? I didn't know he had hazel eyes."

"They're just like the colour of autumn leaves, after the

rain," she said, recalling JJ staring into her own eyes last night.

Rebecca nodded wisely; even on the picture cover of Zone's single she'd never noticed the colour of JJ's eyes. She exchanged a knowing look with Steve, who had finally cleared a space at his desk: it seemed that JJ had had more of an effect on Angie than even she realized!

"Guys like JJ are all talk," Angie continued. "And besides, we've got absolutely nothing in common."

"They do say that opposites attract," Rebecca said mischievously.

Angie paused for a moment, remembering what Stephanie had said about her feelings towards Angie's father. They were both so different, and yet Angie had never seen a happier couple.

Maybe away from the other members of the band, when he didn't feel a need to show off, JJ could be a different sort of person. She thought again of the way he had instantly sprung to her defence when Krupp had threatened to call in the police: that wasn't the action of a selfish, opinionated prig.

"Well, no way do these two opposites attract," Angie claimed stubbornly. "And no matter how many roses he sends me – he can send me the whole of Kew Gardens if he likes – I'm not going to let myself become the latest in his string of one-night stands!"

"You don't know he's like that!" Rebecca said, slightly put out that the integrity of her favourite singer was being brought into question.

"You know what they say about rock stars, don't you?" Angie said, echoing her stepmother's words.

"Yes," Rebecca said dreamily, hoping that at least half of what she'd heard about wild parties and fast living was true.

"And anyway, I've got much more important things to take care of," Angie said.

Rebecca groaned: she'd heard it all before. "I know: revision, articles for the *Recorder*, your work for the kids at Cuttleigh..."

Angie shook her head; there was a wicked twinkle in her blue eyes. "No – Dominic Cairns. Do you think he really does like me?"

5

"OK, Aunt Lizzie, you tell her she's mad as well!" Rebecca demanded and looked over at her aunt. Because her father was so often away on business, Rebecca usually stayed at the house of her aunt, an unconventional fiftysomething woman, who always dressed in long ethnic skirts, and wore long strings of brightly-coloured beads. A wealthy woman, she still looked as though her clothes had been bought from the local Oxfam shop, rather than from some of the trendiest modern designers, and her long greying hair refused any attempts to keep it kempt and tidy.

Angie groaned: Rebecca was beginning to sound like an old worn record now. Couldn't she get it into her head once and for all that she wasn't in the slightest bit interested in JJ and his macho posturing?

Aunt Lizzie peered at Angie through her glasses, as she poured the girls Earl Grey tea from a big china teapot.

"No, Rebecca, I don't think Angie's mad at all," she said. "Unlike certain people – " she darted a disapproving but playful look over at her niece – "Angie isn't just interested in how good-looking or sexy a boy is—"

Angie nodded: for an ageing hippy, Rebecca's Aunt Lizzie spoke far more sense than many other people her own age. She also had a spooky way of knowing exactly what you were feeling or thinking without you ever having to tell her.

"Angie could have her pick of the handsomest boys at that college of yours," Aunt Lizzie continued, and handed the embarrassed Angie a cup of steaming tea. "But I think that for her it's the person underneath that counts. It's not what a boy is that matters to Angie, but *who* he is. Isn't that right, my dear?"

Angie smiled: with the possible exception of Stephanie, Aunt Lizzie was the one grown-up she felt perfectly comfortable with talking about her private life. But whereas Angie always suspected that Stephanie would report back to her dad, she knew that all her secrets were safe with Aunt Lizzie.

"They've got to be more than hunks," Angie agreed. "Sure, JJ's cute and he's got a great body. You can tell that he probably works out at the gym every day. But looks aren't everything. A boy should be kind, and considerate, and gentle too."

"A woman needs to be treated like a lady," Aunt Lizzie said. She looked down as she fondly remembered her own late husband. "Not just as a trophy to be worn on some man's arm, like the latest trendy accessory."

"Exactly," Angie said, with feeling. "Like Dominic Cairns – he's such a nice guy, even after I treated him so badly at the dance the other night. Thoughtful, charming..."

"And a major hunk too," Rebecca pointed out.

"That's an added bonus," giggled Angie, and then added, self-righteously: "But even if he was a spotty fourth-former I'd still like him."

"Oh, yeah?" Rebecca wasn't convinced; for that matter, neither was Angie.

Aunt Lizzie smiled, and offered them a plate of her home-baked muesli flapjacks. "Somehow I think that when Angie falls in love it will be for ever," she said, "and it will be as big a surprise to her as to anyone else!"

"Angie's too obsessed with her work, and getting a good job when she leaves college," Rebecca said. "She won't fall in love for years yet!"

"I wouldn't be so sure of that," said Aunt Lizzie, and peered at Angie over the rim of her teacup, in that creepy way she had when she knew something that no one else did. "I wouldn't be too sure of that at all..."

Angie stared at the phone, as if wondering whether she should go through with her plan, and then, for the third time that evening, started to dial the number. This time she didn't put the receiver down before the last digit, and she heard the ringing tone at the other end.

What's the big deal? she told herself. *This is the 1990s – a girl can ask a guy out for a date! Especially a guy who's obsessed with her! And Rebecca's right – maybe I do need a boyfriend.*

There was a click at the other end as someone picked up the phone, and a dark-brown voice with a slight Scottish burr answered.

"Hello, Dominic, it's me, Angie," Angie breezed cheerfully.

On the other end of the line she could almost hear Dominic Cairns draw in his breath. It seemed like Rebecca was right again: Dominic really did like her a lot! She wondered why he'd never asked her to dance before, or invited her to the cinema or something. After all, they had known each other for several years now. Maybe he was just shy, although it seemed odd that someone as good-looking and as popular as Dominic Cairns could ever be unsure of himself.

"Hi, Angela," Dominic said. He sounded delighted to hear from her, and more than a little surprised. "It's nice to hear from you." There was just a touch of sarcasm in his voice, as if he hadn't really forgiven her yet for leaving him on the dance floor a few days ago.

"Look, Dominic, I'm really sorry about the other night," Angie said, determined to get the unpleasant part of her conversation out of the way first of all. "I was way out of order."

"No problem, Angela," Dominic said generously. "I understand – you had a story to get. Forget about it..."

"That's sweet, Dominic," she said. "But I'd like to make it up to you."

"Oh?"

"It's Christmas Eve tomorrow," she said. "And Rebecca and Adrian are going out for a meal. So I was wondering if you'd like to come along too and make up a foursome – that is, if you're not doing anything..."

"No, I'm not doing anything," Dominic laughed, even though he'd promised to go to a party with the other members of the football team. He made a mental note to cancel.

"Then it's a date! Half-past seven on Christmas Eve!"

"Half-past seven it is," Dominic confirmed. "And Angela—"

"Yes?"

"I can't wait!"

Vito's was a trendy bistro much frequented by the local college students, and indeed anyone else who liked to think that they were in the slightest bit fashionable. Famed for the largest and tastiest pizzas and pasta dishes anywhere in town, it was always crowded by the early evening.

As it was Christmas Eve it was even busier than usual, and Vito had made sure that the restaurant was decorated in a suitably seasonal style. Red and green streamers and balloons decorated the room, and large sprigs of mistletoe hung over each table; awful Christmas muzak came over the sound system, although Vito thankfully kept it to the minimum.

Dominic leant back in his chair and patted his stomach. He had just demolished a huge bowl of fettucine. There was a healthy-looking glow on his face, the result of the three glasses of red wine he had drunk.

Angie gazed at him admiringly: he looked gorgeous in his linen jacket and shirt, and that lock of hair which kept flopping over his eyes made him even more irresistible. She had already noticed several attractive women glance in his direction, but the captain of the football team seemed to have eyes only for her.

Not that he had ignored Rebecca and Adrian, however. For the past hour and a half he had kept them all entertained with stories of some of the antics he and his fellow team-members got up to on their away matches.

He had cracked jokes which made them all split their sides with laughter, had listened sympathetically when Adrian had complained about the grades he was getting at the tech, and throughout the meal had ensured that everyone's wine glass was full.

Even so, his attention inevitably returned to Angie – or Angela as he persisted in calling her, making Angie feel important and ladylike – and Angie felt herself warming even more to Dominic. Dominic Cairns was charming, witty, and, if the tantalizing glimpse of his chest through his shirt didn't deceive her, possessed a body most girls would kill for.

He even had brains and breeding, as he'd demonstrated when ordering the wine for the meal: he'd surprised their snooty waiter by choosing an obscure-sounding wine which proved to be the most excellent bottle on the wine list.

Dominic was the sort of person any girl would be happy to go out with, Angie decided; smart, tidy and responsible, he was the sort of boy she'd even be proud to take home to her dad.

Unlike some other hunks, she thought.

Conversation inevitably got round to Angie's escapade the other night, when she had tried to gatecrash Zone's concert. Dominic was amused: Angie had shown the sort of ingenuity he could never have dreamed of.

"I'd never have the nerve to do what you did, Angela," he said, self-effacingly. "I'm proud of you."

"It was nothing," she said dismissively, although Dominic's compliment made her glow inside. "If I'm going to become a successful investigative reporter then that sort of thing is going to be all in the course of a day's work."

"I'm sorry that you lucked out in the end though," said

Adrian, his arm draped over Rebecca's shoulder. "Do you want me to have a word with my cousin? Maybe he could wangle you another interview."

Angie shook her head firmly. "No way," she said. "After seeing Zone I'm not even convinced that they're going to be that big anyway. They're just another group of pretty boys with so-so voices and average songs."

Rebecca laughed. "And a lead singer who's madly in love with you!"

Angie glared at her best friend. "He was trying to chat me up like the little creep he is, that was all!" she protested. "Don't exaggerate!'

Dominic turned to Angie, a frown on his face. Angie had kept that part of her interview with Zone tactfully out of the conversation.

"JJ was coming on to you?" he asked, and Angie detected a note of jealousy in his voice, and a dangerous look in his eyes.

"It was nothing," she shrugged dismissively, and placed a reassuring hand on his. "And I'm not interested in him at all, if that's what's worrying you. We've got nothing in common with each other, for one thing."

Dominic smiled, and relaxed. "Good, then I'm pleased," he said, and was about to say something else when there was a commotion at the door of the restaurant. They all turned round to see what was happening.

"Well, well, well," said Rebecca, and shook her head in glad amazement. "Talk of the devil..."

JJ and the boys from Zone had arrived and were arguing with Vito at the reception desk. The smooth owner of the bistro was obviously finding fault with the way Zone were dressed. The bistro was by no means a formal restaurant, but Vito did require a certain smartness of appearance: it was obvious that he didn't think that JJ's leathers, Marco and Luke's scruffy jeans and MA flight-jackets, and Danny's back-to-front baseball cap quite came up to the sartorial standards he required of his guests.

Angie groaned, and hid her face behind her menu, hoping that JJ wouldn't catch sight of her. Despite herself, however, she found herself sneaking a glimpse over the top of the menu, and watched with the others as JJ pointed out to Vito that they did, in fact, have a reservation.

Vito, however, was insistent: they could not have a table dressed like that, booking or no booking. Things were starting to get a little ugly, when one of the waiters went up to Vito and whispered something in his boss's ear. Vito's expression changed instantly, and he beamed at the boys, shaking them each by the hand, and welcoming them warmly to his restaurant.

"Now, even I think that is gross," said Rebecca.

"What happened?" asked a puzzled Dominic. "Why's he changed his mind so abruptly?"

"I imagine someone's just told him that Zone are going to be famous one day, and might bring in more business for him," Angie said. "I can't understand how anyone can be so impressed with all that glamour and showbiz hype."

"It's OK for you to say that," said Rebecca. "Your dad works in TV – you're used to celebrities phoning him up, or taking him out..."

"I'd very much like to meet your father one day," Dominic cut in. "Everyone's seen him on those late-night arts programmes. He must be a very interesting man..."

Rebecca, who didn't take kindly to being interrupted, shot Dominic a silencing look. "As I was saying," she continued, "Angie's used to all this showbiz glamour. We common people have to snatch it when we can." She nudged Adrian. "Go on, Adrian, Luke's your cousin! Invite them to our table!"

"Bec!" Angie said, but it was too late: Adrian had already stood up and waved Luke and the others over. The boys swaggered over to their table and Adrian introduced them to Rebecca and Dominic.

It was obvious that JJ didn't think much of Angie's dinner companion; he sneered at his smart and conventional clothes, and obvious good looks. Dominic, for his part, glared evilly at the young rock singer.

"And of course you remember Angie, don't you?" Adrian said.

JJ looked down at the blushing Angie, and smiled his sexy smile. "How could I ever forget her?" he said huskily.

Angie groaned inwardly: what a clichéd line. Even Danny chuckled at his best friend's studied and deliberate crassness.

"You got my roses, did you?" he asked.

"Yes, thank you," Angie replied frostily.

"So maybe you'd like to continue our interview over dinner?" he asked, and crouched down so as to be able to look Angie directly in the eyes.

Marco and Luke exchanged amused glances: JJ was working what he called his "seductometer" at full power. He must really want to win their challenge, they thought.

"And maybe Angela doesn't want to go out to dinner with you!" Dominic said roughly.

Angie looked sharply at him. "I can handle this myself," she said. She turned back to JJ. "JJ, if I get the urge for jelly and custard I'll give you a ring, OK? In the meantime, why not stop trying to be a big boy and go back to your playpen?"

"I guess that means no, then?" JJ asked, while behind him Danny, Luke and Mark sniggered.

"You've got it in one!"

JJ smiled philosophically, and stood up, but not before planting a quick kiss on Angie's cheek. Dominic pushed his chair back, and stood up angrily; the boys from Zone tensed, expecting trouble.

It was Angie who took hold of Dominic's hand, and made him sit down again: she didn't want anyone else fighting her battles for her. She glared angrily at JJ, who just grinned cheekily, and reached up for the sprig of mistletoe that was hanging over Angie's chair. He pulled it down and handed it to her.

Angie's anger turned to amusement, and she smiled too, as, without saying a word, JJ gave her a cute little wave, and swaggered off after the other members of the band to the choicest corner of the bistro where their table was waiting for them.

Angie touched her cheek. The spot where JJ had kissed it felt hot and tingling.

"Angela? Are you OK?" she was vaguely aware of Dominic asking her. "That was a lousy trick to play on you, wasn't it?"

"It's Christmas, Dominic," she said. "It's traditional."

Dominic draped a protective arm over Angie's shoulder. "He's a little creep," he decided, and watched as JJ sat down with the other guys. "And have you seen the way he dresses? Guys who dress in rags like that just show that they don't have any self-respect." With his free hand he self-consciously smoothed the creases of his smartly-cut linen jacket. Dominic knew he looked good in his designer clothes.

Angie followed Dominic's gaze. It was true that JJ and the other guys from Zone stuck out like a sore thumb in the bistro, but they also provided a sort of reverse glamour to the place.

While everyone else was drinking fine bottles of wine they had just ordered two pitchers of beer; and while everyone else had dressed up for their Christmas Eve meal, JJ, Danny, Luke and Marco looked as if they had just tumbled out of a night club at half-past five in the morning. They added a sense of danger and excitement to Vito's stylish but normally laid-back bistro.

No one could take their eyes off the boys, with one surprising exception. Rebecca, of all people, was looking thoughtfully at her best friend, and when Angie turned back to ask her what she was staring at, Rebecca merely pointed to Angie's hands.

Without knowing it, she was still clutching fondly, and almost as if her life depended on it, JJ's sprig of mistletoe.

6

The following day – Christmas Day – was a quiet one for Angie, spent at home in front of the TV as it always was, with her father and Stephanie. Or rather it was spent mostly with Stephanie as her father had sequestered himself in his office, working on the scripts for a new TV programme he had been asked to direct. It was a six-part TV history of fashion in the twentieth century, and it was already being talked about excitedly in the newspapers. It was going to be a major TV series, they said, and it seemed that every famous designer in the world wanted his or her work featured on the show.

Even Angie had been impressed by the number of Christmas cards her dad had received this year. From Calvin Klein in Manhattan, through Gianni Versace in Milan, and even Issy Miyake in Tokyo, anyone who was anyone in the fashion world had sent the Markowskis their warmest Season's Greetings.

Angie idly wondered whether she could persuade her father to get her some cut-price designer clothes from his new-found friends, but realized what his answer would be. That was the trouble with having a dad with principles, she had laughingly complained to Stephanie as they sat in the big front room unwrapping their Christmas presents: you never got any perks.

Stephanie, who had also thought of asking her husband

for the same favour before thinking better of it, agreed. She handed her stepdaughter a medium-sized parcel, wrapped in brightly-coloured paper.

"This was waiting for you on the doorstep this morning," she said.

"I didn't think the postman came on Christmas Day." Angie was puzzled.

"He doesn't," Stephanie said, and handed the packet over to Angie. "Someone must have dropped it off last night or early this morning."

Frowning, Angie tore the wrapping paper off the parcel to reveal a brightly-coloured box. She took off the lid, and peered inside. Another slightly smaller box was inside, and another, and another, like one of those Russian dolls her mum had brought back from St Petersburg where she had been dancing with the Kirov ballet.

Angie finally reached the last box. Inside was a plain unmarked envelope, and she tore it open.

Stephanie looked over her shoulder, by now just as fascinated as Angie was by what the envelope might contain. Angie held up a small cassette tape, and the two of them exchanged puzzled glances. Stephanie nodded over to the stereo system on the far wall.

"Play it," she suggested.

Angie went over and inserted the cassette into the tape deck and tapped the "play" button. She broke into a wide smile as her own voice and then JJ's came over the speakers.

"I don't believe it," she said, delightedly. "He got the tape of my interview back off Joe Krupp! That guy really is too much! Does he ever give up?"

Stephanie chuckled. "JJ must really like you if he defied the fearsome Krupp to help you," she said. "He's certainly determined, almost as much as you can be. Maybe you should take him up on his offer of dinner after all? It could be fun."

"No way," said Angie. She switched off the tape deck and took the cassette out. "After all, you know what they say about rock stars, don't you, Steph? And besides, I've got another date tomorrow afternoon..."

"You have?" Stephanie was immediately interested. There was nothing she liked better than a chat with her stepdaughter.

"He's called Dominic," said Angie, "and he's the kindest, sexiest and most charming guy I've met in a long, long time!"

"Wait a minute, can't you! I'm coming! I'm coming!" Rebecca's Aunt Lizzie called out, as she raced down the stairs to answer the insistent ringing on the doorbell.

Rebecca was still asleep. It was, after all, only half-past eleven: after dinner last night Rebecca and Adrian had gone off to a late-night club and Rebecca had rolled in at four o'clock this morning – she thought she deserved a lie-in.

Lizzie, however, had been up since early morning, preparing the nut-roast that was to be their Christmas lunch. As usual she had several strings of beads round her neck and was dressed in a long flowing kaftan, but, as a concession to the season, she had tied a piece of bright-green tinsel around her waist.

She opened the door, and gazed appreciatively at the caller through her granny-glasses, looking him up and down, as she might inspect a prize piece of porcelain.

JJ was wearing his customary trendy black leathers, and the cheeks of his handsome face were rosy from the cold, and there were flecks of snow in his shock of dark-blond hair.

"Good morning, young man," she said pleasantly.

JJ shifted awkwardly from one foot to the other. "Er, good morning, ma'am," he began, but Lizzie interrupted him.

"Lizzie, my name is Lizzie," she told him, and pulled him inside. "Come into the warm, young man: it must be freezing out there!"

"Thanks, Lizzie," JJ said and smiled: there was

something very endearing about Rebecca's aunt. Most women her age would have been put off by a leather-clad stranger turning up on the doorstep unannounced on Christmas morning; Lizzie, on the other hand, seemed ready to cluck and fuss over him like a mother hen over her brood. JJ liked her immediately.

"I suppose you've come to see Rebecca, haven't you?" Lizzie asked.

"As a matter of fact, yes, ma'am – I mean, Lizzie."

Aunt Lizzie let out a grand theatrical sigh. "Alas!" she smiled. "The handsome young gentlemen callers never come round calling for me!"

"Now that I really can't believe, Lizzie," JJ said, flirting good-naturedly with her. He accorded Lizzie a glimpse of his sexy half-smile which turned all the young girls wild. He was glad to see it had a similar effect on her.

Lizzie went to the foot of the stairs to rouse Rebecca, who called back that she would be down in a minute. While she waited, Lizzie turned back to JJ.

"I didn't catch your name?" she said.

"It's JJ, Lizzie."

"JJ." Lizzie repeated the name, savouring the sound. She recalled the conversation she had shared with Angie and Rebecca the other day, and realized who this handsome young stranger was. *So this is what pop stars look like these days*, she thought approvingly, remembering the long-haired, evil-looking rockers of her own youth.

"And what does JJ stand for, JJ?" she asked.

JJ grinned. "Sorry, Lizzie, top secret!"

Rebecca came down the stairs and gasped when she saw who had come to visit her on Christmas Day. She couldn't have been more surprised if it was Santa Claus himself. She instinctively wrapped her dressing gown more tightly around herself.

"JJ!" she breathed.

What were the other girls back at school going to say when they discovered that the great JJ from Zone had actually come around calling, at her house, at Rebecca

Penswick's own house? She could hardly wait to get on the phone and tell them all.

"I don't understand," she started to babble, and ran a hand through her long blonde hair – *my God, I must look like a real mess!* – "What are you doing here? How did you find out where I live?"

"Luke rang his cousin Adrian," JJ explained. "That's how I got the address."

"That wasn't very clever of Adrian," Aunt Lizzie tut-tutted. "I must have a word with that boy. He should know better than to give out Rebecca's address to all and sundry!"

Rebecca looked at her aunt as if she were mad. *This isn't All and Sundry, Aunt Lizzie*, she wanted to say. *This is a guy who's going to be one of the biggest and sexiest rock stars in the world one day soon. God bless you, Adrian!*

"You look tired," Rebecca remarked: there were dark rings under his eyes, and he looked like he hadn't slept in a long time. *Probably been raving all night long with some sexy girl in tow!* she assumed.

"Yeah, I was up all night, working on a song," he said and looked at his watch. "Listen, Rebecca, I haven't much time. Joe doesn't know I'm here and he'll kill me if he finds out. I know we've only just met, and you don't really know me, but I need a really big favour from you..."

As JJ told her what he wanted, Rebecca's face fell. For a second there, she had thought that JJ had come around to her house to ask her out. She should have known that that was too good to be true.

Still, what JJ was proposing did sound really exciting ... and so romantic that it even made up for the fact that she wasn't the focus of his attentions.

JJ turned to go, and Aunt Lizzie, with whom he had obviously scored something of a major hit, ushered him to the door.

"And the next time you do decide to visit, young man, telephone first," she said. She dived into the capacious pockets of her kaftan, and drew out a grubby and dog-eared business card which she pressed into JJ's hand.

After he had gone, Aunt Lizzie turned to her niece and waved her hand in front of her face as if trying to fan herself cool.

"What a hunk and a half!" she enthused, sounding more like a first-form schoolgirl than the kindly, if eccentric, old aunt she really was. "My dear, if only I was thirty years younger, the things I could show that young man...!"

Rebecca laughed. There were times when Aunt Lizzie acted and sounded like the most un-grown-up grown-up she had ever known.

JJ trudged through the snow, his collar turned up against the wind and the weather. His breath hung in icy clouds before him, as he walked to the posh restaurant where Joe Krupp was standing Christmas dinner for JJ and the other guys from Zone.

There was an ulterior motive, of course: with Joe there always was. It seemed that the editor of one of the most popular teen magazines was up in town today, and at something of a loose end on Christmas Day of all days of the year. Joe had decided that this was the perfect time to treat the influential editor to a slap-up meal and some festive cheer while at the same time introducing JJ, Luke, Marco and Danny to him, and hopefully gaining some valuable press exposure for Zone.

It was the end of December, Krupp had announced to them a couple of days ago; in nine months' time, by the end of September, he wanted the name of Zone to be in every teenage music magazine in the country.

JJ wasn't bothered about impressing the music magazines, although he'd follow Joe's orders, coming on with the tough-guy act that Joe had decided was going to be JJ's image in the band. It wasn't really him, that wise-cracking, street-talking slicker, but Krupp assured him that that was what all the punters wanted these days.

What really mattered to JJ was the music, and he knew that whatever image Zone had, their music would still be successful. But Krupp had managed many other successful bands in his time, so he must know what he was talking about.

JJ's mind wasn't on the band's image, however: it was on Angie. What was it about that girl that was bugging him so? She was attractive, there was no doubt about that, although he'd seen more beautiful women. She was also very bright, something in a woman which always intrigued JJ.

Was it because he couldn't have her? That she hadn't been impressed by his good looks, and glamour, and the fame which everyone said was going to be his soon?

JJ could have had any girl he wanted – he only had to look outside the stage door at any local venue Zone were playing – but Angie was the only one to have turned him down. The only one, too, who didn't gawp at him with lovestruck eyes the minute he opened his mouth; the only one as strong-willed as he was. Hell, she wasn't doing his ego any favours, and that's why he'd accepted the gang's challenge to take her out on a date.

But he remembered how he felt last night when he saw Angie and Dominic together. The guy was a geek, pure and simple, JJ had decided, no matter how good-looking he might be.

With his well-cut and smart clothes, he was the complete opposite of JJ. How could Angie let someone as "solid" and "dependable" as Dominic take her out, let him put his arm on her shoulder? She was wasting herself on him.

She'd said she wanted to be a reporter: if she hung around with Dominic he knew that she might as well kiss goodbye to all those dreams. All Dominic would want would be a wife to wait for him to come home at the end of the day, practically handing him his slippers and telling him that his dinner was ready and waiting for him on the table.

Angie, he guessed, was determined to rise to the top in her chosen career, as determined as JJ was to do the same in his. He had seen that steely sense of purpose in her eyes, that same look that Danny and the others said was in his. He'd hate to see that dream shattered.

But there was something strange about Dominic too, JJ realized, something not quite right, something he couldn't put his finger on. Maybe it was the way he looked at Angie, hanging on to her every word, like JJ's fans did to him. Maybe it was the way Dominic never contradicted her, the way he always seemed to want to please her, always to say the things he knew Angie wanted to hear.

Dominic wanted to please Angie too much, JJ realized. No, it was something more than that: Dominic was *desperate* to please Angie...

Loosen up, man! he told himself. *You want what you can't have and that's what's screwing you about! That's all it is – pure and simple!*

Somehow, JJ didn't quite believe himself.

7

Angie gazed out in wonder at the field of snow before her. It was as if the entire countryside had been clothed in a sheet of white, interrupted here and there only by the black and spidery silhouettes of the bare winter trees, and the low and rough stone walls, which meandered their way across this part of the countryside. A few birds flew in the sky which was cloudless, a brilliant frosty blue and the bright winter sun shining down made the ice and the snow sparkle and glisten even more.

She turned round to Dominic, who was sitting next to her on one of the stone walls. "It's beautiful, Dominic," she said. "So calm and peaceful."

Dominic smiled and nodded. "I know. I come out here a lot when I need to get away from the hustle and bustle of life back at college. It helps me to reflect, get things into perspective."

Angie laughed. "You're certainly not what I expected, Dominic Cairns," she admitted and moved nearer to him for warmth. They were both wearing their warmest leather jackets, and the wind had dropped, but it was still bitingly cold.

Dominic smiled, and turned to look at Angie. She saw that his dark hair had once again flopped into his eyes, and noticed that it was covered with snowflakes. "What do you mean, 'not what I expected'?" he asked in all seriousness.

"Well, when the captain of the football team asks you to go out with him for the afternoon, a girl expects to be forced to spend most of the day standing in a muddy field watching his grotty mates kick an old ball around," she joked. "She doesn't expect to be taken in his car—"

"In his dad's *borrowed* car," Dominic corrected her.

"OK. She doesn't expect to be taken in his dad's *borrowed* car, deep into the countryside, for a wonderful Boxing Day lunch. And then, after lunch, to walk to one of the most romantic spots for miles around," she said, and then added: "I think it's lovely, Dominic; it's a very pleasant surprise."

He put an arm over her shoulder, and cuddled her closer to him. "You're sure now, aren't you?" he asked. "I want today to be really special for you, Angela."

There was a strange urgent tone in his voice, which Angie put down to his desperately wanting to please her: *what a guy!* she thought happily.

"It's the best day of the year for me, Dominic," she said, and reached up to kiss him on the cheek. "And as it's December the twenty-sixth, I've almost three hundred and sixty-five to choose from."

"You should never judge a book by its cover," Dominic laughed. "Appearances often deceive. You thought the captain of the football team could never be romantic. And you were wrong!"

Angie wagged an admonishing finger in his direction. "But you're not just the captain of the football team. You know what they call you around the college, don't you?"

Dominic chuckled. "No. What do they call me?" he asked, although he knew only too well what his nickname was amongst the female students.

"Dishy Dominic!" Angie replied. "Dominic Dreamboat!"

"I'm flattered," he said, laughing off the compliment. "They must all have white sticks and guide dogs," he added self-deprecatingly.

Angie punched him playfully in the ribs. *Modest too!* she thought. *Unlike that rock 'n' roll creep with the divine dimple in the centre of his chin who thinks he's God's gift to women! Was Dominic anything but perfect?*

"Seriously, you're the best-looking guy in school," she told him.

It was something she would never have admitted to him before, fearing that it would make him even more big-headed than she had always assumed anyone that handsome already was. But now that she had got to know him, now that she had seen just how modest and un-assuming he really was, she felt that she ought at least to tell him the truth.

"Are the rumours true – that you'd like to try and become a fashion model after you leave Astor College?"

Dominic shrugged a little self-consciously, as though his modelling ambitions embarrassed him a little, and that working as a model was certainly not the sort of career any level-headed, macho captain of a football team should even contemplate following.

"I'd like to," he finally admitted. "There's a lot of money to be made at the top in that business. But it's a tough, back-stabbing world and I really don't know if I've got what it takes..."

Angie looked at Dominic, from his brilliantly blue eyes, classic profile and Mediterranean complexion, across his broad and powerful shoulders, down his body, which, even though it was clad in a Schott leather jacket, clearly rippled with muscle, down every single inch of his six-foot-four height.

"Believe me, Dominic," she said. "You have most definitely got what it takes..."

Dominic smiled, with those perfectly white teeth of his, and pulled Angie closer to him. She didn't resist, but instead melted into his warm and welcoming arms, as though it was the most natural thing in the world.

They kissed, a tentative enquiring kiss at first, as though Dominic wasn't quite sure how far Angie would allow him to go. Dominic's full and soft lips felt like velvet, and tasted of the fine red wine he had had with his meal. His breath was fresh and warm. His strong hands cradled Angie's head, and he stroked her hair, as tenderly as he would that of a small child or animal. Pulling her hair gently back, he traced the outline of her ears.

They separated, and smiled at each other. Each of their faces was flushed and red, although certainly not from the cold. Indeed, both Angie and Dominic were warmer than anyone should naturally have been in such weather.

Dominic beamed; his hair was mussed, and, despite his efforts, that wayward lock of hair had fallen once again over his eyes, making him look even more devastatingly desirable.

He raised a hand to her face, and with his fingers outlined the contours of her lips. This time it was Angie who reached out and drew him to her, pressing him next to her, enjoying the touch of another body alongside hers, of a strong male body.

She kissed him again, a fuller deeper kiss this time, and wrapped her arms around him, hugging him close to her, tightly as if she feared that he might vanish from her for ever.

Dominic grinned, and massaged the small of Angie's back. Even through the leather of her jacket his touch was like fire.

It felt so good to be with a boy again, Angie thought, so good to know there was someone who was attracted to you as much as you were to him.

It somehow made your life complete: your days could be as busy and as active as possible, but without a boy who loved you, without this confirmation and reassurance of your own worth, then they were as bleak and as unfruitful as the winter landscape Dominic had brought her to.

She drew back and smiled dreamily. "There," she breathed. "I hope that makes up for my leaving you at the Christmas dance a few nights ago."

Dominic grinned. "More than enough," he said gratefully. "I must admit I was a little disappointed when you ran off like that, after I'd been secretly plucking up the courage to ask you out for months."

For months?

This was news to Angie. Even Rebecca, who normally could spot the love-light in someone's eyes before anyone else, would have been surprised.

Dominic chuckled with embarrassment and for a second turned away from Angie, so as not to look her in the eye. "I guess I was ... kinda shy," he said.

The captain of the school football team, shy? The guy who, they all said, ruled his team with a rod of iron, and had turned them into one of the most successful teams in the local college soccer league – this guy was afraid to go up to a girl and ask her for a date? Angie couldn't believe that. However, she didn't pursue the matter.

"You had a right to be upset," she admitted frankly. "It was really bad-mannered of me. If that had happened to me I would have been furious."

Dominic shook his head. "Funnily enough I admired and respected you all the more for it," he said. "You're determined, and you'll do anything which is necessary to become a top journalist." He sighed. "I only wish I had your drive..."

Angie reached out and stroked his cheek; it was only late afternoon but already there were traces of stubble growing there. She liked that, liked the rough touch of his beard as she kissed him.

For some reason she found herself comparing him to JJ: JJ's pale skin was soft and smooth, and, even though he was a couple of years older than Dominic, she doubted whether he shaved more than once every two days. She supposed that that was what all those pre-pubescent schoolgirl fans liked these days. *Let them keep their pretty boys,* Angie thought. *I want a real man like Dominic.*

"I'm sure you'll make it as a model one day, Dominic," she said encouragingly. "After all, you've definitely got the looks..."

Dominic looked doubtful. "Sometimes I'm not so sure," he admitted. "I've sent pictures of myself to all the main agencies, even a couple of the top magazines, but none of them ever bothers to reply..."

"It's the same in journalism," Angie said sympathetically. "If you don't know anyone it's that much harder to get a job..." A sudden thought struck her. "Say, why don't I ask my dad?"

"Your dad?"

"He's setting up this major TV programme about the history of fashion in the twentieth century," she said. "He's been in contact with all the top fashion designers."

"That's right," Dominic said slowly. "I remember reading something about it in one of the newspapers ... I never realized your dad was involved..."

"Well, maybe Dad can help you get your photographs seen by the people who really matter," Angie said excitedly.

"You really think so?" Dominic asked.

"It's worth a try, isn't it?"

Dominic took Angie's hands in his. "Angie, I don't know how I can ever begin to thank you," he said.

"I'm sure I'll think of something," she replied, and kissed him on the lips again. "You could help me out in a couple of days' time, on New Year's Eve, for starters."

Dominic frowned. "New Year's Eve? What's happening then?"

"I'm helping to organize a party for the children at Cuttleigh Hall – you know, the centre for disabled kids," she said. "With Government cuts it's the only bit of fun they get every year, poor things."

Dominic's face fell. "I'm really sorry, Angie," he said, sounding like he meant it. "I can't..."

"Is there something wrong?" Angie asked, trying to understand. "Lots of people feel uncomfortable in hospitals or around disabled kids..."

Dominic shook his head. "It's not that," he said. "Disabled kids are just as good as you or me – why should you feel uncomfortable around them? But ... but ... but I promised my parents that I'd go and see my grandmother that day. She's not very well, and it might be my last opportunity to see her."

"That's OK," Angie said, a trifle disappointed. It would have been so good to have taken Dominic along to Cuttleigh Hall, to show him off to her friends there.

"You know I'd really like to help you," Dominic continued, and added, "especially as you're going to talk to your dad about me..."

"It doesn't matter, Dominic, believe me," she lied, and then held him close again.

She was the luckiest girl in the whole world, she decided. They were made for each other, that seemed certain, and Angie – and certainly Dominic – couldn't believe their good luck.

8

Cuttleigh Hall was a small children's day centre on the outskirts of town, and Angie had been working there on a part-time basis for almost three years now, in fact ever since she had decided that she wanted to become a journalist.

Originally, she had thought that a spot of charity work would look good on her CV, when she started on the dreaded round of job interviews; but, as the months progressed, and as she got to know the staff and children better, she found that she was enjoying her work enormously.

It's typical, she often sharply rebuked herself; I start doing something on a purely "business" level, and I end up getting personally involved!

Most of the children at Cuttleigh were mentally or physically handicapped, but the biggest handicap they all shared was other people's prejudices. Even Rebecca was guilty of this, and while Angie could understand her discomfort, she also knew that it was totally groundless. It was such a welcome relief to find people who treated disabled people just the same as everyone else. She smiled, as she remembered Dominic's words earlier that afternoon: "They're just as good as you or me." What a great, understanding and caring guy he was!

A few days after Christmas, Angie had had to leave

Dominic to go to Cuttleigh, for an appointment with Nurse Clare, the director of the home. No longer a nurse, Nurse Clare was now a successful businesswoman and stalwart of the local community, but she still liked to refer to herself as one. Nurse Clare was a stout and tough seventy-year-old Scot who had run Cuttleigh for the past thirty years. She might have been formidable to look at in her tweeds, short cropped hair, sensible brogues and stern tortoise-shell glasses, but she had a heart of gold, and a highly-tuned sense of humour.

"After all," she would often say, "with the National Health Service receiving less and less money every year, and with my staff obliged to work more and more hours, you'd better have a sense of humour or you'd simply go bonkers!"

Angie had brought a file full of correspondence with her. Nurse Clare sifted through it, and congratulated her. "I don't know how we could manage without you," she said, approvingly. "You've done a sterling job, simply first-rate!"

Angie nodded her thanks. "I've arranged for the caterers to come in at noon on New Year's Eve – jelly, cakes, ice cream, the works!"

"And the entertainment?"

"A conjurer," Angie said, "and one of the very best. I actually got my dad to open his Filofax and pull a few strings for me – for once! The kids will love him!"

Nurse Clare chuckled, and leaned back in her chair, folding her arms and resting them on her ample bosom. "You're a blessed treasure, my poppet!" she said. "The best volunteer we've had since—" she waved her hand vaguely in the air "—since I don't know when. Since Jeremy certainly."

"Jeremy?"

Nurse Clare stroked her chin thoughtfully. "Jeremy? Or perhaps it was Henry? Or Merriman? I can never remember these boys' names. Most of 'em come and go so quickly. No staying power, boys!"

She shook her head dismissively: she was getting on a bit now, she realized, and at her age couldn't be expected to remember everyone's name.

"But whatever his name was, he was a godsend, exactly like you are, my dear. He worked here a few years ago, until he moved out of town."

She started to gather up all the papers Angie had brought in.

"We're all so grateful for all the work you've put in this year, Angie," she said. "It's reassuring to know that there are still people who care about others. All the other lasses your age seem to care about are the latest crooners in the Hit Parade—"

"The charts," Angie corrected her, "and we call them rock stars now." Nurse Clare might have to deal with the horrors of late 1990s Government bureaucracy but some of her vocabulary belonged to an entirely different age!

"—and their beaux," Nurse Clare continued, and then, in response to Angie's look of amusement, added, "Their boyfriends, I mean."

Angie turned shyly away from Nurse Clare. "Well, I might have a boyfriend, now…" she said.

"Really?" There was a note of disappointment in Nurse Clare's voice, as she wondered whether this would mean that Angie would be leaving Cuttleigh.

"You needn't worry, Nurse Clare," Angie reassured her. "Dominic's a wonderful guy, and I'm sure he won't mind me giving up a couple of evenings a week to work here. In fact, he might actually come over and help me!"

"We shall see, my dear," Nurse Clare said quietly. "We shall see…"

"So has dishy Dominic asked you to go steady yet?" Rebecca demanded the following afternoon when she called round at Angie's for a chat and a slice of Stephanie's cheesecake.

"Bec! Don't you think of anything else?" Angie laughed, while over by the breakfast bar in the kitchen, Stephanie stifled a giggle behind her research papers.

"No: what else is there to think about?" was Rebecca's happy reply. "You really are the luckiest girl in the whole of the school, nabbing Dominic Dreamboat like that. Did he take you for a really romantic walk the other day in the snow?"

"As a matter of fact, he did," Angie said.

It felt wonderful discussing Dominic with Rebecca, who obviously thought she was in at the very beginning of the greatest romance Astor College had ever known.

Secret romances were all very well, Rebecca had once told her best friend, but they couldn't even begin to compare with the joy you felt when you realized that the whole world knew that someone loved you.

"He seems a really nice boy, from what Angie's told me," Stephanie said. "Responsible and well-mannered, from a good family. I'd like to meet him sometime soon, Angie."

"You will, Steph, you will," her stepdaughter promised, and joked: "But just remember you're married to Dad and that Dishy Dominic's all mine!"

She turned back to Rebecca and asked her why she had come round: wasn't she supposed to be seeing Adrian today?

"Yeah," Rebecca said, and toyed with her cheesecake. "But I saw him over most of Christmas. I just fancied seeing you."

"Ah." Angie nodded wisely.

After Rebecca's confident announcement that Adrian was the only boy for her, it looked as though their passion was cooling off more quickly than the weather outside. Angie had seen it happen time and time again: Rebecca was always infatuated with one boy or another, but she bored of them easily, and rarely did her interest in them blossom into love.

Now Dominic and me, we're different ... Angie found herself thinking.

"So where's Adrian, now that you've stood him up?" she asked her friend.

"I did not stand him up!" Rebecca protested. "I cancelled

our date a good half-hour before we were due to meet up."
She sliced two more portions of cheesecake, one for her
and one for Angie. "He said it was OK and he'd give Luke
a ring and see what the boys were doing..."

"He's gone out with JJ and the others?" Angie asked.

"He's gone out with Zone," Rebecca corrected her, "not
'JJ and the others'." There was a sly look in her eyes, and
she picked up her plate of cheesecake and headed for the
door.

"C'mon," she said, "let's listen to some music..."

Angie stood up to follow Rebecca when the outside door
opened, and her father came in. He threw his leather-
bound Filofax down on to the breakfast bar, and shuffled
out of his snow-covered overcoat. Stephanie took it and
hung it up.

"Bad day at work, Mr Markowski?" Rebecca asked
sympathetically. Angie's father was an even bigger
workaholic than his daughter, and had been working at
the TV centre all over the holiday, apart from Christmas
Day itself, when he had been working from home.

Peter nodded, and kissed Angie on the cheek in
welcome. Angie looked up adoringly into her dad's eyes,
and Peter sighed: whenever Angie acted like this he knew
she wanted something.

"Dad, I have a really huge favour to ask you," she said.

"I guessed," he said sarcastically.

"You know I went out with Dominic Cairns yesterday..."

"Stephanie told me last night," Mr Markowski said. "I
know his father – he's a member of my club. Dominic
seems a really nice lad. A great footballer too, by all
accounts."

"Well, then you must know how good-looking he is and
he wants to do some modelling work but he's not getting
any positive responses from any of the agencies," Angie
said, without pausing for breath. "And since you're
working on this big fashion series, I thought, maybe—"

"No, Angie," Peter said firmly. "If he wants to succeed in
this life he's going to have to do it on his own. I won't pull

any strings to help you get a job in journalism and I am certainly not going to pull any strings for him."

"He sounds like such a nice boy, solid and dependable," Stephanie said as she returned from hanging up her husband's coat. "Surely it wouldn't do any harm?" She winked at her stepdaughter. "And it would make Angie so happy."

Peter shook his head, and raised a hand to signal an end to the conversation. "Those contacts contained in there –" he pointed to his Filofax on the breakfast bar "– are privileged information. I'm sorry, Angie; if you want to be a journalist, or if your new boyfriend wants to become a top model, you can just go out there and do it yourselves. I am certainly not going to help you!"

"He's as stubborn as a mule!" Angie fumed, after she had stalked out of the kitchen into the lounge, followed by Rebecca. "He won't lift a finger to help either me or Dominic!"

"Chill out, Angie," Rebecca advised her, and took a cassette out of her bag, and slipped it into the tape deck. "You'll just have to tell Dominic the bad news. He'll be disappointed, but it won't break his heart."

"I'm not seeing him tonight," Angie said. "He's in training. Apparently there's a big match in a few days' time."

"A football widow already..." Rebecca joked, and switched on the cassette.

"Dominic's taking me out to dinner tomorrow night though," Angie revealed. "To Vincente's."

"Vincente's?" Rebecca was impressed. Vincente's was a top-rated swanky restaurant which, so they said, was the classiest place to eat this side of the Channel Tunnel. The service was impeccable, the food faultless, and the candle-lit tables in tiny alcoves the perfect places for romantic dinners à deux. The bill could also run into three figures. "I wish Adrian would take me somewhere like that! Dominic must like you one hell of a lot."

"He does," Angie agreed, "and I like him too. He's so

gentle and caring and – what on Earth is that?"

She had just become aware of the music which was coming from Rebecca's cassette. It was a rough cut, obviously done not in a professional recording studio, but in someone's hotel room.

The song was a cheeky, slightly up-tempo piece, technically not particularly brilliant, and it was sung to the backing of a solitary acoustic guitar. And the voice singing it was deep, and soulful – and very, very familiar.

"I don't believe the cheek of him!" Angie gasped, but she couldn't stop the corners of her lips from creasing up into a smile.

"Sssh!" Rebecca urged. "Listen!"

As she listened to JJ's song, Angie's smile became even wider until it filled her entire face.

There is heaven in her eyes
And heaven in her mind
Even in the way she looks
And heaven in her smile.

Heaven's where she's been
I'll need her till I die
I'm lonely when she's not there
I'm haunted by her eyes.

There is heaven when she moves
Like a phantom in the night
I reach out for her when I'm alone
I know our love is right.

I guess I'm just a fool
For the woman I can't win
But a girl who stands aloof from love
Commits a deadly sin

Words cannot describe
What Angie means to me
And if she doesn't call me soon
I swear that I will die...

"What is he *like*?" Angie marvelled. "Won't he ever take no for an answer?"

"Apparently not," Rebecca laughed. She'd been tempted to play the cassette JJ had given her when he had visited her on Christmas Day, but the look on Angie's face made the waiting worthwhile. "So why not go out with him, Angie?" she asked. "After he's tried so hard?"

"He's arrogant, self-opinionated and—"

"No, he's not," Rebecca cut in. "When he gave me that tape he said—"

"And you're just as bad helping him out, Bec!" Angie snapped, although there was no doubt that JJ's song had appealed both to her ego and to her sense of humour.

This creep of a guy had filled her office with roses. And now he had written a song for her. No one had ever done that: after all, it wasn't the sort of soppy thing you expected.

Well, not from people like Dominic, and Adrian, and all the other boys at Astor College.

"When he gave me that tape on Christmas morning," Rebecca continued, "I got the feeling that he really wanted to get to know you. That he was really sincere and genuine..."

"Him? He's about as sincere and genuine as a black widow spider," Angie said flippantly. "The difference is that a black widow spider is prettier."

"Oh, yeah?" said Rebecca.

Angie wasn't pulling the wool over her eyes. Who was it who had said that JJ's eyes were the colour of autumn leaves after the rain?

Who had presumed that JJ spent lots of his time in the gym, because she had noticed his crucifix nestling between his well-developed pectorals?

And who was it who couldn't get that cute little dimple of his out of her mind? Rebecca guessed that Angie was a lot more attracted to JJ than she liked to admit.

"Besides," Rebecca continued, "Aunt Lizzie liked him – and that's good enough for me!"

Angie paused for a moment, and thought. There were those of Rebecca's friends who said that Rebecca's Aunt Lizzie was psychic. Certainly with her long kaftans, the joss sticks which she used to perfume the bathroom, and her unconventional and "hippy" ways, Lizzie didn't do anything to discourage people from believing that she was an excellent judge of character.

There had been times when Angie had gone to Lizzie for advice. Sometimes it was advice on the suitability of a particular boyfriend, sometimes it was advice of a more personal nature which she would have been too embarrassed to ask her parents for.

But whatever words of wisdom Aunt Lizzie had given out, they had always been spot-on. Maybe she was right: maybe, away from the other guys in Zone, when he didn't have to show off and prove his worth as their lead singer and songwriter, maybe JJ was an OK guy after all.

Angie Markowski! she immediately scolded herself. *What do you think you're talking about? Are you out of your mind, or what?*

"Sorry, Bec," she smiled. "I know you've wanted me and JJ to get together ever since I first interviewed him, but I'm seeing Dominic now. Nothing will ever get me to go out for dinner with JJ!"

Rebecca sighed philosophically. "I still think you're wrong," she said. "And Dominic need never know. But, with you out of the picture, I guess that means that we other girls might just be in with a chance!"

"What about Adrian?" Angie asked.

"Oh, yeah, I was forgetting about him…"

Angie was tut-tutting theatrically – Bec was quite simply impossible! – when the telephone rang. Rebecca, who had the ability to make herself at home in anyone's house, answered it. She passed the receiver over to Angie, who mouthed the words, "Who is it?"

"Don't worry, it's not JJ, not this time anyway," Rebecca sniggered. "It's Nurse Clare, from Cuttleigh. She says it's urgent."

Angie put the receiver to her ear, and frowned as she listened to what Nurse Clare had to say. After five minutes, she replaced the receiver and glanced over at Rebecca. There was a resigned and distinctly unhappy look on Angie's face.

"Bad news, huh?" Rebecca asked sympathetically. Angie nodded.

"The worst," she confirmed, and breathed a long theatrical sigh. "It looks like I'm going to have to take up JJ's offer of dinner after all!"

9

The car pulled up outside Angie's house at half-past seven on the dot. Even in the affluent neighbourhood in which she lived, where every second house belonged to someone working in one of the trendy professions, a top-of-the-range limousine gliding up to the kerb was still quite unusual. Add to that the fact that it was being driven by a hired chauffeur, dressed in a smart burgundy uniform and cap, and it was hardly surprising that, when Angie came to the door, thirteen net curtains twitched in thirteen different living rooms.

Angie felt like a queen, as she opened the door. She was dressed in a long, silken white dress, and a black satin waistcoat, the cut of which made her waist seem even smaller than it already was. A beautiful silver chain – understated but definitely classic – hung around her neck, and her hair was glossy and sleek.

A pair of diamond studs sparkled in her ears, glittering in the light from the overhead streetlamps which lined her avenue. Stephanie had loaned them to her especially for the night; or rather she would have done, if she had been around to lend them. Her dad and her stepmother had driven out of town to discuss with a top executive over a meal Peter's plans for his fashion show. They had no idea where Angie was going tonight – or who she was going with.

She looked a million dollars, and when Rebecca had asked her why she had gone to all this trouble for JJ, Angie had simply replied that JJ had told her he was taking her to his favourite restaurant in the whole of the country. It was very exclusive, he had warned her, and the proprietor wouldn't serve just everyone.

When Angie had pointedly and deliberately let slip the fact that Dominic was taking her to Vincente's the following night, JJ had just laughed and told her that, compared to the place he was taking her, Vincente's might as well just be an old greasy spoon stuck in the middle of nowhere.

His restaurant was real swish, he had said, so she'd better dress up like she was going to meet a member of the Royal Family. Or maybe someone even classier, as there was a rumour (and Angie wasn't quite sure if he was joking or not) that this joint was so stylish that one member of that particular family had already been turned away for being improperly dressed.

"And besides," Angie had told Rebecca, "I want to show JJ the sort of class act he's dealing with. What's he going to be dressed in? An off-the-peg suit and scruffy tennis shoes like every other third-rate rock star?"

She couldn't have been more wrong. When she opened the door she gasped at the sight – no, the *vision* before her.

JJ was dressed in a stylish black frockcoat, its inside lined with red satin, and with a tiny red ribbon attached to its dark velvet lapels. Instead of his customary leathers, he wore black Tartar trousers, tucked into knee-length Russian boots, which had been polished so much that, if she had wanted to, she could have seen her face reflected in them.

He wore a linen, collarless white shirt, and, in place of a traditional tie, a green velvet cravat with a pearl pin. His hair, normally so unkempt and wild, had been slicked back, and he had even taken off the crucifix which he normally wore in his right ear.

His whole apparel was wildly unconventional, and yet somehow right for him, and, even Angie had to admit, amazingly stylish. Angie couldn't imagine anyone else having the nerve to wear what JJ was wearing, or getting away with it so successfully.

There was only one word she could think of to describe the way JJ looked: a *star*.

"Wow," was all she could think of to say.

"Your carriage awaits you, my lady," he said in a put-on posh accent. He was holding an unfurled umbrella in his hand, to protect Angie from the heavy snow that was falling down all around them.

Angie forced herself to look past JJ and at the waiting limousine. "JJ, how can you afford all this?" she asked. "You've only just released your first single! You're hardly the big time yet."

"That's right: Zone aren't big time yet," JJ admitted. "But Joe is."

"Joe Krupp laid all this on?" Angie asked in amazement as she allowed herself to be led to the waiting limo. Knowing how fiercely protective he was of his "boys", she couldn't imagine Zone's dictatorial manager sanctioning this sort of extravagance.

"Well, kind of," JJ said sheepishly and opened the passenger door for Angie.

"What do you mean 'kind of'?" Angie demanded.

"I booked the car over the phone on his own personal credit card account," JJ admitted. "I ... er, just forgot to tell him about it before I did it..."

"He'll kill you when he finds out," Angie said, struggling not to laugh, or admire the young rock star's audacity.

"It's all worth it to impress a lovely lady!" he announced dramatically, and beneath his over-the-top manner Angie had the strangest idea that JJ meant what he was saying.

"So, where are we headed for?" she asked, once they were installed in the back seat of the limo, JJ had handed her a diet Coke from the in-car bar, and the chauffeur moved the limo silently off down the street.

"I told you," JJ said. "To the classiest joint I know of. It's about thirty miles out of town. And it's got the best cooking in the world!"

Angie could hardly wait. If the limo, and the chauffeur, and JJ's stunningly stylish and sexy suit – funny that, even in a suit, she could still make out every line, every muscled contour, of his athletic body – if they were all a sample of what was to come, then tonight was going to be one classy night out to remember!

"Fried eggs and chips twice, please, Frank," JJ called out cheerfully.

The man behind the counter, a pot-bellied, unshaven man, a cigarette dangling from his lips, nodded. "You got it, JJ," he said, and repeated his order to the mousy woman by the chip-pan. He looked JJ up and down, clearly unimpressed by the young man's bizarre outfit.

"Say, who's died, JJ?" he asked jokingly. "You going to a funeral or what?"

"No one's died yet, Frank," JJ said cheerfully, and then turned around to look at Angie. *Although from the look on Angie's face I think the first one to die might just be me!* he thought.

Angie had been expecting to be taken to the grill room of the Birmingham Hilton, or the restaurant of some fancy country house. Nothing had prepared her for the caff JJ had taken her to.

She looked around in horror at the tiny formica tables, the rusty tea urn, and the piles of ready-buttered bread slices behind the serving counter.

On the wall hung a dog-eared calendar, with a photograph of a local boxing hero, and a handwritten notice advertising the caff's house speciality breakfast of two eggs, sausage, bacon, mushroom, tomato and fried bread, at an extra-special cheap price if you ordered it before eight o'clock in the morning.

In fact, in Angie's eyes the greasy spoon had only two saving graces: it seemed reasonably clean, and apart from JJ and herself, and the two people she assumed were the owner and his wife, it was mercifully empty. At least no one would know she'd been here!

"Is this some sort of joke, JJ?" she demanded frostily.

JJ tried not to snigger at Angie's surprise and shook his head. "No. Here you get the best egg and chips anywhere in the world!"

"And this is your favourite restaurant?" Angie asked in disbelief.

JJ nodded happily, sadistically enjoying Angie's discomfort. "That's right," he said, and led her to one of the formica tables. He pulled out a chair for her to sit down on. "Frank's Caff is my favourite place in the whole world."

Angie looked at JJ as if he was mad. "I demand to be taken home," she said. JJ shook his head.

"No can do," he said. "We're miles away from anywhere here, it's snowing outside, and I've sent the chauffeur away. He won't be back until ten-thirty!"

Angie was trapped and she knew it. Resigned to her fate, she sat down. It could be worse, she realized. At least her friends weren't here to see her in such a dump.

And then to her horror, the proprietor, Frank, plonked an empty wine bottle on to their table, and lit the stump of a candle which he had stuck into its neck. He nodded over to his wife behind the counter, and as he lit the candle with his pocket lighter, she turned down the lights to create a more romantic atmosphere.

A few moments later, tinny, schmaltzy music came from the ghetto blaster from behind the counter, and Frank and his wife emerged from their tiny kitchen, carrying two plates piled high with egg and chips, and swimming in grease.

Angie felt her stomach heave at the thought of all that cholesterol, even though the food did smell good. *Almost good enough to eat*, she thought ironically.

Frank placed the two plates in front of Angie and her dinner date. "Enjoy!" he said.

Angie raised her eyes heavenwards and sighed. Some romantic evening this was turning out to be.

While Angie and JJ were eating their egg and chips, Rebecca Penswick was having the time of her life. When she'd returned home to her Aunt Lizzie's house there had been a message waiting for her on the answerphone. It had been Adrian, inviting her out for the night.

Deciding that perhaps she had been a little mean to her boyfriend standing him up earlier in the afternoon, she agreed to meet up with him at Vito's, the bistro they had all been to on Christmas Eve.

When she arrived there she had been delighted to find that he'd brought with him his cousin, Luke, as well as Danny and Marco, from Zone. The only girl among four such good-looking boys, she was flirting outrageously with each of them in turn, much to Adrian's evident distress.

As they drank more and more beer the boys began to tell her tales of the band, and especially of Krupp's big plans for them. Image was all-important for them, Krupp always said, and he had chosen an image for each of them, to go with their personalities, and which would help to market the band to as many people as possible.

Luke was meant to be the mean 'n' moody one, which was why he always wore designer stubble, ripped jeans and a grubby T-shirt. Marco was the sensitive one, with his nose always buried deep in a book, even though anyone who had seen him with his shirt off on stage would have guessed correctly that he spent more of his free time in the gym than the local library. Young Danny with his cheeky smile and that baseball cap which he always wore back-to-front was supposed to be the cute one, the one that all the mothers would adore when they bought their daughters a Zone CD as a birthday present.

"And what about JJ?" asked Rebecca, wondering exactly what image Zone's manager had chosen for the sexiest member of the band.

"JJ's supposed to be the baaaad boy," Marco said, drawing out the adjective, "the one your mother always warned you about. He's unpredictable: you're never meant to know what he's going to do next. The sort of guy who kisses the girls and makes them cry..."

"When in fact he's just a big softie," Luke said, a little contemptuously. There had always been a rivalry between the two best-looking members of Zone, and Luke always welcomed the chance to stir things. "He'd never have asked your friend out, if we hadn't bet him that he couldn't do it!"

"*What?*" Rebecca was horrified by what she was hearing. "You bet JJ that he couldn't get Angie to go out with him?"

"Hey, it was just a joke," Danny said quickly, eager to clear up any misunderstanding. "We didn't mean anything by it."

"Oh, no?" Rebecca was unconvinced.

"JJ's not the sort of egomaniac you might think," Danny continued. "I've known him longer than the others. And he's a really nice unselfish guy."

"Music's his life," Marco agreed. "And if a girl says she won't go out with him then he takes it philosophically. After all, there are plenty of others who would be more than willing to date him."

"Then why is he chasing Angie," Rebecca asked sternly, "if not for a bet?"

Danny shrugged. "Who knows? But I've never seen JJ go after any girl like this before... If I didn't know him better I'd say he was falling in love..."

"I'll kill you for this, you know, JJ," Angie said, and glared at her dining companion. She felt like a proper little idiot eating egg and chips in a greasy spoon while wearing a swanky silk dress that had cost her – or to be more precise her dad's credit card – hundreds of pounds.

"Wait until you've finished your meal," JJ said, and took a swig from the can of low-alcohol beer Joe had brought him. "Then you can kill me!"

In spite of herself, Angie laughed. And much as she hated to admit it, the eggs and chips tasted delicious. The chips especially were crisp and dry, not soggy and bland like the ones she'd occasionally had from the local chippy near college. She'd even asked Martha – Frank's wife – for a second helping, and Martha had been only too happy to oblige.

"You like?" JJ asked. He'd already finished his meal.

Angie nodded.

"I thought you would," JJ said. "Like I said, if you want good food Frank's Caff is the place to come."

"I'd never have thought of coming here in a hundred years," Angie admitted and mopped up the remains of her egg with the bread and butter Frank had thoughtfully provided her with. "And I would have imagined a pop star—"

"A third-rate pop star, I think you called me," JJ said.

"How did you know that?" Angie asked.

"Rebecca told Adrian," JJ said. "And Adrian told Luke. And Luke told me! That's three more people you can add to your list of people to kill!"

"Anyway I called you second-rate, not third-rate," Angie said smugly, "so don't put yourself down."

"I'll leave that to you then, shall I?" JJ countered, and grinned, enjoying this sparring with Angie.

"I'd never imagined someone like you in a place like this," Angie continued. "Maybe a trendy bistro or an upmarket hamburger joint, but not a greasy spoon miles away from anywhere."

"I've been coming here for years," JJ said. "Ever since I moved out here when my parents died…"

"I'm sorry…"

"You needn't be," JJ said. "But you see, Angie, you should never judge by appearances. I mean, who would have thought that someone as pretty as you could be such a successful student journalist?"

Angie groaned and put down her knife and fork. "Do

you know that was the tackiest line I have ever heard in my entire life?" she asked in all seriousness.

JJ nodded happily. "It was worth it though," he said, and then added, much more seriously: "And what's more, I meant it."

Angie blushed. There was something about JJ which fascinated her. Away from the other boys he wasn't half as brash and macho as he pretended to be. And he made her laugh too. That was something that only a few other boys could do.

"I need a favour, JJ," she said.

"I thought there might be a catch," JJ joked. "I knew you wouldn't let me take you out to this glamorous five-star restaurant without asking for something in return!" He sighed, and placed his hand on his chest, as though he were heart-broken. "There I was thinking you'd agreed to come out with me because of my charm, my wit and my undeniable sophistication. I should have known that there had to be an ulterior motive!"

"Pig," said Angie jokingly. "Listen, JJ, I've got a big problem."

"Too right you have," JJ agreed. "You're going out with a prize geek when you could be going out with me."

"Maybe," Angie said.

Maybe? What am I talking about? I've got everything I want in Dominic!

"JJ, I do some work at Cuttleigh Hall."

"That little place on the outskirts of town?" he asked.

"How do you know about that?" she asked, curious.

"I come from round here, remember?" he said. "Nurse Clare is famous in these parts. She looks after the disabled kids, doesn't she?"

"That's right. Well, I'm organizing a New Year's Eve party for the boys and girls there," she told him. "Streamers, balloons, party games, that sort of thing. I'd booked a conjurer to entertain them..."

"That's a great idea," said JJ, and sighed wistfully. "I used to love it when Mum and Dad took me to see magicians at the fairground ... before they died..."

"But he's cried off at the last moment," Angie explained. "Nurse Clare rang me up to tell me that he's caught this flu bug that's going round."

JJ looked warily at Angie. "And?" he asked.

God, he's enjoying this! Angie thought. *He knows exactly what I'm going to ask him and he's really enjoying watching me squirm!*

She leaned forward to look JJ straight in the eyes. Those eyes the colour of autumn leaves. He was wearing a sweet-smelling cologne, and for a second she was reminded of the fragrance Dominic usually wore. Dominic's was a much more manly smell; JJ's was a more feminine, more unpredictable fragrance, but he wore it with style and it suited him well.

"JJ, I need someone to entertain those kids," she pleaded. "Their whole day will be ruined if we don't put on a show for them!"

"Now let me see if I've got this straight," JJ said slowly. "You want Zone – tipped to be the next big thing in pop music – you want Zone to be the entertainers at a scrappy little kids' party?"

Angie nodded. The way he put it, it did sound a pretty dumb idea.

"You want me to persuade the other guys to give up their New Year's Eve?" He whistled. "That's a pretty tall order, Angie."

"I know," Angie said, and hung her head. She'd been an idiot to even think of the idea.

"Joe will never let us do it, you know; not unless you're paying big money up front."

"Er, that's another problem. It's a charity gig," she admitted. "You might get leftover jelly and cake if you're lucky..."

"Which I can take back and eat in my playpen, I guess?" he said, reminding Angie of her Christmas Eve put-down in Vito's.

"Er, yes..."

95

JJ took Angie's hand in his; she didn't try to move it away. "Angie, tell me the truth," he said softly. "You wouldn't have agreed to come out with me tonight if it hadn't been to ask me to do this gig?"

Angie wanted to turn away. Instead, she looked straight into JJ's face. "You're right, JJ," she said guiltily. "I'm sorry..."

Or am I? Or am I using the party as an excuse?

JJ stared at her for a moment, as though he was trying to see into her mind, as though he was trying to understand just what Angie was about. She'd just gone and told him the truth, straight out, and not got flustered and come up with excuses or lies. He liked that, he liked that a lot.

Angie returned his stare, and gazed into JJ's eyes, expecting to find there anger, or, at the very least, disappointment. Instead, she saw a flash of delight – and something else too.

JJ took his hand away from Angie's.

"OK," he said simply.

"What?" Angie asked.

"I said OK. We'll do the gig, on New Year's Eve, in two days' time."

"You mean it?" she gasped. "You really mean it?"

"I just said so, didn't I?" JJ was smiling, and seemed almost as delighted as Angie was.

"JJ, this is terrific!" she said. "You are such a great guy!" She leaned over and kissed him.

Kissed him on the lips.

She pulled sharply away, realizing what she'd just done. Without even thinking. Realizing that it had just felt like the most natural thing to do in the world. Realizing that it was what she had wanted to do for days now, ever since she had interviewed JJ in that shabby little dressing room.

What was it Steph had once said to her? Something about how she thought Peter Markowski was the most insufferable man she had ever met. Pompous, arrogant and self-opinionated. And that how, one day, she realized that it was all an act to hide the shy and frightened man underneath.

She'd said something about opposites attracting.

Something about magnets and iron.

Don't be stupid, Angie! she reprimanded herself. *He's nothing more than a randy rock star on the make! And you've got Dominic now! What about him? How would sweet, kind, unselfish Dominic feel if he knew what you were doing now?*

Nevertheless, she kissed JJ again on the lips, briefly, only for a second, before JJ – and not Angie – pulled away. They looked at each other for a half-instant, neither of them quite knowing what to say, but each of them understanding everything.

Finally JJ stood up and looked at his watch. It was half-past ten and outside their limo was waiting.

"C'mon, Angie," he said, "I've got to drive you home." He sighed. "And then I've got some major work to do on Danny, Luke and Marco! It's going to be tough to persuade them to give up their partying."

"It's only for the afternoon," Angie pointed out. "They can still go out on New Year's Eve night."

"Aha, but these guys like to party all day," JJ said. "After all, you know what they all say about rock stars, don't you?"

He came round to her side of the table, and took her hand, leading her to the door like a courtier escorting a duchess to the races.

Unseen by Angie, Frank and his wife winked at JJ as he led her out of the door.

Outside in the cold and the snow, JJ and Angie hurried to the limo. As she climbed into the passenger seat Angie turned to JJ, who was holding the door open for her. "Thank you, JJ," she said. "You've been really sweet. You're a really nice guy."

"Just don't spread it around," JJ said in a stage whisper. "It'll ruin my image!"

They laughed, and then JJ suddenly became serious.

"And congratulations, Angie," he said mysteriously. "You've just passed the test."

Angie frowned, unsure what JJ was saying. Even when he had dropped her off at her house, and given her a friendly goodnight peck on the cheek, she still wasn't sure what he had meant.

Passed the test? Passed what test? What did JJ mean?

10

"Well, how do I look?" Angie asked Rebecca, as she waltzed into Aunt Lizzie's sitting room, and did a twirl. She was wearing a tan Dolce è Gabanna dress, and matching brown leather boots.

Rebecca looked up from her copy of John Donne's love poems, and nodded approvingly.

"You look wonderful, Angie," she said, truthfully, and a little jealously too. Angie, after all, would look good in a bin liner. "Who's the lucky boy tonight?"

"Dominic," Angie said. "What do you mean, who's the lucky boy tonight? Of course it's Dominic. Who else could it be?"

Rebecca closed her book and looked up mischievously at Angie. "I just thought that after your date with JJ last night…"

"Listen, Rebecca Penswick," laughed Angie, sitting down on the sofa next to her friend. In the background music was softly playing: Rebecca was listening to the local pop music station. "That was just a friendly evening out! There's nothing to be read into it!"

"Oh, no?" asked Rebecca. "That's not what I've heard…"

"What do you mean?" Angie asked urgently. How could Rebecca have heard about that "thank-you" kiss that she had given JJ? How could she have known about the way her heart had beaten so much that she thought it would

burst whenever she was close to JJ in that caff? Had JJ –
that louse – been bragging?

"Marco told me," Rebecca replied. "He rang me this
morning to tell me that JJ hadn't stopped talking about
you since last night. Told me how they're all going to give
a concert at Cuttleigh Hall tomorrow afternoon."

Angie clapped her hands with delight. "That's great
news!" she whooped. "I knew JJ could talk them round to
the idea!" she said admiringly.

"He said that JJ had been trying to get in touch with
you all day to tell you," Rebecca added.

"I was putting in some work on the *Recorder*, and then
I was out buying this dress," Angie said, and then
frowned. "Wait a minute. What's Marco doing ringing you
up?" The penny dropped, and she gave her friend one of
her most disapproving looks. "Oh, Bec, you haven't gone
and dumped Adrian for Marco, have you?"

"Of course not," Rebecca said, a little guiltily, and not
very convincingly. "But Marco and I get on so well
together. He's such a nice guy – all the boys in Zone are –
and we had a really good time together in Vito's last
night." She glanced down at the book of love poetry. "And
we like so many of the same things – poetry, music..."

Angie nodded sagely, realizing that within the next few
days Adrian was going to get what she termed as the Big
Heave-Ho. He and Rebecca had been going out for
practically three weeks now: it was almost a record on
Rebecca's part!

And she also knew that Rebecca was not a mean-
spirited person and that, when she did break it off with
Adrian, it would be in the nicest and gentlest way
possible. Rebecca had had many boyfriends, and every
single one of them still remained on good and friendly
terms with her.

Rebecca pointed to the thin cardboard folder Angie was
holding. "Some romantic evening with Dominic it's going
to be, if you're going to be talking schoolwork all the
time!" she said.

"We won't be," Angie said, and took two sheets of computer print-out paper out of the folder. She showed them to Rebecca: they contained a list of names and addresses.

"I promised Dominic I'd get him a list of fashion contacts," Angie said. "You know – so he can try and make it as a model."

"I thought your dad wouldn't help him out," Rebecca said, puzzled.

"Well, he didn't," Angie said shamefacedly. "He and Steph were out last night..."

"So you took them from his Filofax when you got back from your date with JJ!"

Angie shook her head smugly. "No. Dad doesn't go anywhere without his Filofax."

"So how?"

"Dad's so absent-minded at times that Steph is convinced that he's going to lose his Filo one day," Angie explained. "So she's transferred all his contact numbers on to her computer. These sheets of paper are a print-out of his contacts in the fashion business!"

"You crafty ace reporter!" Rebecca said admiringly, before adding: "They'll kill you if they find out, you know."

"Well, they won't, unless you tell them, will they?" Angie said.

"My lips are sealed," Rebecca said. "You know I always keep secrets."

"That's right," Angie agreed. "You're a good friend, Rebecca. One of the very best."

Rebecca's face fell, as she remembered what Marco had told her over the telephone that morning. When JJ had rejoined the others in their hotel last night, he had found out how the guys had let slip that they had challenged him to take Angie out on a date. JJ had exploded and warned that Angie was never to find out about that.

When Marco had phoned Rebecca up he had sworn her to secrecy also. Rebecca was now torn between loyalty to her best friend and her promise to keep a secret.

"So, where did you say Dominic Dreamboat was taking you tonight?" she asked, in order to take her mind off her dilemma.

"Oh, just Vincente's," Angie said casually, as though she was talking about a tiny corner restaurant.

"That's right!" Rebecca marvelled. "The poshest restaurant in town! He must be really serious about you, Angie!"

"Yes," said Angie, "I think he is…"

On the radio, the DJ stopped prattling to his listeners and flipped on another CD. A familiar, dreamy tune emerged from the speakers, the tune Angie and Dominic had danced to together at the Christmas dance. It seemed suddenly that JJ was singing just for Angie:

> *Ask me once, and I'd give you the moon,*
> *For you're my best girl, and you know it's true;*
> *The other guys might fool you, make you dance*
> *to their tune*
> *But, my love, I'd be lost without you.*

"You look wonderful, Angie," Dominic said, and held her hands across the table at Vincente's.

All around them, impeccably dressed waiters minced about, carrying aloft huge silver trays, displaying some of the most delicious-looking dishes that could be had for miles around. A wine-waiter was always on hand to ensure that their glasses were never empty, and in the corner a string quartet played an unobtrusive selection of classical tunes. It was as far removed as it was possible to be from the caff JJ had taken her to.

"Thank you, Dominic," Angie said, her cheeks flushed a little from the wine she had been drinking. "It's been a wonderful meal."

"It wouldn't have been half so wonderful without your company," he said, and gazed into her eyes.

Dominic's own eyes were a startling brilliant blue, real model's eyes: it was funny, but Angie always forgot just how blue they were until she saw him again. They were much more brilliant than JJ's hazel eyes, the colour of autumn leaves after the rain.

"I don't want this to end," Angie said, as their waiter brought them two espressos to round off their meal. "But we both need early nights: we've both got a busy day tomorrow..."

"Sorry?"

"I've got the children's party at Cuttleigh to organize, remember?" she said. "And you've got to make an early start to go and visit your grandmother."

"Oh, yes..." he said.

Angie stroked his hand sympathetically. "I know it's selfish of me, but I can't pretend that I'm not disappointed about you not being able to help me with the party," she said. "But I understand. I really am very sorry about your grandmother. Is she very ill?"

"Gran?" Dominic asked absently, as though his mind was somewhere else. "Her doctors say she's only got a few more weeks to live," he said. "This will probably be the last time I see her alive..."

Angie lifted Dominic's hands to her mouth and kissed them. "I've brought something with me which might cheer you up," she said.

She reached down under the table and picked up the cardboard folder: Dominic had noticed it when she first arrived at the restaurant but hadn't remarked upon it. She handed it over to him.

"Don't tell anyone I've given you this," she warned. "Otherwise I'm going to get into the most enormous trouble!"

"What is it?" he asked excitedly, as he took out the two sheets of computer print-out, and cast his eyes down the list of names.

"My dad's contact list of anyone who's anyone in the fashion business," she said. "Home phone numbers, fax numbers, the works! If these people can't get you a modelling contract then no one can!"

"Angie, this is absolutely fantastic!" Dominic gasped. "How can I ever thank you?"

"I'll think of something," she said.

Dominic leaned over the table to kiss her, a warm, brief kiss on the lips. Angie reached out her hand, and pulled him back to her, for a longer, more passionate kiss. Dominic pulled away, and grinned.

"Whoa, not here, Angie," he said, and glanced shyly at the other posh-looking diners in the restaurant. "What would people think?"

Dominic chuckled and replaced the two sheets of paper in the cardboard folder. He signalled to the waiter for the bill.

"Are we going now?" Angie asked, and looked down at her unfinished espresso. "I wish this night could go on for ever."

"I'm afraid so," said Dominic. "Like you said, we've both got early starts tomorrow." He rolled up the cardboard folder and put it in the inside pocket of his jacket, and smiled gratefully at Angie. "And thank you, Angie, thank you from the bottom of my heart!"

11

Zone are terrific, Angie decided. The funkiest, most exciting and good-looking group she had ever seen, and the kids at Cuttleigh were having the time of their lives as the band performed for them on the makeshift stage at the New Year's Eve party.

And JJ is one of the most charismatic performers I've ever seen! she added to herself.

JJ, whether he was singing steamy rockers or sultry ballads, had his audience in the palm of his hand. He flirted with the young teenage girls, was silly and childish with the younger ones, and winked conspiratorially at the boys when he sang some of his more rebellious lyrics.

Cuttleigh was a small institution and there were only about sixty children in the audience; but JJ and Zone played as if they were performing in front of a crowd of tens of thousands at Wembley Arena, or the Hollywood Bowl.

Zone's act included a section where JJ selected one member of the audience to dance with on stage. As he sang her a love song, promising her that she was the only girl in the world, and gazing dreamily into her eyes, she instantly became the most envied member of the audience. All the girls wished that they could be there, up on stage, with that impossibly sexy man, singing of his wish that this dance could go on for ever.

At Cuttleigh JJ picked on a young girl in a wheelchair. Getting her wheelchair on stage would have posed a problem, so JJ simply leapt off the stage, lifted her up out of the wheelchair, and danced with her in his arms.

Angie brushed a tear from her eye, and hoped that no one had noticed. That JJ had picked someone in a wheelchair to dance with, rather than a more able-bodied person, was wonderful; that he had somehow intuitively zeroed in on the shyest and most insecure girl in the entire building, and was now making her smile like Angie had never seen her smile before, was little short of miraculous.

"The lucky thing," Rebecca said. "What I wouldn't give to be dancing with JJ!"

"He's marvellous," Angie agreed. "And he's so at ease with the kids."

Angie had seen other people give performances at Cuttleigh, and she had often remarked that they were uncomfortable around some of the more seriously disabled children. But JJ showed no such distress, and didn't even seem to notice their disabilities. So much for the image of the dangerous, irresponsible and unpredictable rock star which Joe Krupp was trying so hard to promote!

When Zone finished their hour-long set – Angie and JJ had agreed on twenty-five minutes, but, as he had warned her, once Zone started enjoying themselves they could go on for ever – they didn't leave for their dressing room (which was, in fact, Nurse Clare's office). Instead they jumped off stage and started mingling with their audience, signing autographs, chatting and joking, acting not like stars, but just like the boys you might bump into down at the local youth club.

Rebecca patted Angie on the back. "Well done," she said. "It's been the most successful party ever. Although Heaven knows how the boys got Joe Krupp to agree to them playing here – and for free!"

"I don't care how," Angie said, and pointed out JJ.

JJ was holding a young three-year-old toddler in his arms. He looked totally incongruous, dressed in his leathers, his sweat-drenched shirt open to the waist, as he gave the delighted little girl a kiss on the cheek. Suddenly he was aware of Angie looking at him, and he winked at her, and smiled with flawlessly white teeth.

"He's incredible," Angie gushed. "The way he treats the kids. Who'd've thought it?"

"Who indeed?" said Rebecca, looking suspiciously at her friend. Over by the stage, Adrian had been helping with the sound system, and he came over to join them.

"Thanks, Adrian," Angie said. "You were a great help, coming in at such short notice." Adrian nodded as if to say: *No problem*.

"Wasn't Marco great on keyboards?" Rebecca asked, and Adrian sighed.

Angie smiled. It seemed like Rebecca and Adrian had already had a quiet word about the future of their relationship; and, as she had guessed, they were still remaining good friends.

"I was expecting to see Dominic Cairns here," Adrian said. "Couldn't he make it?"

"His grandmother is seriously ill," Angie explained. "He's gone to see her for the New Year."

Rebecca and Adrian exchanged puzzled looks. "Are you sure, Angie?" Rebecca asked.

Before Angie had the chance to reply, Nurse Clare came up to them. She kissed Angie gratefully on both cheeks, and gave her a hug.

"My poppet, you were superb!" the Scottish woman enthused. "The children loved the musicians!"

"They're called Zone, Nurse Clare," Angie smiled. "And they're going to be very famous very soon."

"I couldn't bear the noise myself," Nurse Clare said frankly; "give me the bagpipes any day." And then she sighed philosophically. "But it's what you young ones want today, I suppose. And I must thank you for bringing the lost sheep back into the fold, if only for the day."

"Huh?" Angie didn't have the slightest idea what Nurse Clare was talking about.

Nurse Clare nodded over to JJ, who was still surrounded by a crowd of adoring and giggling children.

"It was so nice to see Jeremy again. The children do love him so: he was always very good with them, you know."

"Jeremy?"

"That's right." Nurse Clare couldn't understand the look of amazement on the faces of Angie, Rebecca and Adrian. "Don't you recall me telling you about him? One of our best voluntary workers until he left town a few years ago."

Angie looked back at the hunky, leather-clad figure of JJ, trying to reconcile the music scene's latest bad boy with that of the unselfish and diligent voluntary care worker, whom Nurse Clare praised so effusively. So that explained JJ's ease among the children, and the wonderful way he communicated with them.

JJ was Jeremy?

She saw JJ catch their eyes, and he made his way through the crowd towards them, still carrying the little girl in his arms. He was beaming from ear to ear. Angie didn't think she'd ever seen him looking so happy as he did now.

"Hi, girls; hi, Adrian," he said, and then kissed the septuagenarian director of Cuttleigh on the cheek. "And it's really nice to see you again, Nurse Clare."

Angie glared at the young rock star. "JJ," she said frostily. "We have to talk – *now!*"

"Hey, c'mon, babe, what's the big deal?" JJ said as Angie furiously led him to Nurse Clare's office.

"The big deal," said Angie as she slammed the door shut, "is that you lied to me! And don't call me babe!"

"What do you mean, 'lied' to you?" JJ was confused and felt not in control; and that made him just as angry as Angie.

"You didn't tell me that you used to work here!" she

said. "You didn't tell me the sort of person you really are!"

JJ looked at Angie as if he thought she was mad. And then it clicked. "Aha, I see what's eating you up so much, Miss Ace Reporter!" he shouted. "You don't like the wool being pulled over your eyes, do you? You don't like being made a fool of, do you?"

"Of course not," Angie protested. "I mean, of course..." She shuddered with rage. "I don't know what I feel!"

"You thought I was the 'bad boy', didn't you?" JJ continued cruelly. "You believed all the PR rubbish Joe's put out, didn't you? That's your trouble, Angie, you've judged me by what you *think* I am, and not who I am! You thought I was just another big-headed pop star—"

"No," she lied.

"Another big-headed pop star who thought he'd try out his luck on the budding female reporter, see if he could add another notch to his bedpost!"

Angie was dumbstruck. She was so used to boys flattering her, complimenting her, hoping maybe for a date; no boy had ever spoken to her like this before.

"Well, let me tell you, *babe*," JJ continued, and pointed an angry accusing finger at Angie. "I could have any girl I wanted. And no, I'm not being big-headed now, it's the truth!"

Angie nodded meekly: she knew JJ was right.

"But I chose you, *babe*, I decided to go after you, *babe*, someone who was so high and mighty that she wouldn't even look at me twice—"

No, it wasn't like that, Angie thought tearfully. *I thought you were so big-headed that I wouldn't give you the chance to show me who you really were. I didn't want you or the others in Zone to see that I was like everybody else, I didn't want to make a fool of myself. But I was attracted to you from the very first moment I saw you.*

"I chose to make a compete idiot of myself in front of my best mates, in front of your friends," JJ raged, "and all because ... all because..."

"Yes, JJ?" Angie asked softly, hopefully.

JJ shrugged self-consciously, and turned his hazel-coloured eyes away from Angie.

"All because I think I might be falling in love with you…"

An enormous silence fell on the room. JJ raised his head and looked at Angie. There were tears in her eyes; or at least he thought there were, for there were tears in his as well, and everything seemed misty. Angie took a step towards him, and reached out a trembling hand to touch him on the shoulder.

"JJ, I don't know what to say…"

"There's nothing to say," he said sullenly, and turned away. Angie pulled him back, and forced him to look at her.

"You're right," she said. "I thought you were conceited and arrogant and a thousand other things too. And I couldn't understand why I was so attracted to you…"

"You were?" JJ, the future bad boy of British pop, the guy whose picture, everyone predicted, would be pinned up on everyone's bedroom walls within nine months, couldn't believe his ears.

"And that's why I ran from you," Angie admitted. "I thought you were all wrong for me, and I didn't want to make an idiot of myself. That's why I ignored the flowers, and the tapes, and Rebecca begging me to go out with you—"

"But you did in the end."

"Because I wanted something from you," Angie said, and then corrected herself. "No, not from you. From *what* you are."

"From me as a member of Zone, you mean."

Angie nodded. "But if I hadn't I'd've never seen the sort of person you are," she said. "I'd never have seen just how sweet, and kind, and loving you really are…"

JJ chuckled. "Don't tell anyone, will you?"

Angie smiled too. "Come here, JJ," she said.

Angie wrapped her arms around JJ, drawing his face to hers. Their lips sought each other out hungrily, and they kissed, a long, deep and tender kiss that took both their breaths away.

Angie looked up into JJ's face: into his hazel-brown eyes, ringed with long lashes, at his shock of dark-blond hair, wet and shiny with sweat, at his beardless firm jaw, and that divine little dimple in the centre of his chin.

"It's only ever been you," she whispered. "Since the beginning." She giggled. "Since you found me in your dressing room."

"When I found you there, I couldn't believe that anyone could have gone to those lengths to get an interview with me. You were different from all the others. You were intelligent, had a mind of your own – you knew what you wanted and you went out there and got it."

"No, JJ," Angie said. "I didn't know what I wanted – until now."

They kissed again, and Angie ran her hand down the small of JJ's back, over his shoulderblades, then up along his smooth arms and his powerful biceps. She felt his body against hers, felt him breathing out as she breathed in. He nuzzled her neck, nibbling the lobe of her ear, blowing gently into her ear.

Shudders of delight coursed through Angie's entire body. She could have been on another planet. If Rebecca, Adrian, Nurse Clare, if even her dad and Stephanie and Joe Krupp had walked in now, she wouldn't have moved, wouldn't have strayed from the side of this gorgeous man, this blond-haired, pale-faced man who was the exact opposite of her "type", and who she knew now she loved, loved against all reason, loved against all sense, loved against every rule in the book of love.

She broke away from his embrace, and twined her fingers in his dark-blond hair, twisting it into little ringlets.

"Jeremy," she whispered and laughed.

JJ nodded. "Uh-huh," he said. "That's my name. Jeremy Jones."

"But why change it in the first place? And why keep it so secret?"

"Is this an interview, Ms Markowski?" he asked, only half-jokingly. "Hardly anyone knows my real name. Danny's one of the few who do, but then we've known each other for years now."

"This isn't an interview, JJ," Angie promised. "This is very definitely off the record."

JJ smiled, and Angie felt him relax slightly in her arms.

"Jeremy Jones is hardly a suitable name for a sleazy rocker, is it?" he asked. "It was Joe Krupp's idea."

Joe Krupp again. He seemed to control every aspect of the boys' lives.

"How did you persuade Joe to let you do this gig in the first place?" she asked him curiously.

"I have my ways," JJ said mysteriously.

"Tell me!" Angie demanded.

"The ace reporter will have to find that out for herself, won't she?" JJ teased. "But I did this gig for two reasons. For the kids, because I used to work here..."

"Nurse Clare told me you stopped working here several years ago," Angie remembered. "Why did you leave if you loved it so much?"

"My parents died in a car crash, five years ago when I was fifteen," he said. "My aunt and uncle became my guardians after that. When they moved away from the area, I couldn't afford to live here on my own. So I went with them. And I stayed with them, helping them run their business, until last year when Joe Krupp spotted me singing in a local talent contest and asked me to join Zone."

"So you helped them in their business," Angie said, and remembered the conversation they had shared in the greasy spoon two nights ago. Then he had told Angie that singing was his only life, that he couldn't do anything else.

JJ laughed again, and gave his girlfriend – for with a shock he realized that that was exactly what Angie had become in the past few glorious minutes – a brief peck on the lips.

"Their business isn't the sort of business you have in mind, Angie," he said. "They don't work in TV like your dad, or at the local college like your stepmother."

"So what do they do?" Angie asked. "How did you help them in their business?"

"I served the egg and chips."

"What?" asked Angie, and JJ laughed at her surprise. "Wait a minute, you don't mean that greasy spoon – I mean, that café we went to the other night—"

"Which you turned your nose up at when you first crossed over the threshold, because it wasn't what you were expecting, but where you were polite and charming and considerate to Frank and Martha who run the place, because you didn't want to hurt their feelings... And what's more you asked Martha for a second helping."

"They're your uncle and aunt?" Angie asked, amazed. "They looked after you when your mum and dad died?"

JJ nodded. "That's right, Angie. You see, you shouldn't judge by appearances. Remember what I told you at the end of that evening?"

Angie nodded; his words had been puzzling her ever since. "You told me that I'd passed the test..."

"I've taken other girls there," JJ said, "and every one of them has turned her nose up at the place, and demanded to be taken to Vito's or Vincente's, or some other posh joint. And sure, I took them where they wanted to go; but I never saw them again."

"It wouldn't have mattered where I was," Angie said, "as long as I was with you."

"We fought for half of the meal!" JJ reminded her.

"I know. And I enjoyed every minute of it!" she said.

"Frank and Martha loved you, Angie," JJ said. "You passed the test all right. You passed the test with flying colours!"

Suddenly they both started as the door opened. They sprang from each other's embrace, but not before Rebecca, standing in the doorway, had the chance to take in the situation.

"There you are, JJ," she said. "I've been looking all over for you. Nurse Clare says if you wouldn't mind signing a few more autographs..."

"Sure, why not?" JJ said, and headed for the door. "I'll see you girls later, OK?" He waved them goodbye and winked at Angie.

As soon as he had gone Rebecca turned to her best friend. "So?" was all she needed to say.

"So what?" asked Angie and grinned. Nothing else needed to be said between the two of them.

"Well, well, well, what a dark horse you are, Angie," Rebecca said admiringly. "You tell me off for fancying Adrian and Marco. But at least I drop Adrian before I start going out with Marco. Even I don't keep two boyfriends on the go at the same time!"

Dominic Cairns! In the euphoria of the past fifteen minutes Angie had forgotten that Dominic even existed. Dominic was so different from JJ that it sometimes seemed that they lived in two separate worlds.

Angie was going to be forced to choose between the two of them. But how could she make the choice about two people who were as different from each other as could be? How could she make her decision?

12

Angie slammed the phone down for the third time that morning. It seemed that neither Dominic nor his parents were at home, and all she could get was their answerphone. She frowned as she remembered that Dominic had told her that they wouldn't be staying the night at his grandmother's and that they would be back very late on New Year's Eve.

Now it was New Year's Day, and still there had been no reply from Dominic. She had wanted to wish him a Happy New Year, hoping that this year would be the best for both of them, and when she received no answer she started to worry that Dominic's grandmother might have taken a turn for the worse; she was sure that if she had he would have altered his plans to stay with the old lady. But why hadn't he told her? Why didn't he realize how concerned she was about him?

Angie picked up the phone again and prepared to dial the number of JJ's hotel. She had had a restless night, even turning down the New Year's Eve party Rebecca had invited her to. How could she enjoy herself when at the back of her mind was the nagging question: *Dominic? Or JJ?* She had to choose between the two of them: she knew that it wasn't fair on either of them or on herself.

JJ knew that she had been out with Dominic, certainly, but he didn't realize just how much she felt for the captain of the football team. And yet every time she went out with Dominic, she found herself comparing him with JJ, seeing JJ's hazel-coloured eyes when she looked into Dominic's (funny how she still couldn't remember what colour his eyes were), smelling JJ's fragrance whenever Dominic was near to her, thinking how messy and unkempt JJ's hair was when compared to Dominic's.

She started to dial when the door to her bedroom opened. Her father was standing there, an angry look on his face.

"You. Downstairs. Now," he said abruptly, and stormed off to the study where Stephanie was waiting for them. With a sinking heart Angie followed him.

"I thought I told you that the information in my Filofax was totally confidential," he told her. He had his Filofax in his hand and was waving it angrily in his daughter's face.

"You did," Angie said. "And it is." What was the big deal?

"Then why have you been taking names and addresses from my list of contacts?" Mr Markowski demanded.

"I haven't been anywhere near your blasted Filofax, Dad," Angie protested.

"You've accessed the information contained in it and which was stored on Stephanie's computer though, haven't you?" he accused her. Angie looked over at Stephanie, who was standing by her computer.

Angie wished the ground could swallow her up. "How could you know...?"

Stephanie shook her head sadly. "I'm disappointed in you, Angie," she said and pointed to a small text box in the top left hand corner of the screen. "I found this when I switched on my monitor this morning," she explained. "It's a record of the last document which was worked on, and the time it was accessed."

Angie looked at the message in the box: FASHION/ TEL: 30 DECEMBER: 17.19. Sure enough the computer had recorded the time she had opened her dad's file, and taken the information for Dominic. Angie kicked herself. How could she have been so stupid?

"Would you like to explain what you were doing rooting around in my personal files, young lady?" her father demanded, trying hard to control his temper.

Angie decided that honesty was the best policy. "Dominic is going to have a great career one day," she said. "All he needs is a little help... All I gave him were a few addresses."

"Which you gave him against my express wishes?" asked her father.

Angie hung her head in shame. "Well, yes..." she admitted. "But Dominic's a good person, Dad, he'll be very discreet when he rings those people up. And it would be so nice to see him being successful in the fashion world..."

Peter Markowski harrumphed, but in truth he loved his daughter so much that he found it difficult to be annoyed with Angie for long.

"I'm sure Dominic will be discreet," he said. "I told you before, his father's a friend of mine. A more respected, upstanding family I couldn't hope to know..."

Stephanie placed a hand on her husband's shoulder. "Peter, why don't you let me handle this," she said softly. "Sort of – woman to woman?"

Peter nodded and left the room. As soon as he had closed the door Stephanie looked sternly at her stepdaughter.

"Don't think that just because I'm not shouting at you like your father I'm any the less angry with you, Angie," she said.

"I'm sorry, Steph..."

"Why did you do it, Angie?"

"I told you. I wanted to help Dominic. It wasn't as though he asked me: it was my own idea."

"And are you and he serious about each other?" Stephanie asked.

Angie paused. Yesterday morning she would have answered "yes" without even thinking. After the events of the previous day – after JJ – she wasn't so certain.

"Yes, we are," she said finally. "He's such a kind person. Modest, down-to-earth, neat and tidy. Not like some people I know..."

Not like JJ, she thought. *Nothing like JJ in a million years.*

"Good, I'm pleased for you," said Stephanie. "Your father and I would like to meet him sometime. Maybe you should invite him round."

"Yeah, sure," Angie said. She knew that Stephanie and her father would like Dominic. He was solid and reliable, just like Guy, her previous boyfriend, whom they had both adored.

She smiled: she dreaded to think what their reaction would be if she brought JJ round for tea in his leathers and his untidy mop of hair. Her father, who was always so protective of her, would probably have a coronary!

"Why not ring him now?" Stephanie asked. "Invite him around this evening?"

"I tried ringing him before," she said. "He's still not back from his grandmother's."

"That's nice," Stephanie approved. "Spending your New Year's Eve with your grandmother."

"Yeah, it is," Angie agreed. "And he is nice."

"Let's not say anything more about the matter of those phone numbers," said Stephanie. "All girls make idiots of themselves over a boy at one time or another. I know I certainly have."

"You?" Angie couldn't quite believe it: Stephanie was usually so sensible and level-headed.

"When I was your age, Angie – a long, long time ago – there was this boy at university I was crazy about. We went out together, and I thought he really loved me." Stephanie sighed, "I did everything for him, even helped him out with his essays and research. Until I found out he was going out with someone behind my back..."

"That's sad," said Angie.

"Not really," Stephanie said. "He was only going out with me so I could help him with his grades and exams. I was much cleverer than him, you see... When I found out I felt like the biggest fool on the planet. But I got over it, and I learnt my lesson... So let's forget about the phone numbers and start this New Year the way we mean to go on. OK?"

"Thanks, Steph," Angie said, and gratefully kissed her stepmother. She turned to go but Stephanie asked her to wait.

"There was a phone call for you early this morning," she said, and searched around her desk for the yellow sticker on which she had made a note of the caller's name. "Some boy... He was lucky I was up so early working on some papers."

Some boy? Dominic? JJ?

"He said he wanted to be the first to wish you a Happy New Year, but I told him you were still in bed," Stephanie said, and finally found the note hidden underneath a pile of research papers.

"He sounded quite shy on the phone: I got the feeling that he wasn't quite sure whether you wanted to speak to him or not. He seemed relieved when I told him you'd gone to bed early and hadn't gone out partying..."

"Well, don't keep me in suspense all day, Steph!" Angie laughed. "Who was it? Who wanted to be the first person to wish me a Happy New Year? Was it Dominic? JJ?"

"JJ?" Stephanie looked down at the piece of paper on which she had scribbled the caller's name. "No, Angie, it wasn't JJ."

"Then who was it?"

"Jeremy," said Stephanie. "He said his name was Jeremy."

She looked up at Angie, caught the look of delighted surprise on her stepdaughter's face. "Angie, who is Jeremy?"

"Someone who trusts me, Steph," Angie said, and felt her eyes mist over with tears. "Someone who trusts me more than anyone else in the entire world."

13

"Ididn't think you'd come," said JJ, who had been waiting at the bus stop for half an hour now. The shoulders of his leather jacket were covered with snow, and a wisp of hair hung out from the baseball cap which he had borrowed from Danny and which he was wearing to protect his head from the snowfall.

"It's New Year's Day," Angie said, as she stepped off the bus and it drove speedily away. "Everything's delayed by the holiday traffic and the snow." She kissed him on the lips. She shivered. "You're cold."

"You'll have to warm me up then," he said. The words were ones the old JJ might have used; the tone of voice in which he said it was something only the new JJ was capable of.

They held each other close, and kissed again. JJ tasted warm, and sweet and loving, and the feel of his muscular arms wrapping tightly around her made Angie feel safe and secure, and as warm in the falling snow as she might have been on some tropical beach.

"Happy New Year," she breathed, and added mischievously: "Jeremy."

JJ screwed up his eyes in an effort to look menacing. "I trusted you with the biggest secret in the world," he snarled. "And if you call me Jeremy one more time I'll kill you!"

Angie was clearly unimpressed. "Sorry – *babe*," she said.

They burst into a fit of giggles and walked, arm-in-arm down the winding country lane.

Angie looked around. JJ had suggested they meet some distance away from town, in a small village well off the beaten track.

He knew a great village pub there where they could have a late lunch, he had said, when she had returned his call and rung his hotel room; and where there was little chance of him being recognized. Curiously enough, it was very close to the place where Angie had also met Dominic; she wondered how his grandmother was feeling now.

"I love coming out here," JJ said, almost echoing Dominic's earlier words. "Where no one knows me, where I don't have to put on my act..."

"It must be hard being a sex god," Angie laughed.

"It is," JJ said, in all seriousness. "But that's the image I've got to project."

"Joe Krupp's image," said Angie. "He seems horrible."

"He's tough, but he's not unkind," JJ said, and Angie was reminded of her father. "He just wants us to succeed. He's already planned a series of local gigs, and now he's trying to organize a European tour for us. And he's helped us all too."

"How?" Angie was interested: she couldn't imagine Zone's tyrannical manager helping anyone out of the kindness of his heart.

"He helped Danny's parents when they were in financial trouble and it looked as though he couldn't stay on at stage school, for instance."

"But that was to Joe's advantage too," Angie pointed out. "Danny's a great performer, and he'll be a star soon, just like the rest of you. Joe's 'help' was nothing more than a straight financial investment."

"I guess so," said JJ. "But then he helped me out when I had that trouble with the law..."

"The law? You were in trouble with the police?" Angie

asked, and remembered just how concerned JJ had been when Krupp had threatened her with the police.

JJ felt Angie tense up involuntarily, and he cuddled her closer to him. "Don't worry," he joked, "I'm not a serial killer or anything like that. I'm not going to murder you out here in cold blood, miles away from anywhere!"

"I'm relieved to hear it," Angie said, and then was serious again. "What did you do, JJ?" she asked.

They stopped and sat down on a stone wall. JJ looked out into the distance. "It was just after mum and dad had been killed in a car crash, and I'd gone to live with Frank and Martha," he said. "You can't guess how screwed up I was over their death."

"I can," said Angie, and rested her head on JJ's shoulder. "My real mum died as well, remember?"

"Sorry, I forgot…" JJ said, and kissed the top of Angie's head. "Things were tough, and Frank and Martha tried to give me everything I wanted. But the caff doesn't make that much money, and it wasn't enough."

"So you went out thieving?" Angie asked gently.

"I went shoplifting," JJ said. "Once. I tried to steal a designer leather jacket. And I got caught, by a passing policeman. The shopkeeper was going to press charges."

"And Joe bailed you out?"

"I don't know what he did," JJ said. "He probably paid off the shopkeeper to keep the matter quiet. But that was the last I heard of it."

Angie smiled, and sneaked her hands inside JJ's leather jacket, and stroked his firm hard pecs. "So this 'bad boy' image isn't all hype, after all?" she teased.

"I was an idiotic little kid," JJ said. "It was a stupid thing to do, and I could have ended up with a criminal record which would have followed me around for the rest of my life."

Angie thought for a moment; it felt strange talking to someone who, if circumstances had been different, might have turned to crime. Some of her other friends were a little wild, but they never strayed from the straight and narrow, apart from the time when they smuggled bottles of wine into school parties.

"If you'd wanted the jacket so much, couldn't you have saved up for it?" she asked, hoping she didn't sound too much like a disapproving grown-up.

JJ laughed bitterly. "On what? Frank and Martha paid me a wage for working in the caff, but it wasn't much!"

"Well, you could have got another job then..." she suggested.

JJ placed a finger under Angie's chin, and raised her head so that he could look at her eyes. "Angie, I'm not as clever as you," he said. "I only scraped through school and left at sixteen with hardly any qualifications. You're brainy and bright, and you're going to be a great journalist one day! You're going to need all the qualifications you can get!"

"You sound just like my dad!" Angie joked. It seemed odd to hear JJ talk so "sensibly" for once. JJ put a silencing finger to her lips.

"I'm serious," he said. "Don't let anything stop you getting those grades, Angie. There are hardly any jobs out there now. I know – I looked. If it hadn't been for my music I don't know what I would have done.

"Dan, Marco and Luke, they could probably all get other work if they had to. But all I have is my music, that's the only thing I can do. It's my only way out from another forty years on the dole, or serving egg and chips behind my uncle's counter. It's my whole life—" He looked at Angie "—or at least it was – until I met you..."

He pulled her closer to him, kissing her, running his hands along her face, twining his fingers in her hair. Angie responded with equal ardour, her passion increasing with his. Things were starting to get decidedly steamy when Angie stopped JJ.

"No, JJ," she said firmly.

JJ smiled, and nodded. "OK," he said. "Whatever you say. I don't want to do anything that you don't want to do."

Was this guy for real? Angie asked herself. At this point most guys would have thrown a tantrum, or, at the very least, sulked!

JJ reached out and zipped up her jacket. He winked at her. "We don't want you catching cold, do we?"

"I don't think there's any chance of that," she grinned. All around them it was the middle of winter; but they were so warm together that the weather no longer mattered.

They resumed their embrace, delighting in the nearness of each other, delighting in each other's warmth. Then they jumped off the stone wall they had been sitting on, and walked off in the snow, following the path which led to the village pub.

But still there was that nagging voice at the back of Angie's mind. Telling her to make a decision. Telling her to choose.

Between Dominic and JJ.

Damn it! she told herself. *Why didn't I give in to my feelings for JJ when I first met him? Why did I have to be so clever and superior? Why did I have to judge by appearances? If I'd followed my instincts in the first place I wouldn't be in this mess now!*

Angie got home late that night, having spent one of the most wonderful days of her life. She and JJ had had a large and unpretentious lunch sitting in front of a roaring fire at the village pub, a beautiful oak-timbered building.

Away from the crowds, away from anyone who recognized him as the sexy lead singer from Zone, JJ seemed much more relaxed, even chatting away to the young daughter of the landlord, who was most taken with him.

By the time darkness had come and they were waiting for the bus that would take them into town, Angie had decided that she was hopelessly in love with JJ. And, what was more, she was sure that he had exactly the same feelings for her.

She had chuckled to herself and JJ had bent down to nibble her ear, and asked her what the joke was. She had told him that in a few months' time, when Zone had hit the big time, she would probably be the envy of every single girl in the country; she'd probably be known as the girl who used to go out with JJ, just before he became famous.

And then JJ had shaken his head. "No, Angie," he had said. "You'll never be known as the girl who used to go out with JJ just before he became famous."

A troubled look had then passed over Angie's face, a look immediately succeeded by an expression of sheer bliss, as JJ continued: "Because you're going to be known as the girl who is going out with JJ – even though he's famous! It's taken me a long time to find someone like you, Angie, and now that I have I'm never going to let you go. Ever."

Stephanie looked suspiciously at her stepdaughter as she skipped in through the front door. "Good day?" she asked casually.

"The best!" Angie announced, and hung her leather jacket on the hook by the door.

"Who were you with?" Stephanie asked. Angie's stepmother wasn't prying, but showing a genuine interest.

"With JJ," Angie said happily.

"JJ..." The name meant nothing to Stephanie. Unlike Mr Markowski Stephanie didn't keep her finger on the pulse of popular culture; for her, pop music had ground to a halt in the late 1970s when she had been in her early twenties. "You've mentioned his name a lot in the past few days. Is he a nice boy?"

"Kind, gentle, charming," Angie said.

"Just like Dominic, then," Stephanie teased.

No, nothing like Dominic, nothing like Dominic at all!

"Someone rang for you just a few minutes ago," Stephanie told her.

"JJ?" Angie asked excitedly. He had promised to ring her the moment he got back to his hotel.

"No," Stephanie replied. "Rebecca. She said she had to talk to you urgently."

Puzzled, Angie went up to her bedroom, and punched out Rebecca's number on the telephone keypad. The receiver at the other end was picked up almost instantly. Angie asked Rebecca what the urgency was, and at the other end of the line there was an embarrassed pause.

"Look, Angie, we're best friends," said Rebecca, "and if you like you can tell me that it's none of my business..."

"It's none of your business," Angie replied, obediently.

"But I saw you and JJ yesterday in Nurse Clare's office..."

"He is so wonderful, Bec," Angie said. "Thoughtful, and funny, and so handsome, and—"

"Angie, will you listen for a minute! You're starting to sound just like me!" Rebecca snapped. Angie frowned: there was something obviously bothering Rebecca a great deal.

"Adrian and Marco warned me not to tell you," she continued awkwardly. "But you're my best friend, and I don't want to see you get hurt..."

"Get hurt?" Angie was confused. "Tell me what, Bec?"

"Well, it's probably nothing, but ... but ... but when JJ first asked you out, it was all because of a bet..."

"A bet?"

"I'm sure they didn't mean it," Rebecca went on hastily. "But the guys bet him that he couldn't get you out on a date. It was just a bit of fun: you know what boys are like. I'm sure JJ had forgotten all about it ... Angie, are you still there?"

"Yes, Bec, I'm still here." Angie's face had turned a deathly shade of white, and she was finding it an effort to keep her voice steady. There was a long pause and then she finally said, in a stiff and frosty tone: "Thank you for the news, Bec. I'll see you soon."

The instant she replaced the receiver the phone rang again. She picked it up and answered it with a curt: "Yes? Who is it?"

"Hi," JJ's warm voice echoed down the line. "I've just got in this minute. I've had the greatest day with you, Angie, and I'm missing you already—"

"A *bet*?" Angie barked down the phone.

"What?" asked JJ, and then realized what Angie was talking about. "Oh, God, Angie, I should have told you…"

" 'Should have told me'?" Angie shouted. "No, what you should have done, you *creep*, is never to have met me in the first place. It's a shame you didn't get arrested when you tried to steal that leather jacket, because now you'd probably be inside for a very long time and out of my life for good!"

"Angie, I—"

"You've won your pathetic little bet, and I hope you're pleased with yourself. And don't give me all that rubbish about just being a poor misunderstood boy, who doesn't like the pop star image that's being thrust upon him. Save that for the teen magazines – that's if the people who fancy you can even read! Get a life, JJ – one that doesn't include me! We are finished!"

And with that Angie slammed the phone down, and fell back on to her bed, exhausted by her outburst.

And she cried and cried and cried.

14

Thank Heavens there's always Dominic, Angie kept telling herself over the next five days. She'd been a fool to allow herself to fall in love with someone like JJ, with someone so unpredictable, so totally different from herself and the people around her. It had been a silly crush, she tried to convince herself, and perhaps she had been attracted by his glamour. She'd behaved like a silly giggling schoolkid, not like the sensible and level-headed journalist she liked to consider herself.

Much better, she decided, to stay with Dominic. Just as good-looking as JJ, he was far more dependable, far more trustworthy. Going out with Dominic might be less exciting than going out with JJ, but at least Angie knew where she stood with the handsome would-be model.

However, it had been a few days since Dominic had phoned, and Angie was getting worried about his grandmother. The poor old woman must be really ill, Angie decided, and she only wished that Dominic had left her a phone number on which she could contact him. She was sure that he was going to need some emotional support at a time like this.

In the next few days she busied herself as much as possible, going into the *Recorder*'s offices every day, to work on news stories. She'd scrapped the idea of typing up her interview with JJ, of course, and had binned the cassette.

She was constantly reminded of the sexy singer and the boys. Whenever she turned on the radio their single seemed to be playing. She tidied up her desk, and uncovered the photo which had first introduced her to the band.

And then there were the roses. Not huge extravagant bouquets, but a single red rose, waiting for her on her doorstep every morning. There was no card with them, but Angie knew who had sent them.

Five days after she had slammed the phone down on JJ, Angie was sitting at one of the newspaper's Apple Macs, typing up a news feature, when, through the open newsroom door, she heard a commotion in the corridor outside. Rebecca was talking to someone.

"She's in there now," she heard Rebecca saying. "But make it quick. The Principal will have a fit if he finds a non-student on college premises during the holidays."

Rebecca knocked on the open door. "Angie, there's someone here who wants to see you," she said.

Angie spun round on her chair. *JJ? Was it JJ?*

Her face fell when she recognized her visitor.

"Hi, Danny," she said.

"You don't seem so happy to see me," said Zone's young drummer.

Angie apologized. "I just thought you might have been someone else, that's all. Come on in, Danny."

Danny sauntered into the office and Rebecca discreetly closed the door behind him. He walked over to Angie's desk, and sat on it.

"I suppose *he* sent you," Angie demanded, and instantly regretted her frosty tone. She liked Danny and always thought of him as the most down-to-earth and sincere member of Zone.

"He doesn't know I'm here," Danny admitted. "And he'd probably hit the roof if he did!"

"An insult to his macho pride, I suppose."

"Angie, he's miserable," Danny revealed. "He can't write any songs, he's not singing as well as he used to. And he's driving us all nuts!"

"And whose fault is that?" Angie demanded. "It might come as a surprise to you boys, but we girls don't like being treated as something to make bets about!"

"Look, Angie, the bet began as a bit of a laugh. Yeah, sure we teased him when you wouldn't go out with him, and maybe he started out trying to prove a point. But then something happened. I've never seen him behave like this with any other girl he's been out with."

"Not even your sister?" she asked.

"My sister?"

"Yes. He told me that that was how he got to know you. I presumed he'd been dating your sister. Poor girl."

Danny smiled. "Angie, when I met JJ my sister was five years old. She has Down's Syndrome. JJ used to come round and babysit so that Mum and Dad could have a night out every now and then! What's more, he'd do it for free..."

Angie suddenly felt very foolish indeed.

"And if you ever tell him that I told you that, I'll kill you," Danny joked. "Angie, he loves you and he wants you back."

"So why have you come here?" Angie asked. "Why hasn't he?"

Danny smashed his fist into the palm of his hand in frustration. "He's much too proud, Angie," he said. "JJ's a great guy, but he's also stubborn and pig-headed. And I think he's not the only one." He looked directly at Angie: it was obvious who else he meant.

"Well, if he does love me, then he has a funny way of showing it," Angie said.

"Yeah, he has," Danny agreed. "He's prepared to put his career on the line for you."

Do what?

"Didn't you ever wonder why Joe Krupp allowed us to play that New Year's Eve gig at Cuttleigh, for free?" Danny asked. Angie nodded and asked him to explain.

"The night before, JJ and Joe had one heck of a major row," Danny said. "JJ said that if we didn't do the gig then he was leaving the band. He was actually prepared to break his contract with Krupp Promotionals: if he'd carried out his threat Joe could have chased him through the courts for years, and made sure that JJ never worked as a musician again. But Joe's no fool: he knows that without JJ there would be no Zone. So he backed down – and that's why we were able to do the charity gig at Cuttleigh."

Angie stared wide-eyed at Danny. "JJ was ready to do that – for me?"

Danny nodded. "He loves you, Angie, he's crazy about you…"

Angie remembered part of the conversation she and JJ had had on New Year's Day. *All I have is my music, Angie,* JJ had said, *that's the only thing I can do. It's my only way out from another forty years on the dole, or serving egg and chips behind my uncle's counter. It's my whole life…*

And JJ was prepared to sacrifice all that just to make her happy! He must love her, after all.

"Phone him, Angie," Danny urged. "You must have the number of the hotel Joe's put us all in. Tell him you need him, tell him you love him…"

"And why can't he tell me?"

Danny sighed. "Do it, Angie, please…"

He turned to go, and opened the door. Rebecca was standing directly behind it: she had been eavesdropping on the entire conversation. He smiled at Rebecca and then glanced back at Angie who was gazing thoughtfully at her computer screen.

"Try and see if you can talk some sense into her," he whispered to Rebecca. "I don't know who's worse – Angie or JJ. They're made for each other: they're both as proud and as stubborn as each other!"

"Angie, you've got to ring him," Rebecca said gently after Danny had left. "You know you love him."

Angie turned to Rebecca: her eyes were watery with unshed tears. "I don't know what to do, Bec," she said honestly. "How can I believe in JJ after that bet he made?"

"Like Danny said, it was a bit of fun," Rebecca said. "What does your heart believe?"

"My heart?" Angie thought. "My heart says that he is the most impossible, conceited, unthinking man in the world. And also the gentlest, the kindest, the best..."

"Well, that's what love is, Angie," Rebecca said, suddenly sounding wiser than her seventeen years. She pulled up a chair and sat down next to Angie.

"I've been out with lots of boys," Rebecca continued. "And for a few weeks I tell everyone that I'm in love with them. But they all fizzle out in the end like Adrian has, and like Rod before him. Marco will be the same, I imagine. Because I might say I love them, but I don't really..."

"Bec, you've never spoken to me like this before." Angie was genuinely touched by her friend's confiding in her.

"What I feel for them isn't love," Rebecca said. "Because I can only see a boy's good points. Aunt Lizzie once told me that you only truly know you're in love with someone when you love him not *because* of what he is, but *in spite* of what he is..."

Angie reflected on Rebecca's words for a moment, and remembered what Stephanie had told her had been her first impression of Peter Markowski. She'd found him insufferable at first; but they seemed to be one of the best-matched couples in the world.

"Your Aunt Lizzie talks a lot of sense for an ageing hippy," Angie remarked.

"And she's right," Rebecca added. "You know it's right."

"But Bec, it isn't that simple," Angie protested.

"You love JJ. What could be simpler than that?"

"There's Dominic," Angie reminded her. "I love him too..."

"Do you?" Rebecca asked. "Do you feel for him in the same way as you do for JJ..."

"No, but ... Bec, I'm so confused... What should I do?"

"Phone JJ," was Rebecca's advice. "And if it makes you

feel better, phone Dominic as well..."

"I've tried to," Angie told her. "But he's still out of town, visiting his grandmother."

Rebecca shook her head sadly. "Dominic doesn't have a grandmother, Angie."

"Don't be silly," Angie said. "She's very ill..."

"No, Angie, all his grandparents are dead. He's been stringing you along. Wherever Dominic Cairns is now, it's certainly not with his grandmother!"

"Hi, is Dominic there?" Angie asked, as the receiver was finally picked up at the Cairns' house.

"Who's speaking, please?" asked Mrs Cairns.

"It's Angie."

"Angie?"

"Yes, Angie. Surely Dominic's spoken to you about me?"

At the other end of the line Mrs Cairns shook her head. "I don't think so, dear. No, I'm quite sure that Dominic has never mentioned an Angie to me before."

"But we've been going out – oh, it doesn't matter," Angie said. "Is he there?" she asked, although deep down she already knew the answer.

"I'm sorry, Angie," said Mrs Cairns. "But Dominic's down in London. It's so exciting. He's got interviews with two of the top modelling agencies. I'm so proud of him. And it's all down to his own hard work! Is there any message I can give him when he next phones?"

Angie sighed. "No, Mrs Cairns, there's no message..." She replaced the receiver.

Suddenly everything became crystal clear for Angie. Dominic's asking her to dance at the Christmas party when he'd never so much as looked at her for the past two years. His romancing of her over Christmas. His sudden interest in her father's new project. It had all been a carefully calculated plan to get hold of contacts in the fashion business.

Angie realized that she'd been taken in, deceived, well and truly hoodwinked by Dominic's classic handsome looks, his breeding, the way he always knew which wine to order with which meal.

"Kind, considerate, and selfless" Dominic had pulled the wool right over her eyes! It just proved that JJ was right, that you shouldn't judge by appearances. All the time Dominic had only been going out with her for his own selfish ends. He didn't care about her at all, didn't care that she had broken her dad and Stephanie's trust by hacking into Steph's computer; all he was concerned about was his own stupid career. And as soon as he had got what he wanted, he had taken off, and vanished for ever.

Angie felt like a complete fool, but she didn't cry. To cry would have been to waste valuable tears over that smooth scuzzball. To cry would have been to admit that she still felt something for Dominic, to delude herself that he still might love her. No, Dominic had callously taken and taken from her, and had never once given her one little thing.

Angie knew now where her destiny lay. There was only one person who had really said he loved her, only one person she had ever allowed herself to cry over. There was only one person who had given, rather than taken, only one person who had ever been prepared to lay his own future on the line for her. Angie knew now what she had to do. She picked up the phone again and punched out a number.

"Hello," she said with a trembling voice as the hotel receptionist answered the phone. "I'd like to speak to JJ, please. Yes, that's right, the lead singer from Zone. Who's calling? It's Angie – no, no, it's not Angie. Tell him, tell him, it's Babe..."

15

Two months later – March

"JJ, you were wonderful tonight!" Angie said as she ran up to JJ and gave him a great hug backstage. JJ looked around, embarrassed, at the other guys in the band. They had just finished their set and were on their way back to the dressing room, drenched in sweat. They all waved cheerfully at Angie.

"Hey, Angie, I didn't do it all on my own!"

"Sure," Angie said, and winked at the others. "Danny, Marco and Luke had something to do with it, I suppose."

"Thank you very much," Marco said sarcastically, and pecked Angie on the cheek, before moving off to the dressing room.

"Unappreciative woman!" Danny pouted as he followed Marco and Luke. "Sometimes I wish I'd never brought you two back together. Whenever you turn up at a gig you only have eyes for JJ. You never realize just how talented, and devastatingly good-looking his mates are!" He slapped Angie amicably on the back, and moved off.

"Angie, I didn't know you were in the audience tonight," JJ said, and kissed his girlfriend again. "You checking up on me?" he joked.

Angie nodded. "That's right," she said, joining in the joke. "I've read all the Sunday papers. I know what all these rock stars get up to on tour!"

"Yeah, groupies, wild late-night parties," JJ said

wistfully. "Good old sex and drugs and rock 'n' roll. Well, not this rock star. Babe, at the end of a night's gig we're all so exhausted that all we really want to do is fall asleep!"

"You're really going places," Angie said, and drew JJ's attention to the sound of applause coming from the audience. "It's happening at last!"

JJ laughed. "Steady on, Angie! It's just a medium-sized town hall. It's not Wembley Arena!"

"Yet," Angie corrected him. "But the point is that we're a hundred miles away from our home town. You're assured of a great reception back home, where everyone knows you, and half of your old schoolmates are probably in the audience anyway. But to get the same sort of reception out here, where no one's ever heard of Zone, is really something!"

"I suppose it is," JJ said. "Angie, how did you get here tonight?"

"I caught the coach," she said.

Zone had been touring some of the country's small clubs and halls for the past three weeks now, and tonight was the fourth time that Angie had paid a surprise visit to the boys. JJ loved seeing her, but there was one thing that was worrying him.

"Angie, what about your schoolwork?"

"What about it?" she asked. "I'll do it on the coach back tonight."

JJ sighed. "Angie, it's great having you here, but you can't neglect your work. I left school without an exam to my name. You've got all the chances I never had. Don't screw them up just for the sake of me."

"But I love you, JJ," she said. "I want to be with you."

"And I love you too," he said, and kissed her again. "And if I had my way you'd travel with us all around the country, and I wouldn't let you out of my sight for a minute. But your schoolwork's important – you have to get your grades!"

"I've got more time now, and I'm doing fine at school,"

she said. "Now that I've eased up on my work for the *Recorder*, and I've given up Cuttleigh Hall."

"I hear Nurse Clare isn't too pleased about that..." JJ said. "She's almost as upset about that as Joe Krupp is about me going out with you."

"We're keeping it quiet," Angie said. "We're not harming your 'bad boy' image for the fans, are we?"

"No, but I get the impression that if he had his way we wouldn't be seeing each other. But don't worry," JJ said, and kissed her full on the lips, and ran his hand down the small of Angie's back, "because nothing in the world is ever going to take me away from you!"

"And what time do you call this, young lady?" Peter Markowski asked sternly as Angie tiptoed in through the front door later that night.

"It really is very late," agreed Stephanie.

What is this? Angie asked herself. *Some sort of welcoming committee?*

"I'm sorry," she said. "I know it's late. I've been to see JJ and the boys."

"Angie, this infatuation has got to stop," said her father. "It's ruining your schoolwork."

"It's not an infatuation, Dad," Angie said. "And it's not harming my schoolwork!"

"Then what do you call this?" Peter asked. He pulled an envelope from out of the pocket of his jacket. It was Angie's mid-term school report: her face fell.

"You used to get straight As, Angie," he said. "Now it's starting to be Bs, and even B-minuses. You're taking your A-levels in three months' time; you can't afford to let your grades slip now."

Angie smiled. "You sound just like JJ," she said.

"Then he's at least showing some sort of common sense!" her father said, and then adopted a gentler tone. "Angie, I can't forbid you from seeing this ... this singer."

"His name's JJ, Dad," Angie pointed out.

"But try not to see him so often. If only for your exams."

"Yes, Dad," Angie said, sullenly. "I'm tired. Can I go to bed now?"

Peter Markowski sighed. "Good night, Angie."

"Good night, Dad, Steph."

A few minutes later there was a tap at Angie's bedroom door. She opened it to find Stephanie standing there.

"Can I come in?" she asked.

"Sure," Angie said, and invited her stepmother inside.

"He only wants what's best for you, you know," Stephanie said, as she sat down next to Angie on the bed.

"I love JJ, and he loves me," Angie said. "We need to be together."

"But at the expense of your exams?" Stephanie asked. "Even JJ can see that."

"Steph, I've never met someone who cares so much for me," she said. "I can't bear the thought of losing him."

"So that's the problem, is it?" Stephanie said. "You think that if you can't see JJ every day he'll forget about you. Angie, from what you and Rebecca have told me about JJ I think that's the last thing he'll do..."

"Maybe," Angie said begrudgingly. "But what's really bothering Dad is the fact that JJ is in the music business, isn't it? Dad pretends to be all liberal-minded, and reads all the right newspapers and magazines, but deep down he still believes all those tabloid stories about rock stars. He still thinks that JJ's not to be trusted."

"You're his only child, Angie; he has a right to worry about you."

"He's falling into the exact same trap I did when I met JJ, and when I started going out with Dominic," Angie said. "He's judging by appearances, not giving people the benefit of the doubt ... I thought Dominic was a really great, kind-hearted, selfless guy – so did Dad – and we all know what happened there."

"Maybe you're right," Stephanie said. "But try and spend more time on your schoolwork, as your dad suggests – if only for the next few months."

Angie nodded. "I do love JJ so much, Steph," she said. "Dad can't stop me from seeing him, can he?"

Stephanie laughed. "Ban Angie Markowski from doing something? Angie, he wouldn't dare."

Downstairs Peter Markowski had been staring at an open page of his Filofax for the past five minutes. It was against all his principles to ask favours of his contacts in the media industry, but this was a case of Angie's welfare. His only daughter was so much like her mother, always seeing things in black and white, rather than shades of grey. She took things to extremes, and never chose the middle course.

Angie was correct when she had claimed that Peter was wary of JJ because of the business he was in. But his main worry was the declining standards of Angie's schoolwork.

He knew that he couldn't stop Angie seeing JJ. But maybe he could stop JJ from seeing Angie – if only for the next five months.

He ran a finger down his list of telephone numbers until he found the one he wanted. He dialled the number, and drummed his fingers impatiently on his desk as he waited for the connection to be made. Finally someone picked up at the other end.

"Good evening," Mr Markowski said. "I'd like to speak to Joe Krupp please..."

16

"A European tour? JJ, that's wonderful!" Angie reached out and hugged JJ for joy. The other boys were also in the dressing room, and she hugged them in turn as well. Joe Krupp came in carrying a tray on which were two bottles of champagne, and five glasses, opened the champagne with a flourish and two explosive pops, and then discreetly left again.

"The news came through this morning," JJ said, pouring out the champagne. "Five months on the road in France, Germany and Spain, supporting The Lower Depths, one of the top bands of the moment! This is really the beginning, Angie. Joe's promised us massive exposure in all the European music magazines, maybe even a couple of TV spots. When we return to England we'll be really established."

"Three cheers for Joe Krupp!" said Danny and raised his glass to their absent manager. "Even for Joe this is one major coup!"

"How d'you think he wangled it, then?" asked Marco.

"Who cares?" said Luke, and poured himself a second glass of champagne. "Just think of all those French mademoiselles, German fraüleins, and Spanish señoritas!"

JJ glared at Luke, and then took hold of Angie's hand, and led her to a quiet corner of the dressing room.

"JJ, I'm so pleased for you, for all of you," Angie said.

JJ smiled, and shushed his girlfriend. "Angie, you do realize that this means we're not going to see each other for five whole months?"

"I could come with you," she said.

"And give up your A-levels?" asked JJ. "Uh-uh. There's no way any girlfriend of mine is going to throw away her chance of success. You think I'm going to support you when I'm rich and famous?" he joked. "No way!"

"I could always re-sit them next year," she said.

JJ shook his head.

Angie shuddered. She had been so pleased by JJ's piece of news that she had never thought about its implications. It had been hard enough for the past few weeks when Zone had been on this small local tour: how was she going to cope with being separated from JJ for five months?

"I'm going to miss you so much, JJ," she said.

"And I'll miss you too," he said. He glanced over at Danny, Luke and Marco: they were pouring themselves more glasses of champagne. JJ lowered his voice so they couldn't hear what he had to say next. "The contracts still haven't been signed, you know. I could always refuse to go…"

For a second Angie was ready to say yes. She didn't think she could bear not to see the man she loved above all others for five whole long months.

But then she remembered what JJ had been prepared to give up for her two months ago at New Year. He'd been willing to lay his future on the line for her happiness then.

This was JJ's big chance, and he deserved her support every inch of the way. It was now time to sacrifice her own personal happiness for the chance for JJ to fulfil his greatest dream.

Tearfully she nodded her head. "You go, JJ," she said.

"I'll write every day," he promised.

Yeah, sure, she thought. *Every day for a week. And then maybe every two days, and then every other week. Until you meet one of those French mademoiselles that Luke's already talking about. And then I'll have lost you for ever...*

"And Angie?"

"Yes, JJ?"

"Don't worry about me being unfaithful with some silly adoring star-spotter," he said. "You're the only one for me, now and for ever. I'm crazy about you, and now that I've got you, I'd be a fool ever to let you go..."

Their farewell at the airport was probably the saddest thing in Angie's life, second only to the death of her mother. She had tried to keep smiling for JJ's benefit, but still the tears kept falling. Only a few days ago things had been so simple; now everything was going to change.

By the departure gate Krupp and the boys were waiting impatiently for JJ, who was giving Angie one final farewell kiss. He smiled down at her. "You look after yourself, you hear?" he said.

"And you too."

JJ looked over to Rebecca, who had joined Angie at the airport to say goodbye to Marco. Typically, Rebecca and Marco had split up after only a couple of weeks, and, even more typically, they had remained firm friends.

"And make sure she works hard, OK, Rebecca?" he said. "When I return as a world-famous rock star, I want to come back to an ace reporter with a string of A-levels after her name!"

He gave her one final lingering kiss, and then turned and walked smartly over to Joe and the others. Without looking round – he didn't want Angie to see the tears which were already welling up in his own eyes – he waved goodbye, walked through passport control, and was gone.

The days passed long and slowly for Angie. Just seeing JJ once, maybe twice a week, had been like a touch of sanity in her increasingly frenzied world. Astor College was gearing up for A-levels, and the entire place seemed to have been plunged in a maddened chaos of revision and study, as people tried to catch up on work which they hadn't bothered to do over the past two years, and teachers tried to cram their students with all the subjects which they thought might possibly appear on the test papers.

With JJ out of the country, Angie plunged herself back into her school work, and her writing for the *Recorder*, as if all the studying and time she put in would help her to forget JJ and assuage the fact that he was over a thousand miles away.

This did have the advantage of improving her grades though: once again she was getting straight As and her teachers nodded approvingly. If she carried on like this, then she would be able to apply for university in the clearing system, but Angie was adamant that what she really wanted to do was work in journalism.

Mr Markowski and Stephanie kept their secret. Peter had used his contacts in the music and entertainment business to secure Zone's contract for their European tour. With JJ out of the way, Angie would be able to concentrate on her studies, and hopefully get over what he considered to be her infatuation with JJ.

It would all work out fine, in the end, he decided: Angie would forget JJ soon, and meet some nice responsible young man who came from the same background as she did.

Perhaps someone like Dominic Cairns, for instance, who, if the stories were true, was having a great time now that he had decided to leave Astor before taking his A-levels, and had moved down to London, settling into a shared flat with a couple of fellow models somewhere just off the King's Road.

Well, maybe not exactly like Dominic Cairns, Mr Markowski reconsidered. But certainly not someone like JJ. After all, he was a rock star; and Mr Markowski knew what everyone said about rock stars...

For the first few weeks JJ wrote to Angie every day as promised. His letters were full of news of the boys' exploits. They were going down well with the locals of whichever town they played, and he gave her a list of all the places they had played, and were going to play: Paris, Lille, Lyons and Bordeaux in France; Madrid, Barcelona and Seville in Spain; Berlin, Munich, Frankfurt and Cologne in Germany; as well as scores of tiny little towns and villages she had never even heard of.

And then at the beginning of May the letters stopped coming, and he started sending her postcards instead. He was sorry, he scrawled on them in his dreadful handwriting, but things were just so busy at the moment, that he didn't have time to write long letters. They were doing a photo-shoot for this magazine; the local radio station wanted to interview them; they had to make an appearance on that local TV programme.

And then the postcards stopped coming every day, and came every other day. Marco had found himself a girlfriend, he told her, who was following them on their tour; Luke had two girls going at the same time; and even Danny had had a brief fling with a slightly older woman who had fancied him as her toy boy.

And JJ? Angie wondered. Had he found himself someone on the road? Someone who would make his lonely nights warm and comfortable, and make him forget about her? After all, Angie knew as well as anyone what they all said about rock stars.

As Angie became more and more miserable, so she threw herself more and more into her schoolwork. She was working late at night, revising in her father's study at home, when she found out that she'd mislaid one of her term papers.

She searched amongst the files which her dad and Stephanie had left on the desk, and accidentally came across a handwritten note addressed to her father. She wouldn't have paid much attention to it, and certainly wouldn't have read it, if she hadn't recognized the notepaper. It was the same sort of paper that the original press release announcing the coming of Zone had been printed on; it was headed, in bright and bold red letters, *Krupp Promotionals Limited*.

When she had read the letter she stormed upstairs to her father and Stephanie's bedroom, and slammed open the door, without bothering to knock. Her dad and Steph were still awake, reading in bed.

"What the—" began her father.

"No, what's this?" Angie demanded furiously and waved the piece of paper in the air. "You arranged that concert tour for Zone! You and Krupp are responsible for keeping me and JJ apart!"

"Angie, darling," Stephanie said. "Your father only did what's best. Aren't you pleased that Zone are becoming successful? I hear some of the English magazines are even taking notice of them..."

"That's not the point, Steph, and you know it!" she bawled. "He didn't do this for Zone, he did it because he thought JJ was bad for me. He thought a rock singer from the wrong side of the tracks wasn't good enough for his precious little girl!"

"Your schoolwork was deteriorating," her father barked back angrily. "All because of JJ! Your whole future career would have been ruined! If you wouldn't give him up voluntarily I had to think of some other way!"

"How dare you!" Angie cried out. "I love JJ!"

"You're still a child, Angie. You don't know what love is!"

"No, dad, I'm not a child, I'll be eighteen in June. And I do know what love is. And I love JJ just as much as you loved Mum. Just as much as you love Steph now! And I am not going to let you drive me and JJ apart!"

She turned, and stormed out through the bedroom door. Her father leapt out of bed and followed her.

"Angie, where are you going?" he cried after her as he watched her run down the stairs into the hallway and grab her coat and shoulder bag.

"To Rebecca's!" Angie cried. "To someone I can trust!"

* * *

Aunt Lizzie handed Angie an early-morning cup of peppermint tea, and regarded her thoughtfully. Angie had arrived at her house in tears last night, and told Aunt Lizzie and Rebecca about how her father and Stephanie had conspired to keep her and JJ apart. Then she had slept, exhausted, on the futon in the spare room.

In the morning, the discussion continued. Rebecca agreed with Angie: what Mr Markowski and Stephanie had done was terrible. Aunt Lizzie, however, wasn't quite so sure.

"They care very deeply about you, Angie," she said softly.

"Well, I care very deeply for JJ too," Angie retorted. "Don't they ever think about that?"

"I'm sure JJ would say the same thing," Lizzie said. "That you must continue with your studies."

"Then he'll have to tell me so in person, won't he?" Angie said defiantly.

"You're actually going to go through with your plan?" Rebecca asked admiringly. Rebecca had been amazed at the decision Angie had come to last night. It was like something out of a romantic movie! And then she remembered what she had always said about her best friend: what Angie Markowski wanted Angie Markowski usually got!

Angie nodded, and pulled out a photocopied list of all the gigs Zone were playing in the next month. "I'm going to Europe to see Zone."

"And how are you going to get there, might I be allowed to know?" asked Aunt Lizzie. "I take it that you have no money."

"I'll hitch-hike," Angie said, even though she had never hitch-hiked in her life before.

"I see..." Aunt Lizzie looked carefully at Angie, with those spooky eyes that seemed to be able to see through anything. "Hitching through Europe alone is dangerous, especially for a young girl."

"I'll manage," Angie said, her determination hiding the doubt she felt inside. "I can look after myself."

Lizzie nodded thoughtfully, and there was an awkward silence as she continued to regard Angie. She turned away from Angie, and moved to the kitchen window. It was the beginning of May but outside the wind was howling and the rain was falling in torrents: it seemed that a major storm was brewing.

Finally Lizzie seemed to come to some sort of decision and turned back to Angie. "Are you really determined to go through with this, Angie?" she asked.

"I am. I intend to set off this morning."

Aunt Lizzie sighed and shook her head sympathetically. "You have spirit, Angie, I'll say that for you. You remind me of myself when I was your age."

"What Angie wants Angie usually gets," Rebecca said.

Aunt Lizzie took the list from Angie and glanced down at Zone's schedule. "And just where are JJ and his friends playing tonight?" she asked.

Angie consulted the list. "Berlin," she said. "But why do you ask?"

Aunt Lizzie didn't reply, but reached inside the capacious pocket of her kaftan and took out a cheque book and pen. She scribbled out a cheque, and handed it to Angie.

Angie frowned. The cheque wasn't made out to her; it had been made payable to British Airways.

"Then you'd better get down on the next flight to Berlin, hadn't you?" Aunt Lizzie said. "And don't worry – I'll think of something to say to your parents."

Angie threw her arms around Aunt Lizzie. "Thank you, Aunt Lizzie! Oh, thank you!"

Lizzie released herself from Angie's embrace.

"Don't thank me yet, Angie," she warned. "Thank me when you get back. That cheque will only buy you an airline ticket. It cannot guarantee you happiness..."

17

Whenever Angie had travelled abroad before, she had always arrived at the airport laden down with luggage, her pockets crammed full of maps and guide books. When she arrived at Berlin's Tegel airport she was carrying nothing apart from her shoulder bag (in which she always carried her passport) and a wallet containing some Deutschmarks. That was all she needed: that, and her deep love for JJ, and the overpowering desire to see him again.

So Dad thinks he can stand between me and the boy I love, does he? she thought angrily. *Well, here I am in Berlin to prove him wrong!*

She looked down at the list of Zone's gigs which she'd been clutching in her hand all during the flight. Tonight Zone were playing an opening session at the Metropol: apparently it was a big disco somewhere in the city centre. The boys were due to be on stage at 10pm.

She looked at her watch: it was still early afternoon, but she knew that JJ and the others liked to "case the joint", as they called it, checking out the sound systems and getting the feel of a place long before they were due to go on stage. With luck they would be there now.

The Metropol was in a place called Nollendorfplatz – *wherever that might be*, she thought – and she raced through the airport to the cab rank outside, where she asked one of the waiting cabbies in her faltering German to take her there.

She wished that she could speak German as fluently as she remembered JJ once saying Danny could, but nevertheless the cabbie seemed to understand her. As they passed through the wide open streets of Berlin, she wondered what JJ's reaction to seeing her here would be. He would be delighted, of course.

Or would he?

A dreadful nagging suspicion teased away at Angie's mind. What if he had found another girlfriend? What if the fact that she hadn't had a postcard from him for three days now was a subtle hint that things weren't quite the same between them as they had been? What if he didn't love her any more?

When she arrived at the Metropol, a huge grey-stone disco near the Underground – or U-Bahn – station. she was once again faced with a stagedoor bouncer. She recalled the trouble she had had with the bouncer at Zone's concert; but at least that one spoke English. The one at the door of the Metropol, wearing a Guns 'n' Roses T-shirt which barely covered his bulging belly, spoke hardly any English. She dived into her bag to produce her press pass: at least the word "press" was similar enough in both English and German.

The bouncer looked at the press pass and then handed it back to Angie. He shook his head.

"Es tut mir leid, Fraülein, aber hier ist ganz privat. Sie können Zone nicht besuchen. Es tut mir leid..." He searched around for the English words. "Sorry, miss..."

Angie stamped her foot in frustration. "But I must! I have to see JJ!" she insisted. "Tell him it's Angie."

The bouncer shook his head again, and his tone became a little more menacing: "Sorry."

Angie hadn't come so far, hadn't defied her father and Stephanie, to be stopped now. She tried to push past the bouncer, who grabbed her – not particularly gently either – and hustled her out on to the pavement.

149

"Let me go, you big bully!" she cried, attracting the attention of a pair of elderly passers-by who tut-tutted to themselves and hurriedly walked on by.

"It's OK," came a familiar voice, from down the street. *"Lass die Mädchen sein, Klaus. Ich kenne sie: sie ist eine Bekannte von mir. Alles ist in Ordnung."*

The bouncer let go of Angie, as requested, and Angie looked at the person coming down the street.

"Danny!" she cried. "Am I ever glad to see you!" She rushed up to the young drummer and hugged him, knocking his back-to-front baseball cap askew. She kissed him hello.

"What are you doing here?" he asked her.

"What do you think?" she said, feeling suddenly slightly foolish. Danny was carrying a plastic bag full of cans of Cokes: the Coke machine inside the disco had run out and he had been sent out by the others to buy some more from the tiny convenience store down the road.

"Where are you staying?" he asked her, suddenly concerned.

"A little hotel down the road," she lied. The truth was that she hadn't even thought about where she was going to stay tonight, having had the vague idea that JJ would sort all that out when they met.

"It's so good to see you, Angie, here in Berlin," Danny said, and led her past the bouncer at the stage door and into the backstage area. "And JJ is going to be over the moon to see you!"

"You are the craziest, most irresponsible person I've ever met in my whole life, y'know that?" JJ said admiringly, and kissed Angie again.

"Well, you know what they say about ace reporters, don't you?"

After JJ had got over the initial shock of seeing his girlfriend again, he had wound up rehearsals for the day, and taken Angie on a whirlwind tour of the city. They had seen the famous Brandenburg Gate, visited the fantastically ornate Charlottenburg Castle built for Queen Sophie-Charlotte of Prussia, and were now looking over the panoramic vista of Berlin from the top of the 353-feet-high Europa Center in the middle of the bustling city.

"So when are you going back to England?" he asked.

"I'm not."

"What?"

"Aunt Lizzie bought me a return ticket, and my flight leaves first thing tomorrow morning," Angie said simply. "But I'm not going to be on it."

A dark shadow suddenly descended over JJ's face. "But you have to – your A-levels."

"I told you, JJ," Angie said. "I can resit those next year..."

"But won't your parents be annoyed?" he asked.

"They couldn't be more annoyed with me than they are at the moment," she said, and took JJ in her arms. "I love you, JJ, and nothing – absolutely nothing – will send me home. I'm where I want to be, with you, and I never want to be anywhere else ever again."

What Angie Markowski wants, Angie Markowski gets.

"That's ... er, that's wonderful," JJ lied.

So wrapped up in her own joy and love for JJ was Angie, that she didn't notice that he was trembling. JJ was suddenly very worried indeed.

The Berlin audience loved Zone, and JJ in particular. They screamed, they roared, they bawled out their approval, as JJ performed his sexy strut on stage. Angie watched from the wings, dancing in time to the music, mouthing the words to all the songs.

From a distance, Joe Krupp watched her, glowering evilly at her. Angie didn't care: she'd beaten Joe, beaten her dad and Stephanie, beaten the whole world to be with the boy she loved. She had never felt so happy in her life.

After the show she went back to the boys' dressing room to congratulate them all. "You were great – as usual," she said and kissed Danny, Marco and Luke in turn. She looked around: JJ was nowhere to be seen.

"Where's JJ?" she asked.

Danny, Luke and Marco exchanged worried looks.

"Well, where is he, Danny?"

Danny took a deep breath. "He'll be along in a minute, Angie," he said, averting his eyes from her.

Something was wrong, Angie was sure of it. She persisted: "I want to see JJ and I want to see him now. Where is he, Danny?"

Danny looked at Luke and Marco for support. Luke nodded sadly. "Tell her, Danny," he said.

Danny took another deep breath. "He's in the dressing room next door," he finally admitted, and, as Angie walked to the door, he cautioned: "But don't say I didn't warn you, Angie..."

Puzzled, Angie walked down the corridor and opened the door to the next-door dressing room, without knocking.

JJ was there, dressed in his leather trousers and sweat-drenched shirt, which was open to the waist, displaying his smooth and muscular chest. In his arms was one of the most stunning and beautiful blondes Angie had ever seen in her life.

She and JJ were in the middle of a passionate kiss, which they interrupted the moment they realized that Angie was in the room.

"Oh my god!" JJ said, and broke away from the blonde girl. "Angie, I can explain everything!"

The tears were already streaming down her face. "It's perfectly OK, JJ," she said, trying to keep her voice steady, even though her heart had just broken into a thousand tiny pieces. "I understand everything – I understand everything perfectly."

And Angie Markowski, the girl who had travelled over a thousand miles to see the man she believed was her boyfriend, the girl who had thought that JJ was the sweetest, kindest, most unselfish person she had ever met, Angie Markowski, the biggest fool in the world, ran out into the streets of night-time Berlin, sobbing.

There was only one place she needed to go to now, and that was home.

18

Her eyes clouded with tears, Angie stumbled out of the disco and into the Berlin night. It was half-past eleven now, and a light drizzle was falling on the wide open streets. Even though it was May it was still desperately cold and a cruel wind was blowing.

Angie looked this way and that, unsure which direction to take. When she had arrived in Berlin she had assumed that she would have been staying with JJ. Now, with very little money in her pockets, and no one to turn to, she had almost nine hours before her early-morning flight left for London.

Nine hours. Alone in the night. Alone, without JJ, a thousand miles from home. Her breath caught in her throat as she suddenly realized the dangerous situation she had put herself in: a single woman, alone and friendless in a large, foreign city where anything might happen to her. It was a position that only a fool would find herself in; and then she realized that that was exactly what she was – a pathetic little fool for ever thinking someone like JJ would remain faithful to her.

A car driven by a group of jeering young men whizzed past, splattering her jeans with water from the gutter. For a second she considered going back into the disco and seeking out JJ's help. She immediately scolded herself: there was no way that she was ever going to let that louse, JJ, see how much she still depended on him, no way she was going to give him the satisfaction of knowing just how much she still needed him. By now he and his German tart were probably getting ready to go off to some trendy club, while she shivered out here in the rain and the cold.

Danny would help her, surely? Sweet, honest, reliable Danny wouldn't see her left alone in the foreign streets of the harsh Prussian city. She shook her head. Danny was JJ's best friend, and even if he did help her out – as she was sure he would – she knew that tomorrow morning he would be certain to tell JJ.

She walked off to the west, heading for the huge floodlit tower of the Memorial Church at the top of the Kurfürstendamm, the main boulevard of western Berlin. At least in the busy centre of Berlin night-life there would be people, and maybe she could find a bite to eat in one of the many sidewalk cafés she had seen when she first arrived in the city.

She allowed herself one final look behind her at the stage door, beyond which she could hear the music of The Lower Depths, the band that Zone were supporting on their tour. Neither JJ nor Danny, neither Luke nor Marco had followed her out of the disco, and a wave of self-pity crashed over her.

Get real! she reproved herself icily. *They all think I've gone back to that hotel I told them I was staying in! They're all out of my life now – out of my life for good!*

Three hours later Angie was sitting in an up-market coffee house just off the main boulevard of the Kurfürstendamm, numbly staring at the passers-by over the rim of her third cup of coffee. It was half-past two in the morning, and the crowds out there in the street gave the impression that, whereas in other European cities people were tucked up in bed, here in Berlin they were just waking up for the night.

The café was light and airy, and filled not with the sort

of lowlife she might have expected back home in Britain, but bright young things in trendy clothes enjoying a night out on the town. The lady behind the counters serving the coffees looked strangely at Angie, but didn't disturb her. It was obvious from the English girl's pale and tear-stained face that she wanted to be left alone.

Angie felt someone tap on her shoulder. *JJ? Danny?* She looked up hopefully.

"*Warum so traurig, schönes Mädchen?*"

Angie smiled weakly and shook her head at the boy about her age, dressed in leathers and a punk hairstyle. "I'm sorry – I don't speak German," she said.

"I was just asking the pretty young lady why she was so sad," the punk replied. His English was almost perfect, although, like many young Berliners, he spoke with a strong American accent.

Angie shrugged and turned back to her coffee cup. "It's nothing," she said. What she thought was: *It's none of your business, creep!*

"*Ach doch,* on the contrary, it is something," the punk said and put his hand on Angie's shoulder, forcing her to turn around and look at him.

Angie shot a nervous look at the lady behind the counter, but she was serving another customer by the bar and hadn't seen Angie's unwelcome visitor. Angie looked at the rings on the punk's hand: a silver skull, and a plastic eyeball set in copper. It seemed like he was a nasty piece of work.

"A pretty girl all alone on a dark and rainy night like this," the punk continued. "Of course there is something wrong."

Angie stared the punk straight in the face, trying not to reveal just how frightened she was. He was leering at her now, and she could smell alcohol on his breath. He was unshaven, there were dark shadows under his unblinking eyes, and it looked as though he hadn't washed his hair in days.

"Look, just leave me alone, OK?" she said.

"Now you know that I can't do that," he said, and winked at her. Angie felt his hand clasp her shoulder even more tightly.

Alone in a foreign country, Angie felt as though she was living a nightmare. *Somebody help me, please!* she heard herself thinking. She looked over once again at the lady behind the counter, begging her with her eyes to come to her assistance. The lady just smiled at her and continued with her work.

"Just let me be, will you!" she hissed through gritted teeth. The punk shook his head.

"You're frightening her, Wolfgang," came a female voice. "Leave her alone."

Angie turned in the direction of the voice. It had come from a young girl, about Angie's own age. Like Wolfgang she was wearing black leathers, and her hair was also dyed black and dressed in a punk style. She smiled at Angie, and took Wolfgang's hand off the English girl's shoulder.

"He doesn't mean anything," she said. Like the other punk she spoke nearly faultless English. "I hope he wasn't frightening you..."

"Of course not," Angie lied.

"Hey, sure," said Wolfgang. "I didn't mean to upset you." He smiled at her.

Well, you did! Angie thought. *You scared me almost half to death!*

The girl, who introduced herself as Grete, nodded at Wolfgang. "Go get us two coffees, OK?" she said. Wolfgang got the hint and marched over to the woman at the counter. When he was gone, Grete turned to Angie and asked her name, and then said: "OK, so what's the problem?"

Angie feigned surprise. "Problem?" she asked. "I don't understand. What problem?"

"Like Wolfgang says, a pretty girl sitting all alone on a night like this in a café," Grete said, and smiled winningly at Angie. "There has to be something wrong."

157

Angie smiled back. Despite her threatening appearance there was something rather likeable about the young punk girl. "I told you, there's nothing wrong."

"So what's his name?" Grete asked bluntly, ignoring Angie's last comment.

"I beg your pardon?"

"What's his name?" Grete repeated. "I take it you're crying into your coffee over some man, *nicht wahr*?"

Angie smiled weakly. "JJ—" she started, and then corrected herself: "Jeremy."

"And you thought that this Jeremy was the love of your life?" Grete guessed.

"Something like that," Angie agreed.

"Never believe that," Grete cautioned, sounding much older and wiser than she looked. "Always believe the opposite of what men tell you—"

"But you don't understand—"

"Take Wolfgang over there," Grete said, and nodded to her companion who was bringing the coffees over to them. "He scared you – you thought he was up to no good, because of the way he looked and the way he acted—"

"I didn't," Angie lied.

"Of course you did," Grete said. "What you don't know is that Wolfgang is one of the sweetest, most gentle guys around. He wasn't coming on to you there, he was genuinely worried that you were upset." She looked up at Wolfgang, who was just placing their coffees on the formica-covered table top. "*Stimmt das, Wolfie?* Isn't that right, Wolfgang?"

"*Ja, sicher,* of course," Wolfgang replied. "I am sorry if I upset you." He proffered his hand which Angie accepted and shook.

"You see, Angie, like everybody else in Berlin, you are judging by appearances," Grete said. "Just as you believed your man when he said he loved you, when he said he had eyes only for you. Never believe what you see or hear, Angie, always believe what you *feel*."

"But, Grete, you don't understand..." Angie began. "He

was so kind, so gentle … he said he loved me, that he'd do anything for me. And I'd do the same for him. We belonged together…"

"And yet he left you, *ja*?"

Angie lowered her head. "Yes, but…" For the first time she was confused. She knew what she had seen; but what did she really feel deep down? Did she really hate JJ as she had told herself as she had wandered down the streets of Berlin? Or was she prepared to forgive him, if only for the chance of feeling his warm body next to hers once more?

Grete put a hand on Angie's arm. "I understand perfectly," she said. "And when one's heart is broken, we in Berlin have only one solution for that—"

Angie sighed resignedly. She had the strangest feeling that she had just been "adopted" by this young Berlin punk and her boyfriend. "And what might that be?" she asked.

Grete smiled at her. "Why, we go out and party!"

"You are still upset, Angie," Wolfgang said, as he led her from the dance floor. "Why?"

Angie shook her head, and took her drink from Grete who had been waiting for them by the bar. "It's nothing, Wolfie," she said, as she looked back at the dancers bopping away in one of the trendiest discos in the whole of Berlin.

"You were dancing well, Angie," Grete said, as Wolfgang rejoined her and put his arm around her waist.

"I love to dance – my mother was a dancer," Angie said. "Why d'you sound so surprised?"

Grete chuckled mischievously. "With your designer jeans, and your expensive blouse, we thought that you would not want to – *wie sagt man's auf Englisch?* – to let your hair down!"

Angie giggled. "Well, that only goes to show that you should never judge by appearances, Grete!" she said, reminding the young punk of what she had said earlier.

As I did with JJ, she thought, and then reproved herself. *Stop thinking about JJ! He deceived you, left you alone in the big city. He is history, finished! I don't want to think about him ever again for as long as I live!*

"When does your plane leave, Angie?" Wolfgang asked.

Angie looked at her watch: it was half-past five in the morning, and the disco was still buzzing with life. "At 8.30," she said. "I really must thank you and Grete for looking after me..."

"We couldn't leave you wasting your time in a coffee bar, now, could we?" Grete said.

"It's more than that," Angie said. "You took my mind off ... things..."

As Grete and Wolfgang exchanged a knowing look, the DJ changed the tracks on the dance floor and put on a slow ballad. Wolfgang took Angie's hand.

"One more dance before you go to the airport?" he asked.

Angie looked at Grete. "Do you mind?"

"Of course not," Grete smiled, and watched as Angie and Wolfgang started to dance and sway together to the music.

On the dance floor Angie melted into Wolfgang's arms. It felt so good to be dancing with a man again, and, even though she knew that Wolfie was Grete's boyfriend, and that he was dancing with her just as a friend, Wolfgang somehow managed to take her mind off JJ – no, off that *louse* – she had left behind at the Metropol disco.

"Are you happy now, Angie?" Wolfgang asked, as the track ended and the DJ segued into another hit.

Angie nodded. "Thank you, Wolfie," she said. "And thank Grete too. I don't know what I would have done without you."

"Dancing and music," said Wolfgang. "It can take your mind off all your troubles... Never grieve for what has gone, Angie, always think of the future..."

Angie smiled. "You're right, of course," she said. "I've got to look forward..." Suddenly she tensed in Wolfgang's arms.

"Angie, what's wrong?"

Angie heard the track the DJ was now playing, and recognized the singer's voice.

Ask me once, and I'd give you the moon,
For you're my best girl, and you know it's true;
The other guys might fool you, make you dance
to their tune
But, my love, I'd be lost without you.

"What's the matter, Angie?" Wolfgang asked, but it was too late. Angie was already running up the stairs and out of the disco, her eyes flooding with tears.

Oh, JJ, I do love you so! she sobbed silently. *And how can I go on when no matter where I go there will always be something there to remind me of you?*

Angie felt someone gently shake her awake. She opened her eyes and looked up to see the friendly face of the British Airways stewardess smiling down at her.

"We're almost coming into land," she said. "Will you fasten your seatbelt, please?"

Angie sat up and rubbed her eyes. "Sorry, I must have fallen asleep."

"I'll say," the stewardess laughed. "You closed your eyes as soon as we took off from Berlin. Too much partying?"

Angie didn't reply but smiled politely, and did up her seatbelt. The stewardess continued: "Since you've been asleep you won't have heard the announcement."

"Announcement? What announcement?"

"We've changed course," she said. "It's too stormy to land at Birmingham airport, so we've been diverted to London."

Angie nodded: she remembered how bad the weather had been when she had left home the previous day.

"There'll be transport laid on for you," the stewardess said, "so you don't have to worry about getting home."

As Angie had no luggage with her, she was spared the

long wait by the luggage carousel, and was one of the first to pass through passport control and customs.

She walked out onto the main concourse of Heathrow's Terminal Two and looked about her. Even though it was only half-past nine in the morning, the hall was teeming with travellers dressed in their best summer clothes, and chattering excitedly about their forthcoming holidays.

Angie felt out of place amongst so much happiness. She struggled to hold the tears back as she recalled one of the last times she had been at an airport. She remembered waving JJ and the boys off on their European tour and even though she had cried then her tears had been tinged with sweetness, knowing that JJ loved her. Now her tears were tears of bitterness and regret, and anger at having been deceived by JJ for so long, and at having been made a fool.

"Angela?"

Angie froze at the familiar voice. *Not here*, she heard herself thinking, *not now!*

"It *is* you, isn't it? What on earth are you doing here?"

Angie quickly brushed the tears away from her eyes and turned around. Dominic was standing there, and he strode forward and kissed her on both cheeks.

"Hello, Dominic," Angie said frostily. Her former boyfriend was dressed casually in a white linen shirt, opened to the waist, and baggy khaki shorts. His chest and his legs were tanned a deep golden brown.

"I saw you when you were coming through passport control," Dominic said. "I was in the same queue. I tried to call out to you but you didn't seem to hear me..."

"You were on the same flight as me?" Angie asked in disbelief. She knew she had slept through most of the journey from Berlin, but even in her tired and dazed state she would still have noticed if Dominic was on the same plane as her!

"Good grief, no," Dominic said, and then grinned, rather superiorly, thought Angie. "Not unless you've just flown in from Zanzibar!"

"Zanzibar?"

"That's right," he said airily. "We were doing a fashion shoot out there... You've heard that I'm doing modelling work now?"

"Yes I had heard," Angie said, through gritted teeth. "By the way, how's your grandmother, Dominic?"

Dominic frowned. "My grandmother?" he asked, and then the penny dropped. He affected an air of sadness. "She died, I'm afraid: we were all expecting it, of course..."

I can't believe it! How brazen can you get! Angie thought. *He's still sticking to his story!*

"And how are you, Angela?" Dominic asked, skilfully changing the subject. "I hear that you've been seeing that singer – what was his name? EJ?"

"JJ," Angie corrected him. "And no, Dominic, I am not seeing him."

Dominic smiled. "Then I'm glad," he said, and sounded as though he meant it. "Angela, I never really thanked you for getting me that list of modelling contacts..."

"No, you didn't, did you?" Angie said frostily.

"So let me make it up to you," he said. He looked at his watch: Angie noticed that it was an expensive Rolex, something Dominic would not have been able to afford only a few months ago. "There's a car waiting for me outside, but why don't we meet and do dinner tonight? I know a great place in Kensington, where only the best people go..."

"Sorry, Dominic," Angie said. "I have a coach to catch back up north..."

"The food is really first-rate, Angela," Dominic said.

"Do they serve fried egg and chips?" she asked.

"I'm sorry?"

"Never mind."

She considered Dominic for a moment. He was devastatingly good-looking, that was true enough, and it could be fun to be seen with him in a fancy London restaurant. And he seemed genuinely to want to thank her for helping him on his modelling career. Perhaps she should let bygones be bygones ... it was nothing to JJ now.

Will you stop thinking about JJ!

Angie shook her head. "Thanks for the offer, Dominic," she said. "But I have to get back home."

Dominic gave her a dazzling smile, and shrugged. "Some other time then?" he said and pulled a card from out of the pocket of his shorts. He handed it over to her. "Give me a call next time you're in town, OK?"

"Sure..."

He kissed her on the cheeks again. "Well, *ciao*, Angela," he said, and walked away from her to join an equally good-looking man and a dazzlingly attractive woman who were waiting for him by the exit.

Angie saw the woman plant a kiss on Dominic's lips, and the man give him a matey slap on the back. They looked over to her, and Angie struggled to hear what they were saying.

"You're a sly one, Dom," she could just about hear the other man say above the din of the Terminal building. "Who's the cute number off the Berlin flight?"

"Someone I knew a long time ago," Dominic said. "Just an old friend."

"She seemed more than 'just an old friend' to me," the woman said as she took Dominic's arm and all three of them headed for the exit.

"You've no worries on that score," Dominic laughed. "Her old man's something big in TV – I just thought she might be useful to me, that's all..."

19

Five months later – October

"You're quite insufferable, you know that, Angie Markowski?" Rebecca said as they sat eating breakfast in Aunt Lizzie's kitchen.

"Yep," Angie said cheerfully.

"I get three Cs at A-levels, and what do you get?"

"Four As," Angie said, and added cheekily: "Sorry, Bec, I know I've let you down!"

Rebecca laughed. "I'm really pleased for you, and pleased that you've got that newspaper job," she said. "You deserved it."

Angie shrugged. "I worked hard for them," she admitted, and sighed. "But if I'd've done what I was planning to do last March, when I was being a little idiot…" She didn't finish her sentence, but Rebecca knew what she was talking about.

"You still miss him, huh?"

"I thought JJ was the most wonderful person in the world, Bec," she said. "And the minute my back is turned he's messing around with some German girl. He made a fool of me. I loved him – I still do. And I thought he loved me too…"

"Maybe he does," said Rebecca. "Boys are funny, they're not like us. If someone shows them the slightest bit of attention, if a pretty girl starts coming on to them, then it's not their heart they start thinking with."

"I wish I could believe you, Bec, when you say that JJ still loves me," Angie sighed mournfully. "But if he does, why hasn't he called me to apologize?"

"Maybe because he's as stubborn and as proud as you are?" Rebecca suggested and picked up the teen magazine which was lying on the breakfast bar. There was a small picture of Zone on the cover: they were starting to get a name over in England now, and JJ's face, smiling out at Angie from a hundred magazine covers, haunted her every day, reminding her of what a fool she had been, and how she still loved JJ above everything else in the world.

"My dad's trying to fix me up with the son of one of his work colleagues," Angie laughed.

"Nice?"

Angie shook her head. "Twenty-one, a trainee teacher and balding already!"

"Yuck!"

Angie stood up to go. "I have to rush now, Bec," she said. "I'm starting at the local paper on Monday. I'm going to have to buy some new clothes!"

"You're not leaving without me!" Rebecca said. "If you're going to do some serious shopping then I'm not going to be left out of it!"

As they made to leave, Aunt Lizzie came into the kitchen to clear the breakfast things.

She reminded them that they had to be back by six-thirty. Adrian, with whom both the girls had remained on good terms, was due to pick Angie, Rebecca and Lizzie up in his car. There was a big charity variety gala taking place up in Manchester, featuring some of the top stars in the country, and Lizzie, Adrian and the girls all had tickets. They'd originally been bought for Angie and Rebecca by Mr Markowski, as a reward for passing their exams, and, when he and Stephanie unexpectedly couldn't make the date, he had given the two spares to Lizzie and Adrian.

Angie and Rebecca promised that they would be back in time, and left. The minute they left the phone rang. Lizzie picked it up, and she smiled when she heard the voice on the other end.

"Ah, it's you," she said. "You want to know what seats? All right, just hold on one second."

Lizzie put down the phone, and walked over to the note-board on the kitchen wall. Pinned to the board were the four tickets for tonight's gala; she peered at the numbers on the tickets and then returned to the phone.

"Seats J14 through to 17," she said. "And yes, I'll make sure she gets the aisle seat!"

Everyone who was anyone seemed to be at the gala tonight, and even Angie was impressed by the number of famous faces she recognized. There were actors and musicians, newscasters and politicians, as well as several big-name movie stars and high-powered Hollywood agents. There was even a member of the royal family, sitting up in the royal box away from the hoi polloi. As the gala was to be broadcast live on TV, there were scores of cameras dotted all around the theatre.

"I'm really going to enjoy tonight," Angie said as they made their way through the crush of people to find their seats.

"You deserve it," Lizzie said. "Your father's very proud of your exam success and that you've landed your trainee journalist job. Ah, here we are, Seats J14 to J17."

Angie started to move towards her seat, but Lizzie stopped her. "Nonono," she said. "You sit in the aisle seat, my dear!"

"But surely you want to stretch your legs?"

"Nonono!" Lizzie was insistent. Angie glanced at Rebecca and Adrian, who were staring conspiratorially at her. She shrugged: if Rebecca's dotty old aunt wanted her to sit in the aisle seat, who was she to argue? She settled herself down in Seat J14.

The gala began with a dazzling display of virtuoso dancing from a Russian dance troupe, and was rapidly followed by a magician, rather predictably sawing a lady in half. It was all standard variety show fare, impeccably done, stylishly presented, and Angie had seen it all a million times before. She idly wondered why Lizzie – and Adrian, who normally hated this sort of event – had been so keen to go.

Maybe beneath that wacky hippy exterior of hers there's just a boring middle-aged fuddy-duddy waiting to break out! Angie thought rather uncharitably.

The compère – a slick professional who seemed to have been on Angie's TV screen for years – introduced the first singer, a big busty blonde from the late 1960s who was making what Angie calculated was her fifth comeback. The largely middle-aged audience loved it. She was succeeded by a comic, who told the same jokes that he had been telling for the past twenty years.

Angie turned to Rebecca: this gala wasn't quite turning out to be the exciting and memorable evening she was hoping for. "If it gets any more boring I think I'm going to pass out!" she said.

Rebecca giggled. "It could get better," she said, meaningfully.

"If only we had a programme," Angie said, but Lizzie had bustled them so quickly into the theatre that neither she nor Rebecca and Adrian had had the opportunity to buy one. Angie had no idea who was on the bill at all.

Rebecca nudged her, and pointed to the stage. The comic had just walked off to rapturous applause, and the compère was now introducing the next act.

"Your Royal Highness," he began and gave the resident of the royal box an oily smile, "ladies and gentlemen. Now we have something for the younger, more with-it members of the audience—"

"'With-it'?" mocked Angie.

"Ssssh!" Rebecca whispered. Unseen by Angie, Rebecca winked at Adrian and Aunt Lizzie.

"Just returned from a sell-out European tour, I bring you the one, the only, the amazing—"

Oh my God, thought Angie. *I don't believe this!*

"Zone!"

The lights went down, plunging the stage into darkness, and when they came on again in an explosion of colour, Zone were standing there. The girls in the audience screamed: Zone were hot stuff!

Angie stared in horror at the stage. They were all there. Danny, still wearing his baseball cap back-to-front. Marco, his shirt still undone to the waist, showing off his pecs. Luke, still mean, moody and unshaven.

And JJ.

JJ in his leathers, smiling that sexy half-grin, strutting along the stage as though he owned it, singing in that deep masculine voice of his, tossing a cheeky grin to the young girls in the audience, promising them that, tonight, they would be the one.

JJ who she had kissed, and held close like she never wanted to let go. JJ who she had loved above everything else, JJ for whom she would have sacrificed her exams, her career, the love of her parents.

JJ who had betrayed her!

There was no doubting the impact that Zone were having on the audience. Everyone over thirty, with a few exceptions such as Aunt Lizzie, who was happily tapping her feet along to the rhythm, shifted uncomfortably in their seats.

Everyone else gazed adoringly at the new group on stage. At the foot of the stage, cameramen with their mobile TV cameras struggled to get the best shots of Zone, and of JJ as he sang his way into the hearts of millions on live nationwide TV. There was no doubt about it: after tonight Zone were destined to become the biggest stars in the country.

They sang three numbers, all raunchy rockers, and the audience erupted with applause as they left the stage.

In her seat Angie glared at Rebecca, Adrian and Aunt Lizzie. "How could you do this to me?" she hissed. "You know I never wanted to see him again in my life!"

Oh, God, JJ, I've missed you so much! she thought.

"Quiet!" Aunt Lizzie said. "There's more! They're coming back for an encore."

The four members of Zone walked back on stage, and resumed their places. Danny, Luke and Marco started playing the first few bars of a melody Angie didn't recognize.

JJ strode up to the microphone, and with a gesture silenced the applause and the wolf-whistles from some of the more uninhibited female members of the audience.

"Ladies and gentlemen," he began.

Get it right, you idiot! Angie thought irritably. *There's a princess up there in the royal box! You're supposed to address her first! Really, JJ, you've no style at all!*

"Ladies and gentlemen, thank you very much," he said. "It's great to be here. And I want especially to thank all of our fans who've supported us through the hard times. Those last three numbers were for you."

The boys launched into their next song, a dreamy romantic ballad.

"And this next song," JJ continued, "is for one special person. Someone I've treated badly, and someone I love more than I can say. This one's for you, Angie. Come up and join me…"

A spotlight came down on to seat J14, the aisle seat, Angie's seat. The audience burst into spontaneous applause, and the TV cameras swung round to catch Angie's expression.

"This isn't happening!" Angie whispered.

"Go on!" whispered Rebecca. "You have to go on!"

Trembling, Angie stood up, and walked down the gangway. It was a thirty-second walk: it felt like hours. All around her the audience was cheering and clapping, but Angie couldn't hear them. All she was aware of was JJ, waiting for her on stage, his arms held wide open to greet her, tears welling up in his eyes.

Finally she reached the stage and was helped up by a pair of grinning stagehands. And then there she was, back with JJ again, back with the man who she loved and who she hadn't seen in over five months. In front of millions of people on live TV!

"Welcome home, Angie," JJ breathed so that only she could hear. "I love you. More than anything in the world..."

He kissed her on the lips, and put a protective arm around her shoulders. Tears were streaming down her face, as, for the first time in eighteen years, Angie Markowski was rendered speechless.

She kissed him again and then looked over his shoulder at Danny on the drums. There was a big grin on his face, and he winked encouragingly at her.

JJ smiled lovingly at Angie and started to sing, to sing only to Angie, to sing the song he had written especially for her.

You're my lover, you're my woman, you're a tired
lonely child,
A dreamer of dreams I know one day you'll find;
I'm your lover, I'm a liar, I'm nothing but a thief,
I mess around, I play the field, and I waste half of
your time.

But if you ever leave me, if you ever go away
I'd still love you for ever, sure as night must follow day
You're my lover, you're my life, and I'm nothing but
a fool
So take me back, and hold the one who's crazy about you.

Backstage, Angie thumped JJ in the side.

"Ow!" he yelped. "What was that for?"

"That was for—" Angie sniffed. After JJ had finished her song she had had to be led off-stage in a daze. "That was for being so bloody marvellous."

JJ grinned, and took Angie in his arms again. People were milling around backstage, and photographers' flash-bulbs were going off, as the press tried to capture back-stage shots of the nation's latest pop sensation. JJ kissed her.

"I do love you, Angie," he said, "and you don't know how much the past few months have hurt me."

"Sssh," she said, and placed a silencing finger on his lips. "That's all in the past now. We're back together again." She kissed him once more, and then felt someone tap her on the shoulder.

"Ahem! Is this a private snogging session, or can anyone join in?"

"Danny!" Angie said delightedly, and pecked the young drummer on the cheek. "It's so good to see you again! You were fantastic out there tonight!"

JJ pulled Angie back to him. "I'm sorry for what I had to do back in Berlin," he said.

Had to do?

"It doesn't matter, JJ," she said, although the memory of seeing JJ in that German girl's arms still hurt. "You strayed once ... it doesn't matter..."

"Oh, no, he didn't!" butted in Danny.

Angie looked at Danny, and then back at JJ. "What does he mean, JJ?"

JJ glared angrily at Danny, but didn't answer.

"It was all staged," Danny said. "JJ didn't want you to leave home, didn't want you to give up on your studies. But he knew that you're just as stubborn as he is. He knew that there was only one way to make you go back to England. And that was if you thought he was cheating on you!"

"Then that girl?"

"Marco's new girlfriend!"

Angie looked at her boyfriend in disbelief. "You mean you put our relationship on the line, just so that I would go back to my studies?"

JJ nodded. "Remember, I wasted my time at school. I lost my parents, Angie. I didn't want you to waste your life. I didn't want you to lose your parents too..."

"But JJ – you could have lost me for ever..."

"I had to take the risk, didn't I?" he said. "Your happiness, your future was all that really mattered to me..."

The man was unbelievable. So caring. So true. So unselfish. Angie wanted to tell him how much she loved him, how much she wanted to spend the rest of her life with him. She fell into his arms, weeping tears of joy.

"Well done, JJ," came a familiar voice. Angie looked up, to see the last person she'd ever thought to see coming backstage to congratulate Zone.

Dominic Cairns.

Dominic was as hunkily good-looking as ever. He was dressed more stylishly than Angie had ever seen him before, wearing a casual Armani jacket, Cerrutti trousers, a simple black T-shirt – and a devastatingly attractive red-head on his arm. Life down in London was going well for him, she knew: she'd already seen his face in some of the fashion magazines and the rumour was that he was going to go to the very top in the modelling business.

"Hello, Dominic," JJ said. His tone suggested that he was not at all pleased that Dominic had chosen this moment to break in on his and Angie's happiness.

"Hello, Angela," Dominic said. "It's nice to see you again."

"Hi, Dominic," Angie said.

You pig, is what she thought.

JJ looked at Danny. "Dan, join the other guys for a minute, would you?" he said. "Tell the photographers that we're about to do a photo shoot for them, OK?"

Danny nodded. "Sure, JJ. But..."

"Just do it," JJ said. "I don't want any photographers anywhere near me for the next thirty seconds."

Danny shrugged and moved off, leading the press photographers away.

When he was sure that no photographers were on hand to take a picture, JJ accepted Dominic's proffered hand and shook it.

And with his other hand punched Dominic in the face. The model fell to the floor, blood streaming from his nose.

"That was for what you did to Angie, creep!" JJ snarled, and walked away to Danny and the others.

"JJ, you shouldn't have done that!" Angie protested, as she watched a stunned Dominic being helped to his feet by the red-head.

"I enjoyed it."

Angie laughed. "So did I. I love you so very much, JJ."

"Joe's organized a nationwide tour for us, Angie," he revealed. "Do you love me enough to wait for me?"

"Angie won't be waiting for you, JJ!"

"Dad?"

Mr Markowski had turned up backstage, along with Stephanie, Lizzie, Adrian and Rebecca.

"I thought you and Steph were away," Angie said. "What do you mean I won't be waiting for JJ? Dad, I'm eighteen now. You can't forbid me to see JJ! I love him!"

"Let your dad speak, Angie," Stephanie smiled.

"You won't be waiting for JJ," her father said, "because you're going on tour with him!"

"I'm what?" Was her father crazy or what?

"Zone are a local band," her father explained. "And you now work for the local newspaper. It seems the editor thought it might be a good idea if one of his more promising young reporters tagged along with them for the tour…"

"Dad, you used your contacts!"

"I assure you I had nothing to do with it," he lied, and winked at her.

Angie ran up to hug her father, and then returned to the arms of the man she loved. He kissed her once, and then walked up to Danny, Luke and Marco, who were waiting for him with the photographers.

As a hundred flash-bulbs illuminated the smiling faces of the biggest new band in the country, Angie felt someone tug at her sleeve. It was a young girl, perhaps her age, dressed all in black. The ID on her T-shirt identified her as one of the backstage crew.

"He's gorgeous, isn't he?"

Angie smiled. "Who? JJ? Yes, I suppose he is."

"A total hunk... I'd hate to be the girl he marries, though..."

"Oh?" Angie was amused. "And why's that?"

"Well, he's bound to be so full of himself. Big-headed, pompous, arrogant. He probably just uses women and then throws them away like discarded tissues. I bet he's so selfish it's not true."

"And what makes you think that?" Angie asked, as she watched JJ and the boys preen themselves for the photographers.

"Well, they're all like that," she said. "You do know what they say about rock stars, don't you?"

She couldn't understand why Angie was laughing, with tears of joy running down her face.

French Kiss

1

"**S**he didn't!"
"She did!"

Lisa Tyler giggled conspiratorially and took off her reading glasses – as if to attend more closely to the lurid story her best friend, Chrissie, was telling her.

Lisa was seventeen now, and with the start of the summer term and mock 'A' levels looming threateningly on the horizon she knew that she ought to be acting in a much more sensible and responsible manner. Her mother, Maddy, had often told her off for listening to and believing idle gossip. But who cared when the gossip was as juicy as this was! And, as Lisa had repeatedly reminded her mother, it was often fun, at which Maddy had laughed and admitted that when she was a sixth-former she too had enjoyed a gossip as much as Lisa.

Lisa glanced behind her at the two scruffy sixth-formers on the back seat of the top floor of the double-decker. They were both engrossed in the latest computer games magazine, which at least meant that they wouldn't be eavesdropping on Chrissie's salacious piece of news.

And that was just as well, Lisa reflected: when it came to keeping secrets, boys her age simply weren't to be trusted. Lisa could easily understand why some of her more attractive classmates were going out with boys a year or so older than themselves: at least eighteen- and nineteen-year-olds had that level-headed sense of maturity boys a few years younger lacked.

Lisa was a good-looking girl, whose essential prettiness and big baby-blue eyes were often disguised by her glasses, and the fact that she normally wore her long dark-blonde hair tied tightly back in a pony-tail.

As a science student it was an eminently sensible thing to do, but it did have the unfortunate effect of highlighting the more severe aspects of her face. Nevertheless, when Lisa Tyler smiled – which was often – she could be extraordinarily attractive. She was smiling now as she turned back to Chrissie and urged her to continue her story.

The subject of their whispered discussion was the fate of Eliane, the popular young French student teacher from Paris, who had been working as an assistant at the school for the past two terms. Only a few years older than the pupils she was teaching, the glamorous Frenchwoman had impressed and entertained Lisa and her fellow students with her sophisticated tales of the French capital, and her earthy good humour. French lessons, they all agreed, had suddenly become fun again.

But then, Lisa reminded herself, anyone would have been an improvement on their regular teacher, Mr Crowley, whose frosty ways and imposing manner didn't exactly inspire enthusiasm for 'A' level French in his class of nine girls and five boys.

"So what happened?" Lisa asked Chrissie, eager for more dirt.

Chrissie threw back her long brown hair, and grandly paused for effect before continuing: "So Alison Potter went round to her flat – I reckon she wanted a bit of help with this term's project – and the landlady said she'd disappeared, just packed up her bags and left for France, without so much as a by-your-leave—"

"So who's going to teach us French for the summer term?" Lisa asked automatically.

Chrissie tutted. "Lisa! Must you always be so practical?"

she asked, barely concealing her disgust. "There are more important things than schoolwork, you know!"

She shook her head sympathetically, and regarded her best friend. Lisa was a hard worker, there was no doubt about that. After all with French, Chemistry and Biology 'A' levels to study for she had to be. But there were times when Chrissie wished Lisa would let go a little more, and act as a seventeen-year-old girl was *supposed* to act. It had taken practically a war of attrition, Chrissie remembered, to persuade Lisa to go off to the latest hottest disco down in London the other weekend.

On the other hand, Lisa's hard work ensured that in her schoolwork she always got B-pluses and the occasional A. For her part, Chrissie thought it was a cause worthy of major celebration if she managed to scrape through with a B-minus.

Lisa blushed, concealing her awkwardness by replacing her glasses. "Sorry," she said.

Chrissie nodded and continued: "Now you know I'm not one to gossip—"

"Oh yes?" said Lisa, and smiled. Chrissie was genuinely kind-hearted and a loyal friend, but if there was a chance to dish the dirt on anyone then she was always the first in line.

"Well, last term she was off sick a lot during the mornings, and she started to put on weight..."

Lisa's eyes widened with delight at the wicked piece of news. She affected a look of being scandalized. "You don't mean..."

"Well, she didn't get that fat through eating too many cream cakes and missing the odd aerobics class, now, did she? Lisa, you can be so dim at times!"

Lisa aimed a friendly punch at Chrissie's shoulder. "Unlike you, Chrissie Spence," she said in a mock superior tone, "I don't automatically think the worst of everyone... Anyway," she continued, grinning, "I didn't think teachers got up to that sort of thing..."

"I suppose they're human, just like the rest of us," said

Chrissie, and shuddered. "What a horrible thought, though..."

The bus lurched to a halt outside the gates of Applewood School and Sixth Form College, and Lisa and Chrissie stood up to get off. The two sixth-formers pushed rudely past them and clattered down the stairs. Lisa stuck out her tongue at them. So what if it was childish? she thought; it still felt good. She turned back to Chrissie.

"What is it about the average male student of our age," she asked rhetorically, "which makes him behave like a gorilla just let out of London Zoo, searching for his next banana?"

Chrissie smiled and shrugged. "Who knows, Lisa? But for once wouldn't it be nice to have a gorgeous intelligent hunk come over and just sweep us off our feet, instead of a pimply schoolboy whose mind's only on one thing, and who stinks of cheap aftershave..."

"*And* has remembered to clean under his nails," Lisa added, and laughed again. "You're going to have to look a lot further than Applewood if you want that!"

"Yeah, somehow I can't imagine Tom Cruise or a Levi jeans model jetting over and inviting us both out," Chrissie said philosophically. "I suppose we'll have to make do with what we've got..." She shook her head sadly and sighed. "Boys! I don't know why we bother with them sometimes..."

"I don't," said Lisa pointedly. "I've got too much work to do to have time for a boyfriend..."

Chrissie winked at her. "What about James?"

"James is *not* my boyfriend," Lisa said defensively and only half-convincingly. "We're just good friends, that's all."

"That's not the impression I got at Christmas—" Chrissie said as they jumped off the bus.

Lisa blushed as she remembered the way her old friend, James, had cornered her at Alison Potter's Christmas party, and the long lingering kiss they had shared under the mistletoe. They'd had a couple of glasses of wine too many, she reminded herself, and in the festivities their kiss hadn't seemed such a bad idea. It certainly hadn't gone any further.

Even if Lisa had wanted it to go further there was no opportunity for it to do so. James had been Lisa's neighbour since they were both children; now, however, he was a first-year student at Manchester University and only returned home in the holidays.

Besides, Lisa had decided that she had no time for boyfriends if she was going to pass her 'A' levels next year and go on to university.

"Oh, it was just one of those things," Lisa said breezily, trying to sound like a woman experienced in the ways of the world, and to cover up her embarrassment at the incident.

"Oh yeah?" Chrissie joked good-naturedly, calling her friend's bluff. "He could be quite a catch, you know, Lisa. He's not bad-looking and when he qualifies he's going to be a rich doctor..."

"Doctors aren't rich any more," Lisa riposted, joining in the fun. "Haven't you ever watched *Casualty*? Besides, I saw him during the Easter holidays."

"Oh?" Chrissie arched an eyebrow in interest: this was news even to her.

"His mum lives next door – how could I miss him?" Lisa said, before Chrissie could put any significance to the fact.

"It's always the boy next door," Chrissie said wisely, continuing her teasing. "Haven't *you* watched any of the daytime soaps?"

"Do you know what James does in his spare time?" Lisa asked and added grimly: "You're not going to like it..."

"I'm not?" Chrissie asked eagerly.

Lisa nodded sadly, enjoying teasing her friend. "When I first found out I have to admit it shook me up a bit," she said solemnly, and shuddered.

Chrissie couldn't wait to hear. She imagined all sorts of

filthy habits and twisted perversions: who would have thought it of good old innocuous James? It was always the quiet ones, her dad had said every Sunday from behind his copy of the *News of the World*.

"Well, come on. Tell me!" she said, stamping her foot impatiently even though they could hear the ringing of the bell, signalling the start of morning classes.

"Are you sure you really want to know?" asked Lisa, relishing Chrissie's exasperation.

"For goodness' sake, Lisa, just tell me!"

Lisa drew Chrissie to one side, and leant over confidentially to her ear.

"Well, he told me that when he's not working he likes to—" Lisa shook her head, and shuddered – "he likes to go—"

"Yes?" Chrissie was agog.

Lisa took a long deep breath: "Well, he likes to go *trainspotting!*"

Chrissie shivered with revulsion. "Ugh, gross!" she said with feeling, and raced Lisa up the hill which led to Applewood College.

The sky was grey and threatening and they splashed through the puddles from the previous evening's thunderstorm. This sort of weather was only to be expected: it was, after all, the first day of the summer term.

2

Applewood School and Sixth-Form College was much like any other school anywhere in the country. Applewood was a small modern town about fifty minutes' journey north of London, and the college was underfunded, understaffed, and overstretched. Still, alone among all the colleges in the area, it did have a good reputation, especially for languages.

This was due, in part, to Miss Bailey, the principal, who ensured that, no matter how tight the budget was, every year assistant teachers from France, Germany and Italy would come to the school to help the language teachers. Contact with native speakers was invaluable, Miss Bailey insisted, especially as the linguistic experience of some of the teachers at school was questionable, to say the least.

Lisa had once said that the closest Mr Crowley – inevitably rechristened Creepy Crowley by his classes – had ever been to the real France was the hypermarket at Boulogne; it was an uncharacteristically cynical remark on Lisa's behalf; but it was also absolutely true.

These assistants were usually students from foreign colleges who were studying to be teachers themselves, and were very often no more than a few years older than the pupils they were teaching.

Because of the similarity in age, the students found the assistant teachers much more approachable; many of the girls, for instance, had asked Eliane for help in their essays, or just chatted to her about their problems with boyfriends, or asked for make-up tips. Several of the more daring boys had even asked her out on dates. Eliane maintained that she always refused, although some of the older boys had let it be known that they had joined her for a drink once or twice at one of the local trendy wine bars.

Since her first trip to France four years ago, Lisa had fallen in love with the French and their culture. On a school tour to Normandy and Britanny, she had marvelled at the towering gothic splendours of the great Mont Saint Michel, and the magnificent cathedrals of Rouen, and Caen, where William the Conqueror was buried.

The charming narrow streets of the small towns seemed always to be filled with cheerful people, intent on enjoying life to the fullest. Their smiling faces, their long lunches spent outside on pavement cafés, their taking nothing seriously had all appealed to the hard-working Lisa, and they all seemed to exude a certain sort of innate style, even when wearing just jeans and a T-shirt. The ready wit of the Breton peasant had charmed her as much as her cooking, and even though she knew that the people in the north of France were very different from their more sophisticated cousins in Paris, or on the Riviera in the south, Lisa still felt a strange affinity with the country.

It was this love for all things French which had inspired her to study the language at 'A' level – a particularly odd combination with her other two subjects of Chemistry and Biology. Her teachers had advised her against it, recommending her to do a third science subject instead, but Lisa had insisted: only by studying the language would she ever gain a proper understanding of the French and their way of life, she had said.

"You know, Lisa," Chrissie had teased her at the time, "that was probably the most exciting thing you've done in your entire life!"

And this is probably the most boring thing I've ever

done in my life, Lisa thought glumly as she sat at her desk listening to Mr Crowley droning on in that monotonous voice of his about some obscure and minute point of French grammar, a detail she'd probably never have the opportunity to put into practice.

She looked around at her classmates. Chrissie was just as bored as she was and was doodling on the back of her notebook. They exchanged a look of mutual despair, and silently agreed that French lessons had been much more fun when Eliane had been talking about trendy Parisian life, and teaching them some of the juicier words of French slang.

At the back of the class Alison Potter was busy passing a note under her desk to the boy sitting next to her. Alison, with her red hair and startling green eyes, was one of the most popular girls at Applewood, and widely known as the school flirt. Her enemies – who were all less attractive than her, of course – said that if you were male, and had a pulse, then Alison would be interested in you. It was only half-true, Lisa knew, but there was no doubt that Alison enjoyed the company of men: she had actually flirted with a couple of the younger and more attractive teachers, although even Alison would stop at the fifty-year-old Mr Crowley. Lisa and Alison weren't exactly friends but Lisa had to admit to a sneaking envious admiration for her brash and forthright fellow student.

In front of her, even Stuart, the too-good-to-be-true blue-eyed blond who, much to the distress of the entire female contingent of the college, had been going steady with Helen Wilkinson for as long as anyone could remember, was staring blankly into space. If he, who always gets straight As, can't take this much longer, thought Lisa, then what hope is there for the rest of us?

Lisa stared out of the window across the playground and at the staff car park, where all the teachers' cars were waiting in the pouring rain. As Crowley droned on about the finer points of the past preterite tense of the verb *s'ennuyer* – which means to be bored, which is exactly what I am at the moment, she realized – Lisa looked idly at each of the cars, trying to identify their owners and thinking how aptly each one matched its owner's personality.

There was the grey Ford Escort belonging to Mr Ward, the English teacher, as grey and unreliable as the old codger was himself; the push-bike of the vegetarian, eco-friendly, no-smoking, no-drinking, no-anything art teacher; and the mud-brown Mini of the tiny Miss Edwardes, whose explanations of advanced computer programming were about as clear as mud.

All as drab and as colourless as their owners, and this typical English summer's day, thought Lisa as she peered out through the pouring rain up at the bleak and ironically wintry sky.

There was however one car which she didn't recognize: parked somewhat inexpertly between two parking bays, and with a total disregard for allotted parking spaces, was a battered car which Lisa could only describe as an upturned rusty tin bath on wheels.

It was sprayed bright green, bringing a little touch of colour to the dreary car park. Or at least most of the car was sprayed bright green. The doors were white, as though they were left-overs from another car which had been grafted on to it.

Lisa recognized the car as a Citroen 2CV, the cheap, noisy but nevertheless reliable car much loved of university students, and people too poor to afford anything else. In France, she recalled, it was known as a *Deux Chevaux*.

She wondered who the car might belong to, and looked around for other clues; in the background, Creepy Crowley's dreary voice droned on and on. He was still talking about the verb *s'ennuyer*. Why doesn't he start on *s'endormir* – to fall asleep – thought Lisa; because that's what we're all going to do if he doesn't stop soon!

The boot of the 2CV was plastered with stickers from French towns – Cannes, Nice, Marseilles, Paris – and several Lisa had never heard of before, and just above the bumper, at a particularly askew angle, was a large white circle in the middle of which was the letter 'F'. Lisa realized instantly that the car must belong to the new French assistant, who had probably travelled by road all the way from her home town to Applewood.

Well, at least with a car like that she's bound to be more fun than Creepy's boring verbs and past tenses, Lisa thought optimistically, and returned to her lesson.

"Well, has anyone seen her yet?" the bespectacled and pimply Simon Waites asked eagerly, as he, Lisa, Chrissie and Alison sat around in the Common Room during their free period. He was chewing on a piece of gum, as he swaggered up to them, hands hooked in the belt loops of his jeans.

Simon, with his leather jacket, white T-shirt, black 501s, slicked-back hair and an earring in his right ear, thought he looked the epitome of cool. It came from watching too many rock n' roll movies with his dad, Lisa had long ago decided, but realized that there was something casually endearing about him. Chrissie had agreed with her: if Simon would only stop pretending that he had been born in a 1950s rock n' roll musical he might even have something going for him. After all, he wasn't bad-looking in a gawky sort of way.

"Has anyone checked her out yet?" he repeated in his fake American drawl.

"Seen who?" asked Alison, and glanced up from reading her horoscope in that month's issue of *Cosmopolitan*. It forecast that Alison would meet a tall dark handsome stranger, which, knowing Alison, was hardly surprising. She accorded the irksome Simon the same sort of look she usually reserved for a newly-discovered colony of black-heads.

"The new French assistant, of course!" he said.

"And why would she interest you?" Chrissie asked evilly, joining in the fun.

Simon licked his lips eagerly. "Well, you know what they say about French women..."

"No, *we don't*," said Lisa, and winked complicitly at her two companions. "Tell us, Simon, what *do* they say?"

Simon blushed and lowered his gaze but the three girls rounded gleefully on him and urged him to continue.

"Well. She's bound to be glamorous and sophisticated," he said. "And she's a stranger here, and she's going to want someone to show her around the place, maybe take her up West to a movie, or a club..."

"And of course *you'd* fit the bill perfectly, Si?" asked Lisa.

Simon shrugged his shoulders in a nonchalant hey-I'm-a-man-of-the-world gesture. "Hey, if the chick wants an escort who am I to refuse..."

Chrissie winced at Simon's use of what he thought was current American slang: he'd obviously been watching too many old American sit-coms on TV. One day, she decided, she would have to take him aside and give him some words of well-meaning advice.

Lisa, meanwhile, just smiled to herself. The idea of Simon Waites taking a sophisticated and beautiful young Frenchwoman for a night out in London's West End was about as likely as her getting an A double-plus in Biology. Still, *she* could talk: when was the last time a handsome hunk had taken *her* out for dinner?

"Simon," said Alison, from behind her copy of *Cosmo*, "if a woman ever actually agreed to go out with you for a night then she'd either have to be mad, or blind—"

"Or your sister," finished Chrissie, "and even then she'd have to be hard up."

Simon's face fell and he looked ruefully at the two girls before slinking away.

When he'd gone, Lisa light-heartedly reproved Chrissie and Alison for their actions. Admittedly, there were times when Simon could make a complete idiot of himself – and he could also be big-headed in the extreme – but did they have to be so truthful?

"You're too soft, Lisa," Chrissie said, even though she was feeling a little guilty. "Si's like all boys his age. He thinks he's God's gift..."

"Maybe he's just shy," Lisa said charitably. She liked to think that she could sum people up pretty well: and she thought she saw, behind Si's posturing and affected coolness, someone who was very unsure of himself and who just wanted to be liked. "When you're our age, it's expected of us that we should all be going out with someone."

"You're not," Alison pointed out. "And neither is Chrissie."

"I'm too picky," Chrissie said, in a bitchy tone which implied that Alison, whose boyfriend of the week was the captain of the football team from a neighbouring college, wasn't; "and Lisa's too busy with her schoolwork to be bothered with anything so mundane as *boys*."

Lisa glowered at her friend: Chrissie wasn't meaning to be unkind, but nevertheless the comment stung. Certainly Lisa had to admit that she was involved with her schoolwork to such an extent that it did hurt her social life. She always got good grades but it wasn't because of any natural intelligence – like Stuart, for instance; what she achieved was through nothing less than hours and hours of sheer hard work.

Nor was Chrissie right when she said that Lisa wasn't interested in having a boyfriend. The truth was that Lisa would have loved to be going out with someone. She was popular with the boys, there was no doubt about that; but when it came to girlfriends most of the boys at Applewood seemed only to be interested in the glamorous, outward-going girls, like Alison.

Girls like Lisa who were reasonably good-looking but still wouldn't stand out in a crowd were treated as little more than surrogate big sisters, or good mates.

"Boys our age are, like, really superficial," Chrissie had once told her during a heart-to-heart chat. "If you don't look like Demi Moore or Madonna then they're not interested. All they want is to be seen with a trophy on their arm: they don't care about the person underneath."

Lisa shrugged; there would be enough time for boys in the summer holidays and when she'd finished her 'A' levels. She attempted to change the subject.

"So what do you think the new French assistant will be like?" she asked.

Alison shrugged. "As long as she tells me how to chat up French boys when I go on holiday to Paris I'll be happy," she said brightly and returned to her magazine.

"Be serious, Alison!" said Lisa.

"If it's a choice between being serious and being driven down the Champs Elysées by Jean-Michel Jarre you know which one I'd take..."

"No, it's important," insisted Lisa. "A good foreign languages assistant can really improve our spoken French, and help push up our grades."

At the same time Lisa realized that Alison was right and she was indeed being a little too earnest for her own good. Maybe that was why the boys didn't take such an interest in her?

"No one could be as much fun as Eliane," said Chrissie. "With our luck the new assistant will be over fifty, be as boring as old Creepy Crowley, and stink of garlic." She giggled. "She'll have as much dress sense as a scarecrow, and she probably won't even shave under her arms..."

"Well, we'll soon find out," said Lisa, as the bell rang and she picked up her books to go to her Chemistry lesson. "We'll be meeting her tomorrow in the French class."

"I can't wait..." said Chrissie sarcastically.

3

"*Bonjour, mes élèves*," announced Crowley the following day in his heavily-accented French. "*Permettez-moi de vous présenter votre nouveau assistant français...*"

A collective silent sigh of surprise and appreciation went up from most of the girls in the room (and, it has to be admitted, from one of the boys). Each one of them was taken aback; each, that is, except Lisa whose ready ear and linguistic knowledge had caught in Crowley's introduction the vital difference between the expected feminine *assistante française*, and the unquestionably masculine *assistant français* who had just walked into the room.

"OK, I take it all back," Chrissie whispered to Lisa. "The new French assistant isn't over fifty..."

Lisa nodded in agreement, and peered through her glasses at the newcomer. "Not even over twenty-five," she said.

"Isn't over fifty?" said red-headed Alison who had given up on yesterday's flirting with the boy at the back of class, and was now sitting on the other side of Lisa. "Hey, she isn't even a she!"

"No one's going to argue with you there, Alison," Lisa agreed.

Dressed casually but stylishly in Chipie blue jeans and

a red Chevignon sweatshirt, the new French assistant could have easily passed for the elder brother of any one of the students in the class.

He was about twenty-one, tall and slim, with broad shoulders, and the taut firm body of a swimmer. A shock of thick jet-black hair curled over his collar and his swarthy good looks were further accentuated by a deep tan, and a mischievous twinkle which glittered behind his deep brown eyes.

"*Je vous présente Monsieur Jean-Luc Roupie*," announced Crowley.

"*Oooh-la-la*," whistled Alison in the only French she could pronounce perfectly.

Unfortunately she said it just a little too loudly, and Jean-Luc heard her. He looked around the class and met Alison's admiring gaze, and smiled a nervous and embarrassed smile.

With those wonderful white teeth, Lisa found herself thinking, and prodded Alison in the side.

"Behave yourself, Alison!" she reproved in a harsh whisper.

"*Bonjour, mademoiselle*," Jean-Luc grinned, and winked at Alison, calling the girl's bluff. Alison flushed briefly with embarrassment before responding with her own mumbled "*Bonjour, monsieur.*"

"Please," the Frenchman said, "there is no need to be so formal with me. You can call me Jean-Luc." It seemed eminently sensible to the entire class: Jean-Luc, after all, couldn't have been more than three or four years older than any of them.

While Crowley continued to introduce Jean-Luc to the class, Alison licked her lips, and continued appreciating the handsome French assistant from the top of his thick black hair to the tips of his polished trendy cowboy boots.

"I want that," she stated firmly, and only half-jokingly.

Lisa pretended to look shocked but couldn't suppress a snigger. "Alison, don't you ever think of anything else?" she asked.

"No," Alison replied happily, and continued to drool over the young Frenchman standing at the front of the class.

"*Bonjour, la classe,*" Jean-Luc addressed them in a voice as deep brown as his eyes. Lisa noticed that it trembled just a little. She had the impression that Jean-Luc was slightly nervous, and realized just how intimidating a whole classroom full of strangers would appear to a student teacher only recently arrived from a foreign country.

And who'd blame him? she thought sympathetically. Facing thirteen 'A' level students – and Alison Potter! It's enough to give anyone nightmares!

"I thank Monsieur Crowley for the introduction," he continued, still speaking in French, although a little too quickly for several members of the class to be able to follow him. "Let me tell you a little about myself. I come from the town of Cannes—"

"Can anyone tell me where that is?" Crowley butted in, his spoken French, with its heavy English intonation, contrasting sharply with Jean-Luc's natural accent.

Everyone knew where the famous Riviera town of Cannes was of course, but, as the question was asked in French, thereby requiring an answer in French, few put their hands up.

Two who did, however, were Lisa and Stuart. Crowley ignored Stuart – who, he knew, would give the correct answer and in a French so faultless that it would put his to shame – and instead encouraged Lisa to answer.

"*Eh bien, Mademoiselle Tyler?*"

"*Cannes se trouve au sud-est de la France, monsieur,*" Lisa answered, "*sur la plage.*"

She realized self-consciously just how un-French her accent must sound to a native like Jean-Luc. Well, at least my grammar's correct, she consoled herself.

By Crowley's side, Jean-Luc secretly grinned: if everyone's French accents were as bad as Crowley and Lisa's then he was going to have his work cut out for him this summer term!

Still, Jean-Luc beamed encouragingly at the shy and unsure girl in the spectacles who had answered the question. "*Très bien, mademoiselle*," he said, congratulating her, "*tu parles français très bien!*"

Lisa muttered an awkward *merci* and found herself blushing and feeling a little awkward under Jean-Luc's gaze. It felt pleasantly odd to be congratulated on her skill at French. Creepy Crowley never praised any of his students: and praise to Lisa was water to a thirsty man.

Jean-Luc continued to talk about himself, with such a speed and pronounced regional accent that only the very brightest could keep up with him. Crowley noted this: he would have to take Jean-Luc aside later and ask him to slow down in future; otherwise no one – including himself – would be able to follow him.

"Cannes," Chrissie sighed dreamily as soon as Lisa had sat down. "Long golden beaches on the Riviera, the Film Festival, azure-blue oceans, palm trees..."

"Why would someone want to leave all that to come here?" Lisa asked rhetorically and pointed out through the classroom window at the grey skies and thudding rain of another typically English summer day.

"The Riviera must be where he got his tan," gushed Alison, who had decided that Jean-Luc was going to be her sole topic of conversation for the rest of the day. "Lying on the beach all day, sipping Pernod ... occasionally taking time off from his yacht moored in the harbour to go swimming or windsurfing and develop those well-toned muscles of his..."

"How do you know he's got muscles?" asked Chrissie. "We've only just seen him for the first time! And he's wearing a baggy sweatshirt!"

"Anyone that hunky has got to have muscles," Alison replied categorically. "Don't you know anything?"

"Alison, be serious!" laughed Lisa. "He's a student. He's as poor as we are and probably spends most of his time sitting in a dingy old library, reading boring text books and working on a dissertation!"

Beside her Chrissie sighed. "Lisa, haven't you got any sense of romance at all?"

"I'm just being realistic, Chrissie," Lisa pointed out, a little too primly for her own good.

"Boring more like it!" Chrissie smiled fondly at her old friend. "Still, you've got to admit he's a bit of a good-looker, isn't he?"

Lisa pretended to consider the Frenchman for a moment. "He's all right, if you like that sort of thing..." she said begrudgingly, and, in response to Chrissie's challenging look of utter disbelief, added: "Well, OK, he's more than all right."

"Aha!" Alison crowed triumphantly. "Lisa Tyler has feelings and urges and drives! She finally admits to being just like the rest of us mere mortals!"

"He's also our teacher," Lisa continued with a wry smile. "If you think he's ever going to look at us as anything other than his pupils then you're going to be disappointed, Alison!"

"*Mademoiselle Tyler!*" came Crowley's stern voice. "Will you stop gossiping and attend to the lesson please!"

"*Oui, Monsieur Crowley,*" she sighed, and looked reproachfully at Alison. Once again her man-mad fellow student had got her into trouble: the last time had been when Alison had persuaded her to pass a note to a student in the upper sixth whom she wanted to get to know. The boy's girlfriend had seen her do it and had assumed that it was Lisa who was after him: there had been an awful lot of explaining to do that day.

"Pay no attention to Creepy Crowley," Alison whispered to Lisa, after Jean-Luc had left the classroom, and the older teacher had set them some written work. "Listen ... you're good at French, aren't you?"

"I'm OK," Lisa said modestly. "I get my Bs and the occasional A-minus."

"You're better than me, anyway," admitted Alison. "So do me a favour and translate this for me."

Making sure that Crowley wasn't looking Alison passed

a small piece of paper over to Lisa.

"Don't you think that Stuart would be better at this?" asked Lisa, without reading the note and instead nodding towards the good-looking blond at the front of the class whose head was buried deep in his text book.

"No way," hissed Alison, and urged Lisa to look at the note. "This is really important girls' stuff!"

Intrigued, Lisa opened the folded note, and read: Hello there, gorgeous, has anyone ever told you that you have the cutest smile and the most gorgeous eyes this side of the English Channel?

"You want me to translate this into French?" Lisa asked in amazement.

Alison nodded furiously: she was going to get a date with Jean-Luc if it was the last thing she did.

Lisa sighed and raised her eyes heavenwards. Something told her that it was going to be an eventful summer term...

4

"So are you still thinking of asking the new French teacher out on a date, Si?" Lisa asked mischievously the following morning as she, Simon and Chrissie sat around in the common room, waiting for the start of classes.

"I seem to remember you promised you'd be the first one to take 'her' on a wild night out," Chrissie added evilly.

Simon flushed a very vivid shade of red. "Hey, c'mon, girls, leave me alone..." he stuttered, with embarrassment. "I was only foolin' y'know ... he's a guy after all..."

"Any old excuse," said Chrissie, and sniffed haughtily, less at Simon's reply and more at his irritating and obviously fake American accent.

"Some people just don't have the courage of their convictions," giggled Lisa, and returned to the science book she was reading.

"Don't you ever lighten up, Lisa?" Chrissie teased and pointed down at Lisa's text book. "This is the common room! You can get away without doing any work here!"

Lisa smiled. "I've got to get the grades if I'm going to go to university," she reminded her.

Chrissie shook her head. "You're dedicated, Lisa, I'll give you that," she said in admiration. "Once you set your mind to something there's no stopping you." She sighed. "As for me, well, just one episode of an Aussie soap and that's my homework gone for the night..."

Lisa laughed and was about to return to her reading when the door of the common room opened. Simon whistled appreciatively at the figure who was walking into the room; even Lisa and Chrissie had to look twice.

"Will you just look at that?" he gasped.

"I'd rather not," riposted Lisa, and grinned. "It's hurting my eyes..."

Alison had just entered the room, and was dressed to kill in an ultra-short skirt which revealed her long shapely legs, and a tight top which did much the same for her attributes above the waist.

Her red hair was freshly washed, and cascaded behind her as she bounced over to Lisa and the others. Few of the boys could keep their eyes off her; and not a girl in the room could resist glaring at her.

She sat down and grinned at Lisa and Chrissie. Chrissie looked pointedly at her watch.

"It's nine o'clock in the morning, Alison," she said.

"So?"

"The night-clubs don't open for another twelve hours or so..."

"What do you mean?" asked Alison, knowing exactly what they meant.

Lisa smiled. "Don't you think you're just a little over-dressed for school, Alison?" she asked, and looked critically at Alison's short skirt. Underdressed is more like it! she thought and looked down at her own plain but practical sloppy sweatshirt and jeans, which seemed to be the standard uniform of most students at Applewood.

Alison affected a look of disappointment at her friends. "What's wrong with a girl taking a little bit of pride in her appearance?" she asked.

"This wouldn't have anything to do with a certain Frenchman, would it?" Lisa asked with a knowing twinkle in her eye.

"Of course not," said Alison, convincing no one, and continued nonchalantly: "But all Frenchmen are notorious for their appreciation of feminine charms. And who am I to disappoint this one?" She adjusted her appearance in the reflection of one of the windows. "After all, we want to make his stay in our country as pleasant as possible, don't we?"

Lisa laughed and stood up and collected her books as the bell for her first class of the morning rang. Alison was good-looking, there was no doubt about that; and more to the point, she had so much total and absolute confidence in herself that very few boys could resist her charms.

If any one of them was likely to make a date with the handsome Jean-Luc then it was bound to be her. She and Chrissie, and all the others, even if they had wanted to, didn't stand a chance in the face of that competition!

"OK, come on, Alison," Chrissie challenged as she stood up to join Lisa. "Let's see you in action ... it's French conversation now. Let's see you work your charms on Jean-Luc!"

Alison swanned into the French classroom with all the style and grace of a Hollywood beauty queen at a movie première. All the boys looked at her in admiration, and all the girls winked knowingly at each other.

As soon as the early morning hubbub had faded and everyone had taken their seats, Jean-Luc walked into the classroom, carrying his books under his arm. He was wearing blue jeans, and a freshly laundered and brilliantly white open-necked shirt, which shone in the nine o'clock sunlight streaming in through the high class-room windows.

As Lisa opened her text book she found herself idly wondering who it was who ironed and washed Jean-Luc's shirts. Looking around at the other boys in the class, with their scruffy and crumpled T-shirts, most of which also carried the remains of this morning's breakfast, you would have been forgiven for thinking that no male under the age of twenty-five knew what a washing machine or a steam iron was, let alone how to operate them.

But hey, he's French, she realized, and all the men and

women like to make sure that they look good. Why should I presume that it's his girlfriend who irons his shirt? It could just as easily be his landlady. Or even himself! He is French after all!

And Lisa suddenly wondered why the identity of the person who ironed Jean-Luc's shirts mattered so much to her.

It's a great shirt though, she concluded, trying to change her track of thought. Classic French simplicity and elegance, which goes so well with his tanned complexion, and really sets off his dark hair.

And then she pleasantly surprised and shocked herself by adding: and those tiny chest hairs creeping over the tiny 'V' in the open neck which look so cute...

Jean-Luc thumped his books down on the teacher's desk, and turned to face the class. The smile with which he greeted the class suddenly changed to a look of pleasant and interested surprise as his normally mischievous brown eyes took in the sight before him.

Alison was sitting right in the centre desk of the front row, after having unceremoniously kicked out its usual occupant to the back of the class. She was gazing seductively at Jean-Luc with her dazzlingly green eyes.

She flickered her eyelids alluringly at the young French assistant as he moved around the classroom, as though he was the only thing which mattered in the entire world. It was a routine which Alison had played many times before with some of the boys from the upper sixth, and it was a routine which had never once failed.

Jean-Luc, intensely aware of Alison's attention, flushed with embarrassment, and looked to the board as if for moral support. He announced that he was going to tell them a little more about his home town and drew their attention to a large wall map of France, and asked the class, in French, if any of them could point out the location of the coastal town.

Several hands went up, but it was Alison who stood up and left her desk and sashayed slowly over to the map for the benefit of Jean-Luc. A few of the girls giggled at her audacity, but there was no doubt that Jean-Luc was impressed: he gazed admiringly at Alison's slim figure, as she tried to locate Cannes on the map.

Lisa found herself scowling enviously at her flirtatious colleague. Does she have to make it so obvious? she growled to herself. We know she's got everything going for her – and Jean-Luc's no better either, getting an eyeful of her! He shouldn't encourage her!

Alison frowned, searching the south-eastern coastline of France for the town. Finally she found it and with a look of triumph on her face pointed out the town nestling on the Côte d'Azur and looking out over the warm waters of the Mediterranean sea. She glanced over at Jean-Luc for approval; he was beaming at her.

"*Très bien, Mademoiselle ... Mademoiselle...?*" he asked, having forgotten her name.

"*Je m'appelle Alison,*" she said huskily, in an accent which was about as French as a plate of fish and chips.

Jean-Luc smiled. "*D'accord,*" he said. "*Très bien, Alison.*"

Alison turned round to rejoin the class with a look of triumph on her face, as if to say: Round one to me, folks, and Jean-Luc switched into English.

"Now who can tell me the best way one can travel to Cannes?" he asked, in his deep-brown French accent.

"That's easy," piped up Chrissie, who had been to the South of France on holiday some years ago. "You take the plane down to Nice, and then get a train into town."

Jean-Luc's eyes twinkled. "That might be the quickest way, Chrissie," he said, and Chrissie smiled as he remembered her name. "But without doubt it is not the best," he continued. "The flight down to Cannes is most expensive – *très cher*. Poor college students like yourself" – and here he smiled – "and even university students like myself who are much more poorer cannot afford such luxury. No, we must travel by train, and in that way we can also see all the beauties of my great country: the mountains of the Haute-Savoie region, the châteaux of the Loire valley, the rolling hills of the Midi..."

"I know the sort of French beauties I'd like to see," Alison whispered to Lisa.

"Alison! Behave!" hissed Lisa, and kicked her on the shin.

Jean-Luc switched back to French and regarded Lisa. "*Alors, Mademoiselle ... Mademoiselle...*"

"Lisa," she offered. Damn! Why does he have to remember Chrissie's name and not mine! she thought.

"*Bon, Lisa,*" he continued in French, and asked her to come to the front of the class. "So let us pretend that you are a tourist in Paris and you want to come to Cannes..."

Lisa nodded nervously and stood up and left her desk. She hated these rôle-playing games where she had to stand in front of the class; she felt so self-conscious and worried that she would make a fool of herself in front of her classmates.

Jean-Luc was well aware of this, of course; ever since she had answered Mr Crowley's question on the first day of term he had realized that Lisa was potentially a good French speaker, who merely lacked the confidence to express herself properly.

Lisa took a deep breath and looked over at Jean-Luc's encouraging and smiling face. He seemed to be saying, Don't worry, just ignore everyone else in the class. Just pretend that there's only you and me.

"Excuse me, monsieur," Lisa began in faltering touristy French. "Could you give me the directions to the railway station?"

Jean-Luc rubbed his chin thoughtfully with a long-fingered – and ringless – hand, before replying.

"Aha, so you want the directions to the Gare du Nord, mademoiselle?" he asked, referring to one of Paris' railway stations with a mischievous gleam in his eyes – a gleam which Lisa missed.

"*Oui, c'est ça!*" she said, and a brief conversation took place between them in which Jean-Luc told Lisa which

Metro line to take to the Gare du Nord from where she could then catch her train.

Even though Lisa made several grammatical and pronunciation mistakes, the conversation went along surprisingly smoothly. The young Frenchman seemed able to put Lisa very much at her ease, and soon she could almost believe that she was a tourist in Paris asking information from a real-life Parisian.

Finally the dialogue ended, and Lisa returned to her seat.

"Excellent, mademoiselle Lisa!" Jean-Luc encouraged, and Lisa felt her breast swell with pride until he added: "There was just one tiny problem though..."

Lisa frowned, as did several other members of the class for whom Lisa's performance had been an impressive one.

"And what was that – Jean-Luc?" she asked.

"You wanted to go to Cannes, and yet you let me give you directions to the Gare du Nord railway station," he said.

"So?"

"Like London, Paris has many railway stations, each one of which services a different part of the country," he explained. "If you had wanted to go to the South of France you should have gone to the Gare de Lyon. Catch a train at the Gare du Nord and you would find yourself getting off in Germany!"

The class exploded into laughter and Lisa glared at Jean-Luc, not realizing that he and the class were laughing not at her but with her. Jean-Luc noticed her look and instantly realized his *faux pas*; he clapped his hands together for silence.

"It's no problem," he said, and smiled kindly at Lisa. "When I left London to come to Applewood College I got on a train at Paddington station – I nearly ended up in Cornwall!"

The class laughed again and this time Lisa joined in. Jean-Luc looked at her and winked conspiratorially; she smiled back. They both knew that it was a lie told for Lisa's benefit, and that Jean-Luc would have travelled to Applewood in the tiny green CV which she had seen parked outside in the car park a few days ago. At the same time she knew that Jean-Luc would never purposefully set out to hurt her, or indeed anyone else.

There was something about Jean-Luc that Lisa rather liked.

5

Lisa's mother, Maddy, banged furiously at the bathroom door of their two-bedroomed house and looked down at her watch. It was a quarter to eight. If her daughter didn't get out of the bathroom now she would make her late for work – not to mention herself late for school.

Lisa, who normally only spent fifteen minutes in the bathroom every morning had now been in there for almost forty minutes. She'd been doing this for the past week and it was beginning to annoy Maddy.

"Come on, Lisa, be fair on me!" she pleaded. "I do have a job to go to, you know!"

"All right, all right, I'm coming," came Lisa's annoyed voice. Her mother was only about twenty years older than her, and certainly looked much younger, with her short-cut hair and trendy sweatshirts and jeans; but there were, however, times when she could come on annoyingly like – well, annoyingly like a mother.

The bathroom door clicked open, and Maddy was hit by the wave of moist heat flowing out of the room from Lisa's bath. Maddy nodded meaningfully towards the shower.

"I just felt like taking a long bath again this morning," Lisa explained in response to her mother's unspoken criticism. "I felt like pampering myself for a change..."

Maddy looked suspiciously at her daughter, who normally only took long hot baths when she'd been persuaded by Chrissie and the others to do so and to go out for the night. And even then, Lisa had always said, showers were much more efficient and wasted far less time, time which could be spent doing much more useful things.

Maddy remembered when she had been a teenager way back in the seventies: she had loved long luxurious baths then, the tub filled to the very top with foaming suds and exotic bath oils. She seemed to have spent most of her college days soaking up those rich warm waters and making herself look attractive; which was probably why she had ended up getting such cute boyfriends and such bad grades.

If she had taken two-minute showers like Lisa normally did, rather than hour-long baths, maybe she wouldn't be working now as little more than a glorified secretary in a computer company, trying to support herself and Lisa on one person's wage.

Lisa's face was flushed from her hot bath, and her wet hair was loose and dark and poured down her back. She smelt differently too and Maddy guessed that Lisa had surreptitiously borrowed some of her own eau de toilette.

Maddy continued to regard her daughter suspiciously, but decided not to press the subject. For one thing, there wasn't enough time: if she was late for the office again she'd be in for it!

"Have you done all your homework from last night, Lisa?" she asked as she entered the bathroom.

"Homework?" said Lisa guiltily as she crossed the corridor to her bedroom. "Oh, there's just a little bit of Biology left over ... I can do that on the bus into school..."

Maddy arched an eyebrow in surprise and concern. Lisa was usually conscientious to a fault: it wasn't like her to leave her homework to the last minute like this.

"That's not like you, darling..."

Lisa winced under her mother's reproving gaze. "I was reading this book last night, and I suppose I must have got carried away," she said sheepishly.

"And what book's that?" asked Maddy. Knowing her daughter's determination to do well in her exams it was probably some very weighty scientific tome filled with words she, as a mere child of the seventies, couldn't even pronounce, let alone understand.

"It's a French book I borrowed from the library," Lisa offered, "and it's all about this young girl who falls in love with an older man on the Riviera, y'know in the south of France... You ought to read it, Mum, it's really sad..."

Maddy sighed and shook her head. Lisa might not even realize it herself, but there was very definitely something going on.

And if someone had told Maddy that that something was six feet tall, with dark brown eyes, a Mediterranean complexion and a distinctly French accent, then she wouldn't have been in the slightest bit surprised.

Lisa found she was humming happily to herself and there was an unaccustomed bounce in her step as she walked down the corridors to her Chemistry class, threading her way in and out of the hordes of students moving from classroom to classroom in the break between lessons.

A few boys stopped to look at her, as if begrudging her her right to be so happy, but for once Lisa didn't mind them staring; it was rare enough that they did, she thought to herself.

She was in a good mood; after all, outside the sun was shining and it seemed that the summer had finally arrived. To celebrate, she was wearing a medium-length white skirt she had picked up in last year's sales and a trendy mint-green Chevignon shirt which set off her dark blonde hair perfectly.

As she was about to turn into the Chemistry laboratory she heard someone call her name. She turned to see Jean-Luc waving at her from the other end of the passageway, and she shoved her way through the crowd towards him.

"*Bonjour, Lisa,*" he said, and smiled.

"*Bonjour, monsieur* ... er, *Jean-Luc,*" she said. Somehow

it felt odd calling Jean-Luc by his first name, Lisa realized; which was stupid, as she had never felt awkward in calling his predecessor, Eliane, by her first name.

"I hope you have no hard feelings about my playing my little trick on you the other day?" he asked in English.

"Well..." Lisa tried to be stern; after all, Jean-Luc had made her feel like a prize fool in front of all her friends until she, too, had seen the joke.

Jean-Luc pouted and lowered his head, looking pleadingly at her from under his finely-lashed eyelids.

Just like a naughty puppy begging for a bone, Lisa thought, and discovered that she couldn't resist the Frenchman's playful expression.

"Of course not, Jean-Luc," she said and returned his smile, before adding pointedly: "And it'll probably come in handy when I finally do go to Paris — at least then I'll know which train station to go to!"

"And especially will you know where to catch the train which will take you down to all the millionaires on the Riviera," Jean-Luc continued with his good-natured teasing. He smelt fresh, of roses and soap and starched white shirts; it was quite a change from the cheap after-shave worn by most of the sixth-form boys.

Lisa laughed self-deprecatingly. "Millionaires? Me?" she scoffed. "The closest I'm ever going to get to a millionaire on the Riviera is if he wants someone to work as a cleaner on his yacht. And even then he'd have to pay my train fare to get me down there!"

"You shouldn't put yourself down so, Lisa," Jean-Luc rebuked her gently, and his normally mischievous deep brown eyes suddenly turned darkly serious. "If you do it often enough you will end up with yourself believing it."

Lisa flinched involuntarily under the young Frenchman's steady gaze. Jean-Luc had touched a raw nerve. Ever since she had been little Lisa had always considered herself somehow not quite as good as the other girls in her class.

Perhaps it was something to do with her father dying

and leaving her and her mother when she was eleven, while all the other kids were part of big happy families – or so it seemed at the time. But ever since then Lisa had always been painfully aware of what she imagined to be her own shortcomings, and, to ease the pain, had made a joke of it.

That was probably why she worked harder and more conscientiously than anyone else in the class, as though she had to prove something to herself and to the world, and show everyone that even Lisa Tyler could get the As and the Bs in her test scores, and be up there with the best of them.

Trouble is, thought Lisa, as Jean-Luc continued to regard her with his now-serious eyes, if you crack the joke often enough you'll turn around one day and find that the joke's on you and you've become it!

Jean-Luc smiled at her. "I've played that little trick on every class I have taken here at Applewood," he admitted. "And every single person has fallen for it. But not every person's French is as good as yours…"

Lisa looked at the handsome Frenchman in disbelief. "*My* French?" she gasped in amazement, not too sure whether this was another joke Jean-Luc was playing on her. "Come off it now, Jean-Luc! I speak French like Princess Diana understands nuclear physics!"

Jean-Luc laughed at the analogy, but said: "There you are at it again, Lisa. You're putting yourself down!"

Lisa bit her lip. "Sorry," she said, and surprised herself by actually meaning it.

"Your French just needs a little bit of polish and encouragement, that's all," he said.

"They don't have much time for encouragement at Applewood," Lisa said philosophically, warming even more to Jean-Luc. "We're hopelessly understaffed as it is and the teachers spend most of their time trying to come up with schemes to bring more money into the college…"

Jean-Luc nodded sympathetically, and leaned down towards Lisa's ear: Lisa suddenly felt very self-conscious as if everyone passing by them in the corridor was watching her. Jean-Luc lowered his voice.

"And anyway," he said in a conspiratorial whisper, "even without encouragement, your French is still much more better than ... how do you call him – Creepy Crowley!"

Lisa feigned shock. "Jean-Luc! You shouldn't call him that! You're a teacher!"

"Only an *assistant* teacher," he reminded her and his mischievous eyes lit up again. "I know the names you give to all the teachers, Lisa. I often ask myself just what name you give to me..."

"Oh, to us you're just Jean-Luc," Lisa said lightly. And also Dreamboat, the Frog's Legs and French Delight, she added, but only to herself.

"Do you really mean what you said about my French?" she asked, eager both to change the subject and attract more praise her way.

Jean-Luc frowned, as though he was disappointed that Lisa should doubt his word. "Of course I did – I wouldn't have said it otherwise," he said, and grinned.

With those wonderful white teeth, Lisa found herself thinking once again.

"And besides," he continued, "we Frenchmen do not only give compliments just when we are trying to impress pretty young women... Sometimes we actually mean them!"

Pretty young women? Now he really is pulling my leg!

"So stop underestimating yourself, Mademoiselle Tyler," he said mock sternly, and wagged a reproving finger in her direction. "You will promise me that, won't you?"

Lisa smiled, and nodded her head. "OK, Jean-Luc, I promise..."

"*C'est bon!*" he said, and looked at his watch, a Swatch so garishly coloured that only a Frenchman could get away with wearing it. "I have a conversation class with the third year now, and you will be late for your class. *A bientôt, Lisa.*"

"*A bientôt, Jean-Luc,*" said Lisa and fluttered the fingers of her outstretched palm in a gesture of farewell.

As she watched Jean-Luc make his way down the crowded corridor, she felt someone tap her on the back. She turned round to see Chrissie smiling at her.

"Lisa Tyler, talk about a sly one!" she said. "I guess it's true what they say – still waters really do run deep!"

"What do you mean?"

"Now don't tell me that you and French Delight were just talking about work!" Chrissie said accusingly.

Lisa blushed for some unknown reason. "As a matter of fact we were!" she said.

"Oh yeah?" said Chrissie, sounding about as convinced as if someone had just told her that Madonna had joined a convent.

Lisa smiled, privately delighted that Chrissie thought that she might have been trying it on with Jean-Luc, but said: "Let Alison make a fool of herself over Jean-Luc. If he gives me good grades on French Conversation, that's all I'm interested in!"

Chrissie regarded Lisa through narrowed disappointed eyes, and sighed. Lisa was telling the truth after all!

"At least you could help me lay the groundwork for a bit of gossip, Lisa!" she complained.

Lisa shook her head brightly. "Sorry, Chrissie, you're not going to hear any gossip about me and Jean-Luc, so you might as well give up now."

"Shame," said Chrissie with feeling, and looked approvingly at Lisa's white skirt and stylish Chevignon shirt, which made such a contrast to her usual jeans and sloppy sweatshirt. "You look good today, Lisa. If I didn't know you better I'd say you were trying to impress someone…"

Lisa laughed at her friend's insatiable appetite for any sort of titillating gossip.

"Now who would I want to impress?" she asked seriously, and headed off towards the Chemistry laboratory. "It's the start of summer, Chrissie, that's all!"

Chrissie nodded her head slowly at the retreating figure of Lisa, not quite certain what to think. There was one thing she was sure of, however. Her nose had begun to twitch, which meant that she was on to something.

Either that, or it was going to rain.

6

When the half-past three bell rang, signalling the end of yet another working day at Applewood, there was usually a mass stampede to get outside the school gates and home to tea and *Neighbours* as soon as possible.

In this respect the teachers were just as bad as the students they taught; very few of them stayed behind to catch up on their administrative work, preferring to do that at home (over tea and *Neighbours*); those that did usually only did because they had to and often resented the extra unpaid hours they put in.

Jean-Luc, however, sauntered casually out of the main school building and across the sunny playground as though he hadn't a care in the world. In the summer sun he could have been taking a stroll down the promenade at Cannes, rather than walking over to his green 2CV parked on the asphalt car park at dreary old Applewood.

Lisa, who was also leaving the school building, envied him his laid-back attitude to life. She supposed it was something to do with him coming from the South of France; there, with the sun shining down for most of the year and the turquoise waves gently lapping the golden beaches, she imagined it must be pretty hard to get wound up about anything. Maybe she ought to try it one day; as long as she caught the train at the correct railway station, that is.

She watched as Jean-Luc was slowly surrounded by a gaggle of giggling second-form girls. He had just started taking this class of twelve-year-olds, and at least half of them had developed major crushes on the Frenchman.

She sniggered as she watched them, gushing over his French accent and dark Mediterranean good looks, and smiled to herself in a superior way.

She'd been just like them at that age, she remembered with a grimace, "falling in love" with all the handsome sixth-formers at the drop of a hat and, along with Chrissie and Alison and all the other girls in her class, making a complete fool of herself in front of any teacher who just happened to be male, reasonably good-looking and under thirty.

Thank God I've got over that now! she thought gratefully.

Jean-Luc's admirers were still hanging around him and chatting inanely, like a bunch of silly teenagers outside the stage door talking to their pop star hero.

To Lisa it was an amusing spectacle but it was also clear to her that Jean-Luc was getting more than a little embarrassed at all the unwelcome attention, as he tried to make his way through the throng to his 2CV.

He noticed Lisa watching, and waved to her, urging her to come over and rescue him from his fans. Lisa looked around, and then back at Jean-Luc, as if to say: *Who? Me?*

Jean-Luc laughed, and nodded.

As Lisa crossed the playground, the crowd caught sight of her and dispersed, each one of the girls glaring reproachfully in Lisa's direction. The big girls are moving in now, their meaningful looks seemed to say; there's no chance for us now.

It was a feeling which would have surprised Lisa if she had been aware of it; Lisa had never before considered herself serious competition for anyone (apart from in Chemistry class, of course, where there was no one to beat her in analysing complex polymer chains...).

Jean-Luc smiled when Lisa walked up to him. With those wonderfully white teeth.

"*Merci*, Lisa," he sighed with exaggerated relief. "It was getting a little fraught!"

Lisa laughed. "You should feel flattered, Jean-Luc," she said.

Jean-Luc joined in the laughter. "Schoolgirl crushes," he dismissed them. "I'm afraid it comes with the job..."

"But all those pretty young girls after you..." Lisa said, teasing him as she never would another teacher. After all, she reminded herself, he was only twenty-one.

Jean-Luc stroked his chin thoughtfully and pretended to consider the matter quite seriously for a half-second. Lisa noticed that there were the beginnings of a five o'clock shadow on his face.

Finally he replied: "I think twelve-year-olds are a little too young even for me..." He chuckled. "I prefer them a few years older..."

He looked at Lisa and, without either of them knowing why, there was suddenly an awkward silence.

Finally Jean-Luc said: "Lisa, you're not wearing your glasses."

Lisa shrugged. "I don't really need them," she explained. "I only use them for reading, but I usually forget to take them off."

"You should take them off more often," Jean-Luc said. "Wearing them all the time is not only bad for your vision, but they also hide your eyes."

"What?"

"They are very beautiful, Lisa," said Jean-Luc and looked down into her baby-blue eyes. "It is a shame to hide them behind your glasses all the time."

Lisa giggled nervously, sounding exactly like one of the twelve-year-olds she had just seen off.

"Jean-Luc, is that a line you're spinning me?" she asked, rather more breezily than she felt.

I do not believe I just said that! she thought immediately after.

Jean-Luc frowned, not quite understanding. "Spinning a line?" he asked.

Lisa raised her eyes heavenwards, realizing that she was rapidly digging a grave for herself right here and now in the school playground. She searched around for the colloquial French expression which Eliane had taught them all the previous term.

"Spinning a line," she repeated, and then remembered. "You know – *faire la drague!*"

"Ah, I see..." smiled Jean-Luc, impressed by Lisa's knowledge of French slang. He then took a slightly more serious tone: "Lisa, when I say that a woman's eyes are beautiful I am not 'spinning a line'. I'm simply telling her the truth. And the truth is that your eyes are very beautiful."

Lisa nodded, and contemplated her shoes for a minute, not sure whether she was being complimented further, or being sternly told off by Teacher.

"Yeah, well, OK, I'm sorry," she said to her shoes. She felt Jean-Luc's thumb on her chin and he raised her face to look at him. He was grinning again.

"And besides, I'm French," he said, and winked at her. "We do have a reputation to live up to, you know. If we didn't compliment pretty young women—"

Pretty young women? That's the second time he's used those words to me in as many days!

"—If we didn't compliment pretty young women all the time what would people think of us?" he continued. "They might think that we're as cold and wet and unfeeling as a codfish, or – even worse – as you English!"

Lisa stuck her tongue out at Jean-Luc and raised her arm in a mock attempt to hit him for the slight to her entire country. Jean-Luc stepped back, laughing, and raised his hands in a gesture of surrender.

"OK, I admit defeat," he said. "You win the battle, Lisa!"

"We usually do," she reflected. "Think of Waterloo... Think of Agincourt..."

"Ah, but we built our part of the Channel Tunnel first," countered Jean-Luc.

"Yes, and you also gave us reflexive verbs, masculine and feminine endings and the past preterite tense."

Jean-Luc's face fell. "That is a disgrace I and my fellow countrymen shall have to live with for ever ... but we did also give the world great writers and philosophers and singers like Edith Piaf," he said, referring to the legendary singer of the fifties and sixties, whose recordings were still loved today in France by both young and old.

"You like Edith Piaf?" asked Lisa in surprise.

"But of course," he replied. "I am French after all ... but I'm surprised you have even heard of her ... I would have thought someone your age..."

"I'm only four years younger than you, Jean-Luc!" Lisa replied, and explained: "My dad had lots of her songs on CD. Along with our last French assistant that's where I learnt lots of my French slang. I love her songs—"

"Such as?"

Lisa began to sing the words to her favourite French song, the one she always played to herself after she'd seen a particularly sad and romantic movie on TV:

"T'es beau, tu sais,
T'es beau, c'est vrai..."

"Why, thank you," said Jean-Luc, and Lisa blushed as she realized the meaning of the French words: "You're handsome, you know, you're handsome, it's true..."

"It's good to know that you like Piaf," he continued. "But what about other music?"

Lisa mentioned the Lower Depths, a new indy band who had just broken big in the charts, and whose records everyone in the sixth form seemed to be playing. Jean-Luc had never heard of them, and Lisa urged him to search out one of their cassettes, after he reminded her that he didn't have the money to afford CDs.

Lisa attempted to resume their argument. "And do you agree that the English aren't cold and wet?" she asked.

"Well, not all of them," he admitted reluctantly, and added: "Although some of them pretend all the time that they are..."

What does he mean? Lisa asked herself. He can't be talking about me – can he...?

Before she had time to ask, Jean-Luc said: "Look, Lisa, it's getting late—" he gestured around the playground which was now empty – "and you've probably missed your bus."

"That's OK," she said. "I've only missed the school bus. I'll get the public bus – you know, the number nine bus – the one that normal people use..."

Jean-Luc ignored her and continued: "And as you saved me from the manic lusts of the entire second form just there, the least I can do is offer you a lift home." He pointed to the green 2CV.

"Jean-Luc, you don't have to—" Lisa began but the Frenchman put a silencing finger to her lips.

"I insist," he said. "That is, if you can bear to be seen with me in a *deux chevaux*. I know what the English think of these cars..."

"That they're clapped-out pieces of junk only driven by left-wing vegetarian feminists wearing badges banning the bomb and supporting the whales?" Lisa asked with a daring twinkle in her eye.

Jean-Luc burst out laughing again. "Well, something like that," he agreed, and regarded Lisa with renewed interest.

Not only was she pretty in a curious sort of way, but she was also very intelligent, and, when she let herself go, extraordinarily funny. It was a long time since Jean-Luc had laughed with a girl roughly his own age. More often than not when girls came up and introduced themselves to him it was with only one thing in mind; Lisa made a welcome and refreshing change.

"They are also very cheap," he reminded her, returning

to the subject of the 2CV. "And for a poor student like me – even if I am your teacher – that is the most important thing. It is also fast, stylish, unpredictable and totally unique – just like we French!"

Lisa decided that there was only one thing in the world she would prefer to be doing right now; and, as the latest teenage heart-throbs were probably busy somewhere making a video or advertising underwear, she would have to settle for being driven home by Jean-Luc in his 2CV.

They began to walk towards the car when a voice called out from behind them: "Jean-Luc! Jean-Luc, wait!"

Both of them turned around to see Alison running towards them. Today she was wearing a chic leather jacket and a green Lycra work-out suit.

"Bonjour, Alison," said Jean-Luc pleasantly as Alison came up to them. Lisa just stared suspiciously at the other girl; she'd known her classmate long enough now to know that she was up to something.

Alison nodded briefly at Lisa, as if to acknowledge her presence, and then devoted all her considerable attentions to Jean-Luc.

"Am I glad I caught up with you," she said, panting for breath.

Jean-Luc was instantly concerned. "Why? What is the matter?" he asked.

She looked up beseechingly at Jean-Luc while Lisa just continued to glare at her rival.

"Well, it's just that I stayed behind in the library reading up on my French homework..." Alison began, and flicked back her gorgeous long red hair.

Oh yeah? thought Lisa ungraciously. The last time you were in a library anywhere was when you fancied the hunky young librarian in the public library!

However, by her side Jean-Luc seemed to be impressed; although whether it was by the fact that Alison had been pursuing her studies so assiduously, or by her Lycra work-out suit, Lisa couldn't be quite sure.

"And the next thing I know—" Alison looked at her

watch – an expensive one which her father had given her last year as a sixteenth-birthday present – "it's a quarter to four and I've missed the bus home..." She fluttered her eyelids seductively up at Jean-Luc.

"There's always the number nine," Lisa reminded her coldly.

Alison shot an evil look in Lisa's direction before continuing.

"Of course I would get the number nine, but it takes me *soooo* much out of my way – and I do have an aerobics class at the leisure centre tonight which I really don't want to be late for – I do think we should be as fit as we can be, don't you, Jean-Luc? – and I was wondering if..."

Jean-Luc got the hint and smiled. "Well, I was just offering Lisa a lift home," he said. "There's always room for one more..."

Jean-Luc, how can you be so stupid? Lisa thought.

"Jean-Luc, Alison lives miles away from me," she said, and instantly regretted saying it.

"Oh that's all right," Alison said sweetly. "Jean-Luc can drop you off first and then take me home, can't you, Jean-Luc?"

"Well, er ... I suppose so..."

And you really went and asked for that one now, didn't you, Lisa?

Vaguely aware that something was not quite right, Jean-Luc looked at Lisa, who was gritting her teeth and glaring malevolently at Alison. Alison reciprocated by flashing Lisa a triumphant look.

Jean-Luc shrugged his shoulders philosophically, deciding that, like all Frenchmen before him, he would never really understand the female of the species, no matter how hard he tried.

"Well, shall we go?" he asked brightly.

"Why not?" said Lisa in a dark monotone, so frosty that it could have frozen water.

Alison skipped over to Jean-Luc's green 2CV, and stood by the passenger door, which Jean-Luc opened for her.

"Why, *merci, monsieur*," she cooed, and bent down to enter the car, at the same time making sure that the Frenchman had a good look at her almost-perfect figure.

Jean-Luc smiled at Alison's far-from-subtle flirtatiousness. "*Je vous en prie, mademoiselle*," he chuckled.

This just makes me so sick! Lisa fumed to herself as she found herself meekly accepting the back seat of the 2CV, while Jean-Luc sat in the driver's seat, next to Alison, who was already resting a leisurely and familiar arm around the back of his seat. Why does Alison have to go and spoil everything?

Spoil everything? This is just a lift home from my teacher, isn't it?

And suddenly Lisa realized that, for her, Jean-Luc was something more – something much, much more – than just a mere teacher.

7

"Well, here comes the teacher's pet," sneered Simon the following day as Alison strode into the common room with a self-satisfied look on her face.

At his side, Lisa looked up urgently from her French novel. "What d'you mean?" she asked.

"She and the new French assistant, they're like that," said Si and crossed his fingers.

Chrissie, who was also sitting with them, suddenly became interested. If this was gossip then she decided that she ought to hear about it. She urged Si to continue.

"I only saw her last night in Jean-Luc's car," Si said. "Looking very friendly together, if you ask me..."

"That's nothing," said Lisa quickly. "He gave me a lift home too last night..."

"Well," said Si, who had caught the urgency in Lisa's voice. "It seemed considerably more than just a lift home to me..."

"Maybe they're having an affair!" Chrissie suggested gleefully, oblivious to Lisa's feelings, and already looking forward to spreading the gossip around. She looked at Simon with new interest: when he wasn't pretending to be Elvis Presley he loved gossip almost as much as she did! Maybe he was normal after all!

She sighed. "Alison's a lucky so-and-so. But I suppose it was inevitable: the handsome swarthy hunk from the

Mediterranean and the pale-skinned, red-headed temptress from the lower sixth. Typical Barbara Cartland material, really. We should all have seen it coming!"

Lisa stood up angrily, knocking her book to the floor, which she refused to pick up. "Just because Jean-Luc gives her a lift home you automatically think that they're going out together! Men and women can get on very well together without having a raging affair, you know!"

Si flinched at Lisa's outburst. "Hey, I'm sorry if I stepped on somebody's toes…" he said.

"It's nothing," Lisa lied.

Chrissie stood up and took Lisa's arm. "Of course it's nothing," she said, and led Lisa away. As soon as they were out of Si's earshot she said: "OK Lisa, what's the matter?"

Lisa shrugged. "It's nothing," she repeated. "But I wish people wouldn't jump to conclusions … and anyway, Jean-Luc drove me home last night as well. Who's to say he's not going out with me?"

Chrissie nodded wisely, and looked over to Alison who, as usual, was surrounded by an entourage of friends and hangers-on. Lisa wouldn't be the first girl in the sixth form to be envious of Alison's outgoing personality and lifestyle.

"Well, it's just that Alison has a … well, let's say a bit of a reputation for getting the boys," she said tactfully. "And she and Jean-Luc would make a very good-looking pair, you've got to admit that…"

"Meaning I wouldn't, I suppose?" Lisa snapped back.

"Of course I didn't mean that," Chrissie insisted. "You're as attractive as they come, Lisa…" Her voice tailed off.

"But?" demanded Lisa.

"But lighten up a little, Lisa. Life isn't all work, you know. Sometimes you're so serious you frighten people off…" Chrissie avoided Lisa's eyes as she added: "And do something about your hair…"

"My hair?" Lisa asked and flicked back her ponytail.

"Ponytails belong in the fourth form," Chrissie said.

"But it's practical," Lisa said. "It keeps my hair out of my eyes during Chemistry and Biology..."

Chrissie smiled kindly at her friend. "This is Life in the Sixth Form, Lisa," she announced grandly. "It's not supposed to be practical!"

Lisa grinned in spite of herself, and looked over at Alison once more. "Do you really think they're going out together?"

"Who?" asked Chrissie, who had already forgotten the original topic of conversation.

"Alison and Jean-Luc."

Chrissie shrugged.

"She'd certainly like to," she admitted. "But I really don't have a clue. Still, it's a good story to spread around, isn't it?"

Lisa gave Chrissie a look which plainly said: No, it isn't.

"Anyway, why all this interest in Jean-Luc's love life all of a sudden?" asked Chrissie, although she suspected she already knew the answer, even if Lisa didn't know herself.

"Just curious, that's all," said Lisa rather feebly. Chrissie was about to follow up on her line of questioning when Alison left her tiny group and swanned over to them.

"Well, *bonjour mes amies*," she cooed with an over-the-top French accent.

"You look like the cat who's got the cream," Chrissie remarked.

Alison looked meaningfully over at Lisa. "No, just a chauffeur," she said wickedly. "Jean-Luc was *soooo* nice to me last night, driving me home, and then to my aerobics class..."

"He took you to the leisure centre as well?" marvelled Chrissie while, beside her, Lisa just glared at Alison.

"Of course," Alison said, as though it was the most natural thing in the world for a teacher to drive her home, wait while she collected her sportsgear, and then chauffeur her to the sports centre. "He is *such* a gentleman..."

Chrissie imagined, rightly, that Jean-Luc would have had little say in the matter. Alison would have browbeaten him to drive her, especially as the leisure centre was probably on his way home. Indeed it was notoriously difficult to resist Alison when she had set her mind on something.

"Well, *au revoir*, girls, Jean-Luc and I'll see you in French later," Alison said cheerily, satisfied that she had ensured that Lisa knew of her minor triumph. She waltzed out of the common room.

"You can't help admiring her cheek, can you, Lisa?" asked Chrissie, clearly impressed by Alison's coup.

"So he gave her a lift home? So he gave her a lift to the leisure centre? So what?" said Lisa through gritted teeth. "It doesn't mean anything, does it? It doesn't matter."

But Lisa knew that it mattered quite a lot.

For the rest of the day the atmosphere between Lisa and Alison was, to say the least, glacial. The bad feeling finally came to a head in the French lesson, the last class of the afternoon.

Both Mr Crowley and Jean-Luc were taking the class, with Alison once more at the front of the class, openly flirting with the Frenchman, who seemed quite embarrassed by all the attention she was giving him. It was obvious that the news of the lift home had spread all around the class by now, and everyone had drawn the conclusion Alison had wanted them to draw.

Lisa, meanwhile, sat moodily at the back of the classroom, idly looking out of the window and stubbornly refusing to answer Jean-Luc's questions when he addressed her.

This is silly and childish, she reminded herself but continued to do it; so what if Jean-Luc fancies Alison? It's not as if I ever had a chance with him.

But does she have to make it so blasted obvious?

Finally it was half-past three and school was over for the day. As everyone began to bustle out of the classroom Crowley called Lisa over to his desk.

Alison paraded past the desk behind which Jean-Luc was also sitting.

"*Au revoir, Jean-Luc,*" she cooed.

"Good afternoon, Alison," he replied. Lisa noted that the Frenchman was grinning with amusement, and also that he had pointedly replied to Alison in English.

Lisa took a deep breath, sure that Crowley was going to reprimand her for her uncooperative behaviour in class today. Instead he harrumphed and smiled at her.

"I've been looking at your work, Miss Tyler, and it's quite promising," he began, although in truth he had done nothing of the kind; it was Jean-Luc who had drawn Lisa's work to his attention. "You seem to have quite a talent for languages."

"Thank you," said Lisa, surprised at this unaccustomed piece of praise from Creepy Crowley who usually had trouble remembering people's names, let alone their test scores.

"Your grades are good," he said, looking down at the class register on which he entered the students' marks for their essays and class-work. "But I feel—" he looked at Jean-Luc – "*we* feel that with a little bit of extra work they could be even better..."

Oh great, thought Lisa, he's going to give me extra homework!

"What we are proposing – if, of course, you are agreeable, Miss Tyler – is some extra lunchtime tuition in French conversation."

"All free of charge of course," said Jean-Luc and looked up and smiled at her.

With that gorgeous smile.

Crowley glanced curiously at Jean-Luc but didn't say anything.

Vitally aware of Jean-Luc's presence, Lisa still continued to look at Crowley.

"With you, sir?" she asked.

"No, with *me*," interrupted Jean-Luc. "As I told you before, Lisa, all you need is a little more encouragement and practice and you could even be university material."

Lisa looked at Jean-Luc with mixed feelings, wondering how much truth there was in Alison's unspoken claim – that she and Jean-Luc were practically going out together – and then wondered how she would feel working side by side with the handsome young Frenchman with the brilliantly white teeth who smelt of soap and roses and starched white shirts.

Who am I kidding to think that he's got any interest in me? Someone as cute as Jean-Luc could have any girl he wants. And how am I going to feel working alongside him, and knowing that he's going out with Alison? I'd feel frustrated, I'd feel like a fool!

Lisa took a deep breath, and looked Crowley directly in the eyes. "No," she said. "It's a very kind offer, but no thank you."

Crowley briefly raised an eyebrow in surprise and then began to gather up his papers.

"Very well, Miss Tyler, if that is your decision..." He stood up and left the classroom.

"Lisa, why did you say no?" asked Jean-Luc. There was a disappointed expression on his face.

Lisa shrugged. "I've too much work already, Jean-Luc," she said coldly, "and I'm sure there are better things you could be doing than talking in French to me during your lunch break."

"I don't understand you at all, Lisa," he said, clearly mystified, "but if you change your mind the offer's still open..."

He looked at his Swatch. "It's late and I've made you miss your bus home again," he remarked. "Can I drive you home?"

"Thanks, Jean-Luc, but no thanks," Lisa said frostily. "I'll catch the bus." And with that she walked out of the classroom.

Jean-Luc stared after her, and ran his fingers through his thick black hair in desperation. What is wrong with that girl? he asked himself.

And why am I so concerned that she isn't going to study with me?

"Lisa Tyler, you are the most idiotic, senseless, brain-dead thing since fishes crawled out of the ocean and up on to dry land," Chrissie's voice crackled angrily down the telephone line later that evening.

Chrissie had rung Lisa up to ask for advice on some homework and instead had heard the craziest story since Alison Potter had said she was giving up men for Lent.

"No, I'm not," countered Lisa. "I really don't have the time for extra French lessons. And it was you, after all, Chrissie, who said that life shouldn't be all work, wasn't it?"

"Well, yes, but this is different..."

"And just *how* is it different?"

"Lisa, we are talking here about French Delight, the most gorgeous, sexiest, hunkiest guy that ever walked the face of this Earth – well, Applewood anyway – besides that, he's foreign. There are girls in the fifth form who would sell their mothers to have private lessons with him. And what do you do, Lisa Tyler? You say no!"

"You think I did the wrong thing?"

"Too right you did the wrong thing!"

"Chrissie, I'm not interested in how sexy or handsome Jean-Luc is," Lisa claimed.

Oh yeah? Chrissie thought.

"But I haven't got the time..." Lisa continued.

Who am I fooling? Lisa thought. My social calendar is about as exciting as a wet Wednesday in Margate. And Chrissie is right: Jean-Luc is very sexy.

"Look, Lisa," Chrissie said, and her voice took on a serious tone. "You're good at French, right?"

"Right."

"Well, if you accept Jean-Luc's offer you'll be even

better." She laughed ironically. "Forget how gorgeous he is. Forget that two-thirds of the female population of Applewood happen to worship the very ground that he walks on. Forget that Alison Potter would kill to be in your shoes—"

"Alison?" Lisa asked urgently. "What's she got to do with it?"

"Well, you didn't believe that rubbish about her and Jean-Luc, now, did you?" asked Chrissie.

Actually I did, thought Lisa. "Of course not," she said.

"Alison's all talk," said Chrissie. "Grow up, Lisa! OK, she's the best-looking of us all, and a hit with boys her own age – but with someone four years older than her? And a teacher? And French? It's going to take a lot more than her wiggling and fluttering her eyelids for her to get Jean-Luc—"

"You really think so?" asked Lisa eagerly, and quickly corrected herself. "I mean, what's that got to do with me?"

Chrissie laughed down the phone line. "Come off it, Lisa! I've seen how you react when Jean-Luc's around..."

"What do you mean?" asked Lisa.

"The minute he gets anywhere near you, you tense up..."

"I don't," Lisa snapped back defensively.

"I'm your best friend, Lisa, and I know you do," pressed Chrissie. "And in my book that means one of two things. Either you can't stand the sight of him—"

"Or?"

"Well, what do you think?" asked Chrissie and chuckled. "Good luck to you, is what I say. If he was offering me French lessons I'd take them like a shot!"

At the other end of the telephone line Lisa found herself going red with embarrassment. She laughed nervously down the phone.

"And what chance would I have with him?" she asked Chrissie, realizing that what she was hoping for was a positive answer.

"As much as any of us," came the rather disappointing reply. "But get serious, Lisa—"

"You're the one always telling me not to be," Lisa interrupted.

"Go to the lessons," she urged and added sneakily: "If not for French Delight, then for the grades."

"You really think I should?"

"Of course, you idiot... and if you get on well with French Delight, then who knows...?"

So Lisa resolved to accept Jean-Luc's offer of free French lessons. She also resolved to keep the lessons strictly on a business-level.

On the other end of the line, Chrissie laughed silently to herself. She'd like to see anyone keep anything on a business-level with Jean-Luc Roupie!

8

Lisa felt awkward as she sat next to Jean-Luc the next day, poring over a copy of *Paris-Match*, the weekly French news magazine to which the school subscribed. It wasn't just the fact that, as it was a particularly hot day, Jean-Luc had come to school dressed in blue jeans and a white T-shirt which showed off his tan and also proved – as Alison had correctly guessed – that he really did have muscles.

Her conversation with Chrissie on the phone the previous night had hit a raw nerve. Lisa finally had to admit that she was attracted to Jean-Luc. It wasn't just his good looks, although one would have to be blind not to have been struck by them.

Lisa liked the mischievous twinkle in his eyes when he played a joke on his classes; and when his jokes backfired – as had the one about the railway station – the genuine look of concern on his face.

She loved his accent and his inimitable *Frenchness*, the way that no matter what he was wearing, whether it was today's T-shirt, or a collar and tie (when he wanted to impress the principal) he wore it with style and elegance.

And she adored the way in which he encouraged her in her studies, so unlike Creepy Crowley, and always sought to boost her confidence.

But she wondered whether this was a genuine fondness

for the Frenchman, or just a silly schoolgirl crush. Probably the latter, she scolded herself, and I'm a little too old for that now! What signs has he shown that he's even interested in me? Calling me a pretty young woman is hardly a sign of eternal devotion, now, is it? she reasoned.

Whichever it was, she decided that it was a ridiculous concept. After all, apart from the fact that he was a member of the teaching staff he was twenty-one, four years older than her. He'd probably had lots of girlfriends in the past, if the things people said about Frenchmen were even halfway true. And Lisa had never had a serious boyfriend before; that is, if you didn't count last Christmas' kiss under the mistletoe with James.

More to the point, Jean-Luc was quite simply gorgeous, impossibly so. And that, for some peculiar reason, made Lisa feel even more uncomfortable. He was so gorgeous in fact that Lisa bet that he frightened a lot of people off.

She remembered something the undoubtedly very attractive Alison had once said to her and Chrissie during one of her particularly catty and superior moods: "I really wish I was plain! Boys get scared off when you're so good-looking. They're frightened that if they try and chat you up you'll just turn around and tell them where to get off. That's why I seem to do all the running after them!"

Well, Lisa determined that she at least wasn't going to do the running after Jean-Luc. Theirs was going to be a strictly teacher-pupil relationship.

And unlike half of the other girls in the sixth form, she decided, I'm going to ignore his good looks, his hairy muscular arms, that boyish way he licks his lips before he starts to address the class, his cute little smile...

Jean-Luc looked up from the copy of the magazine and smiled: "I'm glad you changed your mind, Lisa," he said in English.

Lisa muttered her acknowledgement and returned to reading out aloud in French from the magazine.

"I'm also glad that you've taken your hair out of its

ponytail," he continued. "It makes your face look much more softer."

Lisa looked up to find herself staring right into Jean-Luc's eyes. She coloured.

"Thanks very much, Jean-Luc," she said a little coolly. "Now can we just carry on with the lesson, please?"

Jean-Luc frowned; why was Lisa being so frosty with him? He was merely complimenting her. And it was true, now that she had let her hair down, her face did look much less severe. Although he wondered why he never noticed when any other of his female students changed their hairstyles.

They turned over the page of the magazine, to an article on Cannes, Jean-Luc's home town.

"It must be wonderful living there," Lisa said, in her acceptable French, the pronunciation of which Jean-Luc would occasionally correct. "Sunshine all day, the sea on your back doorstep, taking life as it comes..."

Jean-Luc laughed. "It would be even better without the tourists," he said. "In August all of France seems to come down to the Riviera. You cannot move for Parisians, and the beaches are littered with cans and rubbish and pale white bodies, and the air is full of car exhaust fumes..."

"What do you expect when you drive a 2CV?" Lisa asked fliply, as Jean-Luc moved over to the bookshelf where he took down a map of France and opened it on the table in front of them.

He pointed to a small town on the outskirts of Cannes. "That is La Napoule," he said in French, "where my mother lives, and where I was born. Many yachts go there, and millionaires often eat in the town."

"You make it sound very glamorous," said Lisa. "Don't you miss it?"

Jean-Luc switched back to English. "Sometimes, when the English summer starts raining dogs and cats—"

"Cats and dogs," Lisa corrected him patiently, but couldn't help smiling. Jean-Luc grinned.

"But there are compensations to living in England," he

continued. "On the Riviera people are so superficial. They are concerned only about appearances, about how people look, and not how they *are*. All they worry about is their money or their tan or buying the latest designer clothing ... I prefer things much more simpler..."

"Simpler," Lisa corrected him again, and when Jean-Luc frowned, not understanding, she explained: "It's 'simpler', or 'more simple', not 'more simpler' ... You're always getting that wrong, Jean-Luc!"

Jean-Luc raised his hands in an affected gesture of saddened defeat. "So, the pupil becomes the teacher!" he said.

"Sorry," said Lisa automatically.

"There's no need to be sorry," he said and laid a hand on her arm, before Lisa quickly moved it away. "If I say something wrong you must correct me, that's the only way to learn. Otherwise I will be convinced that people are laughing at my mistakes behind my back. And I'm sure there's a lot you could teach me, Lisa."

Is he coming on to me or what? Lisa asked herself urgently, not quite sure what to think. Or am I reading too much into this?

"Well, I'd much rather sit on the promenade at Cannes every day than be stuck in boring old Applewood," she said, deftly changing the subject.

"La Croisette," said Jean-Luc.

"What?"

"La Croisette," he repeated, and continued in French: "That is the name of the boulevard in Cannes which stretches along the seafront. It's very famous for its restaurants and nightlife..."

"I can just imagine you in Cannes now," said Lisa in French, "dining off pâté de foie gras in an expensive restaurant, with a glass of Pernod at your side, in the company of an absolutely breathtaking girlfriend."

Jean-Luc laughed. "I'm sorry to shatter your illusions, Lisa," he said with a grin. "We're not all millionaires on the Côte d'Azur, you know. My favourite restaurant on the Croisette is a low-price pizzeria which is always packed, I hardly ever drink alcohol – and I don't have a girlfriend – either in Cannes or here in England."

"Hey, I didn't mean to pry," Lisa said quickly in English, as she suddenly felt her heart leap for joy. She reverted to French: "Your private life's your own concern."

"I didn't think you were prying," claimed Jean-Luc, with a twinkle in his eye. "After all, why should you pry? You're not a gossip like Chrissie—"

"Oh, Chrissie's harmless enough," Lisa defended her friend. "She likes a good story, that's all."

"Nor do you have a personal concern, like Alison…"

"Alison?" asked Lisa, and wondered why it was that she could say things in a foreign language like French which she would never dream of saying in English. "But I thought that you two got on really well…"

Jean-Luc grinned. "She'd like us to, I know that," he admitted. "But I'm not interested in her at all. She's too pushy, too forward. When it comes right down to it she isn't really very interesting at all. People who go about flaunting themselves are usually very superficial: I'm not interested in them, no matter how attractive they might be. I'm not concerned with how people look, Lisa; it's what they are that really matters…"

He seemed to consider the matter for a moment before adding wickedly: "Of course, if they're intelligent, cultured and look like Beatrice Dalle I'm hardly going to say no, now am I?"

Lisa giggled. "You know that Alison's going around saying that you are two are like that—" she crossed her fingers in an imitation of Simon's earlier gesture.

"How childish," he said, and sighed: "Still, I suppose she'll never stop trying."

"We all say Alison's like the Mounties," Lisa said. "She always gets her man!"

Jean-Luc shook his head. "But not this man, Lisa," he said, and looked at her strangely. "Alison will not get *this* man!"

He turned his attention back to the magazine. "And now, Lisa, shall we get back down to work?"

Lisa nodded her head, and resumed her reading. As Jean-Luc turned the pages of *Paris-Match* his bare arm accidentally brushed against the skin of hers. A frisson of delight shot through her.

Suddenly Lisa found it very difficult to concentrate on her work. Indeed, work was now the last thing on her mind.

9

Chrissie groaned and lifted her arms heavenwards in desperation. "Why did I ever let myself get talked into this?" she asked no one in particular.

Standing by her side Lisa tutted good-naturedly. "You volunteered to be on the organizing committee of the summer ball, Chrissie," she reminded her. "No one forced you."

For the sixth form the summer ball was the big social event of the year; even though it was in part financed by the school, and in part from ticket sales, it had the great attraction of being organized mainly by the students themselves with the minimum of adult supervision. Even on the night of the ball, held in the college's assembly hall, there would only be a few teachers present, to check that things weren't getting too out of hand.

Chrissie looked up from the mountain of paperwork before her on a table in the school library. It seemed that every lunchtime for the past three weeks she'd brought the same mound of papers into the library and the pile never seemed to go down.

"But I never imagined it would be so much hard work – I've got to arrange to have tickets printed; I've got to hire a DJ—"

"Try Si," Lisa suggested mischievously. "He's got a great record collection."

"Lisa, grow up!" Chrissie laughed. "Simon still thinks he's living in a late nineteen-fifties movie. This is the nineties, Lisa. We need up-to-date sounds, not crackly old vinyl passed down to him from his dad! I saw his record collection the other day..."

"Oh?"

Chrissie flushed. "I ... er, I had to get a text book off him so I went round to his house..." She changed the subject, indicating the pile of paperwork before her, and looked appealingly at Lisa. "C'mon, Lisa, you're my best friend," she pleaded desperately. "Can't you help me?"

Lisa shook her head sadly; much as she would have liked to have helped in setting up the summer ball there were more important matters to attend to at the moment.

"Sorry," she said, meaning it, "but remember I've got French lessons at lunchtime now."

Chrissie looked curiously at Lisa. The original arrangement with Jean-Luc five weeks ago had been for one lesson a week; now that number had increased to three a week.

Chrissie adopted a superior expression and stared down her nose at Lisa, something which was particularly difficult to do as Lisa was standing and she was seated at the table.

"I think we've all of us by now got a pretty good idea what you two get up to in your 'French' lessons," she said snidely, although not maliciously.

Lisa pretended to be shocked. Secretly she was delighted by the suspicion that her and Jean-Luc's meetings were not as educational as in fact they were.

"*Chrissie!*"

"Well, is he giving anyone else private French lessons?" Chrissie asked pertinently.

"As a matter of fact, yes," revealed Lisa. "Stuart Richardson's having a private lesson one hour a week after school..."

"Aha!" cried Chrissie, spotting the flaw in Lisa's

argument. "But Stuart's dad's paying for that, so at least Jean-Luc's making some money out of it. Yours are free lessons, when Jean-Luc could be charging others for the lessons!"

Lisa blushed: she seemed to be doing a lot of that lately, at least whenever Jean-Luc's name came up.

"Chrissie, we're just good friends," she insisted.

"Of course you are, Lisa…"

"He's my teacher; and if we were more than 'just good friends' his job would probably be on the line," Lisa pointed out. "And I know how you like dishing the dirt, so don't you dare go spreading any gossip around," she added, half-hoping that she would.

"So if you don't – you know – what *do* you get up to in your 'French' lessons then?" Chrissie wanted to know.

"We discuss articles in French magazines, sometimes talk about French politics and cinema…"

Chrissie grimaced. "He's too cute to talk about serious and intelligent things like that!" she groaned, and shook her head dramatically. "It doesn't seem right somehow!"

"Well, that just shows how wrong you are, judging people solely by appearances," Lisa said smugly; and continued: "Sometimes we talk about life in the South of France and his home town—"

This sounded more interesting. "Any more like him back home?" Chrissie demanded urgently.

Lisa shook her head. "Only son, of a widowed mother," she offered.

"Girlfriend?"

Lisa shook her head again.

"Rich? Prospects?"

Lisa burst out laughing. "Chrissie, what is this? A questionnaire?"

"Well, we girls have to be choosy these days, you know, Lisa. You can't be too careful…"

Chrissie continued in a more serious vein. "Whatever he is, he's certainly made a change in you."

"What d'you mean?"

241

"Your French grades have gone up for one thing."

"And?"

"You're wearing your hair long now – it suits you," Chrissie said.

Lisa ran her fingers self-consciously through her long blonde hair. "Well, you did say it would soften my appearance and look more attractive—"

"Yes, I did, didn't I?" said Chrissie, understanding everything.

Not only that, but Chrissie noted that Lisa was remembering to take off her glasses when she wasn't reading, and had started taking more care in the clothes she wore to school every day.

Lisa could hardly ever have been called scruffy, and had always taken a pride in her appearance; but now she dressed less and less in her baggy sweatshirts and had taken to wearing freshly laundered blouses and T-shirts, and, as the weather improved, bright summer dresses. There was a new bounce in her step, and as she walked along the corridors of Applewood College boys who had known her for six or seven years were beginning to take notice of her.

Lisa attempted to change the subject, and gestured towards Chrissie's pile of paperwork.

"So when is the summer ball?" she asked her.

"The week before the final week of term. It's going to be fun – the upper sixth are going to try and sneak some wine in. Are you going to come?"

Lisa hesitated. "Go on, Lisa," urged Chrissie and added wickedly: "You could invite French Delight..." Lisa took a friendly swipe at her friend.

"Or James," she suggested. "He'll be down from university for the holidays..."

Lisa made a face. "Ugh, trainspotter James? What a terrible thought..."

As they burst out laughing (rather guiltily, it must be said, on Lisa's part), Alison entered the library and marched over to Chrissie's table. She eyed the mountain of paperwork curiously until Chrissie explained it was all for the summer ball.

"Put me down for two tickets then," she told Chrissie.

Lisa, in a friendly manner, asked: "So who will you be going with?"

Alison shrugged, and looked at Lisa, pretending to notice her for the first time.

"Oh, I haven't decided yet," she said airily. "There are so many boys who'd like to go with me, you know... And who are you going with, Lisa?"

"I don't know yet," she admitted and Alison tutted sympathetically.

"Well, if you can't get a date, Lisa, just let me know," she said. "I'm sure one of the boys I turn down might be persuaded to accompany you..."

And with that Alison swished out of the library, which wasn't a place she frequented at the best of times.

Lisa stood there speechless, while Chrissie chuckled.

"I don't believe it!" Lisa finally said. "As if I'd want to go out with one of her cast-offs!"

With Alison's reputation, half the boys in the upper sixth are her cast-offs! Chrissie thought.

"Why is she being like that to me, Chrissie?" she demanded. "We've never really been friends before, but I've done nothing to upset her. What reason does she have for being so catty to me now?"

"Isn't it obvious?" asked Chrissie. "She can't wait to get her hands on French Delight... And is he responding? No way..."

"But how can any normal red-blooded Frenchman not respond to Alison?" asked Lisa in disbelief. "She's the most glamorous and sophisticated one of us all. She could have any boy she wanted. The only straight boy who hasn't come on to Alison so far is Stuart, and that's only because Helen would murder him if he did."

"What was it you just told me about never judging by appearances, Lisa?" said Chrissie. "Maybe French Delight doesn't like women to throw themselves at him...

Maybe he prefers women to be more lady-like, and not like a she-devil on heat..."

"He did say that he thought she was too childish."

"Did he now?" asked Chrissie and wondered what else Jean-Luc had told her best friend during their private lessons together.

"But why should that turn her against me?" asked Lisa.

"Alison isn't used to losing," explained Chrissie. "And, as far as she's concerned, in the French Delight stakes, you're winning—"

"But we're—"

"I know – 'just good friends'," Chrissie finished for her although her tone suggested that she clearly didn't believe it. "But that's not how *she*'s seeing it." And with Alison's experience she should know!

"But she's wrong..." I think...

"Watch out for Alison, Lisa," Chrissie warned her as she returned to her paperwork. "What Alison wants she'll stop at nothing to get. Don't make an enemy out of her, Lisa, or you'll regret it..."

Later that night Lisa and her mother, Maddy, were sitting in front of the television watching a particularly weepy movie. Maddy relished these occasions, which were becoming all too rare as Lisa studied more and more for her exams.

She liked to spend as much time with her daughter as possible; now that Lisa was growing up their relationship was becoming much more one of two good girlfriends rather than that of a mother and daughter.

The movie ended and Maddy switched over channels with the remote control. She dabbed at her eyes with a tissue: these old black-and-white films always made her cry.

Curled up on the sofa, Lisa laughed at her mother's sentimentality: Maddy stuck a not-too-motherly tongue out at her daughter.

"So you've got a softie for your mother," Maddy said.

"Those old love stories always get me right there..."

Lisa paused and then looked up at her mother before asking: "Mum, how did you know you were in love with Dad?"

Maddy looked strangely at her daughter. "What's brought this on?" she quizzed her.

Lisa shrugged. "Just watching that old film, I suppose," she said, hoping that she sounded convincing enough. "But how did you know that you were in love with Dad?"

Maddy half-smiled and stared into space, remembering her husband who had died six years ago, and the time when she had first bumped into him almost twenty years ago in the student union bar in her final year at college.

"I was the last one to know," she recalled. "Everyone else seemed to know we were going to be together even before we did.

"I started enjoying his company, looking forward to seeing him every day. I began to feel totally at ease with him..."

"Well, I enjoy James's company, and we get on really great together, but I'm hardly in love with him," said Lisa, remembering once more that Christmas kiss under the mistletoe.

"Let me finish," said her mother, who was clearly enjoying her reminiscences. "And then you find yourself laughing at exactly the same things, and sharing the same interests. Finding that that book you read last year he's reading today; or discovering that you both have the same tastes in music, or painting, or movies."

"I thought people always said that opposites attract?" said Lisa.

"Well, sometimes they do," admitted Maddy. "And when you find that there are certain interests you don't share, then you go out and try to find out as much as you can about that subject – because it's what interests *him*.

"And then you start wanting to know everything about that other person... where he comes from, what he likes to eat, the sort of music he likes..."

"You make it sound like the third degree!" joked Lisa.

Maddy smiled, and continued: "And suddenly there comes a moment when you realize that there's not a single day that doesn't go by when you don't think of him. That you can't even brush against his skin without shivering all over." She glanced knowingly over at Lisa, who was taking in her every word.

"Sometimes you try and convince yourself that it's not love at all, that it's wishful thinking on your part; that someone as wonderful as he is simply couldn't be falling in love with someone as ordinary as you..."

I'm not ordinary! thought Lisa, even though she realized – or hoped – that Maddy wasn't talking about her.

"But deep, deep down inside, you really know," Maddy concluded. "You really know that this is the person you want to spend the whole rest of your life with. You might not be lovers yet, you might not even have kissed each other, but something inside you tells you that this is the one."

"But what is it?" asked Lisa. "What is it that tells you?"

Maddy chuckled. "I don't know. Some unlucky people never have that feeling, some people only experience it late in life. I was fortunate that I met your father when I did..." She sighed, not with sorrow but with fondness. "I still miss him, you know, Lisa."

"So do I..." agreed her daughter. "Do you think you'll ever marry again?"

Maddy shook her head. "No," she said resolutely. "You see, Lisa, I think that in your life there is one person, and one person only, who is absolutely right for you. Your soulmate, if you like.

"Some people never meet their soulmate, but if you do, you know instinctively that he's the right one for you, and you'd do anything for him. Follow him to the ends of the earth if needs be." She chuckled again. "At least that's how I felt about your poor father – still do, as a matter of fact."

"You must have loved him a lot," said Lisa.

"I did, and always will," said Maddy, and changed the subject slightly. "Are you going to pursue this line of questioning every time we watch an old black-and-white weepie together?"

"No..." Lisa smiled.

"You shouldn't really be up this late with school tomorrow," Maddy reproved and glanced at the digital display on the video recorder which read 01.15. She stood up to go to the kitchen to make her customary final cup of cocoa before turning in for the night.

"I was having a word with Miss Greenwood the other day," she said, referring to Lisa's appropriately-named Biology teacher. "She told me that you're not paying enough attention in class these days..."

"Oh Mum!" said Lisa, pretending not to feel concerned. "Greenie's finished with the interesting stuff like reproduction and human biology! Now we're on to boring things like plants and frogs!"

"She said your grades were slipping," her mother continued. "In Chemistry as well, she says."

Lisa averted her eyes from her mother; it was true: in the past few weeks she had indeed received two B-minuses and one C. It was hardly a disaster but, given Lisa's previous track record, it did give a little cause for concern.

"I'm sorry, Mum. I'll try harder," she promised.

"After all, it's you who's always saying that you must get high grades to get on to university," her mother reminded her, far from sternly. She moved towards the kitchen door. "However, there is apparently one subject in which your grades have sky-rocketed, although I can't imagine why..."

Lisa knew what was coming; she pretended to be watching the late-night documentary on TV. "Oh, and what's that?" she asked, trying (and failing) to sound casual.

"French," said Maddy, and vanished into the kitchen.

10

The following day was a Saturday and Lisa had decided to take the day off from studying to go into Applewood's main shopping mall for a spot of window-shopping. If she was lucky she might find the dress which she could wear to the summer ball; if she was even luckier she might be able to go back home and persuade her mother to buy it for her.

As she was walking down the main shopping street she looked casually into the window of Applewood's one and only record shop. Many of the students from college made a habit of meeting in there on Saturday afternoon; and more than once Lisa had been spotted by her friends and persuaded to go off with them to Brucianni's, the coffee shop in the centre of town which was frequented by all those who were seriously trendy, and many of those who aspired to be.

She glanced into the record shop and was disappointed to see that there was no one there she recognized. Oh well, it's no cappuccino and chocolate mousse pie down at the coffee shop for me today, she thought philosophically.

And then Lisa did a double-take. There was indeed someone there that she recognized; it was just that, taken out of the surroundings of the college, he looked so different, and, she had to admit, only a couple of years older than her rather than four. But nevertheless she would recognize those Chevignon jeans, that white Chipie T-shirt with the blue bandana tied casually around his neck, and that shock of thick black hair anywhere.

She walked into the shop and went over to the rock cassette section. She tapped him on the shoulder.

"Jean-Luc!" she said. "How are you?"

Jean-Luc turned round, and when he saw Lisa he beamed, and his brown eyes twinkled even more than Lisa would ever have thought possible.

"Lisa!" he said. "How nice to see you!" He meant it.

Lisa nodded to the cassette in Jean-Luc's hand. "What are you buying?" she asked.

Jean-Luc seemed slightly embarrassed, as though he was a little boy caught with his hand in his younger sister's bag of sweets. Nevertheless he showed Lisa the cover. It was the latest album from the Lower Depths, the art band whose praises she had extolled to him a few weeks ago.

"I thought you'd never heard of them?" Lisa asked a little suspiciously.

"Well, I haven't," he admitted. "But you seemed so much a fan of them that I thought I'd better find out why you liked them…" His voice trailed off.

Lisa couldn't help but smile. "Why, Jean-Luc, that's wonderful," she enthused.

An awkward silence fell between them, as suddenly neither of them knew what to say. Jean-Luc turned his eyes away from Lisa, and looked around the shop, as if he was scared that he might be spotted here.

As if being found in a record shop was a criminal offence for a teacher! he thought.

Lisa regarded the Frenchman with a dawning realization that Jean-Luc was scared of something. But what of? she asked herself. Surely not of me? What's wrong with bumping into just another pupil in a record shop on a Saturday afternoon?

Unless … unless I'm something more than a pupil to him…

Finally Jean-Luc returned to Lisa. "I'm surprised to see you here," he said casually. "I'd have imagined that you would have a Saturday job. We all of us have them in France."

"I should have," admitted Lisa. "I can't expect Mum to support me all through college ... I suppose I'll have to get one in the school holidays..."

Another odd silence followed. It was easy for each of them to talk to each other at school; after all, what was more natural than for a student to talk to her teacher? But here, in that strange and unpredictable environment which Chrissie liked to describe as Real Life, things seemed to be a little different, as if the pupil and the teacher belonged to two different worlds, two worlds which shouldn't really meet.

Think! What would Alison do in a situation like this!

"Well, Lisa, it was nice seeing you," said Jean-Luc.

"Yes. Well..." said Lisa, and looked over towards the door. "I suppose I'd better be going then ... I'll, uh, see you on Monday, Jean-Luc..."

She waved a reluctant goodbye and started walking away.

"Lisa, wait!" Jean-Luc said.

Lisa spun around on her heels and looked eagerly at Jean-Luc. Jean-Luc returned her gaze, and nervously licked his lips, as he always did when he was addressing a new and particularly difficult class for the first time.

"Yes, Jean-Luc?"

"Don't go yet," he urged. "Look, let me buy this cassette ... and then perhaps we can go for a coffee. I believe there's a coffee shop near here called Brucianni's?"

Lisa glanced down at her watch. "Well, I suppose I've got time..." she said, knowing perfectly well that for Jean-Luc she had all the time in the world.

Brucianni's was a short five-minute walk away and as they wandered down the crowded high street Lisa was aware of people's heads turning as they passed them by.

Or, rather, of women's heads turning, for it was obvious to Lisa that most of the women shopping in Applewood this Saturday afternoon found Jean-Luc incredibly attractive. His dark Mediterranean good looks and stylish casualness singled him out from all of the other men on the street with their pasty faces and scruffy jeans and T-shirts.

The strangest thing, Lisa noticed, was that Jean-Luc appeared totally unaware of all the attention. All he seemed to want to do was to chat to Lisa about her tastes in music, films, books, food – the most inconsequential things Lisa could ever have imagined; for all he was concerned the female passers-by might not even have existed.

When they arrived at Brucianni's the place was packed and they had to wait several minutes before a table became free. As they stood in the queue Lisa looked around the coffee shop and recognized a few people from school, people she might briefly chat to on her way to lessons. They acknowledged her presence with a token wave and then returned to their conversations, now punctuated with giggles and knowing side-glances as they speculated on why Jean-Luc and Lisa were having coffee together.

Uh-oh, the rumours are really going to start flying around school on Monday morning, thought Lisa, with something approaching satisfaction. Nevertheless, she began to feel uncomfortable, but once again Jean-Luc seemed to think that there was nothing at all amiss.

"They probably think it's scandalous for a teacher and his pupil to be seen together," Lisa said, as Jean-Luc ordered coffee and cakes.

"Why?" asked Jean-Luc. "I like your company, Lisa, what's wrong with that? We like the same things, the same books, the same music—"

"You hadn't heard of the Lower Depths until I told you about them!" Lisa said and pointed to the cassette.

"Aha, but that is a mistake which I am now rectifying,"

251

Jean-Luc replied with a smile. "You're fun to be with, Lisa: intelligent and sensible too. Unlike the other girls at Applewood you're interested in more things than just make-up and who's number one in the pop charts."

"I'm interested in those things too," Lisa felt obliged to say, as Jean-Luc pulled a film magazine out of the chic backpack he had been carrying with him. Like many French people his age he was passionately interested in the cinema, and would snap up any publication concerning the movies. He opened it at the listings page.

"There's a special screening of *La Belle et La Bête* next Friday at the local art cinema," he said, referring to the famous French film version of the Beauty and the Beast legend.

"Jean Cocteau," Lisa said, remembering the name of the director of the movie. "I love him!" She had seen the classic black-and-white film before on late-night TV, and had been entranced by its fantastic special effects, and had even sobbed a little at its ending.

Jean-Luc smiled inwardly to himself. When everyone else her age was enthusing about the latest Arnold Schwarzenegger blood n' guts epic, or the most recent Hollywood psycho-killer horror, he might have known that Lisa Tyler would be the one to admire an old romantic black-and-white French fantasy film made as long ago as 1946.

"Do you want to go?" he asked hopefully.

Yes, was what Lisa thought.

What she said was: "Well, I don't know..."

Jean-Luc tutted and leant forward, across the table. For one brief second he rested his hand on hers.

"Please?" he said, and then added slyly: "It's all in French, so you can even pretend it's educational..."

Lisa giggled, and Jean-Luc took his hand away from her. Leave it there, please leave it there, she cried out silently.

"Friday night?"

"Friday night," he confirmed.

"Then it's a date!"

Jean-Luc leant back in his chair and smiled.

"Good!" he said, and added impishly: "You know, Lisa Tyler, recently you're easing up a lot more. You're beginning to realize that there are a lot more things in life than just studying for exams. Why, with a little bit of determination you might even start to enjoy yourself."

Lisa stuck her tongue out at the French assistant, and Jean-Luc cuffed her gently on the shoulder, almost – but not quite – as a brother would. They both burst out laughing and then Lisa felt someone tap her on the shoulder. She turned round, and her face fell.

"Having fun?" asked Alison who had just arrived in the coffee shop, laden down with shopping, most of which she'd charged to her father's credit card. She ignored Lisa and instead looked suspiciously at Jean-Luc.

"Good afternoon, Alison," Jean-Luc said wearily. The redhead had still not taken the hint and continued to pursue him; the flirt of the sixth form was now becoming a little tiresome. He glanced down at the film magazine. "Lisa and I were just discussing a movie we're going to see."

Jean-Luc, don't tell her of all people! thought Lisa urgently.

Alison's eyes narrowed and she flashed an evil glare at Lisa, before returning to Jean-Luc. For the first time since Jean-Luc's arrival at Applewood Alison had clearly got the hint.

"Oh, I see…" she said through gritted teeth, but nevertheless still managed to adopt a superior attitude. "French films? How very arty – I much prefer the latest Richard Gere…"

She smiled sweetly at Jean-Luc and said goodbye; before leaving the coffee shop she glared malevolently at Lisa.

"Jean-Luc, you shouldn't have told her that!" Lisa reproved as soon as Alison had left the place.

"Why ever not?" he said. "And if it means that she'll stop bothering me…"

"But she can be so spiteful when she wants to be," Lisa protested, remembering what Chrissie had told her the other day.

"She'll get over her childish crush on me in a very little time," Jean-Luc assured her.

"She'll spread the news all around the school..."

"So what? What could be more natural than two friends going out to see a movie together?" He rested his hands reassuringly on Lisa's.

"You're my teacher, Jean-Luc! If the principal got to hear about it!"

Jean-Luc shook his head. "I'm the foreign language assistant," he corrected her. "And it's not as if we're about to start a raging affair, now, is it?"

"Well, no..." she said.

Jean-Luc's eyes twinkled as they looked into hers. "So relax, Lisa!" he said and then took on a stern tone: "And that is an order from your teacher!"

Lisa laughed and looked down at the table, as if to check with her own eyes what her other sense of touch was already screaming at her.

Jean-Luc had still not taken his hands away from hers.

11

The following Thursday Chrissie looked up at Lisa from the library table, which she had set up as a sort of counter for tickets to the summer ball.

"So you finally decided to go to the ball after all?" she said, as Lisa handed over her £12 for two tickets. "You finally decided to invite Trainspotter James along, did you?"

Lisa gave her friend a wouldn't-you-like-to-know smile, and took the tickets. "I might have," she said sneakily. "And on the other hand I might not have..."

Chrissie hadn't seen Lisa so happy for a long time; there was a mischievous sparkle in her eyes.

"Don't say you've invited French Delight!" said Chrissie.

"Wait and see," Lisa teased, enjoying Chrissie's look of surprise. In fact, Lisa had invited no one yet; James would only be returning from university that coming weekend, and as for Jean-Luc, well, she would decide after tomorrow night when they had been to the cinema...

"You've gone and done it, haven't you! You've beaten Man-eater Alison at her own game!"

"No, I have not invited Jean-Luc," Lisa stated firmly and then grinned, pleased at the thought that she might have. "But what if I have? He's not a teacher, only the foreign language assistant—"

"That's not what you said the other week," Chrissie
reminded her.

"Well, things have changed since then," she replied and
was about to explain further, when Alison waltzed into
the library.

Twice in the library in almost three weeks, thought
Chrissie. For Alison Potter that must be some sort of
record!

"Hello there," she said, positively oozing sweetness and
light, which instantly made Chrissie suspicious, but went
unnoticed by Lisa. She looked at the pile of tickets and
mentioned the summer ball. Chrissie asked her who her
partner was going to be.

Alison studied her nails and affected an air of
nonchalance. "Oh, I haven't quite decided who the lucky
boy is going to be yet," she claimed. She looked at Lisa.
"And how are you looking forward to your date tomorrow
night?"

Lisa blushed, while Chrissie was immediately
interested.

"You have a date tomorrow night, Lisa?" she asked,
surprised that Lisa hadn't confided in her.

"Not just any date," said Alison, scarcely able to conceal
the poison in her voice. "This one is with a certain cute-
looking Frenchman."

"Lisa Tyler, talk about a dark horse!" Chrissie said
admiringly.

"We're just going to see a movie, that's all!" protested
Lisa, for once losing her temper. "What's so special about
that?"

Alison shook her head. "The teacher and his pupil going
out together after school hours," she tutted. "*And* without
a chaperone, too! Why do you think Eliane was asked to
leave? She was showing too much of an interest in the
boys in the upper sixth, that's why."

Lisa and Chrissie looked at each other, uncertain
whether Alison was telling the truth about Jean-Luc's
predecessor or not. Alison fixed Lisa with a steely

threatening gaze. "I don't know what would happen if the principal got to hear about Jean-Luc getting *involved* with one of his pupils..."

Lisa looked to Chrissie for support.

"Well, she's not going to hear about it, is she?" Chrissie said. "As long as you don't open your big mouth!"

"That's right – not unless I open my 'big mouth'," said Alison, and turned round and marched out of the library.

"Alison, wait!" said Lisa, and started to go after her. Chrissie stopped her.

"Forget about her, Lisa," she said.

"But what if she does tell the principal about me and Jean-Luc?" she asked. "He could lose his job..."

"You're just going to see a movie, and a French movie at that, like you said," Chrissie reminded her. "And what's so wrong with that? Listen, Lisa, Alison's only jealous. She'd jump at the chance for a night out with Jean-Luc..."

"But..."

Chrissie clamped a hand over Lisa's mouth. "No buts, Lisa Tyler!" she ordered. "You go to the movies tomorrow night – although why you want to see an old black-and-white French film baffles me. Don't let Alison stop you. You go out and have some fun for a change!"

Lisa followed Chrissie's advice. The following evening she and Jean-Luc had arranged to meet in Brucianni's and go on to the tiny art cinema from there.

Jean-Luc was sitting at a table, drinking a Coke and waiting for her as she arrived, perfectly on time. He was wearing a stylish black leather jacket, draped casually over his broad shoulders, a blue bandana and a spotlessly white T-shirt with black 501s. It was the uniform which every other trendy male under thirty seemed to be wearing, but Jean-Luc carried the look off with typical Gallic panache and somehow stamped on it his very own style.

As Lisa came over to the table he stood up and kissed

her twice on the cheeks in greeting. Lisa felt her heart leap in her breast.

"Lisa, you look wonderful," he said.

Lisa looked down at the soft pale green dress, which complemented her long blonde hair nicely, and the short, smart black jacket she was wearing.

"Oh this?" she said as casually as she could manage. "I've had it for years..."

As a matter of fact it took me three whole hours to get dressed tonight, she thought wryly.

"Well, you still look splendid," said Jean-Luc. "And I'm not the only one to think so."

"What do you mean?"

Jean-Luc indicated a boy sitting near the door, who was staring at her. As soon as she turned around he hastily returned to the book he was reading.

"He's been watching you ever since you came in," Jean-Luc explained. "He must be very jealous of me..."

Lisa smiled with even more embarrassment than the boy by the door was showing. She'd never been aware of turning anyone's head before; and now she found it was really rather pleasant.

Later, as they sat together in the small art cinema, Lisa realized how much she enjoyed the film of the horrible enchanted beast who falls in love with the selfless beauty. For the first few minutes of the movie, sitting there in the cramped and darkened space, she was terribly aware of Jean-Luc sitting close next to her, and his leg which would occasionally (and accidentally) brush against her own.

Jean-Luc, however, soon put her at ease as he pointed out special effects in the film or nuances in the way the actors played their parts which she had missed the first time around. Lisa was impressed by his knowledge and his enthusiasm, and – when the film ended and she noticed his misty eyes – by his sensitivity.

"But I'm French!" he protested, as she teased him.

"We're supposed to be romantic! And it was such a sad ending!"

"You're still a softie," maintained Lisa.

They walked through the throng of couples leaving the cinema to the car park where Jean-Luc's 2CV was parked. Jean-Luc suggested that he drive her home.

"There's no need to, Jean-Luc," she protested, rather unconvincingly.

Who am I kidding? she thought.

"I can catch the bus. And I live out of your way..."

"No, I insist!" said Jean-Luc. He looked at his Swatch. "It's half-past ten and it's a dark night...

"And this time Alison won't be in the passenger seat," he added, leading Lisa gently by the arm to the 2CV.

As they drove along – or rather, shuddered along, with Jean-Luc apologizing for the state of his battered old car – they chatted animatedly about everything imaginable, from music to films, and even gossiped about some of the teachers at school.

It seemed that Jean-Luc was regarded as something of an *enfant terrible* by several of the other teachers, who disapproved of the casual way he dressed and his winning ways with his students, all of whom he treated as his equals. He also confided in her that one of the female teachers had something of a crush on him.

"Mouldy Miss Rutherford?" Lisa giggled in amazement. The fifth-form maths teacher had always seemed such a fuddy-duddy. "Jean-Luc, she's over sixty and at least twice as big as a house..."

"Still, she invites me round all the time to her flat for 'tea and cakes'," he revealed. "Invitations which I have so far refused..." He turned off the main road and into Lisa's road. "I should not be telling you all this staffroom gossip, of course," he chuckled. "After all, I *am* your teacher..."

Lisa turned to look at him. "You're not a teacher, Jean-Luc," she said.

Jean-Luc parked the car opposite Lisa's house. It was now eleven o'clock, closing time for the pubs, and from off the main road they could hear the voices and laughter of Friday-night revellers on their way home.

The local pub, The Lamb and Flag, was popular with many students from Applewood, not least of all because the landlord there was prepared to turn a blind eye to people who were just a little under the legal age for drinking.

Lisa had often been there herself with Chrissie and Alison, although she usually stuck to orange juices or Cokes, while Alison would drink whatever was trendy at the moment.

Jean-Luc sat in the driver's seat, staring out into space. He tapped his long fingers on the steering wheel. There was an awkward silence before he nodded over to the front bay window of Lisa's house. The light was on.

"Your mother will be worrying about you, Lisa," he said.

Lisa was staring thoughtfully ahead. "What?" she asked, and turned to look at the curtained window. "Oh yeah ... sure ... I suppose I'd better go in then..."

"Yes, I suppose you'd better..." he repeated, without any conviction whatsoever in his voice. Neither of them wanted the other to leave.

Lisa unbuckled her seat-belt and looked at Jean-Luc; he was still staring straight ahead, trying not to look at Lisa.

"Thank you for a really lovely night, Jean-Luc," she began, and meant it. "I really enjoyed myself."

"So did I..."

Lisa leant over and kissed him goodbye on the cheek, as a good friend would. She frowned: was it her imagination or could she feel Jean-Luc tense up?

"See you in school then," she said, trying to sound nonchalant.

"Yes..."

She tried to open the passenger door, pulling on the door handle which refused to budge.

By her side, Jean-Luc clicked his tongue in irritation. "It always does that," he said. "This car is getting old – I really should think of getting rid of it – let me try."

He leant over and tugged at the handle. With a grunt, he managed to release it and the passenger door clicked open.

"Thanks..."

"No problem..."

Jean-Luc looked up. His face was now very close to Lisa's and they looked deep into each other's eyes. Like magnet and iron their eyes locked together.

A second passed. Two.

They felt like an eternity.

Uncertainly Jean-Luc moved his lips closer to Lisa's. He paused for a brief half-instant, and looked even deeper into her blue eyes, as if to be sure that she was experiencing the same feelings he was.

Lisa's heart pounded with expectation. Its noise deafened her: she was convinced that the whole world must be able to hear it. But at the same time she knew that there was no other world, there were no other stars, no sun in the sky. Even the noise from the people leaving the pub could have been on a different planet, so oblivious was she to it.

Now there were no other people, there was only her, and Jean-Luc, alone, together. Nothing else mattered.

He kissed her, a long, tender kiss on the lips. His breath was warm and sweet and fresh, and his lips were soft and welcoming.

After what seemed unimaginable years later, but had only been a few seconds, Jean-Luc moved his lips away from Lisa's, while every part of her being screamed out for him to stay.

His black hair was mussed, and fell cutely over his forehead. There was a beatific smile on his face, as he gazed at her seductively with those dark but sparkling eyes.

No, not just seductively, thought Lisa. It's more than

that. He's concerned. He wants to know that I'm happy. That I'm doing what I want to do. That I feel the same way as he does...

Is he crazy or what? Of course I do!

He brought his lips to hers again, this time with more passion. Jean-Luc cradled her face in his hands as Lisa wrapped her arms around him, pressing herself to him, feeling his body against hers, feeling his heart beat next to hers, breathing out as he breathed in.

She ran her fingers through his thick hair, and then along the outline of his firm jaw which was just starting to show the traces of late-night stubble.

He drew back from her again, and gazed into her eyes once more. Now Lisa found that she was smiling too. It was as if her whole life had been leading up to this one moment. This one moment with the gorgeous Frenchman, who cared for her, who liked her, who made her feel good and made her laugh, who...

He gave her a peck on the lips, and grinned.

"T'es belle, tu sais," he said. *You're beautiful, you know.*

"Et t'es beau aussi," she replied. *And so are you.*

He kissed her again on the lips.

"If you only knew how long I've been waiting to do this..." he admitted. "But I thought you weren't interested..."

Now it was Lisa's turn to kiss him on the lips.

"Interested?" she murmured. "From the very first moment when you played that dirty trick about the railway station on me, I knew that I loved – liked you. You're so different from everyone else."

"And so are you," said Jean-Luc.

"But I thought that you'd go for someone like Alison or even Chrissie..."

Jean-Luc smiled. "And how—" he pecked her on the lips – "wrong—" and again – "you—" and again – "were!"

Gently, he kissed her again and nuzzled her neck. Lisa felt his hands run down the small of her back, sending thrills of delight through her entire body. At this moment she would have let Jean-Luc do anything to her.

Jean-Luc looked up, and smiled. "You must go home now, Lisa," he whispered softly. "Your mother will be waiting for you."

Lisa reluctantly released herself from his embrace. As she made for the door, Jean-Luc took her arm.

"I will see you tomorrow?" he asked urgently.

Lisa had a hundred and one things to do on Saturday: she had her homework and studying to do; she was supposed to go out for the afternoon with James, who had returned home from university earlier that day; she had the household chores to do.

"Of course," she breathed.

"I'll ring you tomorrow morning," he promised.

"But you don't have my phone number," she protested.

Jean-Luc grinned. "Oh yes I do," he confessed. "I took it from the records in the school office two weeks ago ... I've been trying to pluck up the courage to use it ever since..."

Jean-Luc gave Lisa one final lingering kiss, and then let her go. She hurried up the short drive to her front door and then turned to watch Jean-Luc drive away in the battered old 2CV. As the car turned the corner Jean-Luc waved and blew her a kiss.

On the doorstep Lisa hugged herself, scarcely able to believe that what had just happened had not been a dream. Her lips still tasted of Jean-Luc's, and she could still smell the fresh aroma of soap and roses. She looked up at the stars in the clear night sky which somehow seemed bigger and brighter than ever before.

It's a dream come true, she thought; but I'm certainly not asleep!

Lisa took one final look at the street corner around which Jean-Luc's car had disappeared, and, with a sigh of decidedly French delight, turned and entered the house.

So caught up in her own emotions was Lisa that she failed to notice the person standing at the other end of the road. Alison Potter had been out at the Lamb and Flag and was now making her way home. When she noticed Jean-Luc's distinctive car parked outside Lisa's front door, she had made her excuses and left her group of friends.

Hidden in the shadows she had seen everything which had occurred between Lisa and Jean-Luc.

12

The following morning, Lisa's mother, Maddy, might have known there was something up. For a start, not only had Lisa got up at seven o'clock on one of the two mornings when she allowed herself a lie-in, but she had also spent over an hour in the bathroom.

When the doorbell rang at ten o'clock, Lisa was up and down to the door before Maddy even had time to put down the newspapers and get out of her chair.

"Don't worry, Mum," Lisa said breezily, as she rushed down the stairs leading to the front door. "It's only for me! I'll see you tonight!"

Earlier that morning, after Jean-Luc had rung, Lisa had said that she and Chrissie were going to go shopping down in London. They were aiming to catch the morning train, she had said, and make the fifty-minute journey down to the capital where they planned to spend the whole day and return late in the evening.

Maddy nodded knowingly; somehow the fine-cut designer jeans and brilliantly white blouse Lisa was wearing weren't the sort of things she could imagine her daughter wearing on a shopping expedition to the capital with her best friend.

Lisa opened the door to see Jean-Luc waiting for her. He was dressed once again in his black leather jacket, this time accompanied by a brilliantly blue shirt, open at the neck to reveal his chest hairs, and some stylish French black trousers. The early-morning sun was already bright and he was wearing a pair of Ray-Bans. He beamed when he saw her.

"You look wonderful," he said, and kissed her on the cheek. He handed her a small bouquet of roses. "For last night," he explained.

Lisa kissed him back, on the lips, to thank him.

"I could hardly believe last night happened," she admitted shyly, feeling like a third-former on her first date, and sniffed the flowers which smelt wonderful.

"Well, it did," he said happily. "And I for one am very glad it did." He offered her his arm. "And now may I escort madame to her car?" he said in a posh English accent.

Lisa affected a curtsy. "Why, monsieur, I'd be delighted," she said, and allowed herself to be led to the waiting green 2CV. Not quite a luxurious Rolls, she thought; but in the company of Jean-Luc it might as well be. "But where are we going?"

"To London of course," said Jean-Luc.

Well, at least that tallies with the story I've told Mum, Lisa thought gratefully.

"That sounds great, Jean-Luc," she agreed and then looked doubtfully at his car. "Do you think she's up to it?" she asked teasingly.

Jean-Luc took his arm away from Lisa's and gave her a playful punch in the side. "That car is the peak of French engineering precision!" he said.

Lisa winked at him. "That's what I'm worried about," she said, as Jean-Luc opened the passenger door for her.

As the car sped away the curtain in the bay window of Lisa's house was drawn aside. Maddy grinned to herself, not at all concerned that Lisa was hiding her new boyfriend from her.

Let Lisa keep her new boyfriend a secret for the time being, Maddy decided. After all, she had done the same thing almost twenty years ago when she had met a fellow student in her college bar, wanting to keep the relationship hidden and special for as long as possible, relishing the secrecy and privacy, and the joy of keeping him for herself.

Finally, of course, she had gone and married him.

The Royal Botanical Gardens at Kew, on the outskirts of London, make up one of the most beautiful places in the whole capital. Set in acres of greenery grow flowers from every corner of the world, and on a warm summer's day, with the sun shining down and glinting off the lily pools and ornamental ponds, it is the perfect place for a pair of new young lovers to stroll, ignoring the other tourists and just delighting in each other's presence.

As Lisa and Jean-Luc walked among the lanes of brightly-coloured flowers, their hands would brush against each other's. They joined hands automatically; it was some seconds before Lisa even realized that they were in fact walking hand in hand – it just seemed so much the natural thing to do that they had done it without even thinking. She and Jean-Luc were now no longer two separate people, they were a single entity, two halves who together made up a whole.

Jean-Luc led her to a pagoda, perched on top of a small hillock, from where they could look down on the people below. He had taken off his leather jacket and, as they sat down, he put his arm around Lisa.

She smiled dreamily, as his hand stroked her back, sending shudders of delight down her spine. The strong taut muscles of his biceps and the firm touch of his fingers massaging the small of her back made her feel as though she were in heaven.

She sighed: she still couldn't quite believe that this gorgeous, intelligent, kind man was actually sitting beside her – beside her, Lisa Tyler – and that he had actually kissed her and held her last night as if he would never let go.

"Are you happy, Lisa?" he asked softly.

"Are you kidding? I've never been happier in my life."

"Then I am pleased," he said in that peculiarly formalized English which he sometimes used unwittingly, and which only went to increase his considerable French charm. He looked her in the eye. "Because I think I may be falling in love with you—"

"Jean-Luc, I—"

Jean-Luc placed a finger on her lips to silence her.

"Let me finish," he said. "When I first came to Applewood you were the only one not to 'pursue' me. And I became intrigued. And as I became intrigued I learnt that, as well as being very beautiful, you were also very shy and lacked self-confidence. So I tried to build up your self-confidence, make you believe in yourself more. And as I did that so I found myself wanting to see more of you, spend more time with you. I wanted to know all about you, about your likes and dislikes—"

"Like the Lower Depths," Lisa interjected brightly, feeling slightly awkward. Very rarely did any of the boys at school express their emotions with such candour; after all, it wasn't quite the *British* thing to do. "And did you like them?"

Jean-Luc pouted sheepishly. "Well, actually, no..." He smirked. "In fact I hated them!"

"That's the trouble with the French," joked Lisa. "They might look good but when it comes to their taste in music – yuck!"

Jean-Luc pulled a face at her, and laughed. He pulled her closer to him, and Lisa snuggled at his side, and with one hand teased at the chest hairs in the 'V' of his shirt.

She nodded down at the people below, all of them admiring the flowers and enjoying their day out; none of them knew her or Jean-Luc, and every single one of them was totally oblivious of their happiness. Jean-Luc realized what she was thinking.

"I would like them all to know how much I love you," he stated.

Lisa agreed, but still a worrying thought was nagging

at her mind. She sat up and looked seriously at Jean-Luc.

"But Jean-Luc, we have to be careful," she urged. "Here in London it's OK, we can be what we want to be, do what we want to do…"

Struck by the concern in her voice, Jean-Luc took her hands in his. "What do you mean?"

"What would happen if they found out back at school?"

Jean-Luc shrugged. "Let them," he said with typically Gallic indifference. "I love you. What is the problem?" He smiled. "There is no problem."

Lisa sighed. Jean-Luc was like all Frenchmen, she decided; he followed his heart – he never thought of the situations it might lead him into. The French might be a passionate and happy race, she decided, but there was one thing which they lacked: basic common sense!

"You're a teacher—"

"I'm *not* your teacher, Lisa," Jean-Luc interrupted with what now had become a familiar cliché.

"But that's the way they'll see it," she explained. "You might lose your job—"

"There's only another three weeks of term left," he said. "So what is the problem?"

"So it might cause you problems back home in France," she said. "Or when you graduate and you want to become a teacher. What would they think of someone who's been going out with one of his students?"

Jean-Luc looked crestfallen. "Are you trying to say that you no longer want to see me?" he asked anxiously.

Lisa stroked his hands reassuringly. "Of course not. But let's just be a little careful for the few weeks we've got left of term. After all, we've got the whole of the summer holidays to look forward to, haven't we?"

Jean-Luc smiled and kissed Lisa on the forehead. "You know, Miss Tyler, at times you can be a very sensible and practical girl," he said affectionately.

"That's always been my trouble," she reflected, only half-jokingly. "But will you promise?"

Jean-Luc sulked playfully, trying – successfully – to look like a cute little boy, being told off by a particularly stern teacher.

"*D'accord* – OK," he said finally. "I promise."

"Good!"

"But when the summer holidays come, Lisa," he continued, "I would like you to come down to France with me ... to meet my friends down in Cannes, see the place where I live."

"Jean-Luc, I can't afford that," she said. "Do you know how much it costs to get a ticket down to the South of France?"

"We drive down," he said. "Just you and me together..."

Lisa looked warily at Jean-Luc. Here was this man – no, this absolutely gorgeous hunk – who she had kissed for the first time only last night, and who was now inviting her on holiday with him! Surely even for a Frenchman he was being a little too forward? Jean-Luc noticed her hesitation and laughed.

"You've no need to worry, Lisa!" he laughed. "If we go on holiday together I will not take advantage of you..."

"'Take advantage of me'?" Lisa repeated. The words sounded as though they had come out of a particularly bad English novel from the 1950s (as a matter of fact, they had).

"That's right," he confirmed. "I will never – ever – make you do anything you do not wish to do... You are much too important for that."

He stood up and led her out of the pagoda, and back into the throng of holiday-makers and day-trippers. Some of them noticed Lisa and Jean-Luc as they walked hand-in-hand along the bright and fragrant flower-lanes of Kew Gardens. Those who did winked knowingly at each other: here were a young couple out for the day; a young couple who were very obviously very much in love.

"This is just too good to be true," Lisa murmured softly to Jean-Luc.

"What is?"

"You and me," she said and looked at him. "I mean, it seems unbelievable that someone like you shouldn't have a girlfriend…"

"I do now," he said simply.

And devastatingly, for Lisa.

"Are you sure that you haven't got some French stunner waiting for you back home in Cannes?" she asked, trying to keep her tone light and nonchalant, but praying for an answer in the negative.

Jean-Luc pressed her hand reassuringly.

"Of course I haven't," he said. "Otherwise why would I want you to come to Cannes with me for the summer?"

"Good point," Lisa conceded.

"And how about you, Miss Tyler?" he said mischievously, turning the tables on her. "Do you have some English hunk waiting for you somewhere?"

Now it was Lisa's turn to reassure Jean-Luc. "No, Jean-Luc," she said firmly, "I promise you that there is no one else…"

"Good." He stopped and turned to Lisa. "Because I don't think I could bear the thought of you being with anyone else, Lisa," he said, and took her in his arms. "If I knew that you were seeing someone else I couldn't even bear to be in the same country as the two of you."

He kissed her long and slowly on the lips, and Lisa responded with equal passion. All around them people walked past them and stared at them.

But for Lisa and Jean-Luc in their embrace, it didn't matter. For all they cared, they might as well have been on another planet.

13

Chrissie looked on disapprovingly as Lisa bounced into the senior common room, her face glowing and her eyes twinkling.

"Lisa Tyler, do you know what day it is?" she quizzed her.

Lisa looked puzzled. "Why, Monday of course," she answered.

"Monday morning to be precise," Chrissie corrected her. "And one of the greatest rules of the entire universe is that no one – and I mean absolutely no one – is allowed to look as happy as you're looking on a Monday morning!"

Lisa blushed, giving away more than she realized to Chrissie. "Do I really look so happy?" she asked.

"Like the cat who got the cream – and didn't put on an ounce either," Chrissie confirmed with a grin.

"I must be full of the joys of summer," she said flippantly, and pointed outside to the gloriously blue and cloudless sky. It was going to be a long hot summer in Applewood – or so she thought.

Full of the joys of summer? Pull the other one, Chrissie thought knowingly, but said nothing.

There was every reason for Lisa to feel happy: she had just enjoyed the most wonderful weekend of her life. After they had spent the afternoon at Kew Gardens, Jean-Luc had driven her into central London, where he had treated her to a meal and then bought some cut-price tickets for one of the recent, more trendy musicals.

Lisa had protested at the expense and had even offered to share the costs, but Jean-Luc had insisted: nothing was too good for her, he declared, and even if he had to live on bread and water for the remaining weeks of term he was determined that Lisa was going to have a good time.

Lisa felt enormously pampered, treated like a princess, something she thought only happened in books or glossy American soap operas. It felt, she decided, pretty good; it was most definitely something she could get used to.

But the greatest thing about that Saturday was being away from Applewood. There in London, where no one knew them, and could disapprove, they were allowed to be themselves.

They could walk arm-in-arm through the crowds of shoppers in Harrods, safe in the knowledge that they weren't going to bump into Alison who, embittered by Jean-Luc's rejection of her, might decide to tell on them.

They could gaze lovingly at each other across a dinner table, hands touching, and know that there was no possibility that Creepy Crowley might be eating at the adjacent table.

And when Jean-Luc suddenly stopped in the middle of Oxford Street, and pulled her close to him to kiss her, they were certain that Miss Bailey, the principal, wasn't going to leap out of the crowds and send Jean-Luc back home to France.

Returning home to Applewood, their farewell embrace in the car was so intense and passionate that Lisa thought she'd died and gone to heaven. When she entered the flat, Maddy had just smiled knowingly: she hadn't been fooled for an instant, but she was glad that her daughter had found someone she could be happy with. Lisa would tell her all about it in her own good time, she decided reasonably. And so what if her new boyfriend did seem a couple of years older than her? Maddy simply assumed that he was a student at the nearby technical institute, or the older brother of one of her classmates.

The following day, Jean-Luc had taken Lisa further afield – to the coast – where they had spent the day swimming in the warm sea or just sun-bathing on the sandy shore. It wasn't quite his home town of Cannes, he had told her, but it was the next best thing.

In a swimming costume Lisa had always been a little too self-conscious of her figure before, comparing it unfavourably to Alison's near-perfect physical proportions. With Jean-Luc, however, it somehow didn't seem to matter that she might have eaten one cream cake too many the other day in Brucianni's.

Needless to say, Jean-Luc's body was firm and muscular, and he was an expert swimmer, the result, he said, of swimming in the sea every morning back home in the South of France.

"With all those beautiful, sun-bronzed, perfect bodies in Cannes, you have to stay in shape," he said, as they lay side by side on the beach.

"I thought you said appearances didn't matter!" protested Lisa and sat up. She viciously tweaked one of his chest hairs.

"Well, no…" he chuckled, "but they do help sometimes!"

And with that Lisa had stuck her tongue out at him and refused to talk to him until he had gone and bought her a strawberry ice cream from the small kiosk on the promenade.

They had even made the acquaintance of some locals who came down to the beach every weekend, and had ended up playing a game of beach volleyball with them. For the first time in her life – and in the company of people who just assumed that she and Jean-Luc were together and thought nothing of it – Lisa felt that strange indescribable thrill of being treated as one half of a couple; and the words "Lisa and Jean-Luc" were suddenly imbued with a powerful sense of magic.

And how wonderful, also, did the words "my boyfriend" sound!

In fact, the only blot on an absolutely perfect weekend was that it had to end so early. Having successfully got out of seeing her next-door neighbour James on Saturday as she had promised, she had made an arrangement to see him on Sunday evening.

When Jean-Luc had asked her who she was meeting she had simply replied "an old school friend who's at university", without mentioning their sex.

Of course there was nothing between her and James, she kept telling herself (at the same time trying hard to forget that kiss under the mistletoe last Christmas); but if Frenchmen were all they were said to be – and Jean-Luc seemed to be living proof of that – she didn't want to arouse his jealousy without good cause.

So their day ended early, with yet another passionate kiss in the car. And who cares who might be watching? Lisa thought recklessly. Jean-Luc had then driven off with a promise to see her tomorrow at college.

"And yes, Miss 'Sensible' Tyler," he had said, before moving off, "I will be discreet – in college at least!"

After a day out with Jean-Luc anything was bound to be an anti-climax. Tea at James's next door was doubly so. Still, Lisa did have a soft spot for James. Kind-hearted and awkwardly handsome in a college-boy sort of way, with short sandy hair, grey eyes and the sturdy body of a rugby player, he had always found Lisa attractive, and had clumsily pursued her for the past couple of years.

The trouble was, Lisa realized, he was just so boring, and didn't know how to treat a girl. Like many boys his age he had only recently discovered the attraction of the opposite sex; until then girls had been a minor inconvenience, getting in the way of his studies, his rugby games and his unfathomable passion for trains.

Even under the mistletoe, he had rarely asked Lisa about her interests or likes and dislikes; and his idea of taking a girl for a day out would probably be the local rugby match followed by hamburgers at McDonalds and a Sylvester Stallone film. In every way, in fact, he was the opposite of the caring, considerate Jean-Luc.

When Lisa finally left him, worn out and exhausted by his discussion of the finer points of the steam engine, she was looking forward to going to school the next day as she had never done before.

She also realized that for the first time in her school life she had let a weekend go by without doing one single piece of homework, or even opening a text book.

And for once, it didn't matter at all.

14

Monday was the day the fun-fair came to Blackchurch – a village about twenty minutes' bus-ride away from Applewood. It arrived every year, usually acting as a temptation for the college's students to forego revision for exams and tests, and go along and have a good time.

At the end of that afternoon's French lesson Jean-Luc had suggested that he and Lisa go and visit the fun-fair later that evening. Lisa was unsure: what if anybody from Applewood saw them there? she asked.

"Relax, Lisa," Jean-Luc reassured her. "Who is going to see us there? Some members of the third form perhaps? Are you seriously worried about their childish gossip?"

Lisa laughed. "No. But what if Chrissie saw us? Or anyone in your French class..."

It was Jean-Luc's turn to laugh now. "With the homework I've given them for tonight?" he said. "They won't have time to watch TV let alone go over to Blackchurch!"

"Yes, that *was* a pretty vicious piece of homework you set us," she admitted. "Translate eight pages of a seventeenth-century play into idiomatic English, and all by tomorrow afternoon!"

"It will keep them busy for a while," he chuckled. "That was the whole idea!"

"But you've forgotten one thing," Lisa pointed out.

"Oh? And what is that?"

"I'm in the same class!" she said. "It's *my* homework as well!"

Jean-Luc winked at her. "But you, Mademoiselle Tyler, have the benefit of a private tutor!" he said, and hugged her close to him. Lisa pulled away.

"Jean-Luc!" she scolded. "Not here in the classroom!"

Jean-Luc's face fell. "Why ever not?" he asked. "I want to hold you. I want to show you what I feel towards you. And besides, there is no one else here. It is the end of Monday afternoon: all anyone is really interested in now is going home to catch *Neighbours*!"

"You crazy, crazy Frenchman," she said. "Start being sensible!"

"I'm French," he grinned. "I don't want to be sensible..."

"You're still my teacher, when all's said and done," Lisa reminded him.

"I'm not—"

"Yes, I know. 'I'm not your teacher, Lisa'," she finished for him. "But that's how it's going to look. Heaven knows what I'm eventually going to tell my mum. Perhaps I could persuade her that you're the older brother of one of my friends. If you kept your mouth shut, and didn't let out that you're French, maybe she'd believe me..."

Who am I kidding? she thought. How could anyone possibly think that someone this good-looking, sexy, and chic could ever be English?

"Let us not worry about tomorrow," Jean-Luc urged her. "Let us think about tonight! Will you let me take you to the fun-fair?"

Lisa shrugged her shoulders in defeat. How could she – how could anyone – resist Jean-Luc, especially when he was looking at her with those big, pleading eyes of his, eyes which said that his entire future happiness would be destroyed if she didn't say yes?

"Well, OK..." she said, and Jean-Luc beamed and kissed her on the lips. As he drew away from her the door to the classroom clicked open. Lisa turned sharply around as she saw Mr Crowley standing there. He cleared his throat loudly and walked over to the teacher's desk.

Oh no, thought Lisa, what if he saw...

"I've left my books behind," he explained, as he rummaged through the drawers of the desk, seemingly oblivious to what had just been happening in the classroom. As he searched, Jean-Luc winked at Lisa.

See, he seemed to say, there's nothing to worry about at all!

"*Eh bien, Mademoiselle Tyler,*" Jean-Luc said, as Crowley started a conversation with him. "*A bientôt, oui?*"

"OK, Jean-Luc, I'll see you later," said Lisa, and reluctantly gathered up her schoolbooks.

While chattering to Jean-Luc, Crowley was still bent down, looking through the drawers for his misplaced books. Unseen by him Jean-Luc mouthed the words "half-past seven" to Lisa, who nodded and, with a smile of anticipation, left the room.

"Calm down, Lisa," Jean-Luc urged her later that night as he parked his battered 2CV in the car-park of the fairground. "You look as though you are in the middle of committing some great master-crime!"

"That's what I feel like," Lisa said only half-jokingly as she undid her seatbelt and thumped open her door on the passenger side. "Leading my teacher astray and getting him to take me to the fun-fair!"

"Aha," said Jean-Luc, and laughed, "I'm not your teacher – as I seem to keep telling you every minute of every day – and it was my idea to come here. So if anyone can be accused of leading anyone astray then it is me."

He got out of the car and looked searchingly at Lisa. "I do hope Mademoiselle Tyler approves?"

Lisa kissed him briefly on the lips. "Yes, Mademoiselle Tyler certainly *does* approve," she said, and felt a certain thrill kissing Jean-Luc in such a public place.

Unlike London, where they were certain not to bump

into anyone they might know, here in Blackchurch there was always the possibility that they might be seen by one of their friends. It gave the act of kissing each other a strangely pleasant sense of danger. Indeed, while half of Lisa was praying that they wouldn't be seen, the other half was secretly hoping that they would be discovered.

I want people to see us kissing, and loving each other, she thought. I want everyone in the whole wide world to know that I love you, and that you love me! I want to shout it from the rooftops! I want every single person at this fun-fair to see us together and to be jealous of us!

Jean-Luc looked around: already the park on which the fun-fair had camped was packed with young couples enjoying themselves. Trashy music blared from the loudspeaker systems of the various rides, mingling with the screams of pleasure of people on the big wheel and the dodgems. The air was filled with the familiar smells of freshly-cooked toffee apples, candy-floss, and burgers and hot dogs.

"So where do you want to go first?" he asked her.

What does it matter, she thought, as long as it's with you?

She shrugged. "I don't know," she said. "Perhaps the dodgem cars? Or maybe you'd like to win me a cuddly toy or a goldfish on the coconut shy?"

Jean-Luc seemed disappointed in her. "I have a much better idea!" he announced and took her by the hand, leading her through the crowds to the ghost train.

Lisa looked uncertain. "Come on, Jean-Luc!" she said. "Don't you think that I'm a little old for that now!" She looked at the youngsters getting on the ride: the oldest must have been about thirteen.

"One is never too old for the ghost train," Jean-Luc declared as he handed over his pound coins to the man in charge. "In fact the older you are the better!" He pulled Lisa into the last of the cars waiting on the track to enter the ghost train. As she sat down he put his arm around her.

"Now you don't really expect me to be scared by all this?" she asked, as the ghost train started up and they entered the ride.

Jean-Luc, his face very close to hers, shook his head, as they passed through the double doors into the darkened interior.

"Of course not," he said. "But one need not only be scared inside the ghost train..."

Just then, an enormous mechanical bat flew down from the ceiling at them, and Lisa screamed, in spite of herself. She clung to Jean-Luc, who held on to her tightly.

"I thought you said that you wouldn't be scared..." he chided.

Lisa laughed. "I'm not, but..." She looked into Jean-Luc's eyes; even in the dark she could see the lovelight gleam from them.

He moved his lips to hers, kissing her softly in the darkness. His arm slid up and down the small of her back sending tremors of delight throughout her whole body. He kissed her neck, burying his face in her long blonde hair.

Finally Jean-Luc released her from his embrace and looked affectionately down at her as the car rumbled on through the horrors of the ghost train.

"Are you still scared?" he asked.

Lisa pulled him back down onto her lips "Not with you around," she breathed.

"Then you shall never be scared for the rest of your life," he promised her. "I shall look after you – make sure that nothing ever harms you..."

And then he yelped as a skeleton rattled down from the ceiling, frightening the life out of him. His face was as white as a sheet. By his side Lisa burst into a fit of uncontrollable laughter.

"You're going to look after me, Jean-Luc?" she giggled. "Haven't you got that the wrong way round?"

"We will look after each other," he decided, and pulled Lisa close to him once more, and they melted gratefully and lovingly into each other's arms.

*　*　*

"Well, I'm waiting, Jean-Luc," Lisa said as she tapped her foot in mock irritation by the rifle range. "I want my cuddly toy!"

Beside her Jean-Luc was peering down the sights of a rifle at the rifle range, trying to hit the moving ducks before him. He had boldly declared that he was going to win a teddy bear for Lisa at the rifle range and had discovered after he had paid his two pounds that as a marksman he was hopeless. He bit his lips, trying to concentrate, and fired, missing the moving ducks by feet. He sighed, and looked over to Lisa who was shaking her head in disappointment.

"I fall in love with the man—" she mused out loud.

In love! I finally said it!

"—and he can't even win me a cuddly toy."

Jean-Luc looked genuinely disappointed, which only made Lisa's heart go out to him even more.

"Alas," he said, "if I cannot win a teddy bear for the fair lady then perhaps she will not want me any more! How can she love someone who cannot even shoot straight!"

Caught up in the moment, Lisa pulled Jean-Luc over to her, and kissed him. She was suddenly serious.

"I love you for what you are, Jean-Luc," she said, surprising herself by her own boldness. "*And* for what you're not. You're not perfect – and neither am I. And that's what love is all about – recognizing a person's imperfections and *still* loving them."

"You're a very wise person, Lisa," Jean-Luc said and was about to embrace her once more when a familiar voice made Lisa freeze.

"Lisa! Jean-Luc! What a surprise!"

Oh no, thought Lisa, now we're done for!

Stuart Richardson, the blond-haired prize student from Lisa's French class, and his girlfriend, the willowy Helen, were standing in front of them.

"Er, hello, Stuart," said Jean-Luc while by his side Lisa flushed with embarrassment.

We've been found out now! Lisa said to herself. I knew it was too good to last...

"What are you two doing here?" he asked.

Long seconds passed. "I ... I was here with Chrissie, and lost her," she lied, making a mental note to ring Chrissie the minute she got home so that she could confirm her story tomorrow. "And then I bumped into Jean-Luc ... isn't that right, Jean-Luc?"

Jean-Luc nodded. "And as I was alone we decided to spend some time at the fair together ... looking for Chrissie..."

Stuart frowned, as though he suspected that there was something not quite right with this explanation. "Oh, I see..." he said, plainly not seeing at all. He looked suspiciously at Lisa and Jean-Luc, and was about to say something when Helen pulled his arm.

"Come on, Stuart," she said. "I want to go on the ghost train!"

"You'll love that!" enthused Lisa. "We've just—" She corrected herself just in time – "Chrissie and I went on it before we got separated from each other..."

As Stuart let himself be led off by his girlfriend, Lisa breathed a sigh of relief while Jean-Luc just chuckled softly to himself. "That was close," she said. "I thought you said that the homework you set would keep everyone in tonight!"

"Aha, but Stuart is the top student in my class," Jean-Luc admitted, clearly not as perturbed by Stuart's meeting them as Lisa was. "If not the most important one..."

"At least it was him," Lisa said gratefully. "He's so besotted with Helen that he'll forget about the whole thing in ten minutes..."

Jean-Luc was looking around the fun-fair at the amazing selection of garish rides. He suddenly grabbed Lisa's hand and pulled her into the crowds.

"Jean-Luc, where are we going?" she asked.

"The perfect place to be alone," he said merrily, like an

enthusiastic little boy going on his holidays. "I know the very place!"

Laughing and giggling Lisa followed as Jean-Luc pushed his way through the crowds to the Big Wheel. As Jean-Luc handed over his money to the operator Lisa looked up apprehensively at the Big Wheel. Jean-Luc took advantage of this to quickly slip the man a ten-pound note and whisper something into his ear.

"I don't know..." she said doubtfully. 'It's very high..." Lisa had always been a little scared of heights.

Jean-Luc put his arm around her waist and led her to one of the waiting buggies. "I shall protect you!" he said dramatically, like a cavalier in an old movie, as the operator made sure that they were securely fastened into the buggy. Jean-Luc winked conspiratorially at him. "With me by your side nothing can go wrong!"

With a grating and a clunk of gears the Big Wheel slowly began to creak into action, and the buggy containing Jean-Luc and Lisa started to rise into the air. Lisa trembled as the Wheel gathered speed, and let Jean-Luc pull her even more tightly to his warm and reassuring body. He kissed her.

"See?" he said, and glanced to the two empty buggies in front and behind them. "Up here we are alone: there is no one to come and interrupt us! Scared now, Mademoiselle Tyler?" Jean-Luc asked.

"Not when I'm with you." She smiled, and then gasped as the buggy began to descend. "I think I've just left my stomach behind!" she laughed.

"No problem," said Jean-Luc. "We will just retrieve it on the next turn round."

The Big Wheel turned and Jean-Luc and Lisa's buggy began to rise again. By now Lisa was enjoying herself enormously: the thrill of the ride and the reassuring and loving presence of Jean-Luc beside her made for a wonderful experience.

They had just reached the top of the Wheel again when something seemed to go wrong. Their buggy lurched and shuddered, and the Big Wheel suddenly came to a jerky halt. A moan of noisy complaint came from the people riding in the other buggies.

"Jean-Luc!" Lisa said nervously, as they sat there in their buggy, suspended at the very top of the Big Wheel. "What's happened?"

"We've stopped," he said, rather unnecessarily. "Perhaps there's something wrong with the ride..."

Lisa noticed that Jean-Luc didn't seem overly concerned. "You mean we're stuck up here?"

Jean-Luc nodded, and kissed her on the cheek. "There's nothing to worry about," he reassured her. "I'm sure the operator will get it working again soon..."

Or in five minutes' time, to be precise, he thought. After all, that was the time we agreed on!

"Now sit back and relax, Lisa," he urged her. "Enjoy the view..."

"It's beautiful," said Lisa. From the top of the Wheel they had a magnificent view of the entire area. In the distance she could see the lights of Blackchurch town and farther off the lights of Applewood; and beyond them the black outline of the hills. Up here the stars seemed even closer and twinkled even more brightly.

She snuggled close to Jean-Luc, and smelt fresh roses and finely starched linen.

"I love you," she said. "When I'm with you nothing else matters... It doesn't matter that I'm not as attractive as someone like Alison..."

"Lisa," said Jean-Luc matter-of-factly. "Alison is merely attractive. You are beautiful." He stroked her blonde hair with his free hand.

Lisa smiled. "It doesn't matter that we have to keep our relationship a secret from the whole of Applewood..."

"Not up here we don't," he pointed out, and kissed her deeply on the lips. He glanced down at the revellers on the ground; they seemed like ants. "No one can see us up here."

"It doesn't even matter that we're stuck at the top of the Big Wheel!"

"Of course not," he agreed. "In fact at the moment there is no place I would rather be." He kissed her again and then turned her face gently to one side. He pointed to a streak of light in the sky. "Look, Lisa," he whispered. "A shooting star."

Lisa pooh-poohed Jean-Luc's suggestion. "Don't be silly!" she laughed. "It's not a shooting star; it's a firework. One of the men from the fun-fair must be letting them off."

Jean-Luc turned her face back to his and wagged an admonishing finger.

"Typically English! So unromantic!" he laughed. "You say it is a firework." He shook his head. "Well, I am French and I say that it is a shooting star. So a shooting star it shall be!"

Lisa chuckled; she could love this man to death! "OK, Jean-Luc, if you say so!"

"And in my country, whenever we see a shooting star we must make a wish," he said. He took Lisa in both his arms and held her fast. "And what do you wish for, Lisa?" he asked.

"Nothing..."

Jean-Luc frowned. "Nothing?" he asked. "One should not let an opportunity like a shooting star pass by so easily!"

Lisa looked into Jean-Luc's deep brown eyes. "There's nothing I want to wish for, Jean-Luc," she said and snuggled closer to him. "Because I have it all. I have you – and I realize that that's all I've ever really wanted. I love you, Jean-Luc."

"And I love you too, Lisa," he whispered, bringing his lips to hers. "And I will never ever let you go."

They kissed and kissed and kissed, holding each other tight, and staring deep into each other's eyes. They became oblivious to everything but each other, so that they didn't even notice when the Big Wheel creaked into motion again, and began its slow descent to the ground.

For Lisa and Jean-Luc there was only each other, alone together, floating high in the warm night sky, the only witness to their love the bright and boundless stars.

15

Alison Potter looked stunning this morning, Lisa and Chrissie decided, as the redhead waltzed confidently into the French classroom. (This was particularly galling as she had taken Monday off 'sick' – though Chrissie and Lisa suspected she'd been up rather too late on Sunday evening...) The class flirt normally wore outrageous, figure-hugging trendy clothes, which would make Cher seem overdressed and dowdy, and which blatantly displayed all the goods she had on offer to any interested boy (and with a good deal of success, it has to be said).

Today, however, she was wearing loose designer trousers, and an equally baggy but stylish white blouse. It was a drastic change of image, and ironically one which, while hiding everything that she normally flaunted, made her even more attractive. So successful was it that every man this morning – from the milkman on the doorstep to the school caretaker in the playground – hadn't been able to take his eyes off her.

She's up to something, thought Chrissie, as Alison waved at her and Lisa and sat down near them.

"Talk about a change of image," she whispered to Lisa. "From Supertart to Miss Demure overnight!"

Lisa, still on cloud nine from her visit to the fairground last night, just nodded and continued to stare thoughtfully at Alison.

She remembered something Jean-Luc had once said to her: "People who go about flaunting themselves are usually very superficial. I'm just not interested in them, no matter how attractive they might be."

An awful thought struck her: was Alison about to make another play for Jean-Luc?

Well, just let her try, Lisa thought, with a confidence she would never have felt until a few days ago. Jean-Luc has said he loves me. And she's definitely not his type. And there's nothing Alison Potter or anyone else in the whole world can do to change that.

The door to the classroom opened and Crowley walked in, followed by Jean-Luc. As they walked over to the teacher's desk, Jean-Luc turned to Lisa who was sitting in the front row, and gave her a tiny, almost imperceptible wink.

Lisa welled up with joy, delighting in their shared secret. But by her side Chrissie had also noticed Jean-Luc's gesture and instantly realized what had happened between the two of them.

And, unfortunately, so had Alison. And something inside the man-mad sixth-former seemed to snap.

An hour later when the lesson had ended and the class began to pack up their books and move on to their next lesson, Lisa went up to the teacher's desk where Jean-Luc was busy in conversation with Crowley. (They were speaking in English as Crowley had realized that, even though he was head of the modern languages department of Applewood, his French would never be as fluent as it should be.)

"*Eh bien, bonjour, Mademoiselle Tyler,*" Jean-Luc said, and immediately regretted his mistake. He had called Lisa by her surname – when everyone in the entire school knew that he preferred to call every last one of his students by their first name! Why should he single Lisa out for such special treatment, unless he had something to hide?

He glanced over at Crowley. The French teacher was

busy collecting up his books and class registers and didn't seem to have noticed anything. Jean-Luc kicked himself: he was just being paranoid!

"I've just been glancing at your homework," he said. "Your translation of Molière was very good..."

That's hardly surprising! thought Lisa. As you helped me out with it!

"Er ... thank you for an interesting lesson, Jean-Luc," began Lisa, observing Crowley out of the corner of her eye.

"*Je vous en prie, mademoiselle,*" said Jean-Luc awkwardly. "Don't mention it..." He also darted a covert look over at the elderly French teacher who was taking an unbearably long time to leave the classroom.

Finally, after what seemed like hours of forced casual talk between Lisa and Jean-Luc – and what had actually only been thirty seconds – Crowley said: "Well, Monsieur Roupie, I'll see you this afternoon with the third form, shall I?"

"*Oui, Monsieur Crowley,*" Jean-Luc said, and breathed a sigh of relief as the French teacher left the room. He turned round and grinned at Lisa.

"I've missed you," he whispered.

"You only said goodbye to me last night!" Lisa chuckled.

Jean-Luc fixed her with those hopeless puppy-dog eyes of his. "I know," he said. "I still missed you though."

Lisa looked briefly around to make sure that no one was eavesdropping on their conversation. Chrissie was looking curiously at them, but turned away when her eyes caught Lisa's.

"Well, I missed you too," she admitted. "I haven't been able to think of anything else but you..."

"By the way, did you meet your friend from university the other day?" asked Jean-Luc.

"My friend?" asked Lisa and then realized who Jean-Luc was talking about. "Oh yes, my friend ... yes, I met them..." she said, careful not to reveal her friend's sex.

Jean-Luc looked searchingly at his girlfriend. "Lisa, is

there anything wrong?"

"Wrong?" she asked, flustered. "Of course there's nothing wrong!"

Damn! Why hadn't she told him she was meeting James on Sunday evening? she asked herself furiously. There's nothing that I should feel guilty about! If he found out now he'd be certain that I was trying to hide something from him!

"When will I see you again?" she asked.

"Wednesday's French lesson?" he suggested, teasing her.

"You know what I mean!" Lisa smiled. "It's going to be so difficult getting a quiet moment with you at school."

"Ring me tonight," he suggested, "and we'll make a date." He took a piece of paper out of his folder, on which he scribbled down his telephone number, and passed it to Lisa. "I'll be waiting. And Lisa—"

"Yes?"

He looked deeply into her eyes. "I love—"

At that moment Alison, who had stayed behind in the classroom packing her books away into her smart leather backpack, came up to them.

"That will be all then, Mademoiselle Tyler," said Jean-Luc hurriedly.

"What's this?" asked Alison suspiciously, as Lisa quickly put the piece of paper in the back pocket of her jeans. "Love letters from the teacher?"

"Don't be silly, Alison!" Lisa laughed nervously, and added rather unconvincingly: "They're just the titles of some French books Jean-Luc's recommended to me..."

"Very conscientious I must say," said Alison snidely, giving Lisa a look which clearly said that she didn't believe a word of what she'd just been told.

Jean-Luc made a great show of looking at his Swatch. "I must go," he said to Lisa and added, purely for Alison's benefit: "I have a fourth-year class..."

"Goodbye, Jean-Luc," said Alison sweetly.

Lisa smiled weakly. "Goodbye, Jean-Luc..."

As soon as Jean-Luc had left the classroom Alison stared accusingly at Lisa. She folded her arms, the way the school principal did when a student was giving a particularly unconvincing excuse for being absent from school.

"OK then, Lisa, what are you playing at?"

"'Playing at'? I don't know what you're talking about," said Lisa, knowing perfectly well just what Alison was talking about.

"You don't seriously expect me to believe that French Delight's just given you a list of books to read in French?"

"Of ... of course he has," Lisa stammered. "What else would he give me?"

Alison didn't answer.

"So where were you on Saturday?" she demanded.

Lisa frowned. Surely there was no way that Alison could have found out that she and Jean-Luc had spent the day in London together?

"I went down to London with Chrissie," she said, repeating the story she had told her mother. "We went window-shopping..."

Alison tutted, shaking her head as though she was disappointed by Lisa's story.

"You'll have to do better than that, Lisa," she said. "You see, I rang you up on Saturday – I needed some help with my French homework – and that's what your mum told me ... that you were down in London with Chrissie..."

Lisa shrugged. "So? That is what I was doing. What's the big problem?"

Alison smiled sadistically: she was obviously enjoying Lisa's discomfort. "The trouble is, Lisa, I met Chrissie for a coffee at Brucianni's on Saturday..."

"Ah..." Lisa suddenly wished that the ground would open up and swallow her. "Well ... er ... you see..." She searched her mind frantically for a half-way convincing explanation of her behaviour.

"Yes, Lisa?" Alison glared defiantly at Lisa, daring her to come up with a believable story.

"Look, Alison," she began in a comradely all-girls-together tone of voice, "swear you won't tell a soul, but you remember James…"

"How could I forget him?" said Alison, and added evilly: "I remember the two of you under the mistletoe at my Christmas party."

"Well, I met him over the weekend, and we went down to London together," she lied. "And because I didn't want anyone to know I told my mum that I was going down to London with Chrissie…"

Alison looked at Lisa through narrowed, disbelieving eyes.

"Oh, of course that must be it," she said sarcastically.

Lisa breathed a sigh of relief; for a moment she believed that Alison was going to buy her story. And then she added: "And I suppose you were with James on Friday night as well…"

"Friday night?" Lisa asked urgently.

Alison smiled and nodded her head.

"In the front seat of a certain green 2CV outside your front door. In the biggest clinch I've ever seen. Talk about tongue-tennis *à la française*! Come on, Lisa, get real! Don't pretend to me that you went down to London with boring old train-spotter James. It was Jean-Luc, wasn't it? You two are having an affair!"

"We are not having an affair!" Lisa protested. "We only spent the weekend together…" she protested, instantly regretting what she'd said, and how it might sound to someone like Alison.

"Aha! So I was right, wasn't I?"

"Look, Alison, keep it to yourself," Lisa pleaded. "If anyone finds out about us Jean-Luc is going to be in *big* trouble. He might even lose his job…"

"Yes, he might, mightn't he?" said Alison, regarding Lisa with a challenging look. "And what's more, if anyone were to hear that you were going out with the French teacher—"

"He's not a teacher," Lisa said automatically.

"If anyone were to hear that you were going out with the French *teacher*," Alison continued, "not only would he lose his job, and be sent back to France, but you might even be expelled."

Lisa felt her heart sinking and her legs shaking. She regarded Alison warily. Was the foxy redhead actually threatening her? She knew that Alison had been piqued when Jean-Luc had spurned her attentions, but would even she go this far?

"What are you trying to say, Alison?" she demanded nervously.

"Just one careless word, Lisa, that's all it would take ... and it could happen so easily..."

"Are you threatening me?"

"As a matter of fact, yes," said Alison with all the affected sweetness of a King Cobra ready to strike. "Stay away from Jean-Luc, Lisa," she commanded. "He's not the one for someone like you."

"Someone like me!" Lisa snapped, uncharacteristically losing her temper. "Excuse me, Alison, but I don't see him taking you down to London for the day, or to the seaside! You tried your best to get your little claws into him and he showed absolutely no interest whatsoever! He doesn't just want someone who looks like she stepped out of a fashion magazine – he wants someone with a few brain cells to rub together as well!"

Alison stood there, unaffected by Lisa's sudden outburst.

"If I can't have him, Lisa, then no one else can," she declared evenly. "So if I so much as glimpse you two together again, if I even catch you staring dreamily into each other's eyes, then I'm going straight to the principal – to tell her all about our randy unprofessional French *teacher* who's gone and seduced one of his pupils! And if you tell Jean-Luc about it, well, I'll do it just the same!"

"You wouldn't dare!" said Lisa, although deep down she knew that Alison was perfectly capable of carrying out her threat.

"Just try me," said Alison sweetly, as she slung her bag over her shoulder, and stalked out of the classroom.

"Lisa, is there anything wrong?" Jean-Luc asked, later that night. Even though he was at the other end of the phone Lisa could almost see the look of concern on his face. She glanced up guiltily at the clock in the hallway where the phone was: it was a quarter to ten.

"Wrong, Jean-Luc?" she asked nervously. "Of course there's nothing wrong. Why should there be?"

"It's just that you promised this morning to ring me at home," he reminded her. "When you didn't I became worried."

"Jean-Luc, I'm sorry – I must have forgotten," she lied.

"Forgotten?" There was a sense of worried urgency in her boyfriend's voice.

"I've ... uh ... had so many things on my mind," Lisa flustered.

"Don't spend all your time on your schoolwork," Jean-Luc's unsuspecting voice laughed down the line. "I thought I'd cured you of that!"

"Yeah, well..." Lisa clenched her teeth; she hated doing this. But she believed Alison's threat: she had to protect herself, and Jean-Luc.

"Look it's not yet ten o'clock," Jean-Luc said. "Maybe I could drive round to your place and we could go and have a drink at The Lamb and Flag on the corner of your road!"

"You know I don't drink, Jean-Luc," Lisa said. What if Alison and her friends were drinking in the pub, as they were more than likely to be doing?

"Well, neither do I," he replied. "So we'll just have to share an orange juice and two straws there, won't we?"

There was nothing in the world that Lisa would have liked to have been doing more.

Instead she said: "Look, Jean-Luc, thanks for the offer ... but I've got such a headache ... I really think I ought to take an aspirin and get an early night..."

There was a disappointed silence at the end of the line. Finally Jean-Luc said: "Fine, Lisa, if that's how you feel..."

No, you gorgeous, gullible lovable Frenchman, that is not how I feel! Lisa longed to scream out.

"Yeah ... an early night might do me good..."

"Very well. Perhaps tomorrow night then?" he suggested. "Maybe we could go and see a movie..."

"Maybe, Jean-Luc," Lisa replied. "I'll see you in school tomorrow..."

"*Bien sûr*," he said and paused for a moment. "And Lisa?"

"Yes, Jean-Luc?"

"I love you."

Lisa felt her whole being tremble. The very words she had longed to hear all her life!

"And I love you too," she said, and softly put down the receiver.

She lifted her eyes heavenwards and swore to herself.

Of course I love you, she said. And there's no one else I'd rather be going out with tonight, or tomorrow night, or for the rest of my life, for that matter. But for the next two weeks if Alison finds out that we're seeing each other it's going to be the end for both of us!

16

The French class the following morning was sheer torture for Lisa. Standing in front of the class, Jean-Luc was so near to her, and yet so unattainable.

She longed to rush out from behind her desk, and hold him in her arms; who cared what the rest of the class, the rest of the school, indeed the rest of the world thought? But sitting just a few places away from her was Alison, watching Lisa and Jean-Luc like an evil vulture ready to swoop down on her prey.

At the end of the period Jean-Luc called Lisa over to his desk. As Lisa approached him nervously she felt Alison's green witch-eyes boring into her back.

"*Eh bien, Mademoiselle Tyler*," Jean-Luc began, and consulted the class register pretending he was discussing Lisa's grades. "And how are you feeling this morning?"

Lisa cast a wary sideways glance at Alison who was watching her. "Fine, Jean-Luc," she said.

"And how is your headache this morning?"

"My headache?" Lisa was puzzled.

"Yes, you said on the telephone that you had a headache," he whispered. "That's why you couldn't go out with me last night..."

"Oh of course, my headache!" Lisa remembered. "It's much better now!"

Jean-Luc frowned. He had the oddest suspicion that there was something Lisa wasn't telling him.

"Are you sure everything's all right?"

"Of course," she nodded furiously, as Alison walked past them and gave Jean-Luc a friendly wave. Jean-Luc waved back, and looked admiringly after the departing redhead.

"She dresses much better now," he said. "Less of those tight figure-hugging clothes. I wonder if she's finally realized that she's much more attractive when she's not being quite so forward all the time..."

Don't you believe that, Lisa shocked herself by thinking; even if she was wearing a nun's habit and acting like Mother Teresa there's no getting away from the fact that Alison Potter can be a scheming witch when she sets her mind to it! If she's dressing much more conservatively now you can bet that she's got an ulterior motive! And only you, you stupid crazy trusting Frenchman, who always likes to see the best in everyone, can't see that!

The classroom was now empty apart from her and Jean-Luc. He stood up and moved to Lisa's side of the desk.

"Maybe now that you're feeling better we can go out tonight," he suggested. "There's a new French movie showing at the art cinema." He raised his arms to embrace Lisa, but she froze at his touch.

"Lisa, what's the matter?" he asked, totally bewildered.

Lisa avoided his eyes. "Let's just play it cool for the next couple of weeks, Jean-Luc, OK?" she said, trying hard to keep her voice steady. Jean-Luc released her from his embrace.

God, I want you to hold me so much, she said to herself. I want you to hold me and just never let me go!

"It's all right," he said and tried to hold her again; she shrugged him off. "No one will see us..."

No one, only Alison Potter! she thought, and looked at her watch.

"Jean-Luc, I'm going to be late for my next class," she said in a trembling voice. "I'll see you later, OK?"

And with that she marched quickly through the open

door so that Jean-Luc wouldn't see the tears, already welling up in her blue eyes. Behind her, Jean-Luc stood alone in the middle of the empty classroom, dumbfounded and deserted as the girl he loved ran off down the corridor.

Unseen by either of them in the corridor Alison smirked. Everything, so far, was going perfectly according to plan...

If that morning had been sheer torture for Lisa then the rest of the week was a living hell. Whenever she and Jean-Luc were together, either in the classroom or even meeting casually in the corridor Alison seemed always to be there, too, watching them like a hawk.

Even when she wasn't there physically her presence poisoned Lisa's life at school. She longed to tell Jean-Luc of the threat the redhead had made towards her; but she was also afraid of the consequences. Alison Potter spurned was capable of anything.

Jean-Luc, for his part, was confused and depressed. Every time he asked Lisa if there was anything wrong, she would rapidly change the subject. Every time he tried to touch her, even on the arm, or kiss her in welcome, as all French people do, her body would become tense, and she would pull away, as though his very touch repulsed her.

Alison, on the other hand, had changed for the better. Jean-Luc noticed her more and more. Her style of dressing had become much more understated, and her former brazenness – which he detested in all women – now seemed but a dim memory. He had always known how physically attractive the sexy redhead was (no man at Applewood could fail to notice that!) but now that it seemed that she had given up any thoughts of pursuing him she seemed much more likeable too. Over the next few days he found himself having friendly chats or sharing a slightly risqué joke with her; she was, he decided, quite a nice girl after all.

But Lisa was still his main concern. Over the next few days she had used a variety of excuses for not seeing him after school. She had another headache, she had claimed, or too much homework, or she had to accompany her mother to visit an elderly aunt. On Friday he thought he had finally succeeded: he had managed to get her to agree to meet him at Brucianni's coffee shop on Saturday evening. But at the very last moment she had phoned him to cancel: she had an essay to finish for Miss Greenwood, the Biology teacher, she'd said, and hurriedly hung up the phone, before he'd had a chance to question her.

So it happened that on Sunday evening there was an urgent knock on Lisa's front door. Maddy opened it, and silently gasped in appreciation, as she sized up the hunk on the doorstep.

If only I was twenty years younger, she thought to herself.

"Good evening, Mrs Tyler," said Jean-Luc. "Is Lisa in?"

Maddy glanced behind her. Lisa was standing in the hallway.

"It's OK, Mum," she said. Maddy stood aside to let Jean-Luc pass, sizing him up appreciatively: the square, determined jaw, the full lips and the shock of black hair; his strong wide shoulders and slim waist, forming the classic 'V' shape. She approved her daughter's good taste; that, at least, was one thing that Lisa had inherited from her mother!

She casually wondered why she'd never noticed him before; Lisa had hinted that she had met an older student from the nearby technical institute, and Maddy was surprised that she hadn't seen him on her way to work which passed by the institute.

Lisa led Jean-Luc into the living room, and closed the door so that Maddy wouldn't hear. She took a deep breath: she wasn't looking forward to what was coming.

"All right, Lisa," said Jean-Luc. "I think I deserve some explanations."

"Explanations?"

"Yes," he said, and there was a note of anger in his voice

as well as a touch of sadness. "You've been avoiding me all week. I ask you to stay behind after class so we can talk, and you suddenly remember that you have a Chemistry assignment to complete. I ring you up to invite you out to the cinema, and you have another of your 'headaches'. And last night, when you finally agree to meet me at Brucianni's, you stand me up..."

"I had a Biology essay to finish for Miss Greenwood, I told you," Lisa said.

Jean-Luc shook his head. "No you didn't, Lisa," he stated quite categorically. "You see I rang Miss Greenwood this morning—"

"You've been checking up on me!" Lisa exclaimed.

"I rang her up about something totally different," he said. "But she told me that, as the school's summer ball is next week, she'd decided not to set any homework for any of her sixth-form classes..."

"Ah..." Lisa hung her head guiltily.

"You lied to me, Lisa," he said, and now there was real pain and anguish in his voice. "What is it? Don't you want to see me any more?"

"No, it's not that..." said Lisa, trying to avoid her boyfriend's eyes.

"Then what is it?" he demanded. "Are you in any sort of trouble? I love you, Lisa, and all I want to do is to help you if I can."

"I'm not in any sort of trouble, Jean-Luc," she reassured him.

"Then tell me what's wrong?"

Don't you think I want to tell you? Don't you think that I want to fall into your arms right now? Don't you think that I want the whole world to know that you love me and I love you!

"Jean-Luc, don't ask me," she pleaded. "Wait until term's over, and then we can sort things out..."

"I don't know if I can wait that long, Lisa," he said sadly. "You see, I believe in absolute honesty in a relationship..."

"Don't you think I do?" she snapped. I'm doing all this for you, she thought. Don't make it even harder on me!

"Then why can't you tell me why you've been avoiding me all week?" he asked. "I thought we had something special between us. That last weekend we spent together was one of the happiest of my life."

And mine, she thought.

"Another week, Jean-Luc," she said, "until term's over. That's all I'm asking you..."

Jean-Luc sighed and looked at Lisa through saddened and disappointed eyes. "Maybe you don't want to see me now?" he said, and added cruelly: "Maybe now that you've won the 'trophy' of going out with 'French Delight' you've lost interest in me?"

"No, Jean-Luc, no," she said, tears welling up in her eyes.

Jean-Luc moved towards the door. "No matter what you've done I still love you, Lisa," he said.

"And I love you too, Jean-Luc..."

He turned around and looked coldly at her. His big brown eyes were glistening.

"Well, you have a funny way of showing it, Lisa," he said and left the room.

Jean-Luc normally didn't touch alcohol, apart from the occasional glass of red wine at meal-times, but tonight he decided he definitely needed a drink. He drove from Lisa's house to the nearby Lamb and Flag, and ordered himself a pint of lager.

Fifteen minutes later he shook his head, as he stared down at his almost empty pint glass. He couldn't understand Lisa at all, he decided. He loved her and she said she loved him; he had thought they were soulmates, bonded together not just by the same interests and passions, but by an indefinable *oneness*, each one half of the same coin. But how could he say that when Lisa wouldn't tell him what was troubling her or why she was avoiding him so much?

He walked over to the bar slightly unsteadily; if he wasn't careful he was going to get drunk.

And what if I do? he thought angrily. I find the one girl I really love and think I might want to spend the rest of my life with and now she's trying to get rid of me!

There was a friendly tap on his shoulder, and he turned around to see the beaming face of Alison Potter.

"Hello, Jean-Luc," she said brightly. "Fancy meeting you here! What a coincidence – I was coming in here to meet some friends."

In fact it had been no coincidence at all. Alison had been walking home from a friend's house when she had noticed Jean-Luc's distinctive green 2CV parked in the pub's forecourt.

"Nice to see you, Alison," he said, genuinely meaning it. "Can I get you a drink?"

"The French teacher getting me a drink?" Alison said coyly, and grinned. "I'm only seventeen, you know. I'm not supposed to touch alcohol yet..." Which has never stopped me before, the redhead added to herself.

"Well, let's bend the rules a little this time," Jean-Luc suggested cheekily. "What would you like?"

"Oh, just a pineapple juice," Alison said. As Jean-Luc ordered the drink, the barman raised an enquiring eyebrow at Alison. This was the first time she had ever had anything non-alcoholic in this pub. Who could she possibly be out to impress this time?

Jean-Luc's seat had been taken by the time they returned from the bar and so they had to sit around a small table in a darkened corner of the pub. Soon they were chatting quite comfortably about general tittle-tattle and their likes and dislikes.

Jean-Luc was surprised to hear that Alison had been to the local art cinema the previous day to see a new French film, and she delighted in telling him all about it. The truth was that she had read a review of the movie in the local paper, and was merely repeating almost verbatim what the paper's reviewer had said.

No matter, she thought. It was obvious that Jean-Luc was impressed and believed he was discovering a previously undetected part of Alison's character.

Inevitably, by the time Jean-Luc had bought another lager and a pineapple juice, talk had got on to school. Alison asked Jean-Luc if he was going to the summer ball and disco next week.

"Alas!" he laughed, and gave her his sad puppy-dog smile, which he knew few women could resist. "No one has invited me!"

"You poor thing!" laughed Alison. *"Quelle dommage!"* She patted his knee in a sympathetic gesture. And left her hand there just a half-second longer than was proper.

"Maybe I should ask Miss Rutherford," he said, referring to the older teacher who had a crush on him.

Alison giggled at the thought of the fat maths teacher bopping the night away. "Can you imagine her dancing to the latest from the Lower Depths?" she asked.

"I can't imagine *myself* dancing to the latest from the Lower Depths either," Jean-Luc smiled. "I hate them..."

"That's funny, so do I," said Alison, who was the Lower Depths' number-one fan. "And don't feel so bad about no one inviting you," she continued, "no one's invited me either..."

"I find that difficult to believe, Alison," said Jean-Luc, slurring his words just a little now as the alcohol started to take effect. "You're a very attractive girl..."

Alison laughed self-deprecatingly. "I feel left on the shelf," she laughed, and gave an exaggerated sigh. "Everyone's got a partner – apart from poor little me. Stuart Richardson's going with Helen Wilkinson, of course. Even Simon's going with Chrissie – although I think she only agreed to do it out of the kindness of her heart – I mean, who'd want to be seen dead with Si?" She eyed Jean-Luc warily, and took a deep breath.

"And of course Lisa will be going there with James—"

"What?" Jean-Luc asked urgently.

"Lisa Tyler," Alison replied. "She'll probably be taking James. He's back down from university for the summer holidays…"

"Who's James?"

"Oh, didn't you know?" asked Alison, all innocence. "They've been going out together since my Christmas party: you should have seen them under the mistletoe… They're practically engaged…"

Jean-Luc's face went white. "'And when did James come back from university?" he asked.

Alison pretended to consider the matter.

"Let me see," she began and stroked her chin thoughtfully. "It must have been last week… Why, Jean-Luc, what's the matter?"

Jean-Luc was staring into space: there was a tear in his eye which he angrily brushed away. Everything had suddenly fallen into place – or so he thought: Lisa's offhandedness with him, her avoiding him and cancelling their date – it was all because James, her real boyfriend, had returned!

Lisa Tyler had made a total idiot of him! How she and James must have been laughing at him behind his back! He felt used and betrayed – and very, very angry. He took a long drink of his beer, and felt the alcohol go to his head.

"How would you feel, Alison," he said, "if someone you trusted completely, someone you thought cared for you – even loved you – suddenly went out and betrayed you? Made you a laughing stock?"

Alison looked into Jean-Luc's eyes, her face a picture of concern. She laid a sympathetic hand on his arm.

"I'd feel hurt and shattered, Jean-Luc," she said softly. "But I'd realize that life goes on. You've got to pick yourself up and get on with your life…" She began to massage his arm tenderly.

"So what if some girl has left you?" she continued. "If she was mad enough to do that then she's not worth your worrying about her."

"You're very kind, Alison," he said. Alison's face was now only a few inches away from his; she was smiling kindly at him, and her striking green eyes gazed longingly into his.

Softly their lips came together in an intense and passionate kiss. It was the sort of kiss that Alison was an expert at, and Jean-Luc felt himself being drawn into her embrace as a swimmer would be sucked into a whirlpool – or as a fly being dragged into the spider's web.

When Alison finally came up for air, she smiled. "I shouldn't be doing this," she said chastely. "Kissing my teacher in the pub..."

"I'm not your teacher, Alison," Jean-Luc told her, now noticeably slurring his words, and drew her closer to him.

Half an hour and several long and passionate embraces later, Alison made a great show of looking at her watch. It was late and it was time to go home, if she wanted to get up in time for school tomorrow.

"But what about the friends you were supposed to meet here?" asked Jean-Luc.

"Friends?" asked Alison, and then remembered the story she had told Jean-Luc. "Oh, it looks as though they changed their minds at the last minute." She looked lovingly at him. "And I'm glad they did. Otherwise I wouldn't have met you..."

Jean-Luc shakily rose to his feet. "Let me drive you home," he offered.

Alison shook her head. "You've drunk too much," she reminded him, and took him by the hand. "There's a taxi rank just down the road. I can get you a cab to take you home..."

They left the pub hand-in-hand, and as they waited for a taxi embraced once more – another long, deep and passionate kiss. Alison ran her fingers down Jean-Luc's back, sending tingles of delight down the Frenchman's spine.

"I feel so depressed and let-down, Alison," he confessed.

"And I don't think I can face being alone tonight..."

"You'll feel better in the morning," Alison reassured him. "Much better..."

The following morning Jean-Luc drove into the school car park after having picked the 2CV up from the pub forecourt. As chance would have it he arrived just as Lisa and Chrissie were walking across the car park to the main school building. They both stopped and stared in amazement as Jean-Luc stepped out and sheepishly went around to the passenger side to allow Alison out.

Alison noticed Lisa and Chrissie and made a great show of kissing Jean-Luc passionately on the lips. Jean-Luc went off to the staffroom, but Alison crossed over to Lisa and Chrissie. There was an unbelievably triumphant smile on her face: it was instantly obvious to the other two what Alison was smiling about.

"Hi there, girls," she said smugly.

"Alison, you haven't ... you didn't..." Chrissie marvelled, briefly oblivious of Lisa's feelings.

Lisa was shaking, and darting a look of pure hatred at Alison.

Alison shrugged, and grinned enigmatically, a move which was calculated to say it all.

"I'll see you later," she said cheerfully. "I got up *sooooo* late this morning and I'm late for a class." She began to move away, and, as she passed by Lisa, whispered in her ear.

"I won," she said simply and cruelly. "And you lost."

17

"**H**ow could he do it, Chrissie?" Lisa asked through her tears as they sat on a bench on the lawn outside the Applewood school building. Fellow students, cheerful and bright in the early morning summer sunshine, stopped to look at her and whisper amongst themselves; but for once in her life Lisa couldn't care less what people thought of her. Her eyes were red and she let the tears run freely.

As soon as Alison had walked out of sight, Lisa had given voice to her emotions and broken down in tears. Chrissie had led her to the bench where Lisa poured out the whole story to her best friend in one long painful sob.

"We don't know what happened," said Chrissie. "They came into school together – so what?"

Lisa looked up. "Don't pretend, Chrissie," she said. "We both of us know what the truth is..."

Chrissie wasn't convinced, but said softly: "Don't blame Jean-Luc. It's that scheming cow Alison's fault. She'll stop at nothing to get what she wants, and she doesn't care who gets hurt..."

"But what's going to happen to Jean-Luc now?" Lisa asked. Even in the midst of her own terrible anguish Lisa was still concerned with her boyfriend's welfare and reputation.

"With a little bit of luck, nothing," Chrissie decided. "If

Alison wants to hold on to Jean-Luc then it's going to be in her own best interests to keep this thing as quiet as possible."

"But he can't love her," Lisa protested.

Chrissie hugged her friend. "Of course he doesn't," she reassured her. "But that's how men are — when they feel they've been betrayed they'll run to the first person who shows them any sign of affection. And when that person is a manipulative witch like Alison Potter..."

"I played right into her hands didn't I?" Lisa said bitterly.

Chrissie nodded. "But when Jean-Luc hears your side of the story, he'll change his mind – that is, if you still want him back."

"I want him back," Lisa said through her tears, With all my heart, she added to herself.

Lisa finally tracked down and cornered Jean-Luc in the corridor just as the twelve-thirty bell rang, and the corridor was filled with students hurrying out of their classrooms to lunch. Jean-Luc saw Lisa and instantly turned away, marching off briskly down the corridor.

"Jean-Luc, wait!" Lisa cried and ran after him. She grabbed his arm, but he shrugged it off and turned around.

He looked at her through hurt and accusing eyes. "Yes?" he asked – a wealth of anger and recrimination in that one syllable.

"I have to talk to you, Jean-Luc," she said.

"So, go ahead and talk," he said frostily.

Lisa looked around at the hustle and bustle in the corridor as people rushed off to lunch; this was hardly the place to talk.

"Can't we go somewhere more private?" she pleaded.

"This is as good as any other place," he said soullessly.

"Look, Jean-Luc, I know how upset you must be," Lisa said – if you're as upset as me then your heart must be breaking, she thought. "But you have to understand why

I've been avoiding you all this past week, why I've cancelled all our dates..."

Jean-Luc looked at her cynically, wondering what ingenious tale his former girlfriend was going to spin now.

"You're my teacher, Jean-Luc," she said and noticed sadly that, for the first time ever, Jean-Luc didn't contradict her as he usually did. "And Alison threatened to tell the principal that we were going out together. You could have lost your job... What I didn't realize was that she was after you as well and was determined to have you..."

There was a disappointed expression on Jean-Luc's face. "Is that it?" he laughed bitterly.

"What do you mean, 'is that it'?"

"You know, Lisa, you're going to have to do a whole lot better than that," he sneered.

"But it's the truth!" she protested.

"I thought I loved you, Lisa," he continued. "I thought I could trust you, and that you loved me too."

"But I do love you, Jean-Luc. You're the best thing that's ever happened to me!"

"And all along you were simply leading me on, using me as a little *divertissement*, a means of passing the time until something better came along."

Lisa was confused. "What do you mean?"

"You've made a fool of me, Lisa," he repeated, stubbornly refusing even to bring James's name to his lips, as if the very sound of it was repulsive to him. He looked at his Swatch. "And I have a lunch date..."

"With ... with Alison?" asked Lisa, and found that her lips were trembling.

Jean-Luc looked at her defiantly. "Yes, as a matter of fact. With Alison."

He turned briskly away and walked off down the corridor, leaving Lisa alone amongst the crowds of students racing off for lunch.

That's it, she told herself with numbing finality. I've lost him for ever. Alison was right: she's won after all...

Her whole body was shaking, and yet she felt somehow detached from what she was experiencing, as if she was looking down on herself from a great height while her heart broke into tiny pieces.

She looked after the departing figure of Jean-Luc. We loved each other. I've kissed him, held him in my arms, told him my secrets. I know every curve of his body, know his smell, his touch, his everything... And now he's grown cold on me, turned me out of his life for ever...

She walked sadly off in the other direction. If she had looked behind her she would have seen Jean-Luc stop at the main door and turn around to look at her through misted and saddened eyes which even now were beginning to moisten with tears.

18

James looked at Lisa by his side, and decided she looked absolutely stunning. There was no doubt about it, he decided, something had happened to Lisa since he'd been away at university.

In that time she'd grown from being a studious, slightly bookish girl who hid her looks behind her glasses and her outdated hairstyle, to a beautiful and vibrant young woman. He'd always found Lisa attractive before; now he felt proud to be in her company, as envious male eyes stared in their direction.

He'd been surprised when she'd invited him to the summer ball, especially as Lisa very rarely went to such events. Still, he'd accepted with alacrity; maybe that kiss all those months ago at Christmas had had its desired effect at long last. Maybe Lisa had decided that she really did want to go out with him, after all.

Of course the reason behind Lisa's invitation was slightly different than the one he'd imagined. After three long days of watching Lisa mope about the school, trying to avoid Jean-Luc wherever possible, and almost breaking into tears when she did see him, Chrissie had decided that her best friend needed taking in hand.

"You can't go on feeling sorry for yourself for ever," she had reprimanded Lisa on the way home from school one day. "You've got to try and forget him..."

"I loved him, Chrissie," Lisa said. "I still do."

"I know that," she replied sympathetically. "But life goes on with or without him. And we've got to get you back into the swing of normal sixth-form life as quickly as possible!"

Or you're going to drive me round the bend! she thought.

"And I know just the thing to take your mind off that Frenchman!" she added cheerfully.

"And what's that then?" Lisa asked doubtfully.

"You've still got your tickets for the ball and disco tomorrow," she said. "You paid me good money for them – it'd be a shame to let them go to waste."

"And who could I get to go with me at such short notice?" asked Lisa, who had originally bought the tickets in the hope that Jean-Luc would escort her. "Everyone chose their partners weeks ago."

"Well, I do know *one* person who would *love* to go with you..." said Chrissie, with a mischievous twinkle in her eyes.

"And who's that?"

Chrissie raised her hands in mock despair at her best friend's lack of imagination. "Come on, Lisa, he's right under your nose – well, right next door anyway..."

"James!" asked Lisa in disbelief. "You're not seriously suggesting that I take James along?"

"Why not?" countered Chrissie. "He likes you a lot. And he's kind of cute – in a trainspotter sort of way. Besides he'll take your mind off Jean-Luc."

"I don't know..." Lisa sounded doubtful, but the idea did have some appeal. James had carried a torch for Lisa for ages, and would do anything for her. And Lisa remembered that kiss under the mistletoe: now *that* had been fun.

Chrissie looked engagingly at her friend. "Do it for me? It's not as if you're going to embark on a passionate romance with him, is it? You might even have some fun."

"Well, I'm not sure..."

"C'mon, Lisa Tyler," Chrissie said determinedly. "When have I ever given you bad advice!"

Plenty of times, thought Lisa, but eventually she agreed.

And so it was that Lisa and James made their entrance at the Applewood summer ball, dressed stylishly in the trendiest clothes their respective parents' credit cards could afford. Lisa was wearing a knee-length white cotton dress, bunched in at the waist with a wide leather belt, while James was wearing a sensible, but nevertheless trendy, black blazer, and Chinos.

The annual summer ball and disco was the one social event of the year when everyone made an all-out effort to dress to impress. Everyone was determined to outdo his or her friends, and each girl who entered the school's assembly hall – where the ball was being held – automatically scanned the room, to see who was wearing what. As the boys were also considered something of a crucial fashion accessory, they also looked to see who was with who.

The hall had been decked out in colourful bunting, and suspended from the ceiling was a huge net of balloons, which would be released at midnight when the disco officially ended. Couples sat at tables which lined the dance floor, and the air was alive with the sounds of the latest dance music.

A few of the younger, trendier teachers were in attendance – to keep a watchful but discreet eye over the proceedings. They seemed more concerned with inter-departmental gossip than with the students they were supposed to be supervising, and only left their own table when a particularly daring student from the upper sixth cajoled them on to the dance floor.

The teachers were also prepared to turn a blind eye to the alcohol which some of the students had discreetly brought in, even though about two-thirds of those present were still under eighteen. The teachers could hardly disapprove; many of them were only a few years older than the sixth-formers themselves and could still remember their own schooldays.

As the evening progressed Lisa found herself warming more and more to James and – as she was drinking orange juices and Cokes she couldn't even blame it on the alcohol – she started to remember why she had kissed him under the mistletoe.

A year at university had done him good, she realized. It had opened him out and made him realize that there was indeed life beyond Crewe railway station. He entertained her all night, delighting her with witty stories of campus life, or making her squirm with pleasurable disgust as he regaled her with descriptions of some of the things he had seen in his studies to become a doctor.

He was kind and considerate too, open about his affection for Lisa. What's more, he had learnt to dance. For James, this was quite an achievement, and it was one that Lisa fervently approved of. She loved to dance, and, as the evening wore on and she was caught up in the heady excitement of the ball, she found herself dancing closer and closer to James.

Looks like Chrissie was right after all, she told herself as they bopped to a track from another Australian soap star turned teeny idol. Coming here was a good idea – and I haven't thought about Jean-Luc once! She also remembered something Chrissie had said on the schoolbus a couple of months ago: James could be quite a catch. Maybe she was right about that too!

They finished dancing and joined Chrissie and Simon at their table. Chrissie and Simon had been getting on surprisingly well over the past few weeks, Lisa had remarked, and Chrissie had been regarding it as something of a challenge to rid Simon of his fascination with all things American. She hadn't *quite* succeeded – Si was wearing a Chicago Bears baseball shirt and jeans for the ball – but she was having fun trying. As they sat there chatting, Chrissie glanced towards the door at the couple who had just entered the hall.

Damn! she cursed. Why did they have to come – just when Lisa was starting to enjoy herself!

Alison was wearing the most expensive, most glamorous, most stylish – and reddest – dress of all the girls at the ball. And on her arm, dressed in a loose-fitting grey cotton suit and a plain black T-shirt, was the most handsome, hunky and stylish man in the entire school.

One of the teachers in attendance raised an eye in surprise as he saw Alison and Jean-Luc cross the hall, and then shrugged.

I suppose it was inevitable, he decided, the sexiest sixth-former in the school, and the handsome young guy from the South of France. And what odds does it make? It's not as if he's her teacher...

Anyway, he had more important things to be getting on with, namely in the attractive shape of the young pretty English teacher opposite him.

Like all the other girls before her Alison surveyed the room, and then smiled, satisfied that she'd won yet again: the classiest dress – a little red Armani number which she'd bulldozed her father into buying for her – and the classiest guy! What more could a girl want? she asked herself.

Then she saw Chrissie's table, and her smile grew even wider. Alison couldn't believe her good fortune. Not only was Lisa here, in front of whom she could sadistically parade her new 'trophy', but so was James!

For the past few days Alison had been slightly worried that Jean-Luc might see through her little deception: it was obvious to her that he still had very strong feelings for his former girlfriend. So seeing Lisa and James together like this – and getting on very well, if you please – would finally give the truth to her lie.

She manoeuvred Jean-Luc over to their table.

"Well, hello there," she cooed. With all the sweetness and sincerity of a hyena ready to pounce, Chrissie thought.

The others mumbled their hellos. At Alison's side Jean-

Luc tensed, and Alison wondered – for the first time – whether she had made a mistake.

Lisa looked away from her former boyfriend, until a not-too-subtle kick under the table from Chrissie forced her to acknowledge his presence.

"Uh ... hello, Jean-Luc," she said; what she thought was: Please, please leave Alison now. I love you and whatever misunderstanding there's been between us let's try and work it out together! I love you so much that I'd follow you to the ends of the earth if need be!

"Hello, Lisa," Jean-Luc's voice was cold and strained, as though he was trying to hide his true emotions. His jaw clenched and unclenched. He looked at Lisa and she was forced to avert her eyes from the anger and sadness in his.

"Have you met James, Jean-Luc?" Alison asked, trying to sound as casual as she could, but meaning: Have you met the man your girlfriend has been two-timing you for?

James nodded a perfunctory greeting and was perplexed when Jean-Luc glared at him. There was a dangerous glint in his eyes, which made both him and Lisa uneasy. He grunted 'hello' to James.

"Sooooo nice meeting you," oozed Alison, casting a triumphant glance in Lisa's direction. "But we've come here to enjoy ourselves..." And with that catty comment she took Jean-Luc's arm and led him off to the dance floor.

"Cow!" said Chrissie.

"What do you mean?" asked James, taking his eyes off Alison as she wiggled off to the dance floor. "She's always seemed quite nice to me."

"Huh?" asked Simon simultaneously.

Only Chrissie noticed that Lisa was visibly shaken by the encounter. She looked disparagingly at the two men. "Look, why don't you two get us a couple of drinks?" she suggested.

"But you haven't finished," protested Simon, gesturing towards Chrissie and Lisa's unfinished Cokes.

There was a large potted palm behind Chrissie, an attempt by the ball's organizers to add a bit of sophistication to the event. She took her and Lisa's Cokes and poured them into the pot.

"We have now," she said.

James stood up and indicated that Si should do the same. "I think we should go to the bar, Simon," he said, and looked questioningly at Lisa. "I think this is girl-talk..."

When the boys had gone Chrissie turned to Lisa.

"Are you OK?" she asked. Her friend's face was white and there were tears welling in her blue eyes.

"She's such a little witch!" Lisa said, and even Chrissie was taken aback by what for Lisa was very strong language indeed. "She blackmailed me into keeping our relationship a secret, and now here she is being blatant about her and Jean-Luc! And what's more" – she glanced at the group of teachers at their table near the doors – "it doesn't matter at all!"

"She's a cow," Chrissie said simply.

"You've got that right," agreed Lisa.

"So don't give her the satisfaction of knowing she's won," suggested Chrissie. "Enjoy yourself as much as you can tonight with James. When Alison sees that you're not concerned, who knows, maybe she'll even lose interest in Jean-Luc..."

"You really think so?" asked Lisa eagerly.

Chrissie shrugged.

For the rest of the evening the atmosphere was tense and electric. Unable to resist taunting Lisa further Alison would try and ensure that she and Jean-Luc were seen frequently with their arms around each other.

Chrissie, on the other hand, was fighting a losing battle to take Lisa's mind off them, steering her away to different parts of the dance floor whenever Alison and Jean-Luc came near. James just remained confused by the whole situation.

Alison's cloyingness was starting to irritate Jean-Luc and he would keep leaving the dance floor to get another drink from the bar. From the Cokes he had started drinking at the beginning of the evening he had graduated to the fruit punch into which some of the upper sixth had sneaked some alcohol.

As the evening drew on he and Alison would stand more and more by the bar, with Jean-Luc brooding, watching Lisa and James together on the dance floor.

Alison tugged at his arm, and gave him a worried peck on the cheek. "Lighten up, Jean-Luc," she encouraged.

Jean-Luc continued to look, not at Alison, but at the couple on the dance floor. He couldn't take his eyes off them.

"She said she loved me," he said, slurring his words slightly.

"But she cheated on you," Alison insisted on her lie. "Forget her, Jean-Luc..."

She took him by the hand, as the music changed tempo. The end of the evening was approaching, and the DJ had started playing slow smoochy songs. Alison led Jean-Luc out on to the dance floor and held him close to her as they swayed and moved to the now romantic music.

The dance floor was now full of embracing couples. Even Simon had persuaded Chrissie to join him on the floor, although she soon found herself regretting it as he stood on her toes for the tenth time. Sometime she was going to have to teach him how to dance. And funnily enough, she was rather looking forward to it...

Lisa and James were dancing too, and Lisa experienced a slight thrill as she felt James's hard firm body press against hers. James had made her feel good tonight, she realized, even though for most of the evening she had hardly been able to take her eyes off Jean-Luc and Alison as they danced close by. He was a good friend, and while he would never replace Jean-Luc in her affections, she found that she liked him a lot.

"I've enjoyed myself so much this evening, James," she whispered as she laid her head upon his shoulder. "Thank you."

"I should thank you," he said. "For inviting me. But there's been something bothering you all evening, Lisa. What is it?"

"It's nothing, James," she lied, painfully aware of how close Jean-Luc and Alison were.

"Because if there's anything I can do you only have to ask."

Lisa looked up and smiled at him. "You're very, very sweet, James..."

James bent down and kissed her on the lips.

And then suddenly several things happened at once.

Lisa felt herself being pulled rudely away from James's embrace. Jean-Luc pushed her to one side and launched himself into James, giving him a vicious blow to the jaw.

Jean-Luc was no match for the burly rugby-playing medical student, but the Frenchman's blow had taken James by surprise and he fell back into the crowd. He quickly reasserted himself and leapt up to defend himself against Jean-Luc, who was pounding away at his body. There was a wild look in Jean-Luc's eyes, and his face was reddened with alcohol. They both fell to the floor, rolling around on the dance floor, raining blows on each other.

"Jean-Luc, stop!" screamed Lisa, as a crowd gathered around them. "Leave him alone!"

Obsessed with jealousy, and with his mind befuddled by the alcohol, Jean-Luc was deaf to her pleas. With a grunt James threw the Frenchman from off his body and staggered to his feet. There was a trickle of blood running down from the corner of his mouth.

"What do you think you're doing?" he barked, as Jean-Luc leapt to his feet.

"Stop it!" Lisa implored once more.

Two teachers had come over to the scene of the fracas and were holding Jean-Luc back from his rival. Jean-Luc shrugged them off angrily. He glared at Lisa, and ignored Alison, who had run after him in concern.

"I can't stand seeing the two of you together!" he cried.

"We were only *dancing*..." said Lisa defensively.

"I love you, Lisa!" announced Jean-Luc. "And I always will! Even when you two-time me with your boyfriend here!"

With a contemptuous snarl Jean-Luc stormed his way through the crowd and out of the hall. The spectators murmured almost approvingly amongst themselves: after all, this was the way all Frenchmen in love were supposed to behave.

Chrissie came up to Lisa and put a hand on her arm: she was trembling.

"Well, how does it feel to have two men fighting over you, Lisa?" she asked in an attempt to defuse the situation.

James joined them as well. "I'm sorry, Lisa," he said. "He just went for me. What's his problem?"

Lisa didn't answer, but Chrissie just shot James a scornful look: sometimes men could be such fools!

"I two-timed him with *James*?" Lisa said aloud to herself.

Chrissie looked accusingly at Alison, who was trying to hide herself in the crowd. Quite a few things were now beginning to fit together.

Lisa made a sudden decision. She ran out of the hall and into the car park, following Jean-Luc.

"Jean-Luc, wait!" she cried. "I have to talk to you!"

But his 2CV was already speeding out of the car park, leaving Lisa standing – alone and deserted – the summer rain falling down like tears.

19

Despite an early promise of long, hot, bright days the summer had turned into one of the worst ever at Applewood. Where the sun had once poured down like golden honey, now the rain threw down in torrents, and the wind blew mercilessly through the narrow streets of the town. The weather exactly matched Lisa's mood: dull, dark, dreary and despairing.

At eleven o'clock the morning following the summer ball Chrissie had gone round to Lisa's to see how her friend was feeling; and, more importantly, to give Lisa some good news.

After James had driven Lisa home from the ball, Chrissie had confronted Alison with her suspicion that she had lied to Jean-Luc to turn him against Lisa. Alison – ashen-faced and concerned that what, for her, had been a harmless bit of fun had ended in violence – had finally admitted her lie.

When Lisa heard the news she was overjoyed, and immediately picked up the phone to ring Jean-Luc and explain the misunderstanding.

And that was the precise moment when Lisa's summer went horribly wrong.

"Can I speak to Jean-Luc, please?" she asked the woman on the other end of the line. She presumed she was her boyfriend's landlady, even though she had never met her.

There was a long pause at the other end of the line – an

unsure hesitation. "Jean-Luc?" the woman asked grumpily. For her it was still early in the morning and Lisa's phone call had got her out of bed.

"Yes, that's right," said Lisa, growing increasingly impatient. "Jean-Luc Roupie. Tell him it's Lisa."

There was another pause. "I'm sorry, I can't do that, my dear," the landlady said, her tone softening as she recognized the concern in Lisa's voice.

"What do you mean?"

"Well ... Mr Roupie left this morning..."

Lisa felt her heart sink. "Left?"

"That's right," said the landlady, more than eager to spread a bit of juicy gossip. "Came home last night – I think he'd been drinking. His suit was dirty as if he'd been rolling about on the floor, and his T-shirt was ripped... Anyway, he started to pack his things. He said he was going home..."

"Home?"

"Back to France... Still, he'd paid his rent in advance so I shouldn't complain..."

"Do you have his address in France?"

"Well, I don't know whether..."

"Do you have his address in France?" Lisa demanded, unprepared to put up with any opposition. "Please..."

"I'm sorry, but I haven't," said the landlady more softly, impressed by Lisa's obvious urgency at this point. If she had had Jean-Luc's French address she would have given it to Lisa. "He said that if he got any post I was to send it on to Applewood College, where he used to work... Do you know it?"

"Yes, I know it," said Lisa. And how! she thought.

"He said that the secretary there would forward it on to wherever he was staying... Is there anything wrong?"

"No, everything's perfectly OK," Lisa murmured, as she tried to stifle her tears, and hung up the phone.

Lisa turned to Chrissie and told her the news. Her friend's face fell when she learnt that Jean-Luc had left the country to return to France.

"Why?" Lisa asked desperately.

"If he thought that you were seeing James maybe he thought there was no point in staying in this country," she suggested. "And after his antics last night he wouldn't exactly be popular in the staffroom, would he? And anyway, there's only one more week of term to go, so what's the point of staying?"

"I love him, Chrissie," Lisa declared boldly, trying hard to keep her voice steady. "And he loves me. And now he's hundreds of miles away … without ever knowing the truth…"

Chrissie moved forward to hug her best friend. "Perhaps it's for the best?" she suggested, even though she clearly didn't believe it; she added reasonably: "After all, you live in England, he lives in France, and you don't even know where…"

Lisa pulled away from Chrissie's hug. There was a deadly serious expression on her face, an expression so fierce and determined that it made Chrissie shiver.

"It doesn't matter where he lives!" she declared. "We belong together!"

Chrissie drew back. There was an urgency to Lisa's words, a determination which she had heard only a few times before, when the old Lisa – the Lisa before Jean-Luc – had boldly announced that she was going to get a B in her exams, and surprised everyone (including herself) by ending up with an A-plus.

Back then Chrissie had been impressed by her friend's determination and her single-mindedness of purpose. That same determination and single-mindedness of purpose were apparent on Lisa's face now.

"But there's nothing you can do, Lisa," she said reasonably.

"Oh, isn't there?"

"No. It's the summer holidays in a week's time," Chrissie continued. "Relax and enjoy yourself – it's the last time you'll be able to – next year is exam year, and we're not going to have a minute to ourselves."

"I can't let him go like this, Chrissie," Lisa claimed, "not knowing the truth..."

Chrissie looked kindly and sympathetically at her friend.

"Look, Lisa, he's a great and gorgeous guy, and what you had together was something special," she said. "And what Alison Potter did was evil – I doubt if anyone's even going to give her the time of day when what she did gets out – and I certainly mean to start telling everyone as soon as possible.

"But he's miles away from you now," she continued, sensibly. "And there'll be other boyfriends. Be glad for what you had with Jean-Luc, no matter how brief it was. Don't grieve for what you've lost: be happy for what you gained. And look to the future. James is really fond of you – he's a lot of fun – why not go out with him? You know he'd jump at the chance."

"No."

"C'mon, Lisa," Chrissie said softly, recognizing what her friend was going through. "Be practical – like you always used to be."

"No," Lisa repeated, and looked at Chrissie.

A sudden plan had already formed in Lisa's mind. She'd had enough of being practical, she decided, enough of being sensible. Now Lisa Tyler was going to do what she wanted to do, to do what her heart told her she had to do.

And so what if she ended up looking like a lovesick fool? Who cared what other people thought of her? If she didn't do what she wanted now she knew she would regret it for the rest of her life.

There was a look of steely resolve in her baby-blue eyes. Lisa remembered a conversation she had once had with her mother, Maddy.

"Chrissie, my mum told me once that she believed that in this life there is only one person for everyone. Their *soulmate*, she called it. Without your soulmate you're incomplete. Well, Jean-Luc is *my* soulmate..."

"But Lisa, he's French," Chrissie protested. "He lives in another country..."

"So what?" said Lisa and shrugged. "We belong together. And if I can't have him then I don't want anyone else."

Chrissie shook her head despairingly. "Get real, Lisa," she said.

"No, Chrissie, for the first time in my life, I don't want to 'get real'," she said adamantly.

"For the first time in my life I know exactly what I want – and I intend to go out and get it."

"You've got a holiday job?" asked Maddy the following morning.

"That's right, Mum," said Lisa. "At Brucianni's. I'll be waiting on tables."

Maddy's face fell. "But Lisa, you don't have to. OK, I might not make the sort of money that Alison's parents do but I do bring home enough to provide you with pocket money for the summer. You've been working hard all through the summer term and you deserve a break – enjoy yourself."

Lisa shook her head. "No, Mum," she said self-righteously. "I think it's time I started supporting myself. You've done enough for me in the past."

"Lisa, is there anything wrong?" Maddy asked, full of concern.

"Wrong? Of course there isn't!"

Maddy looked enquiringly at her daughter. "No boyfriend trouble? That Jean-Luc person who came round the other week..."

Lisa coloured. "Oh, him..." she said nonchalantly.

"I haven't seen him around here before..."

"Oh, he's ... he's a student at the institute, I told you before," Lisa lied. "He's gone home to France for the holidays."

"Oh, I see..." said Maddy uncertainly. She returned to the subject of Lisa's summer job.

"But you've never even had a Saturday job before," she pointed out.

"Then it's about time I started, isn't it?" Lisa said curtly. "And besides, I need to save money."

"Oh? And what for?"

Lisa thought fast. "Chrissie and I are thinking of taking a week or two off towards the end of the summer," she said. "Get away from Applewood for a few days, you know ... James has these university friends who have a cottage in Dorset – he said we'd be welcome to stay there..."

Lisa looked warily at her mother.

"That'll be nice," Maddy said brightly, even though she was slightly put out that Lisa hadn't mentioned this to her before. "You need a holiday..."

My God, she's actually bought it! Lisa thought with relief. Now all I have to do is to tell Chrissie!

The next two months passed incredibly slowly, as Lisa worked every hour possible at Brucianni's, waiting on the tables, and, when there was no work there, lending a hand behind the scenes in the kitchen.

She came home exhausted every evening, and Maddy wondered whether all the work she was putting in at the coffee shop was worth it. All the money Lisa was earning was all very well, she thought, but what was the point if she was too tired in the evenings to go out and spend it on enjoying herself? In the two months she had been working at the coffee shop she hadn't bought herself a new dress, or a new CD, or anything to show for all her hard work. Where was all the money going?

It was Chrissie who, towards the end of the two months, brought the matter up. She had hardly seen her best friend during the whole of the summer holidays; and there were times when she desperately needed to see Lisa, if only to escape from the attentions of Simon who had decided, after the summer ball, that Chrissie was the only girl for him. Strangely enough, as the weeks passed,

Chrissie started to find his single-minded pursuit of her rather endearing.

She cornered Lisa as she was cleaning up a table at Brucianni's late on a Friday night.

"OK, Lisa, what's up?" Chrissie demanded. "I've hardly seen you at all during the summer holidays. In fact the only times I do see you are when I come in here for a cappuccino and chocolate fudge cake..."

Lisa smiled, and sat down at the table. "Chrissie, am I glad to see you! I've been meaning to ring you up for ages... only I never seem to have the time."

"I'm not surprised," Chrissie said disapprovingly. "According to your mum you're working two shifts a day here."

"I'm making lots of money," Lisa pointed out, "and I'm not spending any of it."

"It's not worth it, not at the expense of your social life," Chrissie said.

"Oh yes it is," said Lisa. "And besides, I'm finishing here tomorrow."

"Great. Then maybe we can go out together before the new term starts in a couple of weeks."

Lisa shook her head – she was suddenly very serious. "Listen, Chrissie, I need your help..."

Chrissie regarded her best friend suspiciously. She was up to something, of that there was no doubt. There was a determined expression on her face, that same determined look that had been on her face when Jean-Luc had left Applewood – almost two months ago.

"I've told my mum that you and I are going down to Dorset in a couple of days' time..."

This was news to Chrissie. "And I take it we're not?" she asked sarcastically.

"Chrissie, you've got to back me up on this one," Lisa pleaded. "Why do you think I've been working so hard over the holidays?... It's too important to me for me to be found out now..."

20

The train chugged slowly to a halt in the old railway station, and Lisa stumbled onto the platform, carrying her one piece of luggage – a large black leather holdall – containing two changes of clothes, some reading material, her Walkman and – most importantly of all – her passport and a French phrase book.

All around her people were milling and rushing about, leaving the train, or rudely pushing their way through the crowds to catch a commuter train which would take them from their jobs in the city to their homes in the suburbs.

Even concentrating as hard as she could, Lisa could barely understand their staccato babble as they chatted and traded insults with each other in their own distinctive language and accents.

For the first time the enormity of what she had done struck Lisa like a bolt of lightning.

It was half-past-five in the afternoon.

It was raining.

And she was alone in Paris!

The capital city in a country of almost fifty-five million people.

Fifty-five million!

And of those fifty-five million people she knew only one.

And he was in Cannes.

Another five hundred or so miles away.

Or at least she supposed he was. But Jean-Luc's home address, which she had sneakily obtained from the school secretary by saying that she had promised to send the French assistant some English books, was the only clue to the whereabouts of the man she loved above all else, and for whom she'd spent the entire savings from her holiday job to finance this trip to France and track him down.

It hadn't been easy, or comfortable, fooling her mother into thinking that she was going to Dorset for a fortnight's holiday. She had needed Chrissie to back her up every step of the way. And fortunately Chrissie – when she wasn't gleefully spreading juicy gossip around the school – was a loving and loyal friend, and had backed her story.

By a stroke of luck, Chrissie herself was going to be away from Applewood for the two weeks Lisa was away anyway, which substantiated Lisa's story even further.

"But don't tell anyone who I'm going away with!" Chrissie had begged Lisa. After all, it wouldn't have done Chrissie's image any good at all for it to be known that she was going on holiday with the so retro-cool-it-was-painful Simon who, after stepping on her feet for the umpteenth time at the school summer ball, had since then somehow captured her heart with his charmingly total lack of charm...

The train journey down to Dover and the ferry trip across to Calais had been easy enough. Even the connection to Paris had been trouble-free as she had been befriended by a group of English tourists who had done the Channel crossing many times before. But now the tourists had gone on their way and Lisa was alone, in a country of foreigners, none of whom, she decided, spoke – or wanted to speak – English.

She stumbled through the crowds at the Gare du Nord railway station to look for a map of the city. She remembered what Jean-Luc had told her, all those months ago when he had called her up in front of the class and played his little joke on her. Like London, Paris has several different railway stations, he had said, each one of which services a different part of the country.

C'mon, Lisa, think! she urged herself. Which is the one which takes you down to the South of France? Why didn't you pay attention in class?

Because I was too busy staring into Jean-Luc's deep brown eyes, that's why, she answered herself.

She looked cluelessly up at a map on the wall, hoping that a name would ring a bell in her mind. The Gare Saint-Lazare, the Gare de Lyon, the Gare de l'Est, the Gare d'Austerlitz... None of them sounded familiar.

She turned in desperation to a good-looking, trendy young man who was also studying the map. Back home in England he would have been declared a drop-dead, to-die-for hunk; here in Paris, he was just another good-looking, stylish Frenchman.

"*Eh, pardon, monsieur,*" she began in her hesitant schoolgirl French, "*je veux ... prendre le train pour Cannes. Vous ... savez...?*"

Her French dried up. Why was it that in the classroom, talking to Jean-Luc, she could always get top marks; but here in Paris, talking to a real live Parisian, she fell flat on her face?

The Frenchman smiled generously at her, amused by her attempts at speaking his native tongue. "Perhaps you'd better try in your own language?" he suggested in a heavily-accented English.

Lisa breathed a sigh of relief. "I'm trying to get to Cannes," she said. "Which train station must I go to?"

"Why, the Gare de Lyon, of course," he answered, eyeing Lisa up appreciatively.

"And how can I get there?" she asked urgently.

"It's quite simple, mademoiselle," he said, "you must take the Metro. Travel on line number five to the Bastille, and then change to line number one for the Gare de Lyon..."

Number five to the Bastille, number one to the railway station, Lisa recited to herself, over and over like a mantra.

"But I have a far better idea," the man began.

"And what's that?" Lisa asked innocently, thinking that the Frenchman might be prepared to offer her a lift.

"You are alone in Paris," he said flirtatiously. "Forget about Cannes. There is a nice little bar I know around the corner. Come and have a drink with me. There we can get to know each other better... You are a very attractive woman..."

Lisa's face fell. Only a few hours in this country and already the men were coming on to her! Maybe what everyone always said about Frenchmen was true after all!

The Frenchman shrugged. "Ah well, if mademoiselle chooses not to enjoy my company, what can I do?" he said helplessly. "At the very least I can help you carry your luggage to the Metro..."

"No thank you," Lisa said primly. "I can manage that perfectly well myself, thank you very much..."

"Do not be so English," the Frenchman said. "You are in France now. We do not have so many – how do you say? – 'hang-ups' as you British." And ignoring Lisa's protests he picked up her bag and led her down to the Metro station.

If Chrissie were here now, thought Lisa, she'd say I'm mad – turning down a date with a handsome young Parisian! And how different he is from the English boys. Turn them down, and they're off looking for the next female to chat up. This one offers to carry my suitcase! There was something very different about the French which Lisa liked very much indeed.

After the young man had seen her safely on the Metro to the Bastille she looked around at her fellow passengers in the railway carriage. They were all, men and women, dressed in chic fashions, and every last one of them carried about them that air of casual elegance and sophistication which only the French have.

Many of them were dark and Latin-looking and Lisa, with her fresh-faced complexion, blonde hair and clothes bought from one of the chain stores at Applewood, felt very out of place indeed. Curious French eyes started to stare at this stranger in their midst and Lisa was beginning to feel very awkward when the Metro train lurched to a halt at the Bastille Metro station and crowds poured out of the train, almost knocking Lisa to the ground.

Safely on the platform, Lisa looked around for any indication of where to go next to change trains. The times she had been to London – without Jean-Luc – she had hated the Underground system there, finding its complicated network of interconnecting railway lines confusing for anyone who didn't live there and travel on the system every day of his life. The Paris Metro system had the added disadvantage, thought Lisa, of being entirely French: like Jean-Luc's 2CV it was undeniably fast and efficient – if you could only work out how to use it!

Finally she found the platform for trains on Metro line one and thankfully slumped into a seat with her luggage, as the train started thundering through the tunnels in the direction of what she thought was the Gare de Lyon. It was only when Lisa had been on the train for fifteen minutes or so and had just passed the Champs Elysées Metro station that she decided that something was wrong.

She turned to the person sitting next to her, a chic and glamorous fifty-something woman reading a copy of French *Vogue*, and asked her when they would be reaching the Gare de Lyon.

The fifty-something woman smiled sympathetically at Lisa with all the slightly patronizing affection that big-city dwellers reserve for naïve out-of-towners.

"But you're going in completely the wrong direction, my dear," she said in French. "This train is going west. You need to go east..."

Lisa felt her heart sink. Here she was, trying to cross an

entire country and she couldn't even find her way across town! Maybe her whole trip was doomed from the outset. Tired and exhausted after her long train and ferry trip, she felt herself close to tears.

The woman looked curiously at her. "What is wrong, my child?" she asked curiously.

Grateful for a friendly ear Lisa poured out the whole story of her and Jean-Luc, once again discovering that, when speaking a foreign language, she wasn't half as embarrassed about openly discussing her innermost feelings.

As Lisa told her tale the woman started to smile, and by the time she had finished there was a sympathetic tear in the woman's eye.

"Aha, such courage, such daring! Such love!" she said admiringly. "And who said the British were cold and boring? No wonder he loves you!"

"You really think I'm doing the right thing?" asked Lisa, who had been trying to ignore her doubts all the way down to Paris.

"Of course!" said the woman with conviction. "*Il faut toujours suivre le coeur!* You must always – always – do what your heart tells you, no matter what common sense or others advise!"

As the train rumbled to a halt at the next Metro station the woman stood up and took Lisa's hand. Lisa looked enquiringly at her.

"You have inspired me!" the fifty something woman declared. "Follow me!"

"But where are we going?" asked Lisa, impressed and slightly bemused by the woman's over-the-top attitude. Undoubtedly Lisa reminded her of her own long-lost youth.

"We are getting a taxi," she said. "I am taking you to the Gare de Lyon myself! Nothing – absolutely nothing – must be allowed to stand in the way of true love!"

21

Even with the dry and refreshing Mistral – the wind that blows on from the mountains down to the Mediterranean coast – the heat was oppressive when Lisa disembarked at Cannes railway station early the following morning after the long overnight haul from the Gare de Lyon in Paris to the trendy French town on the Côte d'Azur.

In the distance Lisa could hear the bustling sounds of market porters as they carried their wares to the city market, and the squawks and cries of seagulls as they wheeled and swooped in the blue and cloudless sky.

There was a scent of lavender in the air, and from the café across the road she could smell the wonderful early-morning aroma of freshly-baked bread. Compared to Applewood, or Paris – or rather the little she had seen of it from the window of a Metro carriage or a taxi – with its fuggy smell of car exhausts and American hot dogs, this place was like a heaven on earth.

And somewhere, maybe even just around the corner, there's an angel! she thought.

Clutched tightly in her hand was the scrap of paper on which she had written Jean-Luc's address in Cannes, which she had cajoled the school secretary into giving her: Flat One, 37 rue de la Châtelaine. Although Jean-Luc had told her that his mother lived on the outskirts of the town, he had a flat very near the centre of town. Lisa presumed he shared the flat with other students: she only prayed that he hadn't given up his room in the flat when he had moved to England.

She looked at the notice on the door of the tourist bureau at the railway station. The office wouldn't be open until half-past seven, which meant that she had another hour to wait until she could buy a map of the town and find out the exact location of Jean-Luc's road.

She mentally kicked herself for not having bought a map of Cannes in Paris, or even in England. That was something that the old, sensible and practical Lisa would have done, she told herself; on the other hand, the old, sensible and practical Lisa wouldn't have suddenly taken it into her head to travel all the way down to the South of France in pursuit of the man she loved.

She crossed over the road – narrowly avoiding the cars which were being driven by drivers who had a typically French disregard for the safety of the pedestrian – and entered the café shop opposite. Even this early in the morning it was full of workers from the nearby market, or young backpackers on their way to the coast, who had disembarked from the railway station. There was no free table so she asked if she could share the table of a boy and a girl who were about her own age.

"*Bien sûr*," agreed the girl – a slight, elfin-faced creature with sandy-coloured hair – and offered Lisa a seat.

As the waitress came to take Lisa's order of a chocolate croissant and a café au lait, the girl introduced herself as Lydie, and the young handsome dark-haired boy by her side as her brother, Christophe. They were both science students at the famous Sorbonne University in Paris, Lydie told them; but every summer, in common with so many other Parisians, they came down to the Côte d'Azur where their parents owned a holiday apartment.

"And you, you are from England?" asked Christophe in his faltering English.

"That's right."

"And have you come down for a holiday too?" asked Lydie, whose English was considerably better than her brother's.

"Well ... not exactly..." said Lisa, slightly embarrassed.

"You should do," urged Christophe. "The Mediterranean is beautiful this time of the year. The sun always shines, you can go windsurfing or water skiing..."

"And the beaches are always crowded," said Lydie, and added, "with such good-looking men!" The two girls giggled conspiratorially.

"I'm not interested in chasing any good-looking men along the Croisette," said Lisa, remembering the name Jean-Luc had given to the main boulevard along the seafront at Cannes. She bit into her croissant: it was delicious.

Lydie looked interested. "Oh?" she asked. "And then for what have you come to Cannes?"

Lisa looked slightly embarrassed, and lowered her eyes. Considered dispassionately, her quest to find Jean-Luc might sound laughable to strangers. But when she looked up, after having told Lydie and Christophe the story of her and Jean-Luc and of Alison's evil trick she found that both of them were beaming.

"That is wonderful!" said Lydie, and her brother, to Lisa's surprise, agreed with her.

"I thought the English were all cold and without passion, like the London fog," he said. "Giving up everything in chase of your heart is something which only we French would do. Are you sure that you are not French, Lisa?"

Grinning, Lisa shook her head.

"Then you must have French blood in you," he decided.

Lydie stood up. "And we are going to help you find your man!" she declared, and took the slip of paper on which was written Jean-Luc's address. "37 Rue de la Châtelaine," she read out.

"Do you know it," asked Lisa.

"Oui," she said. "It is only a few minutes' walk from here." She called the waitress over to pay the bill, and made for the door. "Come," she said to Lisa and Christophe.

"It's a quarter-past seven in the morning!" Lisa protested. "We can't go yet!"

"Of course we can," said Lydie. "Don't be so English, my friend. When it is a matter of the heart then it is never too early!"

37 Rue de la Châtelaine was a seedy, run-down white stone building in a side street of Cannes, a stark contrast to the glamorous hotels and shops which Lisa, Lydie and Christophe passed on their way to Jean-Luc's flat. Many students lived here, Christophe explained to Lisa, taking advantage of the cheap rents and the friendly bohemian atmosphere.

They walked into the foyer of the block. Flat One was the first door on the left.

Lisa took a deep breath and looked at her two new friends. "How do I look?" she asked.

"You look beautiful, Lisa," Christophe assured her.

"Go on, Lisa, ring the bell," Lydie urged. "What are you waiting for?"

Because I'm nervous, Lisa thought. Because I don't know what reception I'm going to get. Will he be glad to see me? He still thinks that I two-timed him over James. Is he still hurt and angry?

And there was another nagging and even more worrying thought. What if he's not alone? It's been two months since I last saw him... What if he's forgotten about me? What if he's got a new girlfriend...?

"Ring the door bell, Lisa!"

Summoning up her courage Lisa pressed on the bell, and waited. There was no reply. She tried again. And again. Lisa looked hopelessly at Lydie and Christophe, as an old lady came out of the door of the opposite flat.

She said something to Lisa in a regional accent so

strong and pronounced that Lisa had to look at Lydie for help.

"What did she say?" she asked.

"She says that Monsieur Roupie has left..." she said sadly. "That he arrived back from England two months ago, packed his things and left..."

Lisa felt the whole world spinning around. To have travelled hundreds of miles only to find that Jean-Luc had gone! "Where's he gone to?" Lisa demanded urgently of Lydie. "Ask her where he's gone!"

"I'm sorry, Lisa," Lydie said sympathetically after she had posed the old woman the question. "Jean-Luc left no forwarding address..."

Lisa burst into tears and fell into Lydie's open arms.

22

Lisa sat on the balcony of Lydie and Christophe's holiday apartment, which overlooked the sparkling blue waves of the Mediterranean. She gazed morosely at the silver beaches crowded with bronzed and perfect bodies, at the water skiers and windsurfers further out at sea. Down there people were enjoying themselves, probably having the time of their lives, she decided; it made a stark contrast to her own misery and anguish.

After Lisa had dried her tears, Lydie and Christophe had taken her to their apartment at the far end of the Croisette, the less trendy part where rents were cheaper. When Lisa told them that she had nowhere to stay that coming night they had offered to put her up on their floor. Lisa had responded with relief: when she had arrived in Cannes she had assumed that she would be staying with Jean-Luc; now with Jean-Luc gone a hotel room would eat quickly into the small amount of money she had saved from her summer job.

"What are you going to do, Lisa?" asked Lydie as she came out on to the balcony, carrying two glasses of freshly-squeezed orange juice.

"I have to find him, Lydie," she said as she stared at the palm-lined stretch of the Croisette, hoping against hope that she might suddenly see his distinctive green 2CV. "I love him. And he has to know the truth about me and

James. If Alison hadn't lied to him we'd be together now."

"Do you have any clue as to where he might be?"

Lisa frowned and thought hard. Jean-Luc had told her a lot about his life in Cannes, but there was not one name she could recall. "I remember him telling me that his mother lived just outside Cannes. In a place called ... called ... Napou?"

"La Napoule," said Lydie. "I know it. It's about a twenty-minute bus ride from here... Christophe, where are you going?"

Christophe returned to the balcony, with the Cannes telephone directory in his hand. "You may call me Sherlock Holmes, if you wish," he said and opened the book. With Lisa looking over his shoulder, he ran his finger quickly down the list of people with the surname Roupie.

"There's not one Madame Roupie who lives in La Napoule," Lisa said sadly. "What about looking up Jean-Luc Roupie?"

Lydie shook her head. "If he's just moved – and if he's still in the area – he wouldn't be in the telephone directory yet."

Lisa buried her face in her hands. "It's so hopeless," she wailed. "I'm never going to find him!"

Lydie pressed a soft and comforting hand on her new friend's. "Of course you will," she said. "You're more than just boyfriend and girlfriend, you're soulmates, so you told me, and soulmates belong together. They can never be apart for long."

"You really think so?"

"Of course we think so!" said Christophe. "And tonight you are going to get some rest. And the first thing tomorrow morning we are going to La Napoule!"

To the west of Cannes, La Napoule is a tiny town on the coast, which few tourists know about, preferring the more obvious attractions of the bigger city. Everyone seemed to know each other here and Lydie hoped that by asking around someone would be able to tell them where Jean-Luc's mother lived.

But as the day drew on it seemed that no one could help them. They asked in bars and cafés, they stopped pedestrians on the street, they even went down to the marina where the millionaires moored their yachts but no one had heard of a Madame Roupie whose only son Jean-Luc was a language student.

Lisa became more and more despondent. This is crazy, she told herself. How can I possibly find him? I don't even know whether he's in Cannes or not. For all I know he could have gone and joined friends in Paris or somewhere else!

Even Christophe's regular words of encouragement didn't help to relieve her depression. As they sat together on the bus on the way back to Cannes Lisa began to seriously consider going back home.

"Don't give up hope," Christophe said. "You said he studied at Nice University."

"That's right."

"So we'll catch the train into Nice tomorrow. It's still the summer vacation but there will be students about. Perhaps some of them know where he is."

"You're both so kind," said Lisa. "Why are you doing all this for me?"

"Because we're French," smiled Lydie. "And there's nothing the French like better than a good love story."

She pointed out of the window of the bus, at a hang-glider in the air being pulled along by a speedboat.

Lisa watched the hang-glider swirl and soar in the darkening sky and marvelled at the man's courage: they'd certainly never get her up in one of those!

So intent was she on watching the hang-glider that Lisa completely missed the car which had just overtaken the bus travelling in the direction of Cannes.

It was a run-down and ramshackle green 2CV, driven by a certain dark-haired, brown-eyed Frenchman. And beside him in the passenger seat, her arm draped

casually over his shoulder, was a stunningly beautiful
and glamorous young woman.

23

Another wasted day followed in Nice, the big city about thirty minutes' train ride from Cannes. Lydie and Christophe knew some people at the university there and asked them about Jean-Luc. But as Lydie and Christophe, like Lisa, were science students, their friends also tended to be the same, and very rarely mingled with people like Jean-Luc who studied languages.

At noon they sat down at a small pavement café to have lunch. In front of them young people of both sexes in the latest fashions paraded, greeting friends, or just going to the large McDonalds in the city centre. (Whoever had decided that the French eat delicious haute cuisine all the time had never been to a French McDonalds at lunchtime, Lisa decided.) Everyone in the entire town seemed to know everyone else – every one, that was, except Jean-Luc Roupie!

As Lisa, Lydie and Christophe enjoyed their coffee, a girl of about Lisa's age came up to them.

"You are looking for Jean-Luc?" she asked in faltering English.

"Yes!" said Lisa, replying in French.

"I thought so. You were asking my friends about him earlier."

"Do you know where he is?" Lisa demanded, hope rising in her heart.

"No," the girl said, shaking her head, and Lisa's face fell.

"Have you any idea where he might be?" asked Lydie.

"All I know is that when he came back from England, he was very depressed and moody," the girl continued. "A girl, you understand, a thwarted affair of the heart..."

Lisa nodded sadly.

"He gave up his old flat, and no one has seen him for weeks," the girl concluded. "He could be anywhere now, anywhere at all..."

Lisa walked wearily along the Croisette as the sun set and the lights along the Croisette came on. Everywhere happy holiday-makers and locals, all dressed in the most chic clothes, cruised the famous boulevard with their friends – all intent on having a good time.

Christophe looked at Lisa and then at his own sister. Even Lydie was looking as despondent and maudlin as Lisa. In three days of searching for the elusive Frenchman all they had discovered was that his mother wasn't on the phone and that Jean-Luc had given up his flat. He was starting to think that it might be time for Lisa to admit defeat and go back to England and forget about Jean-Luc altogether.

"We need cheering up!" he announced grandly. "And I know just the thing! I'm buying us all a meal!"

"Christophe, that's sweet," Lisa said. "But you can't afford it..."

"And that is why I'm taking you to Vesuvio's!" he said.

"Vesuvio's?" asked Lisa. "What's that?"

"My favourite pizzeria on earth!" he explained. "The best pizzas in Cannes and at the lowest prices."

Vesuvio's was, in fact, one of the best-kept gastronomic secrets in the entire town. Located on the Croisette with a wonderful view of the beach and the Mediterranean, most tourists would pass by its unassuming façade and presume that it was just another pizzeria, one of thousands along the coast. But once they ventured inside they would find that the pizzas served there were huge and quite simply the most delicious this side of Italy. That was why at seven o'clock each evening there was always a long queue of locals waiting to be allowed in.

After a wait of about twenty-five minutes the three of them were let in and given a table in the corner of the restaurant. The pizzeria was packed with diners, and the waiters wove their way in and out of the closely packed tables, holding the pizzas aloft on huge wooden platters.

Everywhere there was the delicious smell of freshly-baked dough mixed with the tangy aroma of cheeses and tomatoes, and home-grown basil. The air was abuzz with the lively chatter of diners of all different nationalities, and the guttural accent of the waiters as they shouted their orders back to the busy kitchen. It was half-past seven, Vesuvio's had been open only half an hour and the place was already packed.

"See, I told you it was the best place in the whole of Cannes," said Christophe smugly. "Everyone who knows anything about the city comes here."

"There are just *so* many people," Lisa marvelled as she studied the comprehensive menu, wondering which one of Vesuvio's delicious pizzas to have. Christophe and Lydie had no need of menus: they were regulars here every summer and knew the menu off by heart.

When she had finally made her decision and Christophe had placed their order, Lisa looked around the restaurant. It seemed that the whole of Cannes had come to eat at the famous pizzeria.

To the table to the right of them was a group of four poor-looking students sharing two pizzas between them; behind the students there was a family table of two parents and their young children; over there was a beautiful sun-tanned couple, both of whom must surely be models, Lisa decided; and next to them an elderly man dining with his wife, whose ample bosom positively dripped with pearls, and whose long wrinkled fingers were covered with emeralds and rubies.

There was even a table of English tourists, making a hopeless effort to place their order in French. Lisa smiled, as the waiter sighed theatrically, and replied to the tourists in faultless English.

And over in the far corner, through the hustle and bustle of the diners, and the waiters mincing their way through the crowds, was a young dark-haired man with his back to them. He was wearing a red Chevignon T-shirt which hung loosely from his smooth swimmer's shoulders; he was consulting the menu.

Lisa felt her breath cut short, and her whole body began to tremble with anticipation. She felt the blood rush to her head, and her heart began to pound.

She stood up suddenly, and Lydie and Christophe looked at her in concern.

"Lisa, what is it?" asked Lydie, but Lisa had already left their table and was fighting her way through the crowded tables of the pizzeria, ignoring the disgruntled complaints of the waiters or the curious stares of her fellow diners – to the table of the one man she'd thought she'd never see again. Lydie and Christophe followed her.

As she approached the table she felt her legs sinking beneath her. This was the moment she'd been living for – the moment she had been working for for two long and wretched months – the moment she had been looking forward to with all her heart.

It was also the moment she had most feared. The moment when he might turn around and laugh at her. The moment when she might discover that he'd found someone else. The moment when he wouldn't believe her, and when he would reject her, and walk out of her life for ever.

The moment when he wouldn't love her.

She took a deep breath.

"Hello, Jean-Luc. It's me – Lisa."

For a half-instant, unnoticed by everyone except Lisa, Jean-Luc paused. And then he turned around. The moment he saw Lisa his face broke into a wide smile, and he leapt out of his chair.

"Lisa!" he cried out, and reached out his arms to touch her, to see if she was real.

Lisa felt her entire heart go out to the only man she had loved, or would ever love. The joy on Jean-Luc's face was evident: even Lydie and Christophe, who had caught up with their friend, could see that now.

Jean-Luc was at a loss for words. "But what are you doing in Cannes?" he asked.

"I came looking for you," Lisa said brightly, scarcely able to contain her joy. "I tried to find you at your old flat but the lady there said that you'd moved..."

"Yes, I've moved in with—"

Suddenly Jean-Luc drew back suspiciously. Lisa's face darkened.

"You came looking for me?" he asked and there was a sneer on his face, as he tried unsuccessfully to forget the wrong he believed Lisa had done to him back in England. He glanced at the good-looking Christophe. "With your current boyfriend, I suppose?"

"Don't be stupid," said Lydie with uncharacteristic anger. "He's not Lisa's boyfriend! He's my brother!"

"You hurt me, Lisa, you don't know how much you hurt me," he said bitterly. "For the past two months I've been trying in vain to forget you; must you come back now and reopen all those old wounds? And now you are here, expecting me to forgive you?"

"I'm not asking you to forgive me, Jean-Luc," Lisa insisted.

"Oh no?"

"Because there isn't anything to forgive!" she declared.

For God's sake I know how you're hurting, she thought. How do you think I'm feeling? But put away your French masculine pride for a minute and listen to the truth!

"I was never two-timing you with James!"

Jean-Luc didn't say anything, just gave her a look of total disbelief. A look which said: And you expect me to believe that? After what Alison told me about the

Christmas party? And after you stopped seeing me just as James came back from university?

"It was all a lie of Alison's so that she could get her claws into you!" she continued. "She fancied you something rotten, you know that! But I loved you! And I still do! And all I want in this world is for us to be happy. Together!"

Jean-Luc hesitated. What Lisa was telling him he fervently wanted to believe, but he had been made a fool of before and it had hurt his self-esteem very badly.

"Mon Dieu, monsieur!" said Christophe in exasperation. "Why would a girl come all the way from London to the South of France, if she wasn't in love with you?"

Now it was Jean-Luc's turn to look uncertain. And then, just as she thought her former boyfriend might believe her, Lisa's entire world fell apart.

There was a perceptible hush in the restaurant as the doors swung open and a tall and impossibly glamorous and sophisticated woman walked through the doors. She looked in her mid-twenties, with a mane of raven hair and dark-brown eyes. She was dressed in expensive designer clothes, and was as chic and as devastingly sexy as only Frenchwomen can be.

And every man in the restaurant couldn't take his eyes off her. Even Lisa realized that here was a woman so beautiful that she would make any supermodel look dowdy and plain.

The newcomer surveyed the restaurant, seemingly totally oblivious of the commotion and interest she had caused. Finally her eyes alighted on Jean-Luc and she strode over to him, the normally stroppy waiters making a path for her.

She planted a firm and loving kiss on Jean-Luc's lips. "Darling!" she said, in French, and placed her arm around his waist. "I'm sorry I'm late. But one of your friends called around at our flat, and – well, you know how it is, we started talking..."

Our flat?

Lisa felt herself trembling all over. Lydie and Christophe looked at each other, acutely aware of what Lisa must be going through.

Our flat?

Jean-Luc coughed with embarrassment, and looked sheepishly at Lisa. "Er, Adrienne, can I introduce you to my friends..."

Adrienne smiled and held out her hand. "*Enchantée*," she said. "My name's Adrienne. And you are?"

"Lisa Tyler," Lisa said, choking back the tears which were already coming to her eyes.

Lisa Tyler, the girl who came all the way to the South of France to get back Jean-Luc. Not knowing that he's already living with his new girlfriend! And how could I – or anyone else, for that matter? – compete with someone as beautiful, as sophisticated, as glamorous and as self-assured as you?

What an idiot I've made of myself! she thought despairingly. To think that anyone like me could win the love of someone as gorgeous, as sexy and as wonderful as Jean-Luc. Why don't I just go back to England, back to James, and Applewood which is where I belong?

"Sorry, I didn't quite catch your name?" said Adrienne.

Lisa the Fool, Lisa the Hopeless, Lisa the Ridiculous, she thought as she ran out of the pizzeria, and out of Jean-Luc's life for ever.

24

The overnight train to Paris scrunched to a halt at the Gare de Lyon station at a quarter past six the following morning, and Lisa found herself once more stumbling across the station concourse, struggling with her heavy bag. She was bleary-eyed and though she was tired she hadn't slept a wink all night on the journey from Cannes to Paris. Outside the train station the rain was once more coming down in torrents.

After she had run out of the pizzeria Lydie had followed her and they had gone straight to Lydie's apartment, leaving a bemused Christophe to settle the bill. There Lisa had started furiously packing while Lydie looked on helplessly.

"I've made a total idiot of myself, Lydie," Lisa told her in French. "I travel all the way down to Cannes to look for him – and I find that he's already got himself a new girlfriend! And he says he was hurt when he thought I was two-timing him!"

"But, Lisa, perhaps she's only a friend," Lydie had suggested, although she didn't really believe it.

"Did you see the way she kissed him? The way she held him?" Lisa said scornfully. "I know we're in France but that's hardly the way that 'just good friends' behave, is it?

"No, Lydie, Jean-Luc was just a summer fling and I've

got to learn to get over it..." she said, trying hard not to let her tears show.

Get over it? she thought despairingly. How can you get over the most wonderful, handsome, kind and charming man you have ever met in your whole life?

"What will you do?" asked Lydie. "You're welcome to stay here for the rest of the holidays."

"Thanks, Lydie, but no thanks," Lisa replied. "You and Christophe have been so kind to me, and I'll keep in touch. But the sooner I'm out of France, the better."

Because the sound of French being spoken, the people in the streets – even the smell of coffee and freshly-baked baguettes from the café – all remind me of the man I love.

Of the man I can never have.

"I'm getting the train back up to Paris and then to London," she revealed. "With any luck I'll be back home by tomorrow night."

"Won't your mother be suspicious?" asked Lydie. "You're supposed to be in Dorset for another week..."

Lisa shrugged. "I'll think of something," she said, and zipped up her bulging bag. She turned to Lydie and kissed her on the cheek. "Thanks for everything," she said.

"I hope you find happiness, Lisa," said Lydie as she dialled for a cab for which she insisted she would pay. "And I'm sure Christophe would too..."

"He's late..."

"Probably still arguing the bill at Vesuvio's," said Lydie. "But if I know my brother I wouldn't be at all surprised if he's telling Monsieur Roupie exactly what he thinks of him..."

Lisa looked around at the early-morning commuters arriving from the suburbs for work. They were all oblivious to her sadness, as they went about their individual lives; they were all so ignorant of the fact that her heart had been broken, and would never be whole again.

She sighed. No point in thinking about the past, she scolded herself. Must think about the future. A future at Applewood with 'A' levels next year. Who knows – James is a nice guy, after all. If Chrissie can fall for Simon, maybe... She shook her head sadly, as a numbing realization fell on her: a future without Jean-Luc...

She bent down to pick up her bag. It was heavy and it was quite a struggle to lift it.

Suddenly, as though from out of nowhere, a hand appeared and grabbed hold of the strap.

"Allow me, mademoiselle," came a dark-brown voice, a voice Lisa thought she'd only ever hear again in her dreams.

She turned. "Jean-Luc?"

Jean-Luc was standing there, dressed in the clothes he had been wearing last night at the pizzeria. They were crumpled and creased and it looked as though he had slept in them all night; which, in fact, he had. He also hadn't shaved and the stubble on his chin made him look even sexier. He was looking at her with loving, hopeful eyes.

"I ... I don't understand," Lisa babbled. What was Jean-Luc doing here in Paris when she'd just left him last night in the South of France?

"After you'd left, Christophe told me everything," Jean-Luc said. "All about Alison, and James, and how you came all the way down to Cannes to find me..."

"But how did you get here?" she asked.

"Last night I bought a ticket for the last flight from Nice to Paris," he explained. "I've been here all night just waiting for your train to come in..."

"How could you have afforded all that?" asked Lisa, her practical nature reasserting itself even now.

"Adrienne bought the ticket on her credit card," he said. "Otherwise I wouldn't have been able to afford it by myself."

Adrienne.

Lisa suddenly turned cold, anxious not to be made a fool of.

Adrienne.

"And who is Adrienne, then?" she demanded. "Your French girlfriend?"

Jean-Luc seemed surprised for an instant and then grinned.

And then smiled.

And then laughed fondly, adoringly, at Lisa.

"You thought Adrienne was my *girlfriend*?" he asked incredulously.

"Of course I did," said Lisa, suddenly feeling rather foolish.

"You crazy, crazy English girl," he said affectionately, and the love in his eyes for Lisa shone out. "Adrienne's not my girlfriend. Didn't I ever tell you that I have an older sister?"

"*Your sister?*"

Jean-Luc nodded and opened his arms wide. "That's right," he said. "Now come to me, Lisa. I don't ever want to let you out of my sight again."

Lisa fell into his embrace. She looked up into his eyes.

"I loved you, Jean-Luc," she said. "Even when I thought you had left me, even when I thought Adrienne was your girlfriend, I still loved you."

Jean-Luc looked down at her and stroked her hair. He kissed her on the forehead.

"And even when I thought you'd two-timed me, even when I told myself that I should never see you again, I knew that I loved you too. It hurt, but through all that hurt I knew that I still loved you, that you were the only one for me."

Lisa gazed dreamily into the deep brown eyes of the most gorgeous man in the world. "Soulmates?" she asked.

Jean-Luc nodded. "Soulmates," he confirmed. "And more than that. Lovers as well."

He held her tightly to him, so tightly that she hoped he would never let go. He kissed her, a long, passionate kiss which begged for forgiveness as much as expressing the love he felt for her.

Passers-by on their way to work stopped and stared at the young couple so obviously in love. Some tutted disapprovingly: others looked on admiringly. But Jean-Luc and Lisa didn't care; as far as they were concerned the rest of the world didn't exist.

Jean-Luc looked searchingly into her eyes, those baby-blue eyes that Lisa had once hidden behind her glasses.

He stroked her hair once more, that hair that she had once worn in a severe ponytail but now wore loose and free. He smiled.

"I'm not your teacher, Lisa," he whispered.

Lisa smiled too, and pressed herself even closer to her boyfriend's body. There were tears of delight in her eyes as she gazed up at his adorable face.

"And I'm not your student, Jean-Luc..."

IceHot!

1

"I want to die!"

Jackie Taylor looked up indifferently, shading her pretty hazel eyes from the summer sun, and considered the good-looking boy who had just hopped out of the passenger seat of the battered old Mini Metro parked by the open-air café.

He was a little under six feet, which made him about four inches taller than Jackie, and was broad-shouldered and slim-waisted. His complexion was a light coffee colour, betraying his Asian parentage. He was wearing a baggy short-sleeved American baseball shirt (the Baltimore Orioles, although the closest he'd ever been to America was watching cops 'n' robbers shows on TV), a pair of jeans (torn at the left knee) and a pair of scuffed-up trainers which had once been trendy but now were just permanently muddy. A gym bag was slung casually over his shoulder.

"Say again, Vikram?" Jackie asked, and sipped at her cup of coffee.

"I want to die!" Vikram repeated, slightly put out that his declaration of wanting to end it all wasn't having the desired effect on his friend.

"Well, just don't do it here," Jackie quipped. "Not in front of Slinky Jo's, the trendiest caff in this part of the northern hemisphere: it'd get us all a terrible reputation."

She turned to her companion, a girl her own age (which was seventeen) whose short dark hair perfectly complemented her dark gypsyish eyes. "I tell you, Emma, some of these guys have no taste at all!"

Emma smiled, and pulled out a chair for the newcomer. He sat down, breathing out a long and heartfelt sigh of exhaustion.

"Leave Vik alone, Jackie," she said and laughed. She turned to the young Pakistani boy who was running his fingers through his thick black hair which he wore long and curly. Vikram was a year older than them, and when he had still been attending their sixth-form college he had had something of a reputation of being an all-round jock. If you needed to track down Vikram, so common knowledge had it, all you had do was go to the nearest gym or sports field, and there he'd be. Whether he spotted you there or not was another matter: when Vikram was playing sports or working out it seemed that nothing else mattered to him.

"So what were you working out at today, Superman?" Emma asked. "The London marathon or scaling the north face of the Eiger?"

Vikram grinned, revealing a set of perfectly formed white teeth. "Nothing as easy as that, I'm afraid, just a game of five-a-side with Julian and the other guys down the park," he revealed. "But it's tired me out! I'm totally zonked!"

Jackie sighed mischievously. "I can't understand what all this fuss is about," she said mock-wearily. "Grown men kicking a piece of pig's bladder around the park. You'd think you'd have better things to do with your time."

Vikram smiled, and leant forward to give Jackie a friendly punch in the ribs. "And you will never ever understand, because it takes a man to appreciate the finer points of the noble and ancient art of good old-fashioned footie!"

"Chauvinist pig! Sometimes, Vik, you are such a stereotype!" Jackie joked, and smiled. It was a smile which lit up her entire face, making her by far the most attractive girl in the whole café. Jackie wasn't conventionally attractive, with a dimple in her chin which she hated, and long blonde hair which had a tendency to frizz at the ends if she didn't shampoo it sternly every other day; her beauty came from her naturalness and her open character.

Whereas other much prettier girls – and much plainer ones than her as well (Emma for example) – seemed to spend most of their time in front of their bedroom mirrors, Jackie rarely used make-up, and, although she did have one designer outfit, which she'd bought in the last January sales, she dressed mainly in casual, brightly-coloured sweatshirts and well-pressed jeans. It was a look which might have made other girls disappear in the crowd, but in Jackie's case it simply accentuated her happy-go-lucky personality.

"Anyway I haven't got anything better to do with my time," Vikram reminded her. "I've finished college now, and I'm taking a year off before I go on to university."

Jackie shuddered. She still had another year at sixth-form, but the prospect of anyone actually wanting to carry on studying for at least another three years, like Vikram, filled her with something approaching abject terror.

"And who's calling who a stereotype anyway, Ms Taylor?" Vikram riposted, when she told him this. "What are you going to do after A-levels? Find a rich man and marry him?"

Jackie pulled a face at her friend. "No way!" she said defiantly. "I'm not going to get married for ages yet. And when I do it'll be after I've made a career for myself. I'm going to marry for love, not money, and I'm not going to be some rich man's servant!"

"Just don't tell Julian that," Emma muttered under her breath, fortunately not quite loud enough for Jackie or Vikram to hear her.

"Besides I'm not clever enough to go to university like

you," Jackie continued. "I'd never make the grades." Vikram silenced her with a finger pressed against her lips.

"Don't ever put yourself down, Jackie," he said, suddenly all serious. "You've got to believe in yourself in this life. I did. My dad did. When he first came to England from Karachi, he was poor. But he met my mum, and she gave him faith in his abilities. They worked hard, and now they run two small grocery shops. A perfect pair. You can do anything if you believe in yourself and your own talents."

Emma yawned theatrically and took a bite of her chocolate fudge cake: it was loaded with calories, but *hey, what the hell!* she thought.

"Puhhh-lease! We're on holiday! Can we leave all the philosophizing and life-affirmation and calorie-counting until later? The holidays are supposed to be fun! Heck, I might even fall in love!"

Both Jackie and Vikram laughed at Emma: she was always complaining about how overweight she was (in fact, like most girls with the same complaint, she was nothing of the sort) while at the same time scoffing copious amounts of all the fattening foods at Slinky Jo's.

"Just to make up for my being such an obnoxious male chauvinist, why don't I buy us all some more cappuccinos?" Vikram suggested, and winked at Emma. "I might even be able to stretch to some more chocolate fudge cake!" When Emma nodded eagerly, he stood up to enter the café and place his order.

"Make that a double espresso for me," Jackie said. "And easy on the cream on the cake: at least *I'm* watching the calories!"

"*You* don't have to," Emma said pointedly, and gazed jealously at Jackie's slim figure. No matter how much Jackie ate she never seemed to put on a single unwanted ounce; whereas Emma only had to look at a Häagen-Dazs ad on the TV and it was Fat City all over again!

Resigning herself to the fact she'd never attain

supermodel proportions so she might as well keep on scoffing her cakes, Emma glanced up to see a tall sandy-blond-haired boy just locking the door on the driver's seat of a Metro. She waved to him and beckoned him over.

"Three cappuccinos and one double espresso it is then," Vikram said when he saw the newcomer approaching them, and he disappeared into the café.

"Hi, Julian," Emma said, and asked the couple on the table next to them if they could take their other chair. She dragged the chair over next to hers, and then moved places so that Julian could sit next to Jackie.

Julian gave Emma a friendly peck on the cheek, and then kissed Jackie full on the lips. He reached out for her hand under the table and held it; his touch was firm and manly but as he stroked her fingers, Jackie coloured slightly and turned. Recently she'd been wishing more and more that Julian wouldn't express his affection for her in public so much, and she wondered why; last Easter she certainly hadn't minded when he had held her tightly all night at the end-of-term dance like he'd never let her go ("I thought you'd never come up for air!" Emma had teased her the following day. "Who says that you need oxygen anyway?").

Jackie watched a couple of good-looking Italian boys she vaguely knew wolf-whistle at a pair of girls walking down the street. The girls tittered, and the boys hurried after them, all Latin charm and flirtatiousness. Jackie smiled: it seemed like all four of them were having fun. At least they were sure of having a good time this summer!

"You're late," she gently reproved her boyfriend, and looked at her watch (a limited-edition Swatch which was his birthday present to her last year). "We'd arranged to meet half an hour ago. Did yours and Vik's match go on longer than expected?"

Julian smiled and took his hand from Jackie's and reached into the top pocket of his MA1 flying jacket. He pulled out a cassette and handed it to Jackie. She inspected the cover: it was the latest album by

Powerhouse, the hottest band at the moment, whose last single had shot straight to Number One in the charts.

"I knew you wanted it," Julian said and flashed that eager-to-please, little-boy smile which made half of the girls at their sixth-form college swoon with pleasure. His sandy-blond hair flopped over his brilliantly blue eyes making him look even more adorable than usual. "So I drove into town after the game to buy it for you."

Jackie kissed Julian on the cheek. It was soft and smooth, unlike Vikram's, who even at two o'clock in the afternoon sported five o'clock designer stubble. Some of Jackie's girlfriends had said that it made Vikram look dangerously sexy, but she couldn't see it herself somehow. She'd known Vik for years: how could someone like him ever be thought of as sexy?

"That's so sweet of you, Jules," she said. "But you shouldn't have. You shouldn't spend so much money on me."

Julian shrugged. "What does it matter?" he asked, and looked lovingly into his girlfriend's eyes. "Nothing's too much for my little girl..."

"Yuck!" said Emma, who feared that Julian and Jackie were going to indulge in some serious soppiness right in front of her and her chocolate fudge cake.

"Anyway, you know my dad gives me a bigger than usual allowance," he said, and glanced over at the Metro. "He bought me that for my seventeenth birthday last year; he's got so much money he doesn't know what to do with it."

Jackie nodded: what Julian was saying was right. Her boyfriend lived in the big house at the top of the hill with his father who was a successful businessman, and owned a string of fast-food hamburger joints across this part of the country. The weekly pocket money he gave Julian was four times what Jackie's hard-pressed mother could scrape together for her for an entire month. Jackie suspected that Julian's father's generosity was merely a way of assuaging his guilty conscience, to make up for his messy divorce from Julian's mother.

Julian had treated Jackie to unexpected presents ever since they had started going out with each other two years ago, when she was fifteen and he was sixteen. At first she had been delighted by his gifts, but more and more now she was feeling slightly awkward about accepting them. And she wasn't entirely sure why.

"It's really very, very sweet of you, Jules," she repeated, as she read the list of song titles on the back of the cassette. "But I was planning on buying this for myself later... Emma and I have to go into town anyway to see if we can find any Saturday work. I can't expect my mum to keep on supporting me for ever, you know..."

"You don't need a Saturday job," Julian reassured her, and draped his arm over her shoulder in what was almost a protective gesture. "I get enough money to pay for both of us to go out clubbing and partying... And if I run short Dad will always give me some more."

"That's not the point, Jules," Jackie said weakly.

"So what's the big deal then?" Julian asked, not understanding what was troubling Jackie, although it was obvious that something was.

Jackie smiled. "It's nothing, Jules," she said finally. "Thanks again – it was a really nice thought."

"Don't I get another thank-you kiss then?" Julian pouted childishly, his blue eyes twinkling mischievously in his fair-complexioned face.

"Of course you do," Jackie said, and kissed him gratefully on the cheek again.

"Besides," Julian said, and suddenly looked guilty, "it's a sort of way of saying 'sorry' in advance..."

"Sorry?" Jackie asked and frowned. "What for?"

Julian looked around sheepishly, unwilling to look his girlfriend directly in the eyes. He peered back into the interior of Slinky Jo's. Vikram was there, waiting by the counter for his order to be completed, and chatting to a good-looking brunette, who, in her tight red satin T-shirt and close-fitting designer jeans seemed as slinky as the café's owner (Jo, or Josephine) claimed to have been back in the seventies when she had first set up her business. It was just like Vikram to end up chatting to the sexiest girl in the entire café, Julian thought.

Well, the sexiest girl apart from Jackie, that is, he hastily corrected himself.

"Sorry?" he heard Jackie say again. "Sorry for what?"

Julian turned back to Jackie. "For standing you up tonight," he said finally. "It looks as though I won't be able to make it after all…"

Jackie's face fell. "But Julian, you promised you'd drive me out into the country," she said, her voice full of disappointment, as well as a dangerous touch of anger. "I wanted to have a quiet chat with you, maybe at some nice country pub… It was important to me…"

"No can do," Julian said. "A friend of Dad's is coming round tonight – some important person in the medical faculty at the local university. You know I want to study medicine next year if my grades are good enough – maybe he can give me some advice."

"But that's in almost a year's time!" Jackie protested. "You haven't even taken A-levels yet!"

"It's important," he insisted.

Jackie allowed herself the luxury of a childish little sulk. "This is the second time you've cancelled a date in two weeks, Jules!" she reminded him.

"I know," he admitted, and there was a genuine note of regret in his voice. "But I made it up to you, didn't I?"

Jackie nodded. "That new blouse was really nice – I wouldn't have been able to afford it by myself, that's for sure. But it's not your presents I want, Jules, it's *you*. I was so looking forward to going out with you tonight."

Julian brought his hand to Jackie's face, and turned it so she was looking deep into his eyes. "I really am sorry, you know," he said, and Jackie could tell from his expression that he really meant it. "And I'll make it up to you – maybe buy you that dress you saw in that classy store the other day, or take you out for a real slap-up, dress-up meal…"

"But tonight was going to be *my* treat," Jackie said. "I wanted to…"

"Wanted to what?" Now it was Julian's turn to frown.

Jackie shook her head. "It doesn't matter now," she said, and smiled half-heartedly. "Of course, I understand. It's to do with your career and that's what really matters…"

Julian smiled and kissed her again. "I'm glad you understand: I'm really lucky to have you, Jackie," he said, and left the table to go and help Vikram with the four coffees.

Vikram was still talking to the sexy number in the tight jeans, and she smiled appreciatively when she saw Julian approach them, as if, when faced with two such good-looking boys, she didn't know which one to choose.

I should have such luck! Emma thought and finished the last of her cake. She looked sympathetically at Jackie who, after a slight twinge of jealousy at seeing the stranger eye up her boyfriend, had returned to her coffee.

"Men, huh?" she said, impressing upon those two syllables a whole world of meaning.

"Why does he never think of me?" Jackie asked, slightly petulantly. "Why does he always have to put his career first?"

Emma reached out for Jackie's hand. "You know how tough it is to get into medical school," she said. "Julian studies every hour God sends him but he's still going to need all the help he can get…"

"Sure… I guess you're right…" Jackie said, and looked back into the café. Vikram and Julian were still talking and joking with the sexy brunette at the counter. Jackie thought that the two boys were enjoying themselves just a little too much.

"And besides you can't say he isn't sorry – and he always tries to make it up to you," Emma said. "He's always giving you presents – even when he doesn't stand you up! I wish I had a boyfriend like that." She considered the matter for a moment, before adding glumly: "Come to think of it, I wish I had a boyfriend…"

Jackie smiled, used by now to Emma's regular tale of woe. "You'll find a nice boy one day," she promised her. "And you'll find one when you least expect it!"

"With competition like that girl in there?" Emma asked, nodding over to the girl inside Slinky Jo's. "Do us a favour, Jackie!"

"You shouldn't put yourself down," Jackie said, unconsciously echoing Vikram's earlier words to her. "You're as good as any number of brainless bimbos like her..."

"She's slim, and I'm fat –"

"You're not fat!"

"She wears masses of expensive clothes and jewellery, and looks as though she's just stepped right out of a copy of *Vogue*," Emma protested.

"Looks aren't everything, Em," Jackie told her. "It's what a person is deep down that really counts."

"It's still really annoying when you have to turn down party invites because you've got no boyfriend to accompany you," said Emma, "and you know that everyone else at the party is going to be on the arm of some sizzling hunk!"

"Don't be silly, Em," Jackie reproved her. "We've got lots of friends who go to parties by themselves, or with their other girlfriends. It's the 1990s, you know! We don't have to have a mere male to escort us everywhere!"

"Yeah, but the trouble is that they decided to leave their boyfriends at home," Emma carried on, indulging in a spot of self-pity. "At least they have the choice!"

"You've got Vikram," Jackie reminded her. "You like going to parties with him – you told me as much the other week."

"But it's not the same," Emma said. "Vikram's a friend, my mate, he's not my boyfriend. And the moment we arrive at the party, and the other girls cotton on to that fact, they're all over him, like bees around a honeypot, leaving me to play gooseberry!"

Jackie looked at Vikram who was trying to carry two cups of coffee in each hand, while Julian continued chatting to the bimbo. For the moment her jealousy of the other girl was forgotten and she considered Vikram, as he concentrated hard on not spilling any coffee, licking his lips, like a little boy performing a particularly tricky task.

"Vikram?" she gasped in astonishment. "Why would all the girls want to talk to Vikram?"

Emma raised her eyes heavenwards: Jackie was a lot smarter than she liked to believe, but there were times when she could be just so dumb!

"In case you haven't noticed – and from that look of pure amazement on your face, Jackie Taylor, it seems that you haven't – Vikram is one of the best-looking boys in town. Dark-eyed, moody with it, and he's got a body to die for! And I should know – I've been swimming with him down at the leisure centre."

"It's all those sports he plays, I suppose," Jackie decided, and watched Vikram as he wove his way through the crowd of trendies standing outside the café drinking their coffees, or knocking back their bottles of Mexican beer.

"You mean the girls all find him really good-looking?" she asked and chuckled when Emma nodded her head. "When I look at him all I can see is that spotty and snotty-nosed little kid I used to play with when I was young, and he and his parents had just moved into our road. Or the young teenager who always came round to help me with my homework. I can't really imagine anyone finding my next-door neighbour sexy!"

"Uh-huh," Emma said. "Our Vik has quite a fan club of love-hungry females. Not that it does them any good!"

"What d'you mean?" Jackie asked.

"By the end of the evening, instead of being in a corner snogging away with some stunner from out of town, you're more likely to find him in a corner with a couple of cans of cheap cider, watching the late-night football or volleyball results on the telly with a couple of mates," Emma revealed. "Vik is strictly not interested in going out with girls: all he's bothered about is sport, sport and more sport!"

"They must hate him for that," Jackie chuckled, as she gained a new perspective on Vikram. She realized that ever since she'd been going out with Julian she'd neglected her other friends: she couldn't remember the last time she'd been out on her own to a party with Vikram or Emma... They used to have so much fun, and at the end of the night Vikram had always made sure that she got home safely, walking her to her door. She remembered that someone had once teased her about Vikram only walking her home so that he could steal a goodnight kiss; at which point she had exploded in a fit of giggles. *Vikram? A goodnight kiss? Oh, come on!*

"It's a challenge, I guess, and it certainly doesn't stop them trying," Emma said. "If I had a penny for every time some girl's asked me to fix her up with Vik, I wouldn't have to keep reminding my mum to buy a Lottery ticket every week!"

"I don't need a Lottery ticket when I've got Julian," Jackie said wryly, returning to the original subject of their conversation.

"Like I said, you're a lucky girl."

Jackie smiled. "I just wish he'd let me pay for things sometimes," she said wistfully.

"He's got more dosh than you," Emma reminded her practically. "And he likes to buy you things."

"He's been buying me more and more presents lately," Jackie said thoughtfully. "I'd just like to be a bit more independent, and not have to rely on him all the time. It would be really nice for him to let me look after him for a change, and not always have it the other way around. Sometimes I don't even think he needs me apart from as an excuse to spend his dad's money..."

"Never look a gift horse in the mouth," was Emma's cynical reply, although she detected a change in her friend's mood. Jackie's lips were trembling slightly, and there was a faraway look in her eyes.

"That's why tonight was so important," Jackie said. "I was going to pay for the whole meal myself – and we were going to go to a restaurant or a country pub of my choosing, and not one of the swish places he takes me. You see, Emma, for tonight only, I wanted it to be me who was in control..."

"In control? What do you mean, Jackie?" asked Emma, but before Jackie could answer Vikram had returned with the four coffees. He placed them on the table, almost spilling the contents of one as he did so. Jackie smiled, and just hoped that when, and if, Vikram managed to get a temporary job for his year off, as he wanted, it wouldn't be as a waiter in a restaurant: he was so clumsy that he wouldn't last five seconds before accidentally spilling a bowl of spaghetti down some swanky diner's best suit!

"A cappuccino and a double espresso for the two most beautiful women in the world!" he announced grandly, and sat down.

"Liar," said Jackie.

"Julian will be bringing the cakes over in a minute," Vikram told them.

"If he can drag himself away from that bimbo over there, that is," Emma said lightly. By the bar Julian and the girl were still getting on like a house on fire. (Or, as the cynical Emma might have put it, like a Black Widow spider selecting her mate.)

Vikram looked urgently over at Jackie. "Hey, don't get the wrong end of the stick," he said anxiously. "They're only talking."

"I wasn't worried," Jackie said, and at least sounded as though she meant it. After all, they had known each other for so long that she knew there was no danger of Julian going off with the first girl to come on to him. He loved her; otherwise why was he always spending so much money on her?

"I think Vik's just worried that you're going to throw a wobbly like you did last Christmas!" Emma said mischievously.

"I did not 'throw a wobbly', as you put it!" Jackie retorted. It was a sore subject for Jackie and one which she didn't like being reminded of too often. She and Julian had been at a Christmas party at a flat owned by some students at the local tech, when one of the students had come on to Julian in no uncertain manner. Even though Julian had managed to escape the girl's advances, Jackie had seen red, and it had taken all of Emma's reasonable words to calm her down.

"On past form I'd've thought you'd be over there by now, pouring several gallons of espresso down her front," Emma teased, and was taken aback when Jackie suddenly flared up.

"That's enough, Em! OK?"

"Sorry..."

"No, I'm sorry for snapping at you," Jackie said, and started to toy with her teaspoon.

Vikram looked curiously at Jackie, and then continued. "You shouldn't really worry, Jackie. Her name's Linsey and she goes to the tech down the road from your sixth-form," he said. "I've met her once or twice before, at parties. She seems to be a really nice girl –"

"And really sexy too," Emma added. "Or do you mean to say that you hadn't noticed?"

"Is she?" asked Vikram, and looked at Linsey again. "Yeah, I suppose she is kinda attractive ... in a brash and blatant sort of way ... and I guess if you like that sort of thing..."

Emma gave Jackie a knowing, all-girls-together wink which said: *See! What did I tell you!*

"Anyway, she said she knows this job that's going for the next six months," Vikram said. "It could be just what I need to earn some money before I go off to university."

"Vik, that's great!" said Em, and hugged her friend. Jackie congratulated him as well. "What is it?"

"Nothing special," Vikram told them. "It's working in a café-bar, serving food and drinks."

(Jackie groaned inwardly: it looked like Vikram had found himself a job as a waiter after all!)

"Where is it then?" she asked anxiously, as worrying

visions of Vikram dropping bottles of expensive vintage wines, and knocking over the dessert trolley, came flooding, unbidden, into her mind.

"Down at Blades," he informed her.

"Blades?" she asked. "The ice-skating rink?"

"That's right," he said. "They need someone behind the counter to serve teas and sandwiches – that kind of thing."

(Jackie breathed a silent sigh of relief: it seemed that the diners of England were safe for the time being!)

"Vik, that is the most wonderful piece of news I've heard all day!" Emma said, and clapped her hands together for joy. "It looks like this summer is going to be worthwhile after all!"

Vikram laughed at Emma's enthusiasm, and raised his hands, palms-outwards, in a calming gesture. "Hey, I haven't got the job yet," he reminded them. "I've still got to go for an interview later this afternoon!"

"Of course you'll get the job – after all, you're one of my best friends, aren't you?" Emma said confidently, as if that dubious honour automatically equipped him for any task under the sun.

"I'm sure you'll wow them with your charms, Vik," Jackie said, and patted his hand encouragingly. It felt strong and warm and the hairs on it bristled at her touch.

"Thanks, Jackie," Vikram said, and smiled, before turning back to Emma. "But what's the big deal, Em? Why are you so excited?"

"Well, with you working as a member of staff we'll all be able to get in free every day, won't we?" she said.

"Hey, I'm not so sure about that..."

"Of course we will," Emma said confidently. "I've seen the old dragon who runs the place – one flash of those sexy dark eyes and she'll be putty in your hands! You know Jackie and I love to ice-skate. And besides –" here she winked at Jackie – "think of all those men we'll get to meet!"

Jackie laughed. For someone who had never had a

proper boyfriend in her life, Emma certainly thought about the subject an awful lot! She was about to say something when Julian returned, balancing four plates of Slinky Jo's famous chocolate fudge cake.

"Been having fun with your new friend?" joked Jackie, and gestured at Linsey by the counter: she was alone now and sipping thoughtfully on a glass of Diet Coke. She wouldn't be alone for much longer, Jackie realized, as she watched a couple of boys eyeing her up and moving in for the kill. From the looks of Linsey, thought Jackie, were those two boys ever in for a surprise! She looked as if she could eat them for breakfast and still have room for seconds!

Julian's face fell. "Hey, you didn't think that I..." he began guiltily, but Jackie just sighed – sometimes Julian could take things so seriously! – and indicated that he should sit down.

"It was just a joke, OK, Jules?" she said, and wondered why Julian had turned a bright shade of red. Had he really been chatting up the new girl by the bar? And if he had been, why hadn't she been overly concerned about it? Indeed, she had been much more interested in Emma's friendly gossip about Vikram and the news of his new job.

Vikram, as though instinctively aware of some sort of mild tension between his two friends, said: "Linsey's a nice enough girl, isn't she, Jules? It was really kind of her to mention that job at Blades."

Julian nodded distractedly and then, when Emma and Vikram had got down to the much more serious business of demolishing Slinky Jo's cakes, he turned to his girlfriend, a serious look in his eyes.

"You do believe me when I say I wasn't coming on to her, don't you, Jackie?" he asked anxiously. "You know I'd never do anything to hurt you. I love you very much..."

Jackie kissed him on the cheek. "Of course I believe you, Julian," she said. "And I love you very much too..."

But as she sipped at her double espresso, Jackie wondered if either of them was telling the truth.

2

Just as Emma had predicted, Vikram got the job at Blades ice-skating rink, and Miss Crabtree, the cranky middle-aged former skater who ran the place told him he could start on Monday. When he had asked her, rather sheepishly, whether he could let his friends come and use the ice rink for half-price, she had shaken her head firmly.

"Sorry, Miss Crabtree," Vikram said, and hung his head in embarrassment. "I guess it was a pretty cheeky thing to ask, especially as I haven't even started working here yet."

Miss Crabtree beamed a smile that none of her other colleagues would have dreamt her capable of, and said: "Nonsense, Vikram, they must come in for free. I'm sure a young man like yourself will only have upstanding and polite friends – unlike many of the hooligans we attract here nowadays. Call it my welcoming gift to you!"

Vikram couldn't believe his luck, and smiled at Miss Crabtree. The crusty old director of the rink felt her knees turn to jelly. "You really mean it?" he asked incredulously. He stood up to shake the woman's hand gratefully. "Hey, that's great. Thanks very much, Miss Crabtree."

"Think nothing of it, Vikram," Miss Crabtree said, and looked admiringly at the young man before her: if only she were thirty years younger! And he was so polite too, so different to the other young men of his age. If Emma had been eavesdropping on the conversation, she would by now have turned to Jackie and declared that Miss Crabtree had been "well and truly hooked".

Miss Crabtree released her hand from Vikram's, and showed him to the office door. As she opened it, a wave of cold air from the ice hit them, and they could hear the delighted shouts of the Saturday afternoon skaters, as their cries echoed in the huge hall.

"And of course, you have free use of the ice whenever you're not working," she said. "Apart from mornings of course, when lessons are being held."

"That's really sweet of you, Miss Crabtree," Vikram said. "But I don't skate. Every other sport going maybe, but not ice-skating."

"Then you must learn!" she decided. "We should fix you up with one of our instructors – maybe a pretty young girl?" she added with a twinkle in her eyes.

Vikram laughed. "I'm sure she'd find me incredibly clumsy," he said, self-deprecatingly. "I've got two left feet!"

"Well, the offer's still open," she said as she waved him goodbye. "And anything you want, Vikram, just let me know, and I'm sure I'll be able to help. And Vikram, it's Betty – not Miss Crabtree – is that clear?"

Vikram chuckled. "Sure, Miss – I mean, Betty!"

"See? What did I tell you?" Emma said smugly, as she, Vikram and Jackie finished off the last of their noodles in the trendy Japanese sushi bar where they were meeting to celebrate Vikram's job. "Putty in your hands!"

Vikram laughed, and wiped his mouth with a paper napkin: there was a slice of green pepper on his lower lip, Jackie noticed. It made him look cute, like a little boy.

"Don't ask me what I did," he said. "It's not as if I have any experience! Apart from A-level maths of course – I guess that'll be helpful when I come to cash up in the evenings."

Emma shook her head, and placed a hand on Vikram's. "Vik, people like you don't need any experience," she said.

"I don't know what you mean," he replied, and meant it. "But then I guess I've always been lucky."

Lucky where women are concerned, Emma thought. *They all fall over themselves to be as nice to you as possible!*

"Anyway, enough talking about me and my new job," Vikram said, and turned to Jackie, who was idly prodding the last of her noodles with her chopsticks. "You've been quiet all evening. How are you feeling?"

"What?" Jackie looked up, suddenly aware that Vikram was addressing her. She had been distracted, far away from the conversation.

"Are you OK?" he asked, and looked at her with those dark and soulful eyes of his. They were moist and fathomless, yet Jackie could see in them the genuine concern Vikram had for her. He had always looked out for her, even when they had been little kids; somehow she didn't know what she'd do without Vikram around the place. And yet he never dominated her like Julian, he always listened to her opinions. When Julian was taking her out for a meal, she sometimes felt like little more than an adjunct to his social life, almost a pretty accessory, a possession. With Vikram, she felt an equal, a friend.

"You've been looking like this all night," Emma said, and pulled a long face, which made even Jackie laugh.

"I'm fine," she said, and wasn't sure whether she was telling the truth or not. "I've just been thinking."

"About what?" Vikram asked.

Jackie shrugged. "Just things, that's all."

"About all the hunky ice-skaters who are going to take us for a spin around the ice starting next Monday," Emma decided gleefully.

Jackie giggled. "Don't you ever think of anything but boys, Em?" she asked, with a touch of mock-disapproval in her voice.

"Nope," Emma said, and then frowned: "Trouble is, all

the boys are usually thinking of Sharon Stone or Winona Ryder and never little old me..."

Emma's joke defused what could have been a potentially awkward situation, and Jackie finished her meal, rounding it off with a small glass of sake, the Japanese rice wine. Emma loved it but she found it a little too strong for her taste. Vikram was drinking water, as apart from the occasional can of cider he didn't drink at all. Jackie lowered her glass and smiled at Vikram.

"And thanks for inviting me out tonight to celebrate, Vik," she said. "It was so considerate and much better than staying in by myself and watching Saturday night telly."

Vikram smiled and told her not to mention it. "That's what friends are for," he said. "Emma told me how much you were looking forward to going out with Jules tonight – it's the least I could do." He caught the eye of the Japanese waitress by the cashdesk and she came over with the bill.

"Let me pick up the tab, Vik, by way of a thank-you," Jackie offered, and reached for her purse, but Vikram shook his head.

"I can't let you pay for it all!" she protested. That was exactly what Julian would do, she realized, but Vikram shook his head.

"What do you think I am? Made of money?" he asked, pretending to be outraged at the very thought. "We split it three ways."

"OK," agreed Emma. "A third each?"

Vikram turned to her, in wide-eyed horror. "You think I'm crazy, Emma Carter?" he gasped. "You and Jackie had much more than me: the sake for one thing! And you had the –" he snatched at the menu, and tried to pronounce the unfamiliar words – "the hamaguri ushiojiru!"

"The what?"

"The clam soup," Vikram explained. "At least I think that's what it is..."

"I did?" Emma asked.

"No, I did," Jackie butted in, and took the bill from Vikram, and a pen from out of her pocket. "Now let's make a list of what each of us had, OK? Vik, you had the seaweed, right?"

"Sure," he said, and, as Jackie scribbled the price down, added mischievously, "but you and Emma nicked half of mine so you two should go quarters on it!"

"But you tried one of my rice balls," Emma pointed out to him.

"Only one," Vikram said, but Emma wasn't to be swayed.

"I only had six," she said, and quoted a sixth of the price for a serving of rice balls.

"This is getting confusing," Jackie despaired, and for a second longed for the simpler times when Julian would pick up the entire tab.

"No, this is getting ridiculous," Emma corrected her, and laughed. She turned to Jackie and grinned: "It's surprising how much of a male chauvinist pig our Vik can be when he's talking about football; but when it comes to paying for the meal then he's all for equal rights!"

"You two girls have reformed my outmoded and traditionalist outlook on life," he claimed solemnly, with a hand over his heart.

"Got you worried about your bank balance is more like it," Jackie said.

"That as well," Vikram admitted. "We're all as poor as each other: we haven't got super-rich daddies like Jules, you know! We're all equals."

Jackie agreed. "I could still have paid," she said, when the waitress had collected their bill, and a mixed array of crumpled fivers, fifty-pence and five-pence pieces. "After all, I was going to buy for Julian tonight."

"No way," Vikram said. "I don't like to be dependent on anyone. Equals, that's all that matters."

"I know what you mean," Jackie said, half to herself.

Before either Vikram or Emma could ask her what she meant, they spotted Linsey, the girl they had seen earlier at Slinky Jo's, on her way up to their table. She had just arrived with a group of people, both boys and girls, each and every one of them stunningly good-looking and insufferably trendy, and they were being shown to their table by a waitress.

"Fancy meeting you here!" she said, and when Vikram had introduced them gave Jackie and Emma each a brief polite nod, before turning all her considerable attention on Vikram. She was wearing a loud Versace blouse (which must have cost a small fortune, Jackie reckoned), and baggy leather trousers, and she looked a million dollars.

On second thoughts, Jackie seemed to say to Emma as they each exchanged a look, *make that two million dollars!*

"Er, hi, Linsey," Vikram smiled, and gave Jackie and Emma a *hey, what's a boy s'posed to do?* sort of look.

"And where's your other sexy friend, Vikram?" Linsey asked, her voice suggestive and hopeful. "That gorgeous blond guy, Julian?"

Vikram looked helplessly at Jackie, who smiled back at Linsey with all the sweetness and sincerity of a crocodile looking for its next meal.

"My *boyfriend* is at home, preparing for his future," she frostily informed Linsey. She couldn't believe the nerve of the sexy young newcomer! How dare she fancy *her* boyfriend!

Linsey, however, didn't miss a beat. "You must be soooo happy going out with him," she said, and looked Jackie up and down, as though sizing up the competition. "And surprised too. He's got to be the best thing that'll ever happen to you, Emma."

The implication was obvious, but Jackie kept her cool. *Maybe I'm the best thing that's ever happened to him,* she thought, but instead contented herself with correcting Linsey. "And my name's Jackie, not Emma." She nodded over to her friend. "This is Emma."

Linsey looked over at Emma, and then back at Jackie, and then at Emma again, as if she were comparing them.

"Of course, how silly of me," she oozed. "How could I have got you mixed up? You're so different from each other. After all, Jackie, you're so slim…"

At Jackie's side Emma saw red, but Linsey had already turned away from them and was once again addressing Vikram, who hadn't seemed to have noticed that anything was amiss. It seemed that Linsey felt herself honour-bound to put down any females who might be an obstacle in her pursuit of the latest hunk, who in this case, and in the absence of Julian, seemed to be Vikram.

"So did you get the job?" she asked, and when Vikram nodded she let out a screech of delight, and hugged Vikram, planting an enormous kiss on his cheek, and then one full on the lips. Vikram sat back in his seat, totally disconcerted by Linsey's sudden display of affection.

Unwilling witnesses to Linsey's totally over-the-top behaviour, Jackie and Emma winced, but found they couldn't take their eyes off her. Much as they instinctively disliked her, each of them also felt a sneaking admiration. Certainly neither of them would ever have dared to try something like that on a boy they had only just started talking to that very afternoon!

"I knew you'd get it!" Linsey said categorically. "How could Betty refuse someone as good-looking as you? I hope we'll be seeing a lot more of each other now, Vikram."

"Well, sure, Linsey," Vikram said, trying to sound as noncommittal as possible. "But you know, I'm going to be busy, what with this new job, and I play a lot of sports and work out at the gym quite a bit too…"

Linsey's green eyes twinkled mischievously. "I bet you do!" she said, and reached out teasingly, to feel Vikram's biceps beneath the sleeves of his denim shirt. "I really like men with muscles who look after their bodies!"

Jackie and Emma exchanged another look: was this woman for real?

However, Vikram seemed slightly embarrassed by all this teasing, and Linsey instantly picked up on it. She took her hand off his arm, as if it had just turned red-hot.

"But we will be seeing each other a lot more," she said, her voice suddenly less effusive than it had been only a second ago. "How do you think I heard of the job in the first place? I work there occasionally and Betty Crabtree, who runs Blades, is my aunt –"

Emma looked meaningfully at Jackie. She had described Betty Crabtree as an old dragon: it seemed that it ran in the family!

"– and I practise my ice-skating there every day," Linsey continued, and preened herself in front of them all, showing her firm and slim figure to its very best advantage. "I do think it's sooooo important for a girl to stay in shape these days – don't you? Unlike some people."

This last remark was addressed not at Vikram or even Jackie, but at the ever weight-conscious Emma. Somehow Linsey had zeroed in on the one thing guaranteed to upset Emma, who glared daggers at her. Linsey just smiled sweetly and returned to Vikram.

"Look, Vikram, my friends are over there," she said and waved at the group of nine or ten. "You must come over and meet them. I'm sure these two girls won't miss you for a while…"

Linsey wouldn't take no for an answer and hustled Vikram out of his chair. She started to lead him over to the table, when Emma, who had been quietly fuming to herself over Linsey's treatment of her, said: "It's OK, Vik, don't worry about us…"

"Hey, I'm sorry, Em," he said genuinely. "I'll just say hello to Linsey's friends and then I'll be straight back."

"That's right, Vik," Linsey said, and Jackie noticed that she had instantly picked up on their use of Vikram's nickname, and had adopted it herself.

"Of course you have set the VCR, haven't you?" Emma said casually, and Jackie stared at her: what was Emma talking about?

"The VCR?" Vikram's face went pale; this wouldn't be

the first time that he had forgotten to set the video recorder to tape something off the television.

"Sky Sports," she said, and told him that the satellite channel was showing a three-hour special tribute to a famous footballing legend and one of Vikram's all-time heroes.

"But I didn't know..." said Vikram, who always made a point of circling in red in the *Radio Times* whatever sports programmes were being shown on satellite and cable.

"Change of schedule," was Emma's pat reply.

"Vik, forget about it," Linsey urged, and started to pull him towards her table. "It's only a silly little man kicking a football around."

"I can't miss this, Linsey!" he said. "He was the greatest striker of his generation!"

Linsey wasn't prepared to take no for an answer. "So get your parents to tape it."

"No can do," said Jackie, who had caught on to Emma's ruse and was enjoying the look of indignation on Linsey's face. "They've got two late-night shops to run. They won't be home till late."

"For goodness' sake," said Linsey, growing irritated now. "It's only a game of football after all!"

It was the wrong thing to say to Vikram. He released himself from Linsey's hold and looked at his watch: if he hurried he might just make it home in time.

"Look, Linsey, it's been really nice seeing you again," he said, making his exit. "And I'll look forward to seeing you on Monday at the rink."

"But..."

Vikram turned to Jackie and Emma and gave them each a farewell kiss on the cheek. "Thanks for reminding me, girls – you're real mates," he said gratefully, and not without some relief at being rescued from the clutches of the irrepressible Linsey. "I'll see you soon, OK?"

And with that Vikram grabbed the leather jacket he had thrown over the back of his chair, and was out of the restaurant, leaving a fuming Linsey staring angrily at Jackie and Emma.

"You know what boys of that age are like," Jackie said in a sarcastic tone of voice.

"Sports mad," Emma agreed. "No time for anything else – especially not girlfriends…"

Linsey glared at them and then, without saying a word stalked back to her own table.

"You were marvellous!" Jackie congratulated her friend.

"At least it got her off Vik's back," Emma said. "She'd have made mincemeat out of him!"

"Lucky for him that he'd forgotten about that sports programme," Jackie said.

"That's hardly surprising as there isn't going to be a programme for him to tape when he gets back home!" Emma revealed, and giggled. "I made it all up to save our Vik from a fate worse than death!"

"He'll kill you when he finds out, you know," Jackie laughed.

"Either that or thank me for rescuing him from the clutches of our Black Widow Spider over there!"

"Did you see the way she treated him?" Jackie said distastefully. "Like he was a piece of meat, just another notch for her scorecard."

"He is an exceptionally good-looking guy, you know," Emma reminded her.

"Yeah, you said," Jackie said wistfully. "I guess he is…"

"Well, you hadn't noticed until I told you so this afternoon," Emma pointed out.

"He's never had a real girlfriend, has he?" Jackie continued. "Why do you suppose that is?"

Emma shrugged. "We've never discussed it," she said. "I suppose he's just been so busy, what with working hard for his A-levels, and all the sports he does. Some boys are like that – they much prefer to hang out with the rest of the other lads – more's the pity."

"But he must know just how attractive he is to the girls," Jackie said.

"He's like lots of good-looking people," Emma said. "They've no idea of how attractive they are, or the effect they have on others..."

"Unlike some people," Jackie said, and looked over to the table where Linsey and her friends were ordering several bottles of sake. "What gives her the right to barge in here and think she can get any boy she wants?"

Emma looked curiously at her old friend. "Why are you so uptight about it, Jackie?" she asked. "It's not as if Vik's your boyfriend or anything. And I didn't see you getting so upset when she was talking to Julian in Slinky Jo's this afternoon, or when she mentioned just now how sexy she found Jules..."

"Don't mind me," Jackie said off-handedly. "I've probably just had too much sake..."

"Jackie, before Linsey burst in, you were agreeing with Vikram, saying that you didn't like being dependent on anyone," Emma said, choosing her words carefully. "Were you talking about Julian?"

Jackie eyed her friend, and then smiled. "I guess you've known me too well and for too long," she said.

"That's right," Emma said. "You, me and Vik have lived in the same neighbourhood since we were all little kids. And besides I read lots of problem pages!"

"It's not a problem," Jackie said automatically, and then sighed. "It's just that Jules does so much for me, sending me little presents, making sure I'm all right—"

"—And standing you up tonight!" Emma chipped in.

"But he gave me that cassette to make up for it. And no doubt I'll get yet another present tomorrow just to prove how sorry he is," Jackie said.

"He's a sweet guy," Emma remarked.

"But he never lets me do my own thing," Jackie said. "He's always there for me when I need him. But when does he ever need me? When does he ever let me do something for him? Sometimes it's like he's smothering me... And just when I get the nerve to..." She paused.

"To do what, Jackie?" Emma asked softly.

Jackie shook her head. "It doesn't matter, Em," she claimed, and looked over at Linsey's table, no longer bothering to hide the jealousy in her eyes. She turned back to Emma and attempted a brave smile.

"C'mon, Em, let's go home," she said brightly. "And on the way we can call in at Vikram's to apologize for sending him home early!"

"Sure," said Emma, and followed Jackie out of the sushi bar. As she did so, she wondered just what was going on in Jackie's mind. She remembered the conversation Jackie and Julian had had in Slinky Jo's, and all the presents that Julian had recently been giving Jackie.

Could it be that he was trying to ease a guilty conscience? Emma wondered. And then she recalled Jackie's surprise when she had pointed out just how good-looking Vikram was; and how annoyed she had been at Linsey's intrusion tonight. Could it be that Jackie was actually jealous? And what was it that Jackie had found the nerve to do, and wouldn't tell Emma?

Emma Carter, you have been reading too many trashy romances! she scolded herself, as she and Jackie hailed a taxi to take them home. *You're putting two and two together and coming up with five!*

But Emma had never been more wrong in her life, for she and Jackie were just about to discover that two and two most definitely do come to four.

3

"'**G**orgeous blond guy'?" asked Julian in disbelief the following morning, as he and Vikram left the changing rooms of the local leisure centre.

"That's what she called you," Vikram said. "Seemed like she was really disappointed when you weren't at the sushi bar last night."

"Yeah, well, I had to see this friend of my dad's," Julian said off-handedly.

"Fair enough. What did he say? Give you any advice on applying for medical school?" Vikram asked, as they passed an exceptionally pretty young red-head on the stairs, who was dressed in a tight all-in-one Lycra outfit.

"Sorry?" Julian asked, and tore his eyes away from the girl. Vikram gave him a knowing smile. "What did you say, mate?"

"I asked if your dad's friend had given you any good tips on getting into medical school," Vikram repeated patiently.

"Ah that … yes…" Julian coloured. "Well … er … actually he had to cry off at the last moment," he revealed. "Apparently there was some emergency at the hospital and he had to stay in overnight."

"That's a shame," Vikram said, and then a sudden thought struck him. "So why didn't you come out with us? You knew Emma and I had planned to take Jackie out 'cause you were tied up. You could have come along with us. Or gone out with Jackie to that country pub like she'd planned."

Julian stared straight ahead, desperately trying to avoid Vikram's eyes. "I ... I didn't feel like it, that's all," he said rather lamely. "I suppose I just fancied a quiet night in..."

Vikram reached out for Julian's arm and stopped him, making him turn around to look at him. "Jackie was so upset that you couldn't make it last night," he reminded his mate. "She was really looking forward to taking you out for dinner."

"She needn't do that," Julian said, and a tiny nervous tic appeared at the corner of his mouth. "I can easily afford to take both of us out."

"She wanted to do it herself," Vikram insisted. "And if you were just too tired to go out at least you could have rung her to apologize..."

"I ... I know..." Julian said, and then added after a long pause: "Look, Vik, perhaps I just wanted a night in by myself for a change..."

Vikram shrugged. "Sure. No problem." He still hadn't let go of Julian's arm. "Jules, are you sure that you were supposed to meet this friend of your dad's last night?"

Julian flushed even redder. "That's what I said, wasn't it?" he demanded angrily. "Hey, are you accusing me of lying? Of fooling around behind Jackie's back?"

"Forget it, Jules," Vikram said, and released Julian's arm. It was obvious from Julian's demeanour that he was telling the truth. "I mean, it's none of my business really. It's not like she's my girlfriend, is it?"

"Yeah, right on both counts, Vik," Julian said through gritted teeth. Vikram might be his best mate but that didn't mean that he had a right to snoop around into his private life. As it was, he had stayed in last night; but what did it have to do with Vik if he was two-timing Jackie or not? Not that he ever would, of course... "Keep your nose out of it, OK?"

"Just make sure that you don't hurt Jackie, that's all," Vikram warned.

There was a dangerous flash in Julian's eyes. "And what's it to you if I do?" he hissed.

"Look, she might be your girlfriend, but she's my friend," Vikram said, surprised at the force of Julian's anger – and, indeed, at his own. "Jackie and I go back a long way. We used to look out for each other, that's all."

The angry look in Julian's eyes passed, and he was his old self once again. "Of course she is," he said, and took a few deep breaths to control his voice. "I understand that."

"I just don't want to see her unhappy, that's all," said Vikram, still observing Julian through dark, suspicious eyes.

"Why would I want to hurt her?" Julian asked and there was a tremor in his voice which Vikram had never heard before. "She's my girlfriend. We've been going out for over two years. I love her. And she loves me."

Vikram smiled, and offered his hand to Julian. "OK, Jules, no questions asked," he said, his brief doubt past. "Friends?"

"Friends," said Julian, and shook Vikram's proffered hand. "But let's keep this one to ourselves, hey? I promise that I would never cheat on Jackie, but you know what she's like. If she finds out I stayed in last night she'll start thinking all the wrong things…"

Exactly the same sort of things I was thinking just now, Vikram realized, but nevertheless agreed to keep Julian's little secret. Maybe he was telling the truth and he just wanted a night in, although Vikram couldn't see why Julian would rather watch Saturday night telly than have an intimate dinner *à deux* with one of the most popular girls Vikram knew. Vik knew that lots of his mates would have jumped at the opportunity to take Jackie out; some of them had even mentioned to Vikram how sexy they found her. That had puzzled Vikram: he couldn't really see it himself. As far as he was concerned, Jackie was just, well, Jackie – one of his very best friends.

Julian slapped Vikram on the back like one of the lads sharing a private joke with his best mate. "It's all for the best," he claimed. "You've got to handle women carefully, otherwise they go off at the deep end, get the wrong end of the stick, and then it's hell getting them sweet again."

Vikram smiled awkwardly. "Then I'll bow to your wealth of experience on that one, Jules!" he said light-heartedly.

Julian chuckled, like a man of the world, instead of a seventeen-year-old who had only ever had one girlfriend in his entire life. "You'll understand when you start dating the girls!" he reassured him.

"Not much chance of that at the moment," Vikram said, a touch of gloom entering the conversation.

Julian halted on the stairs again (taking the opportunity, this time, of briefly ogling a pretty blonde in a tracksuit who was passing them). "C'mon, Vik, they must be queuing up to go out with you," he said. "Only the other day Clare Bond told me how much she fancied you and asked me to fix her up with you for a foursome with me and Jackie."

"She did?" Vikram knew Clare very well – a pretty girl in a nice self-effacing way. He hadn't the slightest idea that she fancied him, even though they'd spent the past two years studying A-level maths together.

"That's right, Vik, you're a popular man in these parts!"

"Only not as popular as you are, it seems," Vikram said, and instantly regretted what he'd said. If Julian really was cheating on Jackie, as he suspected, then it was none of his business.

Or was it?

However, Julian chose not to pick up on the remark – *a guilty conscience or what?* Vikram wondered – and instead asked: "What did you mean? That there's not much chance of dating anyone at the moment?"

Vikram smiled stoically. "Mum and Dad," he explained. "You know how strict they are."

Julian nodded: he had met Mr and Mrs Pandy, Vikram's

parents, once before, when he was picking Vikram up to go to a party and they had looked disapprovingly at the six-pack of cider he had brought with him for he and Vikram to share. "I didn't think you let that sort of tradition bother you."

"I don't," Vikram admitted. "My parents might still be kinda traditional in some respects but I regard myself as much more English than Pakistani now. But they've picked out a girl they want me to marry."

"An arranged marriage?" Julian asked, and gave a low sympathetic whistle. "Are you going to go ahead with it?"

Vikram shook his head. "No way," he said.

"I heard that some of these marriages can work out," Julian said. "And they grow into love later."

"That's right," Vikram agreed. "But I want to love the person I marry before the wedding."

"So what's the problem?" Julian asked. "OK, you'll get some hassle from your parents, but everyone gets that for one reason or another whether they come from Bangalore or Birmingham!"

"The problem is that the girl they want me to marry – Lakshmi Patel – is the daughter of a friend of my dad's. She's a great girl by all accounts, and the Patels are a respected family."

"Lots of Indian and Pakistani guys refuse to marry the person their parents have chosen for them," Julian pointed out. "Tradition's all very fine, but times change. OK, you might upset your dad for a while, and this Patel guy might strike him off the Christmas card list for a couple of years –"

"We're Muslims," Vikram said with a smile. "We don't send Christmas cards..."

Julian chuckled. "That's never stopped you from going to all the Christmas parties, Vik," he said. "But seriously: they'll get over it. You've got to follow your own feelings in this world, do what you want to do –" he paused for a moment before adding, with a slight touch of regret in his voice – "as long as it doesn't hurt anyone else of course..."

"If it was just a matter of tradition it wouldn't be so difficult," Vikram said. "After all, I've been winding Dad up for years now breaking every tradition in the book. But there's an added complication."

"With you there always is, big buddy," Julian laughed and slapped him amiably on the back.

"Mr Patel is a businessman and he's not short of cash," Vikram revealed. "He's suggested that he might want to invest in a major way in my dad's two stores..."

"Aha," said Julian. "I see the problem. You ditch this Lakshmi girl, and it's bye-bye to your dad's plans to expand his business?"

"Something like that, yes," said Vikram.

"And have you seen this girl yet?" asked Julian.

"Only photos. Her dad's bringing her over to England quite soon to meet my parents and me."

"And?"

"She's pretty – very pretty," Vikram said. "In any other circumstances I'd probably ask her out on a date myself! If it didn't get in the way of football practice, of course."

"But you wouldn't want to marry her?"

"That's right. Not now, at any rate."

Julian frowned. "Not now? What d'you mean?"

Vikram smiled. "Let's leave it, shall we?" he suggested as they finally reached the leisure centre's café area, where Jackie and Emma were waiting for them. "I've said more than I should have done anyway. You don't bring up the subject of Lakshmi again, and I won't mention to Jackie that you stayed in last night. Is that a deal?"

"It's a deal, Vik," Julian said, and walked up and kissed Jackie.

"And how was your game of squash?" Jackie asked.

"I trashed him," Vikram cut in. "As usual!"

"Hard luck," Jackie said. "And how was last night, Jules?"

"Huh?"

"Your dad's friend, remember?" Jackie said, not noticing the look of complicity which passed between the two boys.

"Oh, that was fine, he told me some really useful things," Julian lied. "Let's all have a coffee and then, as the loser, I guess it's my turn to buy us all Sunday lunch!"

"Jules, you shouldn't," Jackie protested, even though Emma hushed her – a free slap-up meal sounded like a pretty good idea to her!

"I insist!" said Julian. "It's the least I can do!"

Definitely a guilty conscience, thought Vikram, as he followed the others to the serving hatch to collect their cups of instant.

And his heart went out to Jackie.

He wasn't quite sure why.

4

Blades Ice-Skating Rink was one of the oldest ice-skating rinks in the country and it showed. Around the oval-shaped ice-rink rose fluted columns which betrayed its previous existence as an old-time music hall; and the domed roof from which paste-glass chandeliers had once hung, now made a perfect echo chamber, amplifying the screams of delight as ice-skaters whizzed round the ice, or their squeals of surprise as the less experienced of them fell flat on their backs.

Beyond the padded crash barriers, there were rows of uncomfortable-looking seats, which were used by spectators. Twice a year Betty Crabtree organized an ice gala, and printed on the tickets there was always an encouragement to the members of the audience to bring their own cushions to sit on. Bruised knees and elbows were hazards of ice-skating which even the most professional ice-skaters couldn't avoid; but bruised backsides were another matter entirely!

At one end of the oval rink there was an organ which, like the elaborate painted designs and fretwork on the columns, had obviously seen better days. It was rarely played now and the ice-skaters moved around the rink to bland and repetitive muzak piped over the PA system, or to the chart sounds of the local independent radio station.

Sitting by the organ, in front of a control board, and

watching the action on the ice, was a weasly-looking man; obviously a former ice-skater, who, like the rest of the building, was dreaming of finer and younger days.

The only concession to modernity was a series of frescoes lining the back of one of the walls, paintings of famous British ice-skaters such as Torvill and Dean, and Karen Slater and Nicky Campbell; or at least that's what Betty Crabtree told all her customers, although, as Emma had once said, "If that's supposed to be Torvill and Dean, then I'm Naomi Campbell!"

Up a small flight of steps, opposite the neglected organ and overlooking the rink, was Blades' café-cum-bar, which served a selection of sandwiches and soft drinks, and where the wall-length window offered diners the best view of the ice-skaters below. It was here that Vikram was working, and as Jackie, Emma and Julian walked into the rink early on Monday afternoon they waved up at him. He smiled and waved back, before returning to his work behind the counter.

Jackie and Emma owned their own skates, and, as they sat down on a pair of slatted wooden benches to tighten up the laces on their boots, Julian went off to the rink's office to hire a pair. Jackie and Emma used the opportunity to eye up the talent on the rink.

A couple of Italian guys – the same two Jackie had spotted in the high street on Saturday – were racing each other around the edge of the rink. They were alone, so it seemed that their flirting with the two girls hadn't gone as successfully as Jackie had predicted.

In the centre of the rink, away from the skating *hoi polloi*, a few small girls, dressed in skating tutus (unlike everyone else who was wearing either sensible tracksuits or jeans and baggy T-shirts), were practising their movements. Accompanying them on the ice were their individual ice-skating teachers, casually-dressed men and women only a few years older than Jackie and Emma. They were whispering words of encouragement to their charges, and giving them a brief round of applause every time they executed a perfect double or triple axel. Watching from the sidelines were the little girls' proud mothers, swapping gossip with the other mothers, and saying just how good their own daughter was. Apart from them there were only about another dozen or so people on the ice, most of them couples.

"So where are all the hunks you said were going to be here, Em?" Jackie asked, as she walked unsteadily on her skates across the rubber-matted floor and to the edge of the ice, where she held on to the surrounding rail for support.

"They'll be here sooner or later," Emma said confidently. "Anyway I'm the one who's supposed to be hunk-hunting, not you! You've got Julian, remember?"

"Of course," said Jackie. She put a tentative foot on the ice. Her feet started to move from under her, and she grabbed a tighter hold of the rail. She looked worriedly at Emma. "Em, do you think this is such a good idea after all? It's been almost eighteen months since I was last ice-skating."

Emma laughed. "It's exactly like riding a bike," she insisted. "You never forget. You just have to get your old confidence back, that's all!"

Then she stepped gingerly on to the ice, positioned her feet into the form of a "T", and pushed off, gliding around the ice with supreme ease, as though she had been born on it and had never done anything else. Jackie watched approvingly: Emma might at times be unsure of herself, but on the ice she moved with confidence and grace. Deciding that if she was going to fall and make a total fool of herself, it might as well be sooner rather than later, Jackie followed Emma on to the main body of the ice.

Contrary to her expectations, she didn't fall, but slid smoothly off after Emma, enjoying the feel of the crisp cold "breeze" as she raced around the ice. The feeling of almost effortless motion invigorated her, making whatever troubles she had seem meaningless, as she remembered in an instant all she thought she'd forgotten.

She wondered why she'd ever stopped ice-skating in the first place: surely this sense of freedom and ease was one of the most wonderful feelings in the world! After a few circuits of the ice she scrunched to a halt by Emma, her cheeks ruddy and healthy with the exercise.

"Wasn't that great?" she said, and then asked Emma why she had stopped. She looked in the direction Emma's finger was pointing.

"Will you look at that!" Emma said. "It seems that my theory about hunks was right after all!"

Skating slowly towards them across the ice was a tall blond-haired guy a couple of years older than them. Even at this distance they could see that he had piercing blue eyes, the clear smooth complexion of a model ("We're talking *GQ* here, Jackie," Emma said confidently), and the sort of body that only years in the gym could have produced.

Emma would have gone even further and described him as "Sex On Ice", if Jackie hadn't got in first.

"Jackie! I'm surprised at you!" Emma said admiringly.

"Just don't tell Jules!" Jackie giggled, and glanced behind her. Julian was still putting on his skates and hadn't noticed them yet. "But he is a bit of all right!"

The handsome and sexy newcomer glided to a halt in front of them, stopping with the sort of smooth ease that Jackie knew she'd never be able to manage, even with years of practice. Without knowing why, Jackie glanced guiltily up at the café: Vikram was serving behind the counter and, like Julian, was too busy to notice them.

The blond boy smiled at each of them in turn, dazzling them with his brilliantly white smile. "Hi," he said. His voice was deep and friendly; he sounded Scandinavian, although there was also the faint trace of an American accent in his voice. He'd probably spent some time in the States where he had perfected his English, Emma guessed, and remembered just how skating-mad some of her American friends were.

"Hi," said Jackie. Emma merely nodded; confronted

with what she'd describe as "drop-dead gorgeousity", for once she was lost for words. That had always been her trouble: she'd rehearsed over and over in her head all the best chat-up lines, but when it came to trying them out on a real-live hunk, she went all to pieces.

"I was watching you out there on the ice," he said. "You were both very good."

"Rubbish," said Jackie.

"You really think so?" asked Emma.

"Seriously," he said, and smiled at her again, with a smile that could make even the ice melt. "And I should know. My name's Adam. I'm one of the skating instructors here."

Jackie smiled and introduced Emma and herself; Adam shook them both by the hand.

"I haven't seen either of you here before," he said.

"That's right," said Jackie. "It's been eighteen months or so since I was last on the ice."

"You wouldn't know it," Adam chuckled. "You skate like a real pro!"

"Flattery will get you nowhere," Jackie said, and found herself blushing. She looked up at the café: she could see Vikram serving one of the skating mothers who was treating her little girl to a strawberry milkshake and telling Vikram what a star her daughter was.

"And you're really good as well," Adam said, and turned to Emma. Emma blushed even redder than Jackie: was this hunk actually *talking* to her? Did her existence even matter to him?

"Er ... thanks," muttered Emma, and wished the Earth would open up and swallow her whole.

Adam was going to say something else to Emma, when they all became aware of someone skating up behind them. Jackie turned, to see Julian approaching. He had only been out ice-skating once or twice before and he was still wobbly on his feet. His brow was furrowed with concentration as he slipped up to the three of them: Jackie held her hand out to him to help him stop, a pretty important movement on the ice which Julian still hadn't quite got the hang of.

Jackie introduced Julian to Adam and the two boys exchanged a polite and cursory nod of greeting. As she did so, the music being blasted through the PA system changed from the usual bland muzak to this year's Number One hit from last year's Hot Teen Idol from Down Under. The weasly guy at the microphone announced that it was time for "pairs" skating, and everyone not with a partner should leave the ice.

Julian groaned. "Can't we sit this one out?" he begged.

"Don't be stupid, Jules," Jackie said. "You've only just got out on the ice!"

"Yes," said Adam. "It'll be fun. We'll make up a foursome." As Jackie was obviously Julian's girlfriend he looked over at Emma.

Emma, however, slid to Julian's side and took his arm. "C'mon, I'll be gentle with you!" she promised, and dragged him away from the others.

As she did so she mentally kicked herself for shyly refusing Adam's offer of a pair-dance: it looked like she was her own worst enemy! Why was it that she always steered clear of boys she found attractive? Was it because she was scared of being rejected, afraid that her more attractive and experienced friends might think she was trying for someone way out of her league?

Adam sighed and gave Jackie a sheepish look. "Well, it looks like you and me, doesn't it?" he said and winked encouragingly at her.

"So it does..." Jackie said, and taking hold of Adam's hand, she allowed him to lead her on to the ice.

It felt good holding Adam's hand as they circled the ice, their fingers intertwined, and Jackie was aware of several girls watching from the side and throwing envious looks in her direction. As she gained confidence on the ice, so Adam increased his speed, and he encircled her waist with a strong muscular arm. She glanced behind her at Julian and Emma, laughing and joking as they sped around the ice. Jackie felt slightly put out at the fact that Julian was grinning, seemingly unconcerned that his girlfriend was skating with the most gorgeous and desirable male on the ice, but when she looked up into Adam's face his smile made her beam even more. The light seemed to reflect off the ice and back into his blue eyes, making them sparkle and glitter like twin sapphires.

Jackie felt Adam's hand softly massage her lower back as he guided her around the ice, and she experienced a thrill of delight as she realized that here she was, skating with the sexiest and hunkiest boy on the ice.

Soon Jackie had forgotten all about Julian and Emma who were skating somewhere up ahead: all that seemed to matter was her and Adam, moving as one in a perfect display of ice-dancing.

"Not bad – for amateurs!"

"Sorry?"

At the cash register in the café, Vikram turned around, after handing his latest customer her change. Linsey was standing before him, dressed as usual in a stylish designer top and jeans.

"Your friends down there on the ice," Linsey said, and nodded over to the large spectators' window. "They're not bad."

Vikram tried to look, but couldn't see from where he was standing. He beckoned to one of his colleagues – a sixteen-year-old girl who, in the two hours she had been working with Vikram had decided that she was totally, a hundred and one per cent, and irretrievably, in love with him.

"Yes, Vikram?" she breathed.

"Do us a favour and look after the till for a minute, will you?" Vikram asked. "I want to see Jackie and Emma do their stuff."

"Sure, Vikram," the lovestruck schoolkid said, and took his place at the till.

Linsey took Vikram's arm and led him to the window. "How was your football programme on TV the other night?" she asked, her voice full of friendly interest.

"What?" he said and then remembered: "Oh, that! Emma and Jackie got the wrong day."

"Did they now?" Linsey asked, and her voice suddenly turned as frosty as the ice below on the rink.

Vikram, however, didn't detect the change in Linsey's attitude, and instead looked down on to the ice. "She's great, isn't she?" he said admiringly, a strange note of fondness in his voice. "I mean, they both are... I wish I could skate like that..."

"I could teach you," Linsey said. "I'm sure I could teach you lots of things." She put a hand on Vikram's arm. He shook his head.

"I'd probably make an idiot of myself and fall flat on my face the minute I got on the ice," he said, self-deprecatingly.

"You should have confidence in your own abilities," Linsey said, looking hard at Vikram's profile – the collar-length hair, the full lips, and the firm chin. Vikram, however, didn't return her look, but continued to gaze out of the window.

"That's what I'm always telling Jackie," Vikram chuckled. "Who's that guy she's skating with?"

Linsey stopped considering Vikram's profile, and turned to look at the skaters. As Vikram knew Julian, it was obvious he was talking about Adam. An evil look came into her eyes.

"That's the new ice-skating instructor," she said, remembering having seen him the other day when Betty Crabtree was showing him around the rink. "I hear he's a bit of a charmer – a real ladies' man. Has all the skating mothers hopelessly in love with him: you should watch out for your two friends down there!"

Linsey frowned when she saw the flash of regret in Vikram's fathomless dark eyes; it disturbed her. "It's odd, isn't it," she continued, "dancing with the hunky skating teacher instead of her boyfriend..."

"What are you trying to imply?" Vikram asked her, a strange edge in his voice, as he protested his friend's faithfulness to Julian. There was also something else there too, Linsey realized, a wistfulness, almost hope. Of a disappointed man clutching desperately at straws.

Linsey smiled. "I was speaking out of turn and I'm sorry," she lied. "I'm sure she and her boyfriend are the greatest couple since Romeo and Juliet! Neither of them would dream of flirting with or looking at someone else..."

"You've got that right," Vikram said, and there was now no mistaking the melancholy in his voice. "Jackie and Julian are as close as close can be."

"Of course," said Linsey, although the way she said it clearly indicated that she didn't really mean it. "It was just that she and Adam looked so good together..."

5

"We were so good together," Adam said as pair-skating ended and he and Jackie slid to a halt by the crash barriers. It was the sort of graceful stop that Jackie knew she could never achieve by herself; but with Adam everything seemed so natural, so effortless.

"Yes, we were," Jackie breathed, and looked up into his face. His cheeks were red, like hers, and there was a happy smile on his face. He was so handsome, Jackie decided, and she scarcely realized that he hadn't yet taken his arm from around her waist. "I've never found skating so easy before."

"That's because you had confidence in yourself," Adam said.

Confidence that you gave me, Jackie found herself thinking.

"I couldn't have done it without you, Adam," she said.

"Of course you could," Adam said, and finally took his hand away from her waist. "You're good – very good –" Jackie started to protest, but Adam silenced her. "You know that Betty – Miss Crabtree – holds an ice-skating gala every Christmas here?"

"Of course I do," Jackie said. "It's her chance to show off her prize pupils to the town, and hopefully get a few more charitable donations to keep the place going."

"That's right," said Adam. "With a couple of months' practice you could even take part in it yourself. You're a

403

natural, Jackie. With extra training and some lessons, you could be very good indeed."

Jackie pooh-poohed the notion. "With you as my teacher, I suppose?" she scoffed. "Adam, I know how much ice-skating lessons cost by the quarter-hour! I've got better things to spend my money on!"

"Have it your own way," Adam laughed. "But Betty always makes sure that there are talent scouts at every one of her galas. You never know, someone might spot your potential..."

"Now I know that you're leading me on!" Jackie said, even though she still couldn't take her eyes away from Adam's handsome face. "I'm seventeen. If a talent scout is going to pick on anyone as a promising professional skater it's going to be one of those skating kids over there –" she nodded over at the young girls, who had returned to the ice, watched over, as usual, by their adoring mothers – "I'm far too old!"

"Whatever you say," said Adam, and pretended to sulk, making himself look even more endearing – *if that's possible*, Jackie thought. "That is, if you really want to turn down my offer of the chance to astound the world – not to mention every ice-skating hunk in the country –"

"I have a boyfriend," Jackie said. "I don't need to impress anyone else."

"Yes, I know," Adam said, and sulked. "That's really such a great pity..."

Jackie laughed. "Are you flirting with me?" she asked happily.

Adam nodded and gave her the sort of smile that any girl in the rink would have died for. "Maybe I am teasing you a little," he admitted. "Only don't tell your boyfriend: I'm sure he'd pick a fight with me..."

"No, he wouldn't," Jackie said. "Julian's not like that." Somehow she could never imagine Julian fighting over her; indeed at times he seemed to take her so much for granted that she wondered if he'd even notice if anyone was coming on to her!

Adam looked slyly at Jackie. "I'm holding some special classes on Wednesday evenings," he said. "I've still got a half-hour window free..."

Jackie paused for a moment, and looked at Julian and Emma who were approaching. Julian had promised to take her out on Wednesday to the movies. After that he'd suggested that they go on to a posh new bistro which had just opened up down the road from Slinky Jo's.

No doubt there he would treat her to a slap-up meal, insisting that she didn't spend a penny, and they would certainly have a great time. He'd choose the wine, usually a Californian rosé which she hated, but she didn't dare tell Jules that because they both knew that it was generally acknowledged to be the trendy drink of the moment.

Afterwards they might even go out to a club of Julian's choice (of course), where they would dance the night away, before Julian would order a mini-cab to take her home. It was a lifestyle which many girls would have killed for, and yet Jackie was finding it more and more oppressive. Sometimes, she felt, she would like to do something for herself, make her own decisions, rather than being constantly looked after by Julian.

"That's a wonderful idea, Adam," she heard herself saying. "Shall we start this Wednesday?"

Adam grinned. "Great!" he said, and greeted Julian and Emma who were skating up to them.

Jackie felt her heart sink. What had possessed her to agree to Adam's suggestion? And how was she going to break the news to Julian that their date for Wednesday was off? And why was she looking forward to her skating lesson with Adam with all her heart?

"You two had a good time?" Julian asked innocently, and Jackie nodded.

"Your girlfriend's a good skater," Adam said, and added: "She's agreed to come to my lesson on Wednesday evening..."

"Wednesday?" Julian asked, and Adam nodded, unsure

of what all the fuss was about. Julian looked at Jackie. "I thought we had a date then...?"

Jackie sighed, and felt her face flush red with embarrassment. "I know, Jules," she started, "but Adam says I've got lots of talent and this is a great opportunity and I'll make it up to you and..."

Julian's eyes narrowed. "I understand," he said emotionlessly, and looked from Jackie to Adam and then back to Jackie.

"It's not what you think," Jackie protested.

"Hey, if I've caused any sort of problem between you two..." Adam began.

Julian glowered at him. "There's no problem," he said, perhaps not as bitterly as Jackie might have expected. "Why shouldn't Jackie take skating lessons with you? After all, that's probably much more important than me taking her out for a meal and to a club..."

"Jules, please..." said Jackie, and considered cancelling her ice-skating lesson there and then.

No, why should I? she scolded herself. *It's about time that I did something I wanted to do! It's about time that I asserted some sort of independence and stopped being continually at Jules' beck and call!*

"I'm going off to change," Julian said, and started to move off the ice. He turned back to look at Jackie. "I suppose I'm still allowed to give you a lift home afterwards?"

Jackie sighed. "Of course," she said, and watched as Julian went off to the boys' changing room.

Adam shrugged. "I'm sorry if I've made things awkward," he said.

"It's not your fault, Adam," Jackie said. "It's Julian's. He always likes to have things his own way ... he gets really grumpy when people start thinking for themselves..."

Adam nodded, and said, in his Scandinavian-American accent, that he could "really relate to that", and then excused himself: he had a class in a few minutes with a seven-year-old girl who showed lots of promise, and could even become a professional skater with the right training.

After Adam had gone, Emma looked disapprovingly at her friend. "What do you think you're playing at, Jackie Taylor?" she asked. "Standing Jules up for someone you've only just met, even if he is so hot that I'm surprised the ice isn't melting?"

"Don't you start on me!" Jackie snapped, and then apologized. "OK, maybe I did get a little carried away then and didn't think things through. But I see Jules every day; why can't I just do something on my own for a change?"

"Jules loves you," Emma said softly. "He only wants what's best for you."

"I know," Jackie said. "But sometimes he smothers me with all his attention... And out there just now on the ice with Adam..."

"Yes?"

Jackie shrugged. "It just felt so natural, so free..." she said. "I've never felt that way with Julian..."

Emma smiled and shook her head. "Typical!" she said, and threw her hands up in the air in a gesture of mock despair. "I come to Blades to find a boyfriend, and who gets off with the hottest and most fanciable hunk on the ice but my best friend – who's already got a hunky boyfriend!"

"It's not like that, Emma," Jackie said, in a voice which carried very little conviction.

"Isn't it?" Emma asked. "I've seen you over the past few weeks. Looking at the other boys in Slinky Jo's. Staring into space when Jules has been talking to you. You're not getting tired of him, by any chance?"

"Tired of him? Of course not," she said, and averted her eyes from Emma.

She stared up at the café. Vikram was still there, watching her; Linsey was standing by his side, and Jackie felt a strange pang. She turned back to Emma.

"Julian is a lovely, sweet guy, and I'd never do anything to hurt him, you know that. I really like him a lot..."

Like him a lot, Emma nodded wisely to herself; only a

few months ago Jackie was declaring her undying love for Julian. She was about to say a few further words when she felt something hit her in the back. One of the Italian boys who had been racing his friend around the ice, collided into her, pushing her forward. She bumped into Jackie and they both fell crashing to the floor.

"You idiot!" Jackie shouted from where she had fallen on the ice, in an undignified heap. "What the hell do you think you're playing at?"

The Italian guy shrugged his apologies, and said something along the lines that if they wanted to stand still on the ice gossiping like a pair of old fishwives, then they should expect to get knocked over. He was remonstrating wildly and from a distance it could have looked as if things were about to turn nasty. He started swearing at Jackie and Emma, when he felt two powerful hands grip his shoulders, and he was forced to turn around, almost losing his balance on the ice.

"Don't you think you'd better apologize properly to the lady, you creep?"

They all turned around to see Vikram; he had rushed down from the café at the first sign of trouble, and there was a dangerous look on his face.

"Hey, look, it was an accident," the boy said. "I couldn't help running into your girlfriend."

"She's not my girlfriend," came Vikram's answer, a little too quickly.

"Vikram, it's OK," said Jackie, who was still sitting on the ice, but Vikram would hear nothing of it. He grabbed the Italian by his T-shirt with one hand, and waved his fist in his face. Sure enough, faced with such a convincing argument, the Italian guy duly made his apologies to Jackie, and Vikram released him.

"Vikram, there was no need to do that," Jackie said, after the Italian boy had left, and Vikram leant over to help her to her feet again. Both she and Emma had been taken aback by his sudden aggression: usually the only thing that got Vikram worked up was the latest Test

Match results, or the woeful performance of his favourite football team.

"He was causing you grief," Vikram said. "I just didn't want to see you hurt, that's all... You know I've always been here for you whenever you needed me..."

His strong firm hands took hold of Jackie's arms and he pulled her gently to her feet. Jackie's feet slipped on the ice, and she fell against Vikram. For a second she remained like that, the full length of her body pressed against Vikram's. She felt his heart beating against her chest, felt his strong hands on her back; she looked up into his face, seeing in his dark eyes something she had never seen before.

Then the moment passed, and Vikram let go of her. They smiled shyly at each other, and exchanged an awkward look.

"You OK now?" Vikram asked.

"Of course," Jackie said, formally, denying the wild, confusing emotions she was feeling within herself, or the outrageous thoughts that were running madly inside her head: *This is crazy! Do you realize what you're thinking of? This isn't supposed to happen!*

"Would a certain hunky gentleman remember his good manners and help a deeply distressed damsel up off the floor?"

Vikram and Jackie both looked down at Emma who was still sitting on the ice, making a great play of tapping her fingers impatiently, and wearing an enormous frown. The tension broken, Jackie and Vikram burst out laughing, and Vikram helped Emma up.

"Thank you," Emma said frostily to her friend, and Vikram affected an extravagant courtly bow, like a gallant seventeenth-century cavalier. As he did so, his feet slipped on the ice, and, after a few moments' un-cavalier-like wobbling, he lost his balance and tumbled to the ground with a – for Emma – delightfully loud *thunk!* Jackie and Emma creased up with laughter.

"C'mon, girls, help me up!" Vikram pleaded.

"No way!" Emma said, and skated away from Vikram, who remained sitting in a cross-legged position as he watched his two friends glide away.

Or rather he watched Jackie glide away, and a troubled frown crossed his brow. Why had he been so anxious to rush down to help Jackie when he had seen her fall on the ice? After all, people fell down on the ice all the time at Blades, and suffered, at the most, a blow to their dignity. And he knew that Jackie was more than capable of shrugging off the unwanted advances of any oversexed Latino teenager.

Hey, she's my mate, of course, he reasoned to himself. *And that's what friends are for!*

But deep down Vikram knew that he wasn't fooling himself. Even though he lacked the courage to admit it, he knew what had passed between him and Jackie just a few moments ago on the ice. And he was just thankful that no one else had noticed it.

But Emma *had* noticed the look that Vikram and Jackie had exchanged. She was full of foreboding for her two friends, and was only grateful that Julian hadn't been there to see it too.

Someone else had, however. Up in the café, Linsey cursed under her breath, and vowed vengeance on Jackie.

6

"And you seriously expect me to believe that he's just your teacher?" Emma asked, as she watched Jackie get ready for her first ice-skating lesson in front of her bedroom mirror.

Jackie coloured, and applied a faint layer of pale-pink lipstick, which, along with the soft blusher on her cheeks, was something she normally never wore. "Of course," she said. "It's only your dirty mind that's reading things into it that aren't there!"

"Adam and Julian – two of the sexiest boys around, and both of them crazy for you!" Emma teased. Yet there was a longing in her voice that her cheery manner couldn't quite disguise. "And I bet Adam's giving you these lessons for free!"

"They're not crazy about me!" Jackie protested a little too earnestly. "Well, at least Adam isn't... And the lessons aren't free either. I landed myself a Saturday job down at the record store in town, so I'm paying for them myself." She looked at herself in the mirror, checking that her make-up was fine, and then asked casually: "Do you really think he is crazy about me? Adam, I mean..."

Emma shrugged. "Vikram thinks so," she said finally. "Not that he seemed particularly happy about it..."

"Vikram?" Jackie asked and then panicked. "What have you been telling Vik, Em? Oh my God, if he tells Jules..."

"Steady on," Emma said. "Vik won't say anything. All he said to me was that he'd seen the two of you out on the ice together, and that he thought that Adam really liked you. He was certainly paying you a lot of attention!"

"But Jules is still upset with me for not going out with him today," Jackie said. "Even though I let him take me out last night instead. Maybe I ought to ring Vik and get him to explain it all to Jules…"

Emma looked curiously at Jackie. "Ring Vik?" she repeated. "Don't you mean ring Jules?"

"Yes, of course I do," Jackie said, and stood up to go to the telephone which was on the landing, just outside her bedroom door.

"There's no point in phoning him," Emma advised. "It's Vik's day off so they've both gone out for the day – to a rugby match."

"God, how boring!" Jackie said, and relaxed again, now that the prospect of another awkward phone call with her boyfriend had been postponed. "I don't appreciate the attraction of football, but I can't even understand the rules of rugby!" She smoothed her hands over her trim figure, made more appealing by the tight T-shirt, and Lycra leggings she was wearing. "How do I look?"

"You look great," Emma said approvingly, even though she wondered why Jackie wasn't wearing her usual outfit of sloppy sweatshirt and jeans. She stood up and followed Jackie out of her bedroom and on to the landing.

"Jackie," she began, and her voice was suddenly serious. "I'm one of your best friends, and you know that I don't want to see you hurt…"

Jackie frowned, both uncomfortable and surprised at Emma's sombre manner and the direction in which the conversation had turned.

"I know that, Em…"

"But I'm also Jules' friend," Emma continued, "and I don't want to see him hurt either. You wouldn't cheat on him, would you?"

Jackie's face turned white – with rage? with

indignation? with the awful knowledge that she had been found out? – and for a second Emma thought that Jackie was going to lash out at her, as she realized that she had hit a very sore point. Then the moment passed, and Jackie sighed and hugged herself, as if for comfort.

"I don't know, Em," she said finally, looking not at her friend, but at the ceiling, as though she was reluctant to look at Emma's face and the disapproving look she was sure she would find there. "Jules is one of the most wonderful guys in the world, and he always treats me like a queen. Especially recently, although heaven knows why. We have some wonderful times together. But when he's not there I never find myself thinking of him... That time I was on the ice with Adam, and Jules was watching, it was like he wasn't there. And yesterday I didn't miss him at all. All that matters is my skating..."

"You've been skating with Adam again since Monday?" This was news to Emma.

"I went yesterday," Jackie said. "I was passing Blades and I went in to say hello to Vikram, and Adam was there and suggested we did a couple of circuits of the ice, as a sort of warm-up to my lesson today. He told me how good I was again; said I should sign up for more lessons."

Emma nodded; that explained why Vikram had told her that he had seen the two of them skating together. She imagined the feel of Adam's strong arm around her waist, and felt a pang of jealousy; what she wouldn't have done to sail across the ice with Adam, as Jackie had done.

"And Adam is so warm and friendly and understanding," Jackie continued. "He's such a nice guy too..."

"You've only known him for a couple of days," Emma pointed out sensibly. "You've known Jules for over two years..."

"Perhaps I've known him for too long," Jackie said sadly. She ran a hand through her long blonde hair. "Sometimes you can know people for a really long time, and still never really know them. But whatever happens,

I promise that I'll never do anything to hurt Julian... Just as I'd never hurt you – or Vikram..."

"You skate wonderfully well, Ms Taylor," Adam said, holding Jackie in his arms as they sped around the rink.

"That's because you're with me," Jackie said, and a shudder of delight ran through her body. "I wouldn't have this sort of confidence by myself!" She grinned, and automatically looked up to the café to see if Vikram was there, before remembering that it was his day off.

Adam took her once more around the rink, helping her to perform a near-perfect figure of eight on the ice, before skating up to the barrier, where they scrunched to a halt. Emma was waiting for them and she gave them a little round of applause as they approached her.

"Pretty classy!" she said.

"Jackie is very good," Adam said, and beamed at Emma, who flushed red with embarrassment and turned away. "I think she should feature in the ice gala at Christmas!"

Jackie smiled, and took her backpack from Emma, who had been holding it while she was on the ice. She drew out her purse, and handed Adam some money – her fee for her half-hour lesson.

"That was really enjoyable, Adam," she said, and shocked herself by giving him a peck on the cheek.

Just a kiss between two new friends, she told herself.

"Even I was impressed," Emma said. She'd seen Jackie's kiss on Adam's cheek: if only she had the nerve to do that! "I've never seen you do such good figures of eight before. If Adam keeps your lessons up you'll be doing double and triple axels next and giving the professionals a run for their money!"

"Maybe you should start doing lessons as well, Emma," Adam suggested encouragingly. "Then you, too, could spin triple axels and do toe jumps and salchows."

He smiled at her again. Emma went weak at the knees.

"Who? Me?" she said, laughing to cover her embarrassment. "I like ice-skating, but I'd never be that good..."

Adam put a hand on Emma's shoulder, just like an older brother. *Well, it certainly wouldn't be like a lover, would it?* Emma thought, as she felt her heart beat faster.

"You shouldn't put yourself down so much," Adam said, his hand still resting on her shoulder. "I've seen you out on the ice – you're good, very good!"

Emma felt herself glowing with pride, and Adam was about to say something else when all three of them became aware of some sort of commotion behind them. They all turned, to see Linsey sweep on to the ice, like some superstar making an entrance for all her adoring fans.

The sexy brunette was wearing an all-in-one Lycra body-suit, which showed off her athletic figure to its best advantage. She was wearing her own skates, and the boots had been polished and repolished until they shone brilliantly in the light.

Every single male at Blades had his eyes glued to her, as she circled the rink in a wide arc, before executing a near-perfect display of skating manoeuvres that left her audience stunned and applauding enthusiastically.

Linsey skated over to the edge of the ice where Jackie, Emma and Adam were watching in astonishment.

"Fancy meeting you two here," she said to Jackie and Emma, before turning all her formidable powers of attraction on Adam. She smiled at him seductively. "Hi," she smouldered. "I'm Linsey. You must be Adam. We've never met but I've watched you loads of times on the ice. I think you're wonderful!"

Adam nodded. "That was a pretty impressive performance out there on the ice too," he remarked.

"Oh *that*!" Linsey said. "It was nothing. I'm sure you could do much, much better..." She hung her head sadly. "Actually there's a part of my technique I'm not too happy with." Here she raised her head and stared at Adam through her dark hooded eyes, suggesting that perhaps she wasn't thinking just of her ice-skating technique. "Perhaps you could help me some time?" she suggested.

"I'd love to," Adam said enthusiastically, and took Linsey's hand. He paused and turned to Jackie and Emma. "Hey, you girls don't mind, do you?"

"Of course not," Emma lied through gritted teeth as she watched Adam and Linsey go off on to the ice hand in hand. As they moved away, Linsey blew them both a sarcastic farewell kiss.

"Can you believe the nerve of that witch!" Jackie hissed as soon as Linsey was out of earshot. "What gives her the right to swan in here, and just take Adam away from us like that?"

Emma shrugged philosophically, and automatically reached up to her own shoulder, feeling the spot where Adam had placed his hand. Just for a moment back there, when he hadn't taken his hand away, she had thought...

Don't be such a little idiot, Emma Carter! she reproved herself. *If he fancies anyone then it's Jackie! Why should a hunk like that think of looking even twice at someone like you!*

"When you look the way Linsey does then I guess that gives you every right," she said. Emma, more so than Jackie, knew what weight sexy good looks could carry with people.

"What's she got against us anyway?" Jackie asked. "We hardly know her and she's acting as though we're arch-enemies."

"Maybe she's just feeling grumpy 'cause she's got the hots for Vik, and he's not showing the slightest bit of interest in her," Emma suggested.

"But why be so horrible to us?" Jackie asked.

"We did tell a little porky-pie to get her off Vik's back," Emma reminded her, and watched Adam and Linsey as they glided around the ice to the sound of one of the summer's biggest hits. "Girls like that never take no for an answer. They're too used to getting their own way. When they don't, they'll take it out on anyone who comes within striking distance. And it looks as though she's picked on you."

"All the same..." Jackie wasn't convinced: how could anyone be that malicious and resentful?

Emma glanced slyly at her friend from out of the corner of her eye. "Who knows? She might think she has some competition..."

"Competition? For Vikram?" Jackie laughed. "Now I know you're talking nonsense, Em! Vik's one of our best mates: we've both known him since we were kids. It's not like either of us fancy him! Is it?"

"Of course not," smiled Emma, and thought quickly: "But perhaps she sees all females as some sort of obstacle to getting her claws into every single male in sight... And who said that she's just jealous of Vik?" She pointed to the spectators and resting ice-skaters who were standing around the rink, watching Adam and Linsey go through their paces. "Look at the boys – they can't take their eyes off her. And all the girls can't stand the sight of her!"

"You're right," Jackie said, as she gazed at the almost salivating males, and the comic looks of annoyance on their girlfriends' faces. It would almost have been funny were it not for the fact that Jackie felt a deep feeling of apprehension well up somewhere inside her.

Was Linsey really going to continue in her attempts to take Vikram out, and would he finally give in to her advances? Or was she now trying to date Adam? She had certainly come on to the handsome Scandinavian in a pretty heavy way just now, and Adam was clearly impressed with the girl's ice-skating skills.

And why are you getting so worried and hot under the collar about it anyway, Jackie Taylor? she scolded herself, although in her heart of hearts she suspected she knew the reason why. *Linsey can do whatever she wants, and it shouldn't bother you in the slightest – after all, it's not as though she's after Julian!...*

Yet...

She turned back to Emma. "She's vile," Jackie stated categorically, and chuckled at her audacity: she rarely had a bad word to say about anyone.

"Not to the boys she isn't," Emma added.

Jackie nodded. "Still, I bet she hasn't got many girlfriends," she said. "They must all hate her."

"Jackie," Emma said, with all the world-weary wisdom of a seventeen-year-old who thought she was much too plain, and would never get a boyfriend, "You saw her the other night in Slinky Jo's with all those trendy boys. With the sort of looks Linsey has do you think she cares how few girlfriends she has?"

A few days later, Jackie was skating on the ice, getting warmed up ready for her lesson with Adam, when she spotted Vikram standing on the edge of the rink. He waved at her, slightly awkwardly, as though he had just been caught spying on someone. She skated over to him; they kissed each other on the cheek, as they always did.

Jackie stepped off the ice, and sat next to him on one of the wooden benches. They were so close that their legs were touching, Vikram's black 501s brushing against her bare skin.

Two young girls, no more than twelve years old, passed by on their way to the café and looked Vikram up and down with all the studied appraisal of a pair of pre-pubescents out on a hunk-hunt. They liked what they saw – firm muscles, lithe body, and thick raven locks to run their fingers through – and giggled to themselves all the way up the stairs. Jackie smiled after them – they'd probably assumed she was Vikram's girlfriend – although Vik appeared not to have noticed them.

"How long have you been watching?" she asked.

"Ten minutes or so," Vikram said. "It's my lunch hour."

"I can think of better things to do in your break," Jackie said. "It's nice and sunny outside; you could go for a walk in the park, or even drop in at Slinky Jo's for a cappuccino."

"Nope," he said, and laughed. "I'd be bound to run into Linsey there! Whenever she's not out on the ice, she seems always to be there."

"Like a spider in its web," Jackie joked.

"An exceptionally pretty spider, all the same," was Vikram's opinion, and for just one half-instant Jackie's face fell into a mask of despair, "if you like that sort of thing," he finished and Jackie brightened up.

"Is she still chasing after you?" she asked, trying to sound casual and nonchalant.

Vikram nodded. "Not as much as she used to, but I suspect she's not the sort of girl who gives up easily," he said. "I suppose it's flattering in a way – although goodness knows why she's interested in me."

Because everyone says that you're the hunkiest, sexiest and most desirable male in town! Jackie thought, but said: "Maybe we should buy her a white stick and a guide dog?"

Vikram laughed and attempted to give Jackie a friendly cuff on the chin. Jackie raised a hand to defend herself, grabbed Vikram's strong, masculine hand and held it in her own, lacing her fingers in his. She felt her hand tingle, as though volts of electricity were being passed from Vikram to her. They looked at each other curiously, in a way that two friends would never look at each other.

Slowly Jackie lowered Vikram's hand, placing it back on his thigh. Still their hands remained clasped for a moment; and then Jackie hurriedly took hers away. She looked away from Vikram, at the other skaters on the ice: Adam was there, taking one of his students around the rink.

"Anyway, I like watching the skaters," Vikram said after a pause. "And you're very good, you know... I often see you from the café up there..."

"Yes, I know you do," she said. "I always look up to see if you're there watching me..."

"It looks fun."

"You should try it."

"Who? Me?" Vikram laughed. "You know I've got two left feet."

"I remember dancing with you at college discos," Jackie

recalled. "By the end of the evening my feet were black and blue from the number of times you stepped on them!" She stood up and took Vikram's hand again, pulling him to his feet.

"Hey, what are you doing?" he laughed, as he allowed himself to be taken to the rink's office.

"Vikram Pandy, you are going to go ice-skating!" Jackie announced, as she hired a pair of size-ten skating boots and blades from the office and handed them over to Vikram. "It's crazy you working in the café and not being able to spend your lunchtimes skating!"

"Look, Jackie, I'm not so sure that this is a good idea," Vikram said doubtfully as he sat down and pulled on and laced up his boots.

"Nonsense," Jackie said and, grasping Vikram's hand once again, she led him to the edge of the rink. Unused to the unfamiliar skating boots and their blades, Vikram waddled across the rubber-matted floor towards the ice looking for all the world like a penguin. Jackie found it a struggle not to laugh. Vikram was usually so cool and collected, a trendy, great-looking smoothie; it was great fun to see him so defenceless for a change! And her heart leapt out for him in his sudden vulnerability, as she realized that all she wanted to do was to be there for him, by his side, helping and supporting him, whenever he needed her, for ever.

But just as friends, of course.

Jackie stepped on to the ice, and turned to look at Vikram who was regarding the slippery surface without much enthusiasm. "It's perfectly safe," she said.

Vikram didn't believe her. "You would say that, wouldn't you?" he said. "I've a terrible sense of balance at the best of times. How do you think I'm going to stay upright on two stainless steel blades less than a quarter of an inch thick?"

Jackie grinned, relishing Vikram's dilemma. "Don't be such a softie, Vik," she said. "When have I ever let you down?"

"Lots of times," he confirmed. "Starting from when we were kids together and you nicked my last Smartie!"

"Aha, but I'm not a little girl any more!"

"No, you're not..."

Jackie placed Vikram's hand on the handrail which encircled the entire rink. "Keep a grip of that," she said, "and you won't fall. And I'll be holding you as well: I won't let you make a fool of yourself."

"That a promise?" he asked warily, and he gripped the handrail with his right hand, while, on his left, Jackie encircled his slim waist with her arm.

"That's a promise!" she said, and started to move slowly along the ice. Vikram tried to follow her, making the same sort of faltering steps as a baby would on "dry" land.

Jackie tut-tutted. "You're on the ice, dimwit!" she teased. "You don't walk – you glide." She looked down at Vikram's two left feet, and instructed him to place them in the form of a "T". "Now, just push with your front foot and then follow with your back one – it's easy!"

Indeed, under Jackie's patient tuition Vikram did find it surprisingly easy, and within minutes the two of them were circling the ice – slowly, certainly and very unsteadily, as Vikram was still half-holding the safety rail, while Jackie's arm was wrapped tightly round his waist (and his around hers).

"Hey, you know this is quite good fun," Vikram said, and looked down into Jackie's eyes.

"The best," said Jackie. "I love the sense of freedom and – whoops! Watch out!"

Vikram had almost lost his balance as they took a particularly sharp curve, and, for a couple of seconds, both of them tottered until they regained their centre of gravity.

Jackie was enjoying her skating immensely, and, even more than that, she was having a great time showing off to Vikram. His lack of skill on the ice gave her confidence in her own abilities, far more confidence than Adam's repeated assurances of her talent had given her. And, looking up into Vikram's happy but nervous face, she saw an expression she had never seen before: Vikram, normally so confident, so powerful and reliable, now looked as helpless as a child learning to walk.

Vikram was depending on her, he needed her, she suddenly realized, and that was a new feeling for both of them. Jackie had never experienced anyone relying on her before: even Julian could get along very well without her, thank you very much, and if anyone was in an inferior position in that relationship then it was Jackie. Julian constantly gave her presents, and did things for her, but there was never anything that she could do for him. But here on the ice, Vikram had placed all his trust in her: it felt good to be needed, she decided.

"See, I told you it was easy!" she grinned at him, and felt his arm tighten its hold on her waist. "I knew you'd get the hang of it in –"

Vikram yelped, and lost his balance, crashing to the floor. In a panic he grabbed hold of Jackie's free arm, and tried to pull himself up. With a shriek Jackie lost her balance too, and smashed down on to the floor on top of Vikram, much to the delight of several spectators. At the far end of the ice, Adam, who was still with his younger pupil, turned around and grinned.

"Easy, huh?" Vikram grunted sarcastically, and found himself staring right into Jackie's eyes – hardly surprising as her face was only an inch away from his. "You told me I could trust you!"

"First rule of ice-skating: trust no one. And the second rule is never grab hold of another skater when you've just decided to make an idiot of yourself," Jackie giggled. "It's not particularly dignified doing a prat-fall on the ice – especially when yours truly wants to make a good impression on her tutor!"

"Not dignified, huh?" Vikram joked. "It feels pretty 'dignified' from where I am!"

He shut up abruptly. He had gone too far, said too much, and suddenly the joke was no longer a joke. He stared up into Jackie's eyes; her long blonde hair flopped down and swung over his mouth. He tasted Jackie's freshness on his lips, smelt her natural fragrance. They were so near that they could hear each other's breathing, feel the beat of each other's hearts.

Jackie felt a pair of strong arms lift her off Vikram and help her stand up. The same pair of arms then restored Vikram to his upright (if very wobbly) position.

"So when my back's turned you're two-timing me with my best friend?" Julian cracked, and gave Jackie a peck on the cheek.

"Julian, it's not like that at all!" Jackie protested, and Julian laughed.

"Of course it's not," he said, and glanced sideways at Vikram. "Vik would never try to steal you away from me. Would you, big buddy?"

"Of course not," said Vikram, and smiled nervously.

"Besides he's already spoken for, from all accounts," Julian added and realized, when Vikram glowered evilly at him, that he'd hit a raw nerve by reminding him about his forthcoming arranged marriage to Lakshmi.

"What do you mean?" Jackie asked and looked questioningly at Vikram.

"Skip it," he said, and started to stagger off the ice.

Jackie looked questioningly at Julian: there was a secret here, she would ask Julian about it later.

Julian took a small envelope from the back pocket of his Chinos, and presented it to Jackie, who looked at it curiously. She opened it: it was a pair of tickets for the next Powerhouse concert.

"Call it my way of saying sorry for the other night," he said, "when I stormed off the ice. It's been bugging me for a couple of days now – I was way out of order then."

"It's me who should be sorry," Jackie insisted. "I shouldn't have stood you up like that on Wednesday just for my silly old ice-skating class."

"It's OK," Julian said, and he tried to forget how he had also let Jackie down the previous Saturday. "I should have realized that you wanted your own space. And if Adam's right and you could make that Christmas gala then it's important for you."

Jackie leaned forward and kissed Julian on the lips. "Thanks, Jules, you're so good to me," she said. "So understanding."

Julian held Jackie in his arms. "It's entirely my pleasure," he told her. "I do love you, Jackie."

Jackie smiled, wanting to tell Julian that yes, she loved him too, and wondering why she couldn't bring herself to say the words. She glanced over his shoulder: on the ice Adam had finished his lesson, and he was skating up to them. She released herself from Julian's embrace.

"I have to go now," she said, "it's time for my lesson."

Julian smiled understandingly. "And afterwards we can go out, maybe to Slinky Jo's?"

"Yes, of course, Jules, that would be wonderful," Jackie said half-heartedly, and went off to join Adam for her lesson.

But Jackie had learnt a lesson in those few minutes, a lesson which had just changed her life for ever.

7

Jackie looked at herself in the bathroom mirror, and nodded approvingly. She was wearing her favourite leather jacket (a present from Julian for her last birthday), tight black 501s and boots, and a baggy white shirt. Her blonde hair had been swept back, and her make-up was subtle but effective, with just a hint of glitter on her eyelids. She knew that she looked a million dollars for the Powerhouse concert and, as she checked her pockets for her money, she felt the two tickets that Julian had bought: they were in the front row, naturally: nothing was too good for Julian.

Jackie and Julian used to love going to rock gigs, losing themselves in the music, and the company of other fun-loving people. *Perhaps tonight some of that old magic would return*, she thought hopefully, *perhaps tonight she would realize that Julian really was the man for her*. She smiled, as her mind turned its attentions, unbidden, to Vikram. Vik hated Powerhouse, calling them a "bunch of talentless goons": there'd certainly be no danger of bumping into him tonight!

Jackie was about to go downstairs to wait for the taxi that Julian had said he would order for her, when the phone rang. Frowning – she wasn't expecting a call at this time – she picked up the receiver.

"Hello?"

"Hi, Jackie, it's me," Julian introduced himself at the end of the line. As soon as she heard Julian's voice, Jackie felt her heart sink.

"What's up?" Jackie asked, even though she had a fair idea.

"Jackie, I'm really sorry, but I can't make it tonight," Julian said.

Jackie sighed. Somehow she'd had a feeling that this was coming. "Why not, Julian?" she asked peevishly. "What's wrong?"

There was a pause at the other end, before Julian said that he had an emergency assignment for college, which he had to hand in the first day of the forthcoming term. It couldn't be put off and might even go some way to helping him get a place at medical school next year.

"But I've already rung up Emma," he said quickly before Jackie could say anything. "She's more than happy to go with you tonight: I told her to come straight round to your place..."

You've got it all tied up nicely, haven't you, Jules? Jackie found herself thinking. *But what are you really up to? Is it another girl? Or is it that you just don't want to see me?*

"Look, Jackie, you don't know how sorry I am," Julian said. "But I promise you, I'll make it up to you."

"Yes, Julian, I'm sure you will," Jackie said coldly. "You always do..."

With a heavy heart she hung up the phone, just as Emma rang the front door bell. On the other end of the line, Julian replaced the receiver and sighed. It was all a lie, of course. But there was no other girl, there wasn't even an emergency assignment. It was simply that, much as he cared for Jackie, he just didn't want to see her tonight. What was happening to him? he wondered. Why could he not admit the truth to himself and to Jackie? He no longer loved her the way he once had...

And yet to see Jackie hurt would break Julian's heart...

"Look, I'm really sorry I couldn't make it, Jackie," Julian

said a few nights later when they all met up in Slinky Jo's.

"Oh, that's quite all right," Jackie said icily. "You buy me tickets for the hottest gig of the year and then you don't turn up!"

"I had a lot of studying to do," Julian claimed. "And it's not as though I stood you up — I let you know beforehand, didn't I?"

"And am I ever glad you did, Jules!" gushed Emma. "We had a great time. That lead singer is just so hunky!"

"I really am sorry, Jackie," Julian repeated. "But you know how important my work is..." He took her hands in his.

"I know, Jules," Jackie said, unwilling to continue the argument; in fact she hadn't had a passionate argument with Julian for months now. "But sometimes I just wish..." Her voice trailed off.

"Wish what, Jackie?"

I just wish that I could feel something when your hands touch mine, that's all, Jackie thought.

"Oh, nothing," she said.

"Forgiven?" Julian asked and winked at her with those pretty-boy eyes of his. How could anyone resist them?

"Forgiven," Jackie smiled, and stood up to go. She and Emma were going down to Blades. Did he want to come? Julian shook his head, reminding Jackie just how unsteady he was on the ice. The girls laughed and left.

"OK, so what's up, Julian?" asked Vikram after Jackie and Emma had left Slinky Jo's.

"What d'you mean, 'what's up'?" his friend asked, although he knew perfectly well what Vikram was talking about. He looked around the café: a group of exceptionally pretty girls were sitting around one of the nearby tables, laughing and joking and sharing a jug of sangria. When they caught sight of Julian looking at them they started to giggle. Julian reached out for his own glass of wine, but Vikram moved it away, making Julian turn around and look at him.

"Standing Jackie up like that," Vikram said. "That's the second time you've done it in as many weeks with no apparent reason at all."

Julian took his glass and gulped at his wine. "I told you," he said, "I've got lots of studying to do."

Vikram shook his head. "Sorry, Jules," he said. "Jackie might fall for that but not me. So why are you lying to Jackie?"

Julian gritted his teeth in an effort to control his temper. What gave Vikram the right to probe him about his personal life like this?

"Look, I just wanted some time to myself, that's all," he said finally. "We see each other practically every single day."

"Because you invite her out," Vikram reminded him. "And then you get cold feet and come up with these wild excuses to cancel. As if you don't really want to see her any more."

"Hey, stop hassling me, Vik," Julian pleaded. "I've got my reasons."

"So tell them to Jackie," Vikram urged him. "I'm sure she'd understand."

"And I'm sure you don't understand women," Julian snapped. "She'd automatically assume that I'm carrying on with someone behind her back – someone like Linsey maybe."

"And are you?" Vikram challenged.

"No," was Julian's firm reply. "I'd never two-time Jackie. I ... I love her..."

"We all do."

"What?" Julian stared accusingly at Vikram, and Vik realized that he had said too much.

"As a friend, I mean," he said hastily. "We all love Jackie as a friend."

Julian looked thoughtfully at his mate for a moment, before saying: "Yeah, well, I love her as more than a friend – I love her as my girlfriend..."

Well, you sure have a funny way of showing it, thought Vikram.

*   *   *

"This is quite a surprise, Jackie," Adam said, as he settled back into the plush seating of the sushi bar, having devoured an enormous bowl of noodles.

"I was at a loose end tonight, so I came to the rink on the off-chance of seeing if you were free," she said.

"And I was!" Adam laughed. "But I certainly didn't expect to be taken out for a slap-up candle-lit Japanese meal by one of my students! You spend enough money already on your classes!"

"They're worth every penny, and besides, the record store pays good money," Jackie said and sipped at her glass of sake (Adam had ordered it, and she hadn't wanted to tell him that she didn't like the taste). "Especially if you think I'll be good enough to take part in the Christmas gala," she added uncertainly.

"Of course you will be," Adam said and rested his hand on hers. He laughed: "With me as your teacher you can't fail!"

Jackie looked down at Adam's hand, and her head started swimming in a sea of conflicting emotions, and an awful feeling of guilt. There was something wrong with her relationship with Julian, she was beginning to realize now, and that was why she was reaching out for Adam, just as earlier the thought of Vikram had fired her body with strange new feelings. What was she doing here with this man, when she knew that Julian was working hard at home, in his efforts to set up some sort of future for them? And what would Vikram think if – if – well, what did it matter what Vikram thought? He was her friend, that was all.

Wasn't he?

Vikram didn't place his hand on hers, Vikram didn't hold her tightly round the waist when they circled the ice, like equals. Vikram had been there for ever, as much a part of her life as her mother, her family, her friends. Adam was something new and exciting in her life, with his Scandinavian-American accent, and the way he made her feel so confident out there on the ice.

She glanced up: Adam was smiling at her now, and the candlelight caught in his long blond hair, making it shine and glisten like finely-spun gold. His steely blue eyes sparkled in the light.

Adam was one of the most attractive men she had ever seen, Jackie suddenly realized, possessing cool good looks which reminded her of snow at Christmas, or beautiful frost-patterns on a window pane. His beauty was so different from Julian's sandy-haired boyish looks; and a million miles away from Vikram's wild and brooding darkness.

"I hope you're not just my teacher, Adam," she breathed softly. "I hope you're also my friend."

"Of course I am," Adam reassured her warmly.

Moments passed, as Jackie struggled with her emotions, painfully aware that Adam, this man who was so different to Julian, had not yet taken his hand away from hers. Finally, she closed her eyes and leant forward to kiss Adam lightly on the lips. She felt Adam tense, and draw back; he took his hand away from hers.

Jackie opened her eyes, and saw the look of surprise on Adam's face, and instantly realized her mistake.

Adam smiled. "Jackie, I think you've got your wires crossed somewhere," he said, not unkindly.

Jackie suddenly felt like the biggest fool ever. She wished the ground would open up beneath her. "I ... I thought..." she stammered, and then found that there were no words to express what she felt.

"Hey, it's OK," Adam said. "It's a natural mistake to make."

"I just thought ... it felt so good skating with you, having you hold me in your arms," Jackie said. She grimaced. "I guess I've just made a right idiot of myself, haven't I? Just like a little kid, having a crush on the teacher!"

"You're not a little kid, Jackie – you're only a couple of years younger than me," Adam said. "And like you said,

I'm not just your teacher – I also hope I'll be your friend. It's just that you're not my type –"

"Well, thank you very much," Jackie quipped in a half-successful attempt to relieve the tension.

"And you have a boyfriend – Julian," Adam continued. "And somehow you don't seem to me to be the sort of person to cheat on him."

Jackie sighed. "It feels so right when we're going round the ice together, you holding me by the waist," she said. "Feeling your touch. It's just so different…"

"Different?"

"Julian hardly ever holds me now, not the way you do…" she said. "When he touches me it no longer means anything… There's no thrill, no excitement, no passion…"

"He seems to love you very much indeed," Adam said. "Vikram and Emma tell me that he's always giving you presents."

Jackie grimaced. "Yeah, the most expensive clothes, the trendiest CDs, tickets for the hottest gigs," she said. "But that's not what love is, is it? It's not about material things, or possessions, or getting the biggest present for your birthday. Sometimes I think that he's trying to buy me off with all those presents…"

" 'Buy you off'? What d'you mean?"

"It's as if that's the only way he can express his feelings for me," she said. "Whenever he cancels a date for whatever reason, I know for sure that he'll give me an expensive gift the next day to make up for it. But how many times have you seen him hold me on the rink, or kiss me anywhere other than on the cheek?"

"I take your point," Adam said.

"He doesn't hold me the way he used to when we first started going out," Jackie despaired. "He's not as tender as he used to be… At times he's on another planet."

"He seemed pretty upset when you cancelled your date to take your first skating lesson," Adam pointed out.

"That was just his silly pride," Jackie decided. "And he apologized for it afterwards –"

"With another present?"

Jackie nodded.

Adam reached out for Jackie's hands again, and she let him take them. There was no misunderstanding this time: she realized that this was just Adam's way of showing affection, of making contact with people – he had no ulterior motive.

"How long have you been going out with Julian?" he asked.

"Two years – three years next January," she replied.

"People change, Jackie," Adam said. "And when they do there are no heroes and no villains. Sometimes they just grow out of love with each other. It's sad, but that's the way it is. And it's hard and painful to break out of that love, but you have to do it."

"But how do I know, Adam?" she asked. "How do I know if I have grown out of love with Julian?"

Adam looked kindly at her, a knowing smile on his face. "I could tell you," he said, "but it's up to you to find out for yourself..."

Jackie smiled back, aware that she had made a new friend. It seemed odd telling a boy all her troubles, but there was something trustworthy about Adam which inspired confidence.

It was the same sort of confidence that enabled her to skate so well when she was with him. They made a team, she realized, and even though Adam was a much better skater than her, on the ice he brought out the best in her. On the ice they were equals, partners, each relying on the other: neither one inferior to the other, neither one superior. That was what friendship was all about, Jackie realized; but what was love all about?

Did she still really love Julian? she wondered. There was an aching deep inside her, she knew that; and if she truly had fallen out of love with Julian then she knew that it would break his heart – and she couldn't do that, could she? She shook her head, and looked at Adam, misty-eyed.

"You're wrong, Adam," she said. "Julian is so kind to me, so generous, I do love him, I really do love him."

Adam smiled kindly. "I'm sure you do, Jackie," he said. "But are you *in* love with him?"

And Jackie no longer knew the answer.

Jackie and Adam stayed in the restaurant for another half hour, happy that they had reached a new understanding. Adam was a charmer, of that there was no doubt, but, as he had said, he needed to be if he had to convince what he called the ice-skating mothers to pay good money to send their spoilt daughters to his lessons.

Bizarrely, as Adam talked, Jackie found her mind returning to Vikram, as she realized just how different Adam was to Vikram, who simply wasn't aware of the devastating effect he had on the opposite sex. Vikram with his muscular physique, and the way his chest hairs peeked out over the top of his T-shirts sometimes; his firm jawline, and his million-dollar smile which could turn even the dreariest October day into the first day of the summer holidays. The way he never went out to impress anyone, or put on an act, and was always himself; but was invariably polite and considerate, even with pushy little witches like Linsey. Kind, intelligent and straightforward, with the proportions of a Greek god: the spotty little kid from next door, on whose shoulder she used to cry, had turned into a prize catch for some lucky girl, and the crazy thing was that he didn't even realize it himself!

And while there was now no doubting Adam's sincerity in his friendship with her, she still found Vikram's unassuming manner preferable and his good looks all the more appealing because of his total ignorance of them. Whoever Vikram eventually fell in love with would be one lucky girl, she decided.

As they left the sushi bar, they failed to notice Linsey who had just arrived, with her usual entourage of trendy and good-looking boys and girls. Linsey, however, noticed them, and scowled when she spotted Adam helping Jackie on with her coat.

She saw red. She'd had her eyes on Adam, ever since she'd realized she was on a losing streak with Vikram, and thought she had made a start by impressing him out on the ice. And now here Jackie was, stealing the hunky ice-skater right from under her nose!

Quivering with fury and jealousy, Linsey plotted her revenge.

8

As the evening drew to a close, the music in the trendy club, to which Julian had taken Jackie, changed to a slower and sexier beat. The two of them looked at each other as if to say: *Shall we?*

All around them other couples were pairing off for the last slow-dance of the night. They'd both look fools, they silently decided, if they joined the other couples who were slinking off to the bar, embarrassed, or unwilling to indulge in some decidedly untrendy and intimate touch-dancing. Jackie and Julian were boyfriend and girlfriend; sharing the last dance of the night was only what was to be expected of them.

Julian put his arms around Jackie, pressing his warm body hard against hers, and Jackie reached up to run her fingers through his fine, sandy-blond hair. They swayed dreamily to the music, and Jackie rested her head on his shoulder, watching the other smooching couples on the dance floor.

Over by the bar, Vikram was chatting to a couple of his mates, and ordering a low-alcohol cider from the pretty barmaid: it was obvious that she was very attracted to him.

Obvious to everyone apart from Vik, Jackie realized, as her handsome friend – *my handsome friend, and that's all!* – took the drink from the girl, barely acknowledging her, and continued chatting with his mates. No doubt they were debating the merits of various football teams, she decided. Vikram hadn't come with her and Julian to the disco, but it had been a pleasant surprise when they had run into him; for the first hour they hadn't danced, but had just sat chatting.

"Are you happy?"

The voice seemed to come from a long way away, and Jackie looked up at Julian.

"Sorry?" she asked.

"I asked you if you're happy," Julian said, and ran his fingers distractedly up and down Jackie's spine. Jackie smiled, and gave a brief sigh of pleasure; after all, that was what girls were supposed to do when boys as handsome as Julian massaged the hollow of their back, wasn't it?

"Of course, I am," Jackie said, and kissed Julian briefly on the lips. "It's been a lovely evening, Jules. I've really enjoyed myself."

It wasn't a lie, Julian certainly knew how to give a girl a good time: he had picked her up in a cab, taken her to a new exclusive restaurant where he had blown his father's money on a candlelit dinner for two, and then taken her to the trendiest of clubs in town. Jackie calculated that he must have spent a small fortune on her.

"I just wanted to make tonight really special for you," Julian said, and glanced over to the pretty barmaid making eyes at Vikram, before turning back to his girlfriend. "We seem to be seeing less of each other lately – I was wondering whether there was something wrong…"

For a second Jackie froze almost perceptibly in Julian's arms, and then resumed moving back and forth to the music.

"Of course there isn't," she said. "It's just that I've been so tied up with my ice-skating recently, that I haven't had time to go out." It had been three weeks now since she had had her chat with Adam in the sushi bar, and he had been constantly encouraging her in her skating, saying that she had a lot of talent.

"Maybe I should be jealous of Adam?" Julian said, but when he saw the worried look on Jackie's face, he smiled, and kissed her on the forehead. "Hey, it's just a joke," he claimed. "I realize I was wrong when I thought that you preferred your ice-skating tutor to me!"

Jackie stopped dancing, and shrugged herself out of Julian's arms. *Did he suspect something?* she asked herself, and then considered. But what was there to suspect? After all, there was nothing going on between her and Adam and there never would be.

"Hey, what's up, Jackie?" Julian asked.

"Nothing, Jules," she said. "I'm just tired of dancing now. Shall we sit this one out?"

"Whatever you say," Julian said indulgently, and allowed Jackie to take his hand and lead him off the dance floor. They threaded their way through the dancing couples, and back to the bar and Vikram. He smiled when he saw them, and Jackie took her hand away from Julian's.

"Touch-dancing!" he scoffed with a look of disgust on his face. "How yuckky can you get?"

"Some romantic you are, best buddy," said Julian, and accepted a glass of cider from him. "You'll never know how good it is until you try it!"

"Alas, I have no fair maiden like Jackie to dance with!" Vikram moaned theatrically.

"I'm sure Jackie wouldn't mind dancing with you," Julian said, all innocence. "Would you, Jackie?"

A beat. A brief exchange of glances between Jackie and Vikram. And then: "Of course not."

"It doesn't matter," Vikram said quickly. "I don't really want to dance at all..."

Julian looked strangely from Vikram to Jackie and then back at Vikram again. "What is it with you two?" he asked finally. "You're both about as jumpy as each other!"

"I ... I twisted my ankle playing football tonight," Vikram lied. "I couldn't dance even if I wanted to..."

Julian made sympathetic noises. "Tough luck, Vik," he

said. "I guess it was Jake Bond's fault, huh? He's a mean mother when he's playing."

"Er, that's right," Vikram said, and made a mental note to get Jake to back him up on his alibi. "I guess he's never forgiven me for refusing to take his sister Clare out on a date!"

"The poor girl must have been devastated," came a familiar voice, and they turned to see a flash of scarlet and black designer clothes. Linsey had spotted them and had come over in order, so she said, to say goodnight.

Pull the other one! Jackie thought.

"Oh, hi, Linsey," Vikram said, as she pecked him on the cheek, as she would a friend. It was hard to think that only a few weeks ago she was practically throwing herself at him. Linsey turned and acknowledged Jackie pleasantly, which immediately set Jackie's alarm bells ringing.

And then Linsey looked at Julian, fixing all her sultry charms on him. "I haven't seen you down at Blades recently," she said, casually.

"I've been catching up on some work," Julian said and smiled. "It's Jackie who's the skating champ around here."

"Of course," Linsey said. "She and Adam look so good together on the ice – real partners. I guess it's because they get on so well socially too. I see them all over the place, at Slinky Jo's, at that trendy sushi bar on the high street –"

Julian frowned. He'd been out with Jackie and Emma and Adam occasionally to Slinky Jo's, but never to the sushi bar.

"Oh, about three weeks ago now, I think it was," Linsey said sweetly, as though butter wouldn't melt in her mouth. Jackie glared hatefully at her.

"You didn't mention this to me," Julian said to Jackie.

"I must have forgotten," Jackie said, who had purposely not let Julian know of her meal with Adam out of embarrassment. "It wasn't important anyway."

Linsey put a hand on Jackie's shoulder. "Oh dear,

Emma –"

"It's Jackie."

"Of course it is; how silly of me to forget. I haven't dropped you in it, have I?" she asked, and, before Jackie could reply, she took her hand from Jackie and offered it to Julian. "Don't get the wrong idea," she said. "There was nothing out of order about it."

"Of course not," Julian said. "Jackie isn't like that."

A bizarre thought sped through Jackie's mind: *how dare he take me so much for granted?*

"Especially not with someone as handsome as you are," Linsey smarmed, and finally took her hand off Julian, satisfied that she had sown a seed of doubt in his mind. And with that she made her excuses and left them standing at the bar.

"She's a nice girl," Julian said, and Jackie looked curiously at him.

"And how would you know?" she teased.

Julian coloured. "I've seen her at the ice rink when I've been watching you," he said.

"You couldn't miss her in those tarty clothes," Jackie said, unkindly but truthfully.

"I think she's lonely," Julian said thoughtfully, and watched Linsey's departing figure – along with most of the other men in the place. "She's always by herself."

"No, she just doesn't have any friends – real friends anyway – 'cause she's so unpleasant to people – other girls at least," Jackie said. "Look at the way she latches on to anyone's boyfriend – even Vik here!"

"What do you mean, 'even Vik here'?" Vikram asked, and laughed. "I have been able to pass as quite presentable-looking occasionally!"

Gorgeous-looking, more like, Jackie thought.

My gorgeous-looking friend.

"Anyway, Vikram isn't anyone's boyfriend," Julian said, as if Jackie needed any reminding. "And Linsey hasn't been giving him the eye like she used to..."

"Alas, she has decided that I'm a lost cause!" Vikram

chuckled, and then slapped his mate on the back. "It seems, however, that she thinks you're a different case!"

The atmosphere froze, and Jackie and Julian exchanged worried looks. It was as if Vikram had unwittingly put his finger on a truth neither of them had been willing to admit. When he noticed the effect of his words, Vikram clapped his hands together, in an attempt to change the subject.

"Enough of psycho-analysing man-mad Linsey!" he said. "Let's make arrangements for tomorrow night. We're all still going to see this dreary old movie, aren't we?"

Earlier that day, Jackie and Julian, Vikram and Emma, had all agreed to go to the cinema to see one of the latest blockbusters the following night. It was, so Emma read from the reviews in the local newspaper while sitting in Blades café, "a tender and haunting vision of romance and betrayal and a passion that wouldn't die". Vikram had replied that, if it was all the same to them, couldn't they just go and see the latest blood 'n' gore sci-fi action fest instead?

Emma had shaken her head firmly, and declared that it wasn't surprising he didn't have a girlfriend if that was his taste in movies. Vikram had finally conceded, after some brow-beating from Jackie and Emma, even though Julian had been mildly on his side.

"Of course," Jackie said.

Vikram sighed. "I was thinking perhaps you'd changed your mind," he said dolefully, and looked at Julian, hoping for some loyal masculine support.

"You never know, you might enjoy it, Vik," Julian laughed, betraying Vikram's faith in him. "It's even up for some Oscars!"

"Big deal!"

Jackie joined in Julian's teasing of Vikram. "You've just no soul, Vik," she said. "You've got no heart, no sense of romance!"

"Oh yes I have," he replied.

There was a momentary pause in the friends' chatter,

unnoticed only by Julian.

"So prove it, Vik!" Julian said. "Be at the cinema at seven-thirty tomorrow as arranged! Afterwards we can go on to Slinky Jo's – it'll be my treat."

Vikram rammed his hands into the pockets of his Chinos, and affected a pretty convincing sulk. "If I have to..." he grumbled. "Although give me an Arnie actioner any day!"

Julian smiled, and looked at his watch: it was almost one-thirty in the morning. It was time to go home, he said, and, despite Jackie's protests that she could get a cab, he insisted that he take her home. He reached out to put an arm around her waist, and then turned to Vikram.

"You want a lift too?" he asked. "After all, you're practically Jackie's next-door neighbour."

Vikram smiled gratefully. "Thanks, but no thanks. You two will want to be alone," he said; was it regret that Jackie could detect in his voice? "I'll walk it. It's not far and I've got some thinking to do."

"Have it your own way," Julian said, unconcerned by Vikram's sudden change of mood. He started to walk off with Jackie towards the exit. As they left, Jackie turned and saw Vikram, who was watching them go.

Suddenly he looked so alone, so vulnerable, surrounded as he was by kissing and dancing couples, or laughing boys at the bar. There was a look of yearning on his face, and of sadness too, as though he would break down at any moment into tears of longing and regret. Her heart went out to him, and Jackie suddenly knew that she didn't want to go home, that she wanted to stay here with her friend, with Vikram.

"C'mon, Jackie, it's getting late!" said her boyfriend, and, casting one last look behind her, Jackie let herself be escorted out of the club.

9

"You're doing really well, Emma," Adam approved the following day as Emma executed a perfect figure of eight on the ice under Adam's critical gaze. She came to a halt and beamed gratefully at the handsome skating instructor.

"You really think so?" she said.

"I wouldn't say so if I didn't mean it," he said truthfully. "Ever since I started teaching you, you've improved by leaps and bounds."

Emma gulped: was this impossibly handsome Viking actually speaking to her and complimenting her? And was it her imagination or was he really spending more and more time with her, stretching her lessons out more than the quarter-hours she had paid for? Of course it was her imagination: she would have to be a fool to think that someone as gorgeous as Adam could be attracted to someone like her!

"I've loved ice-skating since I was little but I've always been such a klutz before," she admitted. "If I have improved then it's all down to you!"

Adam chuckled as he took her hand and skated with her towards the edge of the ice; it was the end of their session and he had another lesson to take in a couple of minutes.

"Jackie said something very similar a couple of weeks ago!" he remembered. "I'm afraid all this praise is going to go to my head!"

When they reached the barrier, Emma stopped and sighed. "But even with all your teaching I'm never going to be as good as Linsey," she complained. "Or as pretty," she added.

Like a good mate, Adam chucked Emma under the chin. "Linsey's a great skater if something of a show-off," he said. "And what if she is conventionally attractive? Some men don't like their women to be sizzling sex-bombs—"

"Aha! So you have noticed then!"

"—They know that beauty's only skin-deep," Adam finished. "It's what a person is like underneath that really counts. Their wit, their intelligence, their personality – not how many heads they can turn on the ice or when they're walking down the high street."

There was a pause, and, for want of anything better, Emma looked at her watch – six o'clock – and then asked: "Where is Linsey for that matter? She's usually on the ice by this time, putting on a show for all those sex-crazed pimply adolescents who come here to ogle and drool over her."

Adam shrugged. "I never even noticed she wasn't here," he said. "I've been watching you all the time!"

"Yeah, well, you are my teacher, aren't you?" she said. *After all, why else would a hunk like Adam want to look at a frizzy-haired, plain Jane like me?* she thought.

"Of course, that's all I am – just your teacher," Adam confirmed, and kissed Emma goodbye as she went off to the girls' changing rooms to take off her skating boots and have a shower.

Adam skated back into the centre of the ice, and looked around for his next pupil, a nine-year-old girl who, in common with most of his other pupils, was hopelessly in love with her Scandinavian skating instructor. She hadn't yet arrived, and as he circled the ice, he spied Julian waving at him from the side. He skated over to him.

Julian was dressed smartly in a pair of freshly-pressed Chinos, and a black unstructured designer jacket which had probably cost him – or rather his father's credit card –

more than Adam earned in a month. He was also carrying a rolled-up umbrella: it was raining outside.

Julian nodded briefly to him: while he had now realized that Adam was no threat to his relationship with Jackie, and had indeed shared a cappuccino with him a couple of times, the two boys weren't particularly good mates. (In truth, Julian was a little jealous of the admiring looks which Adam, a far better skater than he would ever be, received from the girls at Blades.)

"Is Jackie here?" he asked, and Adam shook his head: he hadn't seen her all day. "I tried contacting her at home but there was no reply."

"Is there something wrong?" Adam asked: there was an anxious look on Julian's face.

"Er ... no ... well, yes, as a matter of fact there is," Julian said guiltily. "I'm supposed to be meeting her, Emma and Vikram tonight at the cinema," he continued, and mentioned the romantic film they were all planning to see.

"And you can't make it?" Adam guessed, and looked searchingly at Julian, who nodded, and averted his eyes from Adam's gaze.

As if he's hiding something, Adam realized.

"That's right," he said, and looked up at the café; Adam told him that it was Vikram's night off.

"Emma's still around," Adam said. "You could tell her."

"Sure..." Julian said, not sounding very sure at all. He looked at his watch. "Look, Adam, I'm going to be late. Do us a favour and tell Emma for me, will you?"

Adam smiled to himself: did Julian really think he was fooling him with his tale of a science project that he hadn't even started yet, with only three weeks to go before it was due to be handed in? Nevertheless Adam promised he would tell Emma so that they wouldn't waste their time waiting for him at the cinema.

"You're a mate, Adam," Julian said, relieved that he would be spared the embarrassment of having to lie to Emma. "I owe you one!"

"Any time," Adam said, and, as Julian made to go, he stopped him and asked: "You're just supposed to be meeting Jackie, Emma and Vikram at the movies, yes? No one else?"

Julian frowned, wondering why Adam was suddenly so interested in who he was due to be meeting that night. But Adam had seen the looks that passed between Jackie and Vikram, and could see things in a much clearer light than Julian.

"That's right – just me, Jackie, Emma and Vik," Julian confirmed, and, taking another look at his watch – "My God, I'm going to be so late!" – he made his goodbyes and raced out of the ice rink.

Emma came out of the girls' changing rooms, her skates slung over her shoulder, just as Julian left the hall. She joined Adam by the barrier; Adam was stroking his chin thoughtfully, and when he saw Emma, his face lit up…

"Was that Jules I just saw running out of here like a bat out of hell?" Emma asked. "I've never seen him run that fast except on the football field!"

Adam said it was. He smiled sympathetically at Emma. "He's just been in to say that tonight's cancelled," he said. And then Adam took a deep breath, as though lying was something he wasn't accustomed to, and said: "Something about a project he's got to hand in. He told me to tell you that Jackie and Vikram can't make it either…"

Emma's face fell. "I was so looking forward to that movie as well!" she said.

"You can always see it another time," Adam told her.

"Just my luck," Emma said miserably. "Stood up by my three best friends! Thank goodness I haven't got a boyfriend – or he'd stand me up too!"

Adam laughed and patted Emma on the back. "I can't see why any boyfriend of yours would ever stand you up," he said. "You're pretty, intelligent and great fun to be with."

"No, I'm not," Emma protested, even though she felt a little buzz of pleasure at being told how pretty she looked by a guy as gorgeous as Adam. *Even if he is only being nice to me!* she added. "And besides, I'm fat."

"No, you're not."

"Yes I am," Emma insisted. "Compared to someone like Linsey, I'm enormous!"

"So stop comparing yourself to her then," Adam said sensibly. "Not all boys fancy pencil-thin, empty-headed bimbos, you know!"

That shut Emma up, and there was an awkward pause, before Adam said: "I've got a lesson to take, but after that I'm going to be free for the rest of the evening. Your evening's been called off, so why don't you hang around and then we could go around the ice a few times? Maybe we could go for a coffee at Slinky Jo's?"

Emma shook her head. "I can't afford any more lessons, Adam," she said sadly, choosing to ignore the ice-skating teacher's final suggestion. Why would he want to go out with her? she asked herself, as a wild hope sprang in her breast.

"And I'm not offering lessons," Adam said. "We can just go ice-skating – with a little bit of determination, Emma, you might even begin to enjoy yourself!"

Vikram wiped a tear away from his eye, hoping that Jackie hadn't noticed. They were sitting side by side in the movie theatre, having decided that they couldn't wait any longer for Julian and Emma to turn up; and Vikram had decided that what he called the "decided slushiness" of the movie they were watching perhaps wasn't so bad after all.

"Aha! Caught you!" Jackie giggled, a little too loudly, ignoring the protests of the couple sitting behind them. "You're a bigger softy than I am!"

Vikram gave her a friendly punch in the ribs, and continued to watch the movie, the tale of a nineteenth-century farm girl forced to choose between two men. He found it strangely moving, and by his side Jackie's bare arm accidentally brushed against his. The hairs on his arm stood up on end, as he became aware of Jackie's warmth next to him. She moved her arm away, but he could still feel its presence there, as though he had been branded with a mark that nothing would ever remove. Vikram shifted uncomfortably in his seat, crossing his legs, and trying to focus all his attention on the screen.

And how could he do that when sitting next to him was a girl who was a hundred times more beautiful than the heroine on the screen?

He turned and looked at Jackie, who was watching as the movie's heroine lost her beau to the wiles and machinations of the local scarlet woman. The actress playing her looked a little like Linsey, Jackie decided.

Suddenly Jackie was aware of Vikram looking at her in the dark, and she turned, smiled at him, and then returned to watching the film.

Jackie's eyes were bejewelled with tears as she watched the events on screen, and Vikram had an almost irresistible desire to reach out and gently dry them, and to run his fingers through her fine blonde hair. Jackie always complained about how unmanageable her hair was, and about her split ends – *whatever they are!* Vikram thought – but to him her hair seemed beautiful, as fine as gossamer and as golden as summer sunlight.

What the hell am I thinking of! Vikram thought angrily to himself. *She's the girlfriend of my best friend!*

He turned back to the screen, folding his arms as if to contain within him the emotions that he was finally admitting to himself. And as he turned his eyes away from Jackie, Jackie looked at him, and wondered why the normally so cheerful Vikram was frowning. He was troubled by something, of that she was sure, and she would have done anything in the world to unburden him of his problems. She sighed, and resumed watching the film.

They stayed like that, staring ahead at the movie screen, in silence, each of them alone with their own thoughts, until the credits rolled up on the screen and the movie drew to a close. The lights came up (but not as quickly as Vikram's hand which wiped the tears from his face before Jackie could see), and they stood up to go.

In the narrow aisles of the local cinema, Vikram found himself placing his hand on Jackie's back as he ushered her out of the seats. It was the most natural thing in the world to do – something Vikram had done hundreds of times before – but now he froze, and drew his hand away.

It was raining outside, a soft summer shower, and Vikram unfurled his umbrella to protect them from the rain. Jackie hadn't brought hers, so she hooked her arm around Vikram's, pressing herself close to him so that she would be protected by the umbrella.

"That was a wonderful film," she said. "Emma and Julian will be so mad that they missed out on it!"

"It's odd that neither of them rang up to cancel," Vikram said, as they started walking down the road.

Jackie shrugged. "Who cares?" she said. "I've had a wonderful time with you, Vik."

"Yes, so have I..." Vikram said, and looked down at Jackie. *Just friends, and that's all*. And why did he not believe that any more? "Where to now, Ms Taylor?"

"If we were with Julian, we'd probably all go off to a posh bistro or restaurant," Jackie said teasingly.

"What d'you think I am, made of money?" Vikram feigned outrage. "It's a cappuccino at Slinky Jo's – if you're lucky!"

"Then Slinky Jo's it is!" Jackie decided, and she walked off down the rain-swept streets, arm-in-arm with Vikram.

Just friends, and that's all.

"Do you remember when we were kids, Vik?" Jackie reminisced. "Whenever there was a big storm and it started to thunder, I'd climb over the fence and into your dad's garden shed. It was your little 'den', and I always knew that you'd be there."

Vikram chuckled at the memory. "I remember – you were always frightened out of your wits. And only big brave Vikram could comfort you!"

"Liar! You were as scared as I was – that's why you were in the shed in the first place, hiding from the thunder and the lightning!"

"Maybe I was a little bit frightened..." Vikram admitted with disarming candour.

"I knew that we were like each other, you see," Jackie continued. "And that I didn't have to pretend to you. Mum would fuss over me and tell me there was nothing to worry about. But you were as frightened as me, and that was good because I could look after you, just as you could look after me."

Just friends, and that's all.

"A couple of scaredy cats, that's what we were."

"And sometimes I even used to look forward to thunderstorms, because then I knew that I could be *there* for someone, and that they'd be there for me. We needed each other, y'see."

They walked on in silence for a few seconds, and then Vikram said: "You've got Jules now."

Jackie sighed – with what emotion neither she nor Vikram was quite sure – and rested her head on Vikram's shoulder. "Julian looks after me, buys me things, makes sure everything's all right—"

"Even holds your hand in thunderstorms, I bet," Vikram said, attempting to make a joke of it.

Just friends, and that's all.

"But he never lets me look after him," Jackie said. "He never lets me pay for meals – unlike you, for instance."

"Hey, even with the job at Blades, I'm still on the breadline!" Vikram laughed. "If anyone's offering, this guy will take any free meals that are going!"

"And I bet he wouldn't have cried at the movie tonight the way you did," she said.

"That wasn't crying!" Vikram claimed. "That was merely an altruistic and noble attempt on my part to comfort a sobbing female in her hour of crisis, and make her feel comfortable in her great distress!"

"Yeah, and the rest," Jackie gloated. "For all your

bravado, in my mind you're still the frightened little boy in his dad's shed—"

"Just don't spread it around, OK?" Vikram said. "I don't want anything to harm my reputation as an all-round all-purpose jock!"

"I wouldn't dream of it," Jackie said, and cuddled up closer to him.

Just friends, and that's all.

"Besides, until you learn to ice-skate you're not all-round and all-purpose!" she added. "And from your performance on the ice a couple of weeks ago, I don't think you ever will be!"

And that's when I knew, thought Jackie. *That's when I knew that you needed me. That's when I knew that I needed to be needed too.*

"The Leaning Tower of Pisa has a better sense of balance than you, Vik!" she said.

"Please, woman, spare my blushes," Vikram said flippantly, at the same time deciding that he didn't quite like the turn the conversation was taking. "And less of the thunderstorm stories too! I don't want to be reminded of my days as a snotty-nosed, spotty kid!"

They stopped walking, and Jackie looked up into Vikram's dark eyes. "You're certainly not that now, Vik," she murmured.

"Jackie, I..." Vikram did not know what to say.

Just friends, and that's all.

He looked nervously about, at the passers-by walking briskly past them, more concerned with getting out of the rain than the conversation between two friends sheltering under an umbrella; he glanced over at Slinky Jo's across the road, its candle-lit tables glowing warmly and invitingly; he looked at anything, in fact, except at Jackie.

Vikram was suddenly aware of Jackie's hand as it reached up towards his stubbled chin (even though he had shaved earlier that evening), and made him turn round to face her.

"Jackie..."

Just friends, and that's all.

It was inevitable, as certain as the night giving way to day, the sea rushing to shore, just two people finally following the dictates of their hearts. Vikram lowered his face to meet Jackie's and they kissed, a long, deep, passionate kiss, acknowledging the feelings they had for each other that they had never before dared express.

Jackie felt the rough touch of Vikram's stubble against her cheeks, and ran her fingers through his dark raven curls, and down around his strong and muscular neck. She swayed with him, as if they were dancing, and not standing sheltered under an umbrella on a busy and rainy street.

That world of rain, of dirty wet pavements and of passers-by no longer seemed to exist for them. Vikram and Jackie: there was nothing else. There was no Adam, no Emma, no Linsey and certainly no Julian to intrude upon their happiness.

Vikram smiled, and caressed Jackie's soft cheeks, outlined her chin with his fingers, as gently as if he were handling prize porcelain. He had lowered the umbrella and the rain fell down on him, plastering his hair to his head, and leaving tiny raindrops lingering on his long dark eyelashes. To Jackie, Vikram appeared as some wild and beautiful creature of the deep, a handsome sea-god risen from the ocean.

They kissed again, more urgently this time, and Vikram held her tightly to him, as he nuzzled her neck, burying his face in her hair. And then he seemed to tense, and pulled back from her. He stood there for a long while, staring into the face of the woman he knew he loved. Jackie could see the love written on his face plain for all to see; she could also see the guilt and the fear.

"Nonono," he said, and shook his head. He released Jackie from his embrace.

"Vikram, what's wrong?" Jackie asked, and reached out for him. Vikram recoiled at her touch.

"We can't," he said, almost to himself. "We mustn't – it's

not right..."

"Vikram, I love you," Jackie said. "I never knew before now. You were always around, the boy next door; I could never appreciate what was always under my nose..."

"You're my best friend's girlfriend," Vikram said, and his voice was breaking with emotion. "Don't you see? There's no future for us."

"But..."

"Do you love Julian?" Vikram asked, and he made no attempt this time to hide the tears which were already welling up in his eyes.

"Vik, I don't know..."

"I can't betray him," Vikram said. "You don't understand. We're mates, he's the guy I play football with, go out drinking with."

"Vik..."

"Let's just forget tonight, shall we?" Vikram said. "Pretend it never happened."

"But we won't. And it did."

"We're friends and that's all we are," Vikram said coldly, and turned and walked down the road, the rain concealing his tears which were now flowing freely.

Just friends, and that's all, Vikram had thought.

And now friends no more.

Just two broken hearts.

10

What followed was a living hell for Jackie, long weeks of bleakness and despair. Unable to admit to herself that she loved Vikram, she now tried to avoid him, as if not seeing him might make her ignore and then forget the longing for him which gnawed at her heart, a pain eating away at her soul. Torn between her love for Vikram and her feelings for Julian she didn't know which way to turn.

And it was so hard to avoid Vikram, for, in her efforts not to see him, she threw herself into her ice-skating at Blades; which was, of course, where Vikram was working. And every time she circled the ice she found her eyes looking involuntarily up at the window of the café, hoping that Vikram would be there, watching her.

At times he was, and when he caught sight of her looking at him, he would turn away, and return to his work, and chat distractedly to the adoring girl behind the counter who wondered why it had been weeks now since she had last seen Vikram smile that irresistible smile which turned her knees to jelly.

Jackie's ice-skating was improving daily now, and Adam was pleased with her progress. He had a special routine already worked out for her, he told her, and, even though she had had to cut down on her training because the winter term had started, he was sure that she'd be in fine form for the Christmas gala.

Dancing on the ice with Adam felt good, and Jackie could relax in his arms like a child cuddling up to her favourite brother. The two were becoming good friends, now that Jackie realized that there would never be any passion between them. She had been a silly fool all those weeks ago, Jackie now knew. And if she had been so mistaken in the feelings she had had for Adam why couldn't she have been wrong about her feelings for Vikram also?

She had tried approaching Vikram to discuss their situation, but whenever she had entered the café he had turned away, or immediately found an urgent job to carry out. Even when they met by chance at Slinky Jo's he had found some excuse to leave shortly after she had joined him and their other friends at their table. And when Jackie had shrugged philosophically and turned back to Julian, or Emma or Adam, to hide the sadness she felt, she failed to notice the look of anguish on Vikram's face as he took one final look at her before venturing out into the night.

"Boy, Vik's so moody these days!" Julian said, after one of these encounters.

Emma nodded. "You've noticed it too?" she asked. "I'm worried about him. But when I've asked him what's the matter, he's snapped my head off!" She turned to Jackie. "What do you think is up with him?" she asked.

Jackie toyed with her cup of double espresso. "Me? I've really no idea," she lied, and reached out for Julian's hand under the table, as if that physical expression of her affection for Jules might take her mind off Vikram. She re-membered there had been a time in the summer holidays when she had recoiled from Julian's touch. Now she needed him there; and yet it was an act of desperation that was without any passion.

Julian pressed her hand lightly, and then withdrew his. "It's the start of a new term," he said.

"So what?" Emma asked. "It's we three who are going back to college, remember! Lucky old Vik's taking a year off!"

"He's probably going to miss you two," Julian said. "After all you won't be coming to Blades quite as regularly as you have been doing."

"Look, can we all stop talking about Vikram!" Jackie erupted. "If he wants to walk around looking miserable then that's up to him, isn't it?"

She stood up angrily, and in doing so, knocked over her cup of espresso. She cursed, and raised a hand to her brow, to soothe away the headache she knew was going to come any second.

Julian was suddenly all concern, and he put his arm around her shoulder. "Hey, Jackie, are you OK?" he asked.

"I'm fine!" she said, although at least to Emma it was patently clear that she wasn't. Julian, however, seemed to be convinced, and he returned to his seat. After a few seconds, wondering whether she should just rush out into the street after Vikram, Jackie sat down as well.

Julian beckoned to their waitress for the bill, and Jackie reached for her bag. Julian shook his head, and placed his hand on hers, preventing her from opening her purse.

Jackie sighed. "Julian, you paid for the last coffees, and the ones before that, and that meal two nights ago," she protested.

"It's my pleasure," Julian said airily. "Nothing's too good for you!"

"But..." Jackie said weakly.

"We're seeing so little of each other lately," he said. "It's the least I can do."

"I understand – your studies," Jackie said, and across the table only Emma noticed just how embarrassed Julian had suddenly become. Jackie was too concerned with asserting her own independence to notice the worried look in her boyfriend's eyes.

"So let me pay, OK?"

Jackie sighed her assent: she knew she was fighting a losing battle. While Julian sorted out his change with the waitress, Emma groaned and stood up shakily.

"Look, guys, I'm feeling a little faint," she said.

"You are?" Jackie asked. Emma didn't look ill at all; indeed for the past few weeks there had been a rosy glow in her cheeks and a happy spring in her walk. That was when she had seen Emma, of course; recently she seemed to have been keeping rather a low profile. They often used to meet up in the evenings at Slinky Jo's for coffee; now Emma was spending more and more time away from their regular haunt. If Jackie had not been so concerned with her own troubles, she might also have remarked that she was seeing less of Adam in the evenings too.

"Yes, I am," Emma said, and exchanged a conspiratorial look with Jackie. "I think I'd better go to the bathroom. Are you coming?"

"Sure," Jackie said, and stood up to follow Emma into the bathroom.

When they had gone, Julian smiled at the waitress who had brought them their bill. "What is it about you women that you always have to go to the loos in pairs?" he asked.

"It's so we can talk about you men in private," she giggled.

"And what do you say about us?" Julian teased.

The waitress – she was really very, very sexy, Julian decided – tapped the side of her nose. "Wouldn't you like to know!" she said.

Julian smiled at her and turned on his charm. "Well, maybe you should let me know sometime," he suggested.

"Sorry, we girls don't like divulging trade secrets to the weaker sex," she said in a friendly manner. "And besides, I think your girlfriend might have something to say about it if we did!"

Julian chuckled, but there was a suggestion of regret as he turned his eyes away from the sexy waitress, and to the swing doors through which Jackie and Emma had gone on their way to the bathroom.

"Oh, yeah, my girlfriend," he said. "I forgot..."

"OK, what's the big deal?" Emma demanded as soon as they had walked into the Ladies'.

"'Big deal'?" said Jackie, and checked her complexion in the bathroom mirror. "I don't know what you mean. And besides, I thought you said that you were feeling ill."

"That was just a lie to get you on your own, and away from Jules," Emma said. She glanced approvingly at herself in the mirror: she seemed to have lost a few pounds in the past few weeks. "What's happened between you and Vikram? Have you fallen out over something?"

"I don't know what you mean," Jackie said, and now started to examine an imaginary blackhead.

"Don't give me that!" Emma said. "Every time your name's mentioned he comes over all moody and withdrawn. And what was the matter with you just then – biting our heads off simply because we were talking about Vik?"

"It's just that I think there are more important things to discuss than Vikram's moods," Jackie said.

"Well, I don't think there are, Jackie Taylor," was Emma's reply. "He's my friend. So are you. And I don't like it when two of my closest mates suddenly look as if they can't stand the sight of each other!"

"It's not like that, Em," Jackie said wearily. "If anything it's the exact opposite..." She bit her lip: she had said too much.

Emma stared at her friend for a moment: a few things were starting to become clear. "Jackie," she said softly, "what is there between you and Vikram?"

Jackie paused for a moment, and then realized just how much she had been hurting over the past few weeks, keeping her secret to herself, going through all manner of torments to deny to herself and to her closest friends the reality of her love. She wanted to climb to the rooftops and shout it to the whole world: she loved Vikram, and she would love him for as long as there was breath in her body!

"It started a few weeks ago when Vikram and I went to

see that movie," she began.

"I remember," Emma said. "Adam apologized to me the day after. He said he must have got Jules' message all wrong, and thought that the entire evening had been cancelled." Emma smiled to herself, remembering the first night she and Adam had gone out together; she would die if she couldn't tell someone about it soon, although Adam had advised her to keep quiet. After all, Betty Crabtree might frown on Adam seeing her outside "working" hours and his skating mothers might get so jealous of him spending time with her rather than with their beloved daughters, that they might stop the lessons in a fit of pique. Emma urged Jackie to continue.

"Well, after the cinema, we sort of…"

Emma didn't need to be told anything else; her face fell. "Jackie, you've been cheating on Jules!" she said.

"No, I haven't," Jackie retorted. "We kissed – and that was all… But Emma, it felt so right, so natural, so different from what I have with Julian. It felt as though Vik and I *belonged* together."

Jackie closed her eyes and involuntarily shuddered with delight, remembering Vikram's firm masculine body against hers, recalling his deep passionate kisses and the raindrops which lingered on his eyelashes.

"Jackie, you can't lead both of them on," Emma said.

"Don't you think I know that! Don't you think that I'm terrified of hurting either of them," Jackie snapped. "But every time I'm with Jules I keep finding myself thinking of Vik … and he won't have anything to do with me!"

"He's scared," Emma realized.

"Scared? Of what?"

"Scared of losing his best friend," Emma said. "If Julian found out there'd be all hell to pay. You've seen how possessive he is of you, calling you his 'little girl', buying you all those presents, constantly making sure you're all right…"

"Jules is so sweet, and I really appreciate everything he does for me," Jackie admitted.

"And maybe he's also scared of commitment," Emma said. "Boys are funny like that; they'll run around with as many girls as they can, but when things start to get serious they go all cold on you."

"Vik doesn't run around with the girls," Jackie said. "He's never had a girlfriend before."

"Just a wife-to-be," Emma said darkly. The arranged marriage Vikram's father wanted to set up with Lakshmi wasn't something they usually talked about. Jackie and Emma had decided it should be a taboo subject, ever since Julian had confided in Jackie and she had told Emma.

"Vik won't marry that girl," Jackie stated categorically. "He's told us so."

Emma stroked her chin thoughtfully. "You know, this might explain Linsey's behaviour over the past few weeks," she said.

"Linsey?" Jackie had been successfully trying not to think of the sex-bomb of Blade's ice rink.

"Remember how she made a play for Vik when she first started coming to the rink?" Emma asked, and Jackie nodded.

"It's hardly surprising," Jackie said. "He is the sexiest and most handsome man in the place." She smiled wryly to herself: only a couple of months ago she hadn't even noticed Vikram's good looks; now they seemed to be part of that beautiful centre around which her entire life revolved.

"And then she suddenly left off," Emma continued. "Linsey may be like a cat on heat, but she's no fool. If a guy isn't going to be interested in her – because he's in love with someone else, for instance – she's not going to make a laughing stock of herself over him. She's the kind of girl who doesn't like to appear a failure, so she'll just look elsewhere."

"Like with Adam?"

"Adam?"

"Remember how she always used to show off whenever he was around?" Jackie said.

"Do I ever." Emma's voice was frosty as she recalled Linsey's stunning performance on the ice, and her suggestive remarks to Adam. Adam had certainly appreciated the performance; she hoped that the suggestive remarks had been a different matter. "And you're right, she has left Adam alone recently… She must have realized that he's a lost cause too as far as she's concerned. Maybe he's gone and got himself a girlfriend we don't know about yet?"

Emma was lost in reflection for a few moments, and there was a secret smile in her eyes; how she longed to tell Jackie her secret! She turned her attention back to Jackie.

"You have to sort it out with Vikram; you two can't carry on like this any longer," she advised her. "Tell him that that kiss meant nothing, that it was just two friends who went a little bit further than they should have."

"But it wasn't nothing," Jackie protested. "It meant more to me than anything in the world. I would give anything to feel Vikram in my arms again…"

"You can't love two men, Jackie," Emma said. "Maybe Vik's doing the right thing, staying away from you."

"You can't mean that!"

"You're his mate's girlfriend," she said. "How do you think you'd feel if your best friend stole Jules away from you?"

"I'd…" Jackie began, and then stopped. How would she feel? Angry? Outraged? Betrayed?

Or relieved? Because then the field would be clear for her and Vikram?

"Do you love Vikram?" Emma asked.

A pause. "Yes, I do," Jackie said finally. "I never realized it before – but I've loved him ever since we were kids and he was the boy next door."

"And do you love Julian?"

"He loves me, Em."

"That's not what I asked," said Emma. "Do you love Julian?"

Another pause, slightly longer this time. "Yes, I do."

Emma shook her head sadly. "You can't love both of them, Jackie. This is the real world, not some fairy-tale romance. You have to choose – for your sake, for Vikram's, and for Julian's."

Jackie was close to tears now. "But whatever choice I make, I lose out. If I pick Vikram then I'll have lost Julian as a friend, and Vik will have lost his best mate. And if I stay with Julian, then I'll never see Vik again. I can't stand losing either of them, Em!"

"You must make your decision, Jackie," Emma said. "Like I said – this is the real world!"

11

As the new term got under way, Jackie found herself far too busy to think about Vikram, or even about ice-skating as she threw herself into her college work. For a while things seemed to be going smoothly – she and Julian were getting on very well, helping each other with their course work (although his medical studies meant that their dates together became fewer and fewer). When they did get together, they had a good time, almost as good as they had had in the days before Jackie started noticing Vikram.

Yet Vikram was always there at the back of her mind, and if she had thought that staying away from Blades would make her forget the handsome young Pakistani then she was very much mistaken.

Wherever she went there seemed always to be some reminder of him; his favourite records were still being played over the PA system at Slinky Jo's; his favourite noodle soup was still on the menu at the sushi bar they all used to frequent; and of course Vikram himself was still working at Blade's, watching her as she skated with Adam on the ice, but never once coming near her, and only giving her the briefest of welcomes whenever he did see her. It was as if, by keeping as far away as possible from her, he would somehow conquer the feelings that Jackie knew he had for her.

Julian was aware that something was troubling her, but, as his studies were taking up more and more of his time, the subject was rarely broached when they did meet. He still continued to treat her like a princess, of course, and whenever he was forced to cancel a date Jackie always knew that the following day there would be an expensive present waiting for her by way of apology.

"A penny for them?" Adam asked one night as he skated up to Jackie who had been watching him from the barrier. He kissed her on the cheek.

"It's nothing," she said, and looked across the ice to where Linsey was performing one of her usual spectacular double axels. Linsey was wearing a floppy sweatshirt and jeans, similar to the ones Jackie was wearing: it was a marked change from the brash and tight Lycra cat-suits she had been wearing only a few weeks ago. Linsey had mellowed somehow, and didn't seem to be chasing the boys any longer – or at least not the ones who came to Blade's.

Maybe she's found a boyfriend now, Jackie thought, although she had never seen Linsey out alone with a boy; she realized that she'd seen less and less of the sexy skater on the ice too.

That puzzled Jackie for a moment until she remembered Vikram saying that Linsey was a science student at the local tech down the road; she supposed that now, in the initial run-up to her mock A-levels, Linsey would be just as busy as the rest of them.

Adam put his hand on Jackie's shoulder. "Who are you trying to kid?" he said. "You've been looking miserable ever since our lesson finished half an hour ago."

"I guess I'm worried about the Christmas gala," Jackie said.

"You'll be fine," Adam reassured her. "You're one of my best students: you'll knock 'em dead in the aisles."

"I'll probably fall flat on my face!" Jackie joked. "I've never skated in front of an audience before – I bet I'll be terrible!"

"Believe in yourself," Adam reminded her once again. "You do want to be in the gala, don't you?"

"Of course I do," Jackie said. "At first I thought it was only because I wanted to prove that I could be just as good as people like Linsey over there. And because—" she coloured.

"And because you thought you fancied me?" Adam laughed, and Jackie joined in.

"But now it's because I enjoy it so much, all the freedom, with no one in control but myself!"

"That's the spirit!" Adam cheered. "Always follow your heart. And always keep in control."

"Yes."

Jackie's eyes were drawn instantly up to the café, which was in semi-darkness. She'd never stayed so late at Blades before, but she knew that Vikram was usually there alone at this time, cashing up for the night.

Adam looked at his watch. "Jackie, I'm meeting Emma later down at Slinky Jo's," he said.

Jackie smiled: Adam had been seeing a lot of Emma recently. She wondered if anything was going on between the two of them, and then remembered just how radiant Emma had been looking recently: surely that was proof enough?

"Come along with me," he urged. "We need to talk anyway."

"About what?"

"Blades is going to be closed for a few weeks, for resurfacing, and re-icing," he told her. "It'll re-open at the beginning of December just in time for the gala. We'll have to find another rink for you to practise on."

"What about Vikram?" was Jackie's first thought. "Is his job going to be safe?"

Adam assured her that it would be, and walked off to the boys' changing rooms. As he did so, Linsey came off the ice and made her way to the girls'. She flashed a smile at Adam, and even nodded a hello to Jackie. Linsey had changed from the bitchy man-chaser of only a few weeks ago into someone who was much more subdued, at least whenever Jackie was around: and "subdued" was a word that Jackie had thought could never be applied to Linsey.

The ice-rink was empty, and eerily silent now that the PA system with its steady stream of chart pap had been switched off for the night. The overhead lights faded one by one, until the only illumination left was a stream of white coming from the café window. Slowly, Jackie climbed the stairs, and pushed open the door.

Vikram was sitting at one of the tables, poring over the till receipts and counting the cash he had taken during the evening session. From the piles of screwed-up balls of paper in front of him, it seemed that the former A-level maths student was having a major problem in getting the takings to balance. As the door creaked open, he looked up to see Jackie standing there.

"Vikram, we have to talk," Jackie said.

Vikram shook his head. "We've got nothing to talk about," was his awkward reply.

"We've lots to talk about!" she countered.

"Not now, Jackie," he said, and returned to his calculations. "I have to work."

"This is important," she said firmly and sat down opposite him. She took the pen from out of his hand, and pushed his till receipts to one side, so that he was forced to look at her. She placed his hand in hers, took a deep breath, and said:

"I love you, Vik. I don't care about Julian, I don't care about what anyone else thinks, I love you with all my heart."

Vikram's lips trembled and, from the look in his eyes, it was clear that all he wanted to do was to take Jackie in his arms and hold her like he'd never let her go.

"We've had all this out before," he said, a pained expression on his face. "You're the girl of my best friend."

"For heaven's sake, Vik, I love you!"

"What could I give you?" he said. "Julian's rich, he's good-looking—"

"So are you," Jackie insisted, and stood up and walked to his side of the table. "The handsomest, most caring boy in the world."

"He's got a great career ahead of him as a medical student and then as a doctor," Vikram said, and twitched uncomfortably for a moment when Jackie went behind him and put her hands on his shoulders. Slowly she began to massage the tense muscles of his neck, easing out all the stress and pain inside him. He could feel her breath on his neck, and he closed his eyes.

"Don't you think that it hurts me to deceive Julian, to fall out of love with him?" Jackie asked. "I love him, and I'd do anything to spare him any pain... But in the end all that really matters is you and me, Vik..." She buried her face in his neck, and kissed him there, smelling his freshly-washed hair and drinking in his scent. Julian had always smelt fresh and lemony, reminding Jackie of clear-running country streams; Vikram's scent was far earthier, far wilder, the tang of the storm-tossed sea, or the excitement of wild, unscaled mountains.

Vikram shuddered, but did not say a word. Instead he stood up, turned around, and kissed Jackie passionately on the lips. Jackie melted into his arms, knowing that here was her space, here was where she truly belonged. She felt her head spinning as Vikram's strong masculine arms held her tight; she felt the salt taste of his tears on her tongue.

"I need you, Jackie," he whispered. "I need you like I've never needed anyone before. Ever since we were kids, ever since the thunderstorms... These past few weeks have been agony for me – wanting you, needing you, and knowing that I could never have you, knowing that you were in the arms of my best friend..."

"I just want to be with you for ever," Jackie said. "For the rest of our lives..."

Vikram drew slightly away from her, as though he had come to some sort of decision. "So will you tell Julian?" he asked, and Jackie tensed.

"It's not the right time," Jackie said, her voice breaking. Why did she lack the courage to give up her boyfriend? She knew that she didn't really love him. So why couldn't she bring herself to tell him? "It's not that simple, Vikram," she pleaded.

"Yes, it is," Vikram said, and his manner had suddenly turned cold. "We both lose one of our best friends."

"It's not that," Jackie insisted. "Julian loves me. It would break his heart if he found out."

"And what about my heart, Jackie?" Vikram asked, and wiped a tear from his eye. "What does my heart count for in all this?"

"Please, Vikram," Jackie begged. "Don't make me choose between the two of you. Not now."

"Then when, Jackie?" Vikram demanded angrily. "Are you going to string both of us along for the rest of our lives like a coward? That's not what love is about. Love is about sacrifice, about being brave enough to make difficult decisions; it's about following your heart, about doing what you want to do, not what you think you should do."

"Vikram, I..." Jackie made no attempt to wipe away the tears which were flowing from her eyes. Why was Vikram putting her through this torment? Why was he suddenly being so horrible to her?

Because he loves me, she realized. *And I'm tearing his heart apart.*

"What is it with you, Jackie?" Vikram demanded angrily. "Sometimes I think you're worse than Linsey. At least she sets her sights on only one boy at a time. But you're teasing both of us!"

"That's a horrible thing to say!" Jackie said. "I love you!" *But I love you both ... and I can't bring myself to hurt either of you!*

"And don't you think that what you're doing to me is horrible too?" Vikram said. "Just a few minutes ago you were saying that I was the only boy for you. But will you ditch Julian? Oh no, you want the best of both worlds!"

"Vikram, I'm confused," Jackie said. "Don't try and

make me out to be some sort of cheap tart... Julian makes me feel good, but it's only you who makes me feel alive. When I'm with you I know I could do anything. You never smother me like Jules, you let me be my own woman, you treat me as your equal."

"You have to give things up for love, Jackie," Vikram said. "If there's any future for us, you have to break up with Julian..."

"Soon," Jackie moaned. "I have to pick the right moment: I can't hurt him..."

Long uncomfortable seconds followed in which Vikram did nothing but glare accusingly at Jackie. Jackie looked at him through a mist of tears, and watched as his fists clenched and unclenched in an effort to control the storm of passions rising within him.

"Thank you, Jackie," Vikram said, in a strange tone of voice.

" 'Thank you'?" Jackie didn't know what Vikram was talking about. "What for?"

"For helping me to make up my mind," he said, and, with the tears streaming down his face, he turned and ran out of the café, leaving Jackie alone.

She stood there for a few moments, and then the door opened again and Emma and Adam walked in. They were by her side in seconds, as they saw the obvious distress on her face.

"What's wrong?" Adam asked and he pulled out a chair for Jackie to sit on. He looked at the table, taking in at a glance the pile of money and the unbalanced till receipts. "We've just bumped into Vikram running out of here..."

"What's happened, Jackie?" Emma asked.

Jackie buried her face in her hands. "I've just broken the heart of the one man in the world I really love," she said. "And now I know what I must do..."

12

It was several days before Jackie and Vikram saw each other again. Jackie had gone round to his house several times, but when his father had answered the door she had been told repeatedly that Vikram wasn't at home. It was a lie, she knew, because on the last occasion she had seen a light in his bedroom window, so it was obvious that he was trying to avoid her.

Nor could she see him at Blades. The rink had now closed for resurfacing, and when she went out with Adam or Emma to Slinky Jo's the waitress told her that she hadn't seen him for several days now.

Julian was also proving difficult to get hold of. His telephone seemingly either constantly engaged or switched to the answerphone. She had left several messages, stressing that it was important that they meet up, but so far he hadn't rung her back. For a shocked moment, she thought that Vikram might have told Julian about them, until she realized that no matter how angry and betrayed he might feel, Vikram would never do anything like that.

Due to the temporary closure of Blades, Jackie was now taking her ice-skating lessons at the rink on the outskirts of town. Several of Adam's pupils had followed him there, and Jackie recognized many faces from Blades, including Linsey's. When Linsey had seen her, however, she had immediately left the ice; *probably out on the hunt for some poor unfortunate male,* Jackie had guessed, and thought nothing more of it.

To take her mind off Vikram (and Jackie still wouldn't tell Emma or Adam exactly what had taken place between them in the café), Adam had given her some free lessons, spending most of his spare time in the evenings coaching Jackie on the ice. She was getting better every day, he told her, and when the gala took place in five weeks' time she would be the star of the show.

"Betty Crabtree always invites some talent scouts to the gala," Adam reminded her. "They could spot you."

"And do what?" asked Jackie. "Sign me up for the next Winter Olympics?"

"You never know," Adam said. "You'll be good enough to star in a Holiday on Ice show at the very least – with a little extra coaching from me!"

"Now I know you're winding me up, Adam! The only skaters they'll spot are little cutesy kids they can train up to competition standard!"

"No, I'm not winding you up," Adam said in all seriousness, and Jackie was uncertain whether to believe him or not. She was looking forward enormously to the gala, and training for it at least took her mind off Vikram.

After her lesson had finished she went into the women's locker room where she showered and changed. Adam's compliments had cheered her up considerably, and, as she prepared to leave the rink, she was whistling a cheery tune.

She turned the corner, and her life changed for ever.

She took things in slowly, little by little. Julian was there, partly turned away from her. He was as attractive and as innocent-looking as ever, and for a moment Jackie wondered what he was doing at the ice rink when she knew that he only ever went skating with Emma and herself. What was more, someone as conscientious and as hard-working as Julian should have been studying at home.

He was wearing a baggy green Chevignon sweatshirt –

Jackie remembered saving up to buy it for him last Christmas – and the colour enhanced his sandy hair which she always thought looked so cute when it flopped over his eyes.

Long, red-nailed fingers were winding through that sandy hair, stroking his neck. In Julian's arms, in the middle of a serious clinch, was Linsey, her lips pressed tightly to the lips that Jackie had tasted time after time.

Jackie felt the whole world spin sickeningly around her as she finally took in the complete image of her boyfriend and Linsey in their treacherous embrace. She felt somehow removed from the scene, as though she wasn't really witnessing this betrayal; she broke out in a cold sweat, and leant on the wall to support herself.

Her lips quivered, as if wanting to say something, but no words left her mouth. Her eyes stared, wide-open and unblinking, at Julian and Linsey who still hadn't noticed her.

No tears appeared.

She had been a complete and utter fool, Jackie realized suddenly. While she had been agonizing over her illicit love for Vikram, not wanting to hurt Julian, he had been playing around behind her back.

And with this...

This slut!

Jackie remembered what Emma had told her about Linsey, that she never fought a battle she knew she would lose. When Linsey had discovered that Vikram was attracted not to her but to Jackie, she had given up on him, while swearing revenge on Jackie.

She had then set her sights on Adam, thinking that he and Jackie had had a thing going (as if everyone was as cheap with their favours as she was! Some people still lived by certain standards – Vikram, for instance!) Linsey had tried to impress Adam with her skating skills, and, when it was clear that he was more interested in Emma, she had gone for the biggest prize of all: Jackie's own boyfriend.

Several things became clear to Jackie. Julian's cancelling several of their recent dates – presumably to spend time with Linsey. She'd remarked that his skating had improved recently: presumably he had been here skating with Linsey.

The little gifts he would give her after each of their broken dates were obviously his way of easing the guilt, and to stop her asking too many questions. And they had worked – up until now.

Only a few months ago, if anyone had asked Jackie what her reaction would be if she caught Julian cheating on her, she'd always imagined that she would break down in tears, or fly into a white-hot outburst of anger. She did neither of these things. She felt neither anger nor resentment, neither sadness nor hurt. She felt elation, happiness.

And an enormous sense of relief.

Julian and Linsey were suddenly aware that they were being watched, and they turned round. Julian's face fell, and he quickly released himself from Linsey's embrace. Linsey smiled in triumph – and then frowned, as she realized that her evil little scheme had not had the desired effect on Jackie. Jackie's eyes were dry; for heaven's sake there was even the hint of a smile on her face!

"Hello, Jules," Jackie said, keeping her voice steady and emotionless. "Hello, Linsey."

"My God, Jackie!" Julian said. "I can explain!"

"I'm sure you can," Jackie challenged him.

By Julian's side, Linsey gave a nervous little cough. "Er, Jules, I'd better be going now," she said. "Somehow I think you two might have a lot to talk about..." And with that, Linsey left Jackie and Julian to confront each other.

"Jackie, I know how it must seem," Julian said. There was a wild and desperate look in his pretty-boy eyes; their assumed innocence might have fooled Jackie once, but no longer.

"I know exactly how it is, Julian," Jackie replied icily.

"Darling, I'm really sorry," he said, calling Jackie "darling" for the first time in many months.

"How long?"

"What?"

"How long has this been going on?" Jackie said. "How long have you been cheating on me with that person?" She couldn't even bring herself to utter Linsey's name.

"A few weeks..." Julian said. He gazed down at his feet, like a naughty schoolboy brought up in front of the headmaster, rather than a sneaky two-timer who'd just been found out by his lover. He remembered the first time Linsey had come on to him, and what a louse he had felt when he'd passed on the message that he couldn't make the movie because he had some homework to catch up on.

"I can't believe that you were kissing her here," Jackie sneered. "Practically right under my nose, in the ice-rink I train at!"

Julian looked nonplussed. "I didn't know you'd be here today," he said, as if that somehow made everything all right. "Linsey said you didn't practise today..."

That witch, Jackie thought. Linsey knew perfectly well that, in the run-up to the ice gala, Jackie trained at the ice-rink practically every day. Not content with stealing Julian from her, she wanted to rub salt into the wound as well, by making sure that Jackie would catch her and Jules in the act.

Julian raised his head, and looked up at Jackie. "Look, darling, I'll make it up to you – I promise."

Jackie gave a scornful laugh. "Like you did all those times before?" she sneered. "Little expensive presents to keep me sweet? And to think I fell for it, fool that I was! How many other girls have you been seeing behind my back?"

"Only Linsey," Julian insisted. "She was the first..."

"And to think I thought you loved me," Jackie said, and allowed the first hint of emotion to creep into her voice. "To think that I even worried myself sick over ever hurting you..."

Julian stepped forwards and took Jackie by the arms: she pushed him off, not in anger, but with an odd sort of weariness. When he spoke to her, there was pain in his words, and absolutely sincere regret.

"This isn't really to do with Linsey, Jackie..." he began.

"Oh, isn't it?" she said. "You should have been where I was standing!"

"C'mon, Jackie, face it," Julian said. "It goes back much further than that, doesn't it? We both of us know it, but we were each of us too cowardly to admit it."

"What do you mean?" Jackie knew exactly what Julian meant, but she needed to hear him speak the words out loud.

"There's been something missing in our relationship for months now," he said. "The magic we first had is gone. We were young then – you were my first girlfriend, I was the first boy you'd ever been out with. Perhaps we were too young. People change and little kids grow up."

"Like Vikram..."

Julian ignored the comment. "I remember a time when I had eyes only for you –"

And I for you, thought Jackie, and for the first time a tear appeared in the corner of her eye.

"And then I started noticing other girls, started fancying them, and I always felt guilty because I was your boyfriend, and I didn't want to hurt you, because you seemed so faithful, never flirting with the other boys. And so I started thinking that maybe we were meant just to be friends, and not lovers... But I still couldn't bring myself to tell you; because I didn't want to lose you as a friend, I didn't want to break your heart..."

"I was going to tell you weeks ago," Jackie revealed, and now her eyes were brimming with tears. She noted, with some satisfaction, that so were Julian's. "Back when I wanted to take you out for a meal at a country pub, but you had to see that doctor friend of your father's."

Julian remembered, and also recalled how he had spent that night alone, rather than go out with Jackie. If only they had told each other, instead of carrying on with this ludicrous play-acting! All along they had been lying to spare each other's feelings; if only they had expressed what their hearts were feeling, if only they had told the truth! He experienced intensely once again all the guilt he had felt at lying to Jackie, cancelling dates because of "studying" when, in reality, he was seeing Linsey.

He attempted an ironic laugh. "I guess we've been a couple of prize idiots, haven't we?"

"The biggest fools around," Jackie agreed.

"I loved you, Jackie," Julian said. "And I still love you as my first girlfriend, as a sweet and caring person, and as one of my best friends. But I'm not *in* love with you any more... Can you understand that?"

"Oh yes, I can understand that," Jackie said, and Julian was taken aback by the depth of feeling in her words. Jackie recalled Vikram's question to her: *You love Julian, Jackie. But are you* in *love with him?* Julian had made her realize what her answer was.

"I'm sorry you had to find out this way," he continued. "And that it had to be with Linsey: I know that you two don't get on..."

Jackie smiled. "I have a lot to thank Linsey for," she said, "even though she doesn't know it yet!"

"I don't get it," Julian said. "What have you got to thank Linsey for?"

"For finally showing me where my heart lies," Jackie said. "For finally bringing me to my senses."

And then Jackie completely bowled Julian over by kissing him on the cheek, no longer the kiss of lovers, but the kiss of the best of friends who have been through a lot together and know that they will remain friends for the rest of their lives.

"I hope you're happy with Linsey," Jackie said (although she suspected that they wouldn't be for much longer), "and now I have to go and track down Vikram!"

"Vikram?" Julian frowned, as a sudden suspicion dawned on him. "You mean – you and he..." He no longer knew what to think. Jackie and Vik together? Part of him felt betrayed. Part of him felt relieved that he and Jackie no longer had to pretend to each other. And yet another part was so glad that Jackie and Vik – his two best friends had found what he and Jackie never could.

"Yes, do you know where he is?" Jackie asked. "I haven't seen him for days."

"I talked to him on the phone the other day, arranging a five-a-side match," Julian said slowly. "He's been away – 'on business'..."

"Business? What sort of business?" Jackie asked. "Never mind. Is he at home now?"

Julian shook his head. "No. I agreed to meet up with him later at Slinky Jo's..."

"Then that's where I'm headed," Jackie said and started to move to the exit.

"Jackie, don't..." Julian pleaded, but Jackie had already gone. He ran after her, only to see her hop on the bus at the bottom of the road.

Julian cursed, and ran over to the car park. It was essential that he catch up with her before she reached the café-bar. Julian might not feel for Jackie as a lover any longer, but as a friend he loved her with all his heart.

And he didn't want that friend's heart broken.

Slinky Jo's was crowded at nine o'clock that night when Jackie arrived. Winter was drawing on now, and the place was usually full of people attracted by its warm and friendly ambience. She walked through the door – *glided* might have been a better word, as she was so happy that she felt as if she was walking on air – and looked around for Vikram.

She panicked for a moment, as he didn't seem to be there. A mutual friend was passing and Jackie grabbed her, and asked if she had seen Vikram. The girl, who had carried a torch for the good-looking Vikram for ages said, yes, he was here, in the small chill-out room at the back of the bar, where people went to escape from the noise and the bustle of the larger bar; and didn't she think it was such a waste?

Not understanding the girl's last remark, Jackie pushed her way through the throngs of trendies around the bar to the chill-out room. There were several tables there, at some of which couples were huddled in candle-lit conversation.

Vikram was sitting at a corner table; he was dressed in a loose-fitting black jacket, and matching trousers, and a white designer T-shirt. Jackie hadn't seen him looking so smart for ages.

Or so drop-dead gorgeous! she thought, and noticed that his normally unruly mop of raven curls had been combed and slicked back. There was a glass of orange juice in front of him, which was unusual, as he normally drank only coffees or bottles of designer cider whenever he went to Slinky Jo's.

He wasn't alone. Sitting at the same table, each of them cradling a glass of orange juice, were Vikram's father and a smartly-suited, slightly balding Pakistani man, who Jackie guessed was about the same age as Vikram's father. Unconcerned by their presence, Jackie caught Vikram's eye, waved at him and then walked over.

"Hi, Vik," she said happily and leant over and kissed him full on the lips. "Listen, I have the most wonderful news!"

Vikram sat back and nodded over to the stranger. "Er, Jackie, this is Mr Patel," he said politely, all the time wondering just what Jackie was doing here and why she was looking so happy.

Hadn't she heard from Julian? Didn't she know?

"Hi," Jackie said, and wondered why the man's name sounded so familiar; a glimmer of doubt came into her mind but she chose to ignore it, and continued to look lovingly at Vikram. She wanted to take him in her arms, tell him how much she loved and needed him, and beg his forgiveness for all the hell she had put him through. Finally free of Julian, Jackie no longer felt guilt over her love of Vikram; all she knew was a wonderful sense of release, a marvellous, instinctive conviction that their life together was now about to begin, a life in which every day would be a hundred times better than the one before.

"Julian and I have split up!" she announced importantly, as though it was the most earth-shattering piece of news she could ever deliver. As, indeed, it was.

"I shouldn't think that is something to be happy about, young lady," Mr Patel harrumphed, but Jackie paid no attention to him. As far as she was concerned there was only one other person in Slinky Jo's, in the whole of the universe in fact, who mattered now.

There was a wary gleam in Vikram's dark eyes as he took in Jackie's news. "You ... you told him?" he asked, and Jackie wondered why he had suddenly turned very pale.

"No, but I've found out that he's going out with Linsey," Jackie said, blissfully happy. "Isn't that wonderful news, Vik? It means that there's nothing standing in our way now!"

"Vikram, who is this?"

Jackie turned to see a gracefully petite Pakistani girl approach their table; she'd obviously just returned from the ladies'. Her silk trousers and tunic, shot through with filigree lengths of gold, made her look very classy indeed; her noble profile, almond eyes, and sensual mouth marked her out as breathtakingly beautiful. For the first time Jackie noticed the fourth glass of orange juice on the table, as the girl took her place, in between Vikram and Mr Patel.

"Vikram, who is this?" Now it was Jackie's turn to ask the question.

Vikram looked mournfully at Jackie, and back at Mr Patel; then to his father who had remained silent throughout the conversation, an uncomfortable expression on his face; and then, finally, at the gorgeous woman sitting on his left.

"Jackie, this Lakshmi Patel," he said with a heavy heart.

"Lakshmi?" The name rang a bell with Jackie, a bell that tolled doom for her heart and happiness.

"My daughter," explained Mr Patel proudly. "And Vikram's wife-to-be!"

Vikram's wife-to-be.

Jackie wasn't hearing this; she refused to believe it. This was a nightmare, a cruel trick played on her by fate. It was the end of everything, the end of her future happiness, the end of her life together with Vikram.

And it's all your own fault, she realized. *If only you hadn't been such a stupid little coward, if only you had told Julian how you felt earlier and split up with him. If only you'd given in to your passions. If only you'd admitted to yourself that the person you love most in this world is Vikram. If only you'd done what you wanted to, rather than what you thought was right... If only... If only...*

Jackie looked at Vikram. "Your wife-to-be?" The words came leaden to her lips.

Vikram nodded, and there were tears of regret – and of raging anger – in his eyes. "We're to be married in the New Year," he said, his voice cracking with emotion. "It's all been arranged..."

For Jackie there was nothing more to live for. From the heights of happiness she had been blasted down to the depths of despair. The world dissolved before her eyes into a tearful blur, and she was only dimly aware of someone coming up behind her and taking her arm.

"C'mon, Jackie, let's go home," said Julian, who had just arrived at Slinky Jo's. "The car's outside."

Jackie looked at her former boyfriend through a daze, as he guided her through the crowds of happy, smiling people.

"You knew, didn't you?" she said.

"I tried to tell you," Julian said. "But you left the rink so quickly..."

"It doesn't matter now," she said. "Nothing matters any more..."

And after Julian had brought Jackie home, she threw herself on her bed and cried and cried until she thought that she could cry no longer, until she thought that she would drown in her own tears.

And then she cried a little more.

13

To admire and to love a boy from afar, and know that your love will never be reciprocated is a terrible thing. But to love someone and to know that he loves you; and to be faced with the terrible knowledge that you have lost him for ever, entirely through your own fault, is too much for anyone to bear. Jackie withdrew into herself, as she tried to answer a whole series of whys.

Why had she never realized just how much she loved Vikram before? Why had she ever gone out with Julian, when the only man for her had been living so close by, the boy-next-door for almost fifteen years? And why, when the relationship between her and Julian had so obviously broken down, had she not called a halt to it, instead of letting it stagger on, and ruin her life? If only she had done that, she and Vikram would be together now – no guilt, no shame, no Lakshmi and no wedding scheduled for early January.

Why? Because she had been scared, frightened of following her heart. She had been sensible, responsible, adult about the whole affair; and it was only now that Jackie realized that true love is never sensible, responsible and adult. It simply *is*, a force as inexorable as the ebb and flow of the tide itself. Follow it, go with the flow, do as your heart and not your head bids, and you will eventually be washed up on the shores of some tropical paradise; fight it, try to resist the pull, and you will surely drown.

Jackie was drowning now, in a sea of regret and bitterness. Even comforting words from Emma and Adam (and Julian, who knew what she was going through, and towards whom Jackie felt no bitterness) didn't help her; all that got her through the next few weeks, as the first snowflakes started to fall, was her ice-skating. She threw herself into it with an almost maniacal obsession, as if the faster she sped around the rink the quicker she could escape the mocking ghost of those saddest words in the English language: *what might have been.*

So it was a further blow on the bruise when, only a week before the ice gala and Blades' reopening, Adam came up to her one evening at their training rink.

"We're double-booked," he told her, gritting his teeth to keep his anger in check.

"Double-booked? What do you mean?"

"Betty, Miss Crabtree, called me into her office back at Blades this morning," Adam said. "It seems that a charity five-a-side football match has been booked for that same night."

"Don't be stupid," Jackie said, as she skated over to the edge of the ice. "I've heard of hockey on ice, but never football on ice."

"Remember we're resurfacing the rink," he said. "There's still no ice on it, and Blades is the biggest indoor venue in town – it would be ideal for the match."

"Well, it'll just have to be cancelled," Jackie said practically. "The ice gala's booked for one week's time: it has to go ahead."

"The charity match is being organized by a wealthy foreign businessman," Adam said. "In return for the use of the rink he's willing to give Blades a handsome donation."

"But tickets have already been sold for the gala!" Jackie protested. "And you said that some talent scouts are coming up from London!" She remembered Adam telling her how proficient she had become; for the past few weeks she had been entertaining the notion that maybe she was good enough, even at the grand old age of seventeen, to be spotted as a promising young player in the sport she loved so much.

Adam rubbed his thumb and forefinger together. "We need the money," he said sadly.

"There has to be a way around it," Jackie said. "The gala can't be cancelled – not after all the effort I've put in. Not after all those lessons I've paid you for. We've both worked really hard for this!" She rubbed her chin thoughtfully. "Can't the venue for the gala be moved?" she asked. "We could have it here, where we've been practising ever since Blades shut down." Adam shook his head.

"There has to be a way around this!" Jackie reasoned. "Who is this businessman willing to put up the money anyway?"

"Someone called Patel," Adam said: the name meant nothing to him. "I think he owns a chain of grocery stores or something like that."

Vikram's father-in-law. Or rather he soon would be, Jackie realized. For one wild, unthinking moment she wondered whether Vikram had had anything to do with the double booking, to spite her. And then she remembered that Vikram loved her, even though she had not seen him since the news of his wedding, and that he would never stoop to such a mean, low trick. In fact, there was only one person she knew who could ever be so unscrupulous and wicked.

"Look, how did this double booking happen in the first place?" she asked. "I thought Crabtree was too efficient to let something like this happen."

"It wasn't her fault," Adam said. "It seems that–" he hesitated a second, as if debating whether to spare Jackie even more bad news "– it seems that Linsey has been helping her out in the office in the evenings. It was her fault. A clerical error, so they say."

I'll kill her, thought Jackie. *The little tramp isn't content to ruin my love life – now she's trying to destroy my ice-skating life as well!*

"Then get Crabtree to apologize to Patel," Jackie said. "I'm sure he'll understand..."

"That's the other problem," Adam said. "One of Betty's favourites is playing in the football match. She doesn't want to let him down either..."

"Vikram?" She remembered how Emma had once said that the old dragon-lady would be putty in the dark-eyed boy's hands. It seemed she had been right after all.

Jackie missed school the following day: it was nearing the end of term and she was sure she wouldn't miss anything she couldn't catch up on during the Christmas holidays. For most of the morning she looked out of her front-room window at the snow falling in the road outside, waiting for Mr and Mrs Pandy, Vikram's parents, to come out of their house, get into their cars and drive off to work.

This was the easy part. The hardest thing then was to gather up all her courage and walk around to Vikram's house and knock on his door. There was no response, and she was about to walk away when the door creaked open.

Vikram was standing there, still in his dressing gown, which was opened to the waist, and which he quickly gathered around him when he saw Jackie standing there. His hair was still wet from the shower, and there was a small nick on his cheek where he had cut himself shaving: it made him look innocent and vulnerable.

This was the man she loved, she knew, the man she could never have. The man she had not seen for weeks in the flesh, and the man she saw every night in her dreams. The man without whom her life would never be whole; the man who was marrying another woman.

Taken aback, Vikram let Jackie into the house, forgetting to shut the front door in his confusion.

"Vikram, you must give up the football match," she said, after he had led her into the living room.

"Why?" he asked in a monotone. He looked at her with

eyes which seemed to bore deep down into her very soul; at the same time he kept his distance from her. It was almost as if he was scared, Jackie thought, as if he was terrified of the passion he might express should he let himself come any closer to her.

"It clashes with the ice gala," she told him.

"So?"

"This is my big chance, Vikram," Jackie said. "Adam says I'm very good. There'll be important people down from London, who might be able to give me some work. This is my opportunity to make something of my life, Vikram, it could be the start of something big."

"You'll be in the gala?" This was news to Vikram.

"Of course I am," Jackie said irritably. "Why do you think I've been taking all those lessons with Adam? I wanted to keep it a surprise until the night—"

"Why?"

Always these damn monosyllables! Jackie thought. *As if he's scared of what else he might say!*

"I don't know – to impress you, I suppose," she said helplessly.

Again: "Why?"

Jackie threw her arms up in frustration. "What's the point in hiding?" she said. "The football match and ice gala aren't the real reason I've come around this morning; they're just excuses. I've come round to see you, Vikram. We belong together. It's not too late – you can still refuse to marry Lakshmi!"

Vikram tensed, and his jaw clenched. "I can't do that," he said.

"Of course you can!" Jackie exploded. "For heaven's sake, the marriage has been arranged between your two fathers! You can't love her!"

"What do you know about love?" Vikram shouted, even though he was breaking up inside. "It's your fault we all got into this mess in the first place!"

"What do you mean?"

"You thought you loved Julian, when all the time he was

carrying on with Linsey!" he reminded her. "If you had followed your heart, done what you wanted to, if you had found the courage to tell Jules, then we'd be together now!"

"You're a fine one to talk about following your heart!" Jackie countered. "I didn't see you following your heart. Heck, it was you who tried to stop our affair!"

"You were my best friend's girlfriend! I had a duty to Julian!"

"Forget your stupid masculine pride and loyalty for a moment!" Jackie shouted. She made a halfway successful attempt to calm down. "Look, for whatever reasons, we've both been too scared to give in to our emotions. You're even doing it now."

Vikram stared wildly at Jackie: he knew exactly what she meant.

"This is our last chance, Vikram."

"To do what?" he sneered. "To 'follow our hearts'?"

"Well, you're certainly not following your heart by entering into an arranged marriage with Lakshmi, are you?"

"Leave Lakshmi out of this!"

"She's the whole reason I'm here, you idiot!"

"If I marry Lakshmi, then that will be the seal on a business deal my dad wants to enter into with Patel," Vikram said. "Patel has promised to invest hundreds of thousands into Dad's business. It means he could expand his chain of shops. It could make him very rich indeed..."

"I love you, Vikram."

"And what do I get if I follow my heart, as you call it?" he asked rhetorically.

"You told me once that love was all about making sacrifices," Jackie said.

"If I follow my heart, my dad stands a chance of losing his business," he said. "Do I have to sacrifice my family for you, Jackie? Can you really be that selfish?"

Jackie didn't know what to say; he was right. Why should he give all that up for her? "Vik, I'm sorry..."

"I love you, Jackie," Vikram said. "And I'll love you till the day I die. But I love my parents too. And someday maybe I'll be able to love Lakshmi as well…"

"Vik … we have to be true to ourselves…"

Jackie moved forwards and reached out for him. He turned away, but Jackie pulled him back, and drew him into her embrace. Their lips met, and they kissed a brief kiss; and then a longer, deeper one, the last kiss they knew they would ever share. When their lips parted, Vikram's eyes were wet with tears.

"If only, Jackie, if only…" he said, echoing her own earlier thoughts. He stroked her fine blonde hair with his hands. "I have to marry Lakshmi…"

There was a click at the door, and Vikram and Jackie drew apart quickly. Lakshmi and her father were standing there: they had let themselves in by the front door which Vikram had neglected to close. Mr Patel opened his mouth wide, speechless, but Lakshmi took in the situation at a glance, and stared icily at Jackie.

"I think you'd better leave – and now," she said, and she and her father escorted Jackie to the door, leaving Vikram alone with his thoughts.

14

"Well, Jackie, I don't know what you did, but congratulations anyway!" Adam said the following day, and planted a friendly kiss on Jackie's cheek. They were in Slinky Jo's, sharing a cappuccino with Emma, and sheltering from the heavy snowfall outside.

"What have I done?" she asked, nonplussed.

"Why, got the football match cancelled, of course!" he said. "Betty's just told me. It's been postponed to the week after next – and to a different venue. The ice gala can go ahead after all!"

"Vikram."

"What?"

Jackie stood up, and excused herself. She went to the phone at the back of the bar, and punched in a familiar number. As she waited for the connection to be made she drummed her fingers impatiently on the receiver. He had thought of her after all, she realized; to give her a chance, he had risked the wrath of his father and Mr Patel by cancelling the match. She had to tell him thanks, if nothing else; and who knew what else she would tell him? But when the phone was answered the voice at the other end made her heart sink.

Vikram's father answered the phone, and when she asked for Vikram, he told her that he was out. His tone became even more frosty when he recognized her voice,

and he informed her that no, he didn't know where
Vikram was, and that he had stormed out of the house
the previous morning after an argument. It was obvious
from Mr Pandy's manner that the argument had been
over her, and he put the phone down abruptly, making it
clear that he wanted nothing more to do with her.

Jackie returned, ashen-faced, to her table, where Emma
immediately asked her what was wrong.

"Vikram's vanished," she said, as she eased herself back
into her seat. Her legs were shaking, and she felt faint.
She took a sip of her cappuccino. "He and his father have
had an argument."

"Over what?" Emma was all concern.

"Isn't it obvious?" Jackie said, and told her and Adam
everything that had happened the previous morning.
"He's running away from his marriage."

"But that's great!" said Emma, not thinking through the
consequences of Vikram's actions. "He's cancelled the
match for you, probably upsetting both his dad and
Lakshmi's father along the way; and now he's not going
through with the wedding. He's doing it for you! He's
proving once and for all that he really does love you!"

"And by doing that he's risking losing the love of his
family," Jackie sobbed. "I can't let him sacrifice all that
just for me."

Emma took hold of Jackie's hands. "Jackie, you and
Vikram belong together," she said. "You always have done
since you were kids, first as friends, and now as lovers.
You can't let anything else stand in the way of that love.
Love is all that matters, nothing else. Things will sort
themselves out, they always do..."

"But where is he?" Jackie asked. "If he's doing all this
for me, then why hasn't he come to me?"

"Is there anywhere you think he might have gone?"
Adam asked practically. "Any friends he might stay with?"

"There's Jules," Jackie guessed, and also gave him the
names of some other friends.

"We'll try them first of all," he said. "And then we'll look in all the places he usually goes – the gym, the leisure centre. And in the meantime you must continue practising for the gala."

Jackie nodded. "I know, it could be my big chance," she said. "And after all, it's to give me that chance that Vikram cancelled the match."

"Ah, yes, that..." Adam said and blushed with embarrassment.

"Adam, what is it?" asked Jackie.

"I'm afraid I might have misled you a little on that one," he said shamefacedly. "You're good, Jackie, one of my best pupils ever. But like you said, you're too old now to ever make championship level..."

"But you told me..."

"I needed the money from your extra lessons," he admitted. "And then when I got to know you, and when I saw your confidence grow on the ice, I continued to tell you that because I saw just how happy it made you. I'm sorry..."

"So Vikram's done all this for nothing," Jackie said, and wondered why she felt no anger towards Adam, only a sad acceptance of the way things were. Would she have gone to see Vikram if she hadn't thought she had had a chance at the gala? And if she hadn't seen Vikram, would he still be going ahead with his wedding plans with Lakshmi?

It seemed that Jackie's whole life was cluttered now with deceptions and misunderstandings – from kidding herself that she still loved Julian when she should have done the brave thing and called it a day, to Julian's cheating on her, to Adam's little white lies about her skating abilities. If only everyone had been straight with each other since the beginning – if only everyone had followed their heart – none of this would have happened. Yet in the midst of this sea of confusion one thing shone clear and steady, like a lighthouse beacon, guiding the weary storm-tossed sailor home: her love for Vikram.

For the man she knew she could never have.

*   *   *

The day of the ice gala dawned, and Betty Crabtree was in a state of excitement, ensuring that the newly resurfaced ice was ready for the big event. Banners and decorations were festooned around the rink ("making it look like a crazy and particularly naff Christmas tree," Emma had said in a superior fashion), and even the PA system had been given such a major overhaul that some of the music blaring out from it actually sounded half-listenable.

In fact the only cloud on Betty's horizon, as the hall began to fill with the ticket-holders coming in from out of the heavily falling snow, was the absence of Vikram. It had been a week now since the rink had re-opened, and ten days since he had disappeared from home, and still there was no sign of him.

Betty had replaced him as manager of the café with his assistant, and when Jackie had asked her if she knew where he might have gone to, she had said that he'd probably run off with some girl. After all, she must have seen just how good-looking and sexy Vikram was, and didn't she know that all the girls were crazy for him? She had no idea why Jackie had then burst into tears.

Jackie had contacted everyone who knew Vikram, but no one had heard from him. Even Julian claimed not to know where he was, although the guilty look on his face as he told Jackie this had made Emma suspect that he knew slightly more than he was letting on. She kept her counsel on that, though, anxious not to raise any false hopes in Jackie. But when she and Jackie had left Julian's house, Jules had picked up the phone and dialled a number. The conversation that followed had been heated.

Now Jackie was waiting in the changing room of Blades, dressed in a stylish all-in-one leotard, and wearing her skates, as she waited for the piece of music which was her cue to go out on to the ice and perform the routine that she and Adam had been working on for the past few months.

All around her, other excited skating pupils were

talking nervously to each other, wondering which big talent scouts might be out there in the audience; in the first half of the programme, someone said, a couple of promising seven-year-olds had already been picked out for special praise. Others, of a more practical nature, like Jackie, just hoped that they wouldn't fall flat on their faces as soon as they stepped out on to the ice.

Jackie could hardly hear them: their excited chatter sounded like the buzzing of faraway bees. Not only her hearing was dulled: her whole body felt numb and cold. She could hardly feel her own limbs as she stretched and warmed up, before going out.

There was only one thing on her mind, only one thing which could make her forget this aching emptiness. Vikram. Vikram who had risked his father's wrath, who had sacrificed everything, just so that she could have her chance out there now on the ice. Vikram who had given her the greatest gift of all – not presents or jewellery or CDs, but the willingness to put her own happiness and success before his own. Vikram who had always been there for her, through their childhood together, through the thunderstorms, and now, even though he was far away, in her own heart. Vikram had sacrificed so much for her: how could she now go out and perform on the ice?

She creaked open the door of the changing room, and looked out on to the rink. A young boy and girl, dressed in spangles and frills, were coming to the end of their ice-dancing routine: Jackie was due on in less than a minute.

In the front row of seats she could see Emma and Julian who had come to watch her performance; Linsey was nowhere to be seen, which hardly surprised Jackie. She'd guessed that Linsey would soon tire of Julian, and she was sure that Linsey wasn't the sort of person to come to an ice gala and watch other people being the centre of attention.

She closed the door. If she had kept it open for just one moment longer, she would have seen a familiar figure sneak into the hall. Vikram took his place at the back of the rink, but not before Emma had spotted him. Emma nudged Julian and whispered something to him, but Julian just nodded and smiled knowingly.

The two young kids sped off the ice to tremendous applause (none louder than that from their own adoring parents), and Adam glided into the centre of the ice to announce the next performance. He nodded to the organist at the far end of the rink, who launched into a fanfare, which was Jackie's cue to step out. With an exaggerated flourish, Adam invited Jackie on to the ice.

Jackie didn't appear. Adam appeared flustered, and nodded over to the organist to play the introduction again, as, for a second time, he announced Jackie.

Still no Jackie. A dissatisfied murmur arose amongst the crowd. Adam, ever the professional, looked down at the clipboard he was carrying to check who was the next act on the list: a pretty nine-year-old, for whom he held great hopes. He skated over to the organist, and instructed him to play the young girl's introductory piece of music. Jackie Taylor was ill, he announced, and he was very sorry that he hadn't known before. Unable to leave the ice as the master of ceremonies, Adam cast an urgent glance towards Emma, who had already left her seat and was making her way to the changing room.

"Jackie, what the heck do you think you're playing at?" she demanded, when she found Jackie, sitting disconsolately on a bench, her skating boots unlaced and lying on the floor before her. Her face was white and her eyes were red with crying.

"I'm not going on, Em," she said.

"Why ever not?" Emma said. "You heard what Adam told you: you'll knock 'em dead!"

"How can I go on after all that Vikram's given up for me?" she asked. "He's sacrificed his family for me."

"What d'you mean?"

"If it wasn't for him the gala wouldn't have gone ahead," she reminded her. "How do you think he explained that to Mr Patel, his future father-in-law? 'Sorry for postponing the charity football match but the woman I love – not your daughter, of course, but this cute number from next door – wants to go ice-skating'?"

"But, Jackie –"

"The least I can do is give up my skating. The only reason I agreed to do the gala in the first place was to impress him. And now that he's gone there's no point any more…"

Emma took Jackie in her arms. "But Jackie, that's what I'm trying to tell you if only you'd listen to me!" she said. "He's back! He and Jules spoke on the phone last night. He's come back to see you perform!"

"Vikram? He's out there in the rink?"

"That's right," Emma confirmed. "I saw him arrive about fifteen minutes ago."

Jackie leapt up and rushed past Emma, a wild look of delight on her face. She ran out of the changing room, ready to throw herself into the arms of the man she loved with all her heart.

And he wasn't there.

She looked all around the rink, at the happy, smiling faces of the spectators, but there was no sign of Vikram. At the back of the rink, one seat was empty, mocking her, telling her that once again she had been too late, once again her hopes had been dashed, once again happiness could have been hers and she had let it slip through her fingers.

Jackie fell into Emma's arms and cried and cried and cried.

15

Jackie walked from the rink, her skating boots slung over her shoulder, having refused Julian's offer of a lift home, wanting to talk to no one about her loss. To have been so close to Vikram and then to have lost him yet again was too much. And the laughing faces at the gala, every single one of them unaware of her loss, made her sadness even more acute; in the distance she could still hear the blaring music and the rounds of applause, which seemed to be laughing at her, taunting her.

The snow was falling heavily now, and she could hardly see for the blanket of white which lay before her eyes. She wrapped her coat around her for warmth: it seemed as though it was going to turn out to be one of the coldest winters for a long time. Even the small pond, which she always passed on her way home from Blades, had frozen over.

But no matter how cold the weather was it could never match the coldness in her heart, the bleak emptiness she saw lying before her. A lump of ice had encrusted her heart, freezing it in its sub-zero grip, and only Vikram could thaw it. But she no longer knew where he was. He would certainly not be at his father's; Vikram's dad was a stern man who would not have taken kindly to his son having disobeyed his wishes; and even if he did forgive Vikram, she suspected that Vik would have been much too proud to return home.

She had been a fool all along, she realized. Why hadn't she listened to her heart? Why did she always have to do what she thought she ought to do? Now she had lost the one man in the world she wanted, the one man in the world who was her equal and who could make her whole.

"There are other boys," Emma had told her when she had fallen, sobbing, into her arms, but Emma was wrong. There was only Vikram, and, fool that she was, she had lost him for ever.

It was getting dark now, and she quickened her pace, taking the short cut across the park to her home. The trees swayed in the winter wind, their bare charcoal-black branches as bleak and fruitless as the life that Jackie saw stretching before her. On the edges of the park, lights from distant houses shone invitingly with a warmness that Jackie would never know again.

The winter would pass, Jackie knew, and the trees would bloom and bear fruit again. But her soul was in the grip of a terrible Ice Age that would last her whole life long.

The path took her past the frozen pond. It was iced over more than she had ever seen it before. In other winters some local kids had tried to skate on its frozen surface, before being warned that it was too dangerous, but tonight it looked strong enough to support any weight.

There was a scrunching sound behind her, and Jackie froze. Slowly she turned around, to see who was approaching her through the snow. She couldn't see clearly – the snow was falling too fast and thick – but she recognized the broad shoulders, the slim waist, and the long shock of curly black hair.

Vikram stepped forward, and, as he did so, the full moon came out from behind a cloud, suffusing his handsome, manly face with a silvery-white radiance. Snowflakes crested Vikram's hair like a crown of flowers, or a halo. He looked like an angel, returned from heaven, or an elemental earth-spirit in whose eyes burned a passion red and wild.

Neither of them spoke. They just stared at each other,

lovingly, knowingly. There was no longer any need of words.

Finally Vikram spoke. "Dance for me, Jackie," he said.

As if in a trance, Jackie bent down and took off her shoes. Keeping her eyes fixed on Vikram – she would never take her eyes off him again, she vowed – she slipped her skates off her shoulder, and pulled them on, and walked over to the frozen pond.

As she had guessed, the ice was thick and firm, and there was no chance of it cracking. With Vikram watching, she stepped on to the ice, and circled the pond, performing the routine she had learnt with Adam. But this was now no longer just a display of ice-skating prowess intended to please the crowds. Now she was playing for an audience of one, and the dance was nothing less than an expression of her love for Vikram. The moon illuminated her like a spotlight, and the sound of the winter wind rustling through the branches of the trees provided a greater musical accompaniment than any organ or tape could ever do.

When she had finished, she stepped off the ice, unlaced her boots, and replaced them with her normal everyday shoes. She walked up to Vikram – she still had not said a word – and there, with only the moon and the falling snow for witness, she embraced him.

He felt warm and comforting, and Jackie pressed herself against him, melting their bodies into one body, their hearts and souls into one heart and one soul.

"I love you," he whispered, "and I'll never let you go as long as we both live. It's taken me all my life to realize it."

Jackie still didn't say a word: she just smiled blissfully at Vikram, knowing that whatever happened now they would always be together. This winter's night had proved it. Vikram was her winter and her spring, her summer and her autumn, her very world itself.

"You didn't do your piece at Blades tonight," he said.

"How could I?" Jackie said. "How could I be so selfish when I knew what you'd given up for me..."

Vikram frowned. "But you've given up your chance of a career in ice-skating," he said, and Jackie shook her head.

"That was only Adam spinning me a line to get me to pay for more lessons," she said, and chuckled. "I've as much chance of being an ice-skater as you have!" She stroked his hair tenderly. "But you've sacrificed much more than me..."

Vikram frowned once more. "What do you mean?"

"Your father... Lakshmi..." she said, and wondered why Vikram was grinning so.

"Lakshmi's called the wedding off," he said. "She realized that it would never work – as long as I loved you. It seems that she saw what no one else – ourselves included! – could: that we belong together, now and for always!"

"But your father?"

"Lakshmi told Mr Patel that it was her decision to call off the marriage," Vikram said. "He and my dad are still going to go into business. Even though my dad isn't too pleased about Lakshmi's decision: we had an argument about it and I stayed with friends for a few days to think things over."

"And the football match? Wasn't Patel angry about that?"

"I told him that several of the players had come down with the flu, and that the match had to be postponed for a few days. It'll still go ahead, and he'll still raise money for his charity."

Jackie feigned a look of discontent. "And there was I thinking you'd told him that it was because the woman you loved wanted to show off her skating!"

Vikram laughed, and pulled her closer to him. "No way!" he chuckled, and then became deadly serious. "But the point is that I would have done. And if Lakshmi hadn't have called off the wedding I would have done – no matter what I would have lost: my father, my future, everything. That's what love is all about, Jackie: it's about devoting your whole being to only one other person, and forsaking all others. And that's what I'm offering you, Jackie – my entire devotion until the very end."

"I love you, Vikram," Jackie said.

"And I love you too," Vikram said. "And one wedding might have been called off; but another one can be arranged..."

And as they kissed again, on that cold winter's evening, with the snow falling all around them, the ice in Jackie's life finally melted.

Pointing the way forward

More compelling reading from top authors.

The Highest Form of Killing
Malcolm Rose
Death is in the very air...

Seventeenth Summer
K.M. Peyton
*Patrick Pennington - mean, moody and out
of control...*

Secret Lives
William Taylor
Two people drawn together by their mysterious pasts...

Flight 116 is Down
Caroline B. Cooney
Countdown to disaster...

Forbidden
Caroline B. Cooney
Theirs was a love that could never be...

Hostilities
Caroline Macdonald
*In which the everyday throws shadows of another, more
mysterious world...*

Flash Fire
Caroline B. Cooney
Things are hotting up...

His Dark Materials: 1 Northern Lights
Philip Pullman
*Winner of the Carnegie Medal &
Guardian Children's fiction award*

Point

Kick Back
David Hill
It's the strong heart that wins...

Comfort Herself
Geraldine Kaye
She's got a long way to go...

P●INT CRiME

If you like Point Horror, you'll love Point Crime!

A murder has been committed ... Whodunnit? Was it
the arch rival, the mystery stranger or the best friend?
An exciting series of crime novels, with tortuous plots
and lots of suspects, designed to keep the reader
guessing till the very last page.

Kiss of Death
School for Death
Peter Beere

Avenging Angel
Break Point
Deadly Inheritance
Final Cut
Shoot the Teacher
The Beat:
Asking For It
Black and Blue
Missing Person
Smokescreen
Dead White Male
David Belbin

Baa Baa Dead Sheep
Jill Bennett

A Dramatic Death
Bored to Death
Margaret Bingley

Driven to Death
Patsy Kelly Investigates:
A Family Affair
End of the Line
Accidental Death
Anne Cassidy

Overkill
Alane Ferguson

Deadly Music
Dead Ringer
Death Penalty
Dennis Hamley

Concrete Evidence
The Alibi
The Smoking Gun
Malcolm Rose

Dance with Death
Jean Ure

13 Murder Mysteries
Various

POINT FANTASY

Read Point Fantasy and escape into the realms of
the imagination.

Doom Sword
Peter Beere
*Adam discovers the Doom Sword and has to face a
perilous quest...*

Brog the Stoop
Joe Boyle
Can Brog restore the Source of Light to Drabwurld?

Book of Shadows
Stan Nicholls
Magic so terrible as to be beyond imagining...

The Renegades Series:
Book 1: Healer's Quest
Book 2: Fire Wars
Book 3: The Return of the Wizard
Jessica Palmer
*Journey with Zelia and Ares as they combine their magical
powers to battle against evil and restore order to their land...*

Realms of the Gods
Tamora Pierce
The barrier's gone ... and no one's in control...

Elfgift
Elfking
Susan Price
The cry went out for vengeance...